## POE MUST DIE

Poe sat across from the grave-robber and his cronies, wishing desperately for a drink and knowing that to have even one now could cost him his life.

'Got more for you to look at, poet. Under the table. Go on . . . You wanted proof, poet. Now, goddam you, *look*!'

Under the table, the ghoul held the head of Rachel's husband with bits of ice gleaming in its long black hair and on its pale skin. The opened eyes glittered like polished glass and stared at Poe who used every ounce of willpower not to scream. *It had been at his feet all the time.*

MARC OLDEN

# Poe Must Die

Futura

For my mother Courtenaye Olden,
who is always there and whom I
love very much.

A *Futura* Book

Copyright © 1978 by Marc Olden

This edition published in Great Britain in 1989
by Futura Publications, a Division of
Macdonald & Co (Publishers) Ltd
London & Sydney

ISBN 0 7088 8299 4

Printed and bound in Great Britain by
Cox & Wyman Ltd, Reading

Futura Publications
A Division of
Macdonald & Co (Publishers) Ltd
66–73 Shoe Lane
London EC4P 4AB
A member of Maxwell Pergamon Publishing Corporation plc

History and legend, scripture and fable have all ranked Solomon as the wisest and wealthiest of kings. But it is within the occult lore of both east and west that one finds mention of the darker side of Solomon, for he is said to have commanded spirits, demons and evil forces to obey his every wish.

Of all his treasures, none was the equal of his throne, a marvel surpassing any treasure owned by all the world's monarchs. There are varying accounts of the throne's appearance, for marvels are created by writers more often than they are by kings or even gods.

One scroll describes the throne as made of ivory, with a golden lion by each arm and twelve golden lions on its six steps. Giant eagles covered the golden lions on the stairs and when Solomon mounted his throne, the eagles spread their wings to shade him from the sun.

Another account says the throne was made of more gold and silver than the mind can dream of.

The throne is also described as being made entirely of precious stones and is the size of a mountain. Over this throne hovers a large crown of more jewels and because of the throne's size, one must enter it by one of seven doors.

Someone else tells of a gigantic throne supported by large columns of rubies and diamonds and each time Solomon mounted it, the twelve golden lions roared, shaking the earth around them.

In keeping with Solomon's power over the world of darkness, which authors of black magic have written of for hundreds of years, it is said that books showing the evocation and control of devils are buried beneath the throne and he who possesses the throne possesses more than all of the riches of the greatest sovereign who ever lived. He possesses power equal to that of Satan and rivalling that of God.

**Marc Olden**

# CHAPTER ONE

## LONDON, January 9, 1848

Jonathan's eyes were bright, alert. He stared across the cluttered table at Arthur Lecky, whom he had just hypnotised and would soon kill.

'Tell me about the Throne of Solomon,' Jonathan said.

'I know of no throne, sir.' Lecky frowned at the sound of his own voice. 'The American never mentioned a throne to me.'

Jonathan inched forward in his chair, palms down on the table. The little fingers were missing from both hands. 'The American sought your services. I know this to be true.'

'To steal books for him, sir. Only books.'

'Tell me about those books.'

Arthur Lecky shivered. 'Works of darkness I would say, sir. Books on demons and devils. Books for them what loves Lucifer and the anti-Christ.'

Jonathan thought: This fool reeks of onions, tu'penny gin and bread piled high with lard, and the opium pipe in front of him means as much in his useless life as do the small boys who warm his bed at night. Yet he presumes, *dares* to speak of Lucifer, whom I serve.

*But when Solomon's Throne is mine never again shall I have to serve Lucifer, for he and all demons will be at my feet and even Asmodeus, king of all demons, will be forced to bow to me.*

Asmodeus, whom Solomon the master magician forced to build the Temple of Jerusalem, who later took his revenge on Solomon, sending him into exile and ruling in his place.

Asmodeus, the fiend of Persian and Hebrew scriptures, who filled men's hearts with anger, lust, with the desire for revenge.

Asmodeus, whom Jonathan had twice attempted to conjure from the world below, failing to do so each time, and who Jonathan knew wanted revenge for those attempts to force him into submission.

Which is why Jonathan desperately needed Solomon's Throne; without it he was doomed to a horrible death for having dared to enslave the king of demons. The throne was survival and it was

7

more. It was immortality and power equal to that of Lucifer, power surpassing that of all demons including the dreaded Asmodeus.

Jonathan.

Spiritualist, psychic, devil-worshipper, hypnotist, doctor, murderer.

Jonathan.

Conjurer of demons and a witch, a master black magician who exalted evil above all good, a man with an obsession for dominance and supreme power.

But even his powers could not long resist those of Asmodeus, who would never stop seeking vengeance on Jonathan for trying to subjugate him. To get Asmodeus to bow as he had once bowed to Solomon, Jonathan had to possess the throne and the books of magic hidden beneath it.

Solomon's Throne. Hidden for thousands of years, its untold wealth and power eluding all. But it wouldn't elude Jonathan, who now knew how to obtain it, who now knew how to bring it from the other world into this. *He knew.*

But first he needed those books that Arthur Lecky had stolen and passed on to the American. Lecky was a kidsman, the manager of a band of child thieves whom he forced to climb down narrow chimneys where panic meant being trapped and suffocating to death. Ugly little Arthur Lecky, with his toothy, squirrel-like face pitted by smallpox and framed by a shoulder-length red wig.

A wooden leg was attached to Lecky's right stump by a thick, brown strap, whose brass buckle was polished daily by one of his tiny thieves. Tonight his unwashed bony body was wrapped in a filthy, lice-ridden brocaded robe of yellow silk and, like others living in Victorian slums and eating the poisonous foods of those harsh times, Lecky looked much older than he was. He was thirty and looked sixty.

Some of his child thieves were purchased from parents too poor to raise them, or from other kidsmen; the rest were street orphans willing to steal in exchange for food and a place to sleep. Tonight only two were in the dirty, cluttered room used by Lecky as living quarters and storeroom for his stolen goods. Barefoot and in rags, the pair slept on the floor in front of the dying fire, drugged into sleep by 'Godfrey's Cordial', a combination of molasses and opium used to quiet children.

To the right of the fire and half in darkness, a grey rat, its eyes pinpricks of light, silently watched the sleeping children and waited.

Jonathan and Lecky were on the second floor of a decaying tenement in 'The Holy Land', London's worst criminal slum. Stretching from west London's Great Russell Street to St Giles High Street, The Holy Land was a dangerous and disease-ridden congestion of passages, lanes, courtyards and vile housing all overcrowded with thousands of starving, unemployed poor. Sharing the slum with them was the nation's largest collection of thieves, whores, beggars, gamblers and murderers, who only left The Holy Land to prey on the city surrounding them. Having struck, the predators quickly retreated back to the sanctuary and asylum of the infamous area, knowing its reputation would discourage all pursuit.

'Books belonged to Sir Norris Davy, sir,' said Arthur Lecky. 'The American come to his house and he seen 'em and he requests that I pinch 'em for 'im, me and me little ones. The American told me where they was, the books, and he told me when Sir Davy and the missus would be gone and where the servants slept. Sent in one of me little ones, I did, and she come down the chimney, opens a door and the others they come inside.'

*Damn the American.* Like Jonathan the American had spent long months pursuing the throne, and like Jonathan the American had a strong reason for risking everything to get it. Justin Coltman of New York was wealthy, young and dying, a doomed millionaire obsessed by spiritualism and the occult, by a belief that only the Throne of Solomon could cure his terminal cancer.

The men had never met, but each knew of the other.

Jonathan, wrapped in a black cloak, his face hidden by a hood and the chilled darkness of the room, pushed an oil lamp across the table and closer towards Arthur Lecky.

'You were paid well for stealing?'

'Most handsomely, sir.'

'Tell me what you saw when you read the books.'

'Devil books they was, sir. Books to summon devils and demons, to make 'em do your bidding.'

'The names of the books.' Under hypnosis, even a dirty pile of rags like Lecky could remember things eluding his brain in a waking state.

The kidsman, rigid and upright in the stolen church pew he used as a chair, blinked and remembered as the soft voice insisted that he do so. 'Yes sir, I did look at 'em, I did. Three books. Very expensive pieces of work. A Smagorad was one, and two had Solomon's name.'

He paused. Dearest Jesus, allow me to sleep, to enter that warm darkness this most sweet voice lures me into. But ... but the voice is also holding me back, *holding me back*. Yet I must please it. I must do as it commands.

'*The names.*' Jonathan's voice was a hard hiss, a knife drawn quickly from a sheath. He needed answers, *now*; there was no time to spare and he had enemies. There was Asmodeus and there was a mortal enemy, an Englishman whose life had been touched by Jonathan's evil and had vowed to kill him for it. The mortal was Pierce James Figg, a prizefighter with no power except that in his fists. Jonathan, who feared little on this earth, feared Figg without entirely knowing why. Two days ago Jonathan had killed Figg's wife.

'*La Clavicule de Solomon* was the second book,' said Lecky. 'And the third was *The Lemegeton of Solomon*.'

Jonathan inhaled with excitement. The very books he had traced to London and now had just missed.

'What did the American say to you?'

'Say, sir? He seemed most pleased. The books appeared to be important to 'im. He stares at 'em for a time and he ignores me. He speaks to the books, sir. He says, "Soon, soon." Then he says, "I'll have it. It *will* be mine." '

Jonathan, tense, angry, quickly stood up. *The American knows.* He knows that these books can lead him to the throne.

*Smagorad.* A 700-year-old book of magic and spells said to have been given Adam by God in consolation for the loss of Abel.

*La Clavicule de Solomon.* The Key of Solomon, a collection of writings on magic dating from the fourteenth century. Said to be the work of King Solomon, to be used in finding treasure and in summoning good or evil spirits.

*The Lemegeton of Solomon.* The Lesser Key of Solomon. Writings on magic dating from the seventeenth century. Used in summoning good or evil spirits.

Jonathan had sought these books for years, never getting closer than one more clue, one more trail to follow. And then his cunning had told him to stay close to Justin Coltman, to let the dying American's wealth and determination lead Jonathan to the throne.

Did Coltman know that their power lay in *combining* their knowledge? For hundreds of years, those who owned one or more of the books had lacked the knowledge to effectively use them. But Jonathan, who challenged God and demons, had that knowledge of the black arts; he knew how to use the three books to find the Throne of Solomon.

Find Justin Coltman. Find him before he stumbles across the secret in those writings. Coltman was no sorcerer, no magician; he was only a man driven by desperation, by fear of death, but his wealth gave him power to buy any knowledge he needed. Sooner or later he would find someone to pull Solomon's Throne from the pages of the three books he had just paid to have stolen.

Suddenly Jonathan froze, listening carefully, every instinct on edge. He heard angry noises coming from the muddy, uncobbled street, from scrawny cows and pigs rooting in the garbage in front of the tenement. Someone had savagely pushed and kicked the animals aside, someone who now ran into the building. Male footsteps. Heavy boots speeding along a dark, foul-smelling hallway and towards the stairs leading to Arthur Lecky's room. *Danger.*

Was it the boxer? Was it the ring-scarred Pierce James Figg, the only mortal Jonathan had ever feared? For a few seconds that fear tried to rule him, but he forced it down deeper and deeper inside himself and now he was again in control.

He quickly looked around the room. Only one door and not even one window.

The one door would lead Jonathan straight towards – *the boxer?*

In front of the fireplace one of the child thieves now sat up, rubbing sleep from her eyes. The long-tailed grey rat, which had been just inches from her face, turned and scampered back into darkness.

Stolen loot—clothing, furniture and bric-à-brac, from a silver-mounted ostrich egg to a collection of stuffed birds under glass—filled almost all of the room. Even thieves like Arthur Lecky shared the Victorian passion for possessions and clutter.

Jonathan blew out the oil lamp, leaving only the tiny fire to light the room. Now he was on his knees in front of Lecky, fingers moving quickly in the darkness, finding the leather strap that held the wooden leg to the kidsman's stump.

Seconds later, the door to Lecky's room crashed open and a male voice screamed, 'Magician, you are a dead man! I will have your life *now!*'

To the left of the door, Jonathan stood flat against the wall in total darkness, one end of the strap wrapped tightly around his left fist, the heavy buckle dangling at his side and lost in the folds of his cloak.

'Magician!'

Jonathan waited. *Not my life, fool, but yours.*

The footsteps rushed through the door, into the room and past Jonathan, who lifted his arm high. The brass buckle gleamed brightly, catching the eye of the grimy-faced little girl who sat on the floor and stared up at it.

# CHAPTER TWO

## LONDON, January 19, 1848

Charles Dickens, fighting a sore throat and a growing cold in his chest, sipped warm gin and lemon. His head throbbed, his voice was hoarse and he longed for a soft bed in a quiet, dark room. But quiet darkness would have to wait.

This morning the 35-year-old Dickens had stood in a cold rain with a crowd of twenty thousand people and watched as a fourteen-year-old boy was hung in front of Newgate Prison. Tonight the boy's grieving father sat in Dickens's book-lined study.

Dickens coughed phlegm from his raw throat. He was small, slim, with a thin, handsome face, and still in the red velvet waistcoat, blue cravat and tight grey trousers he'd worn to the hanging.

'Thank you for coming, Mr Figg.'

'Thankin' you for askin', Mr Dickens, sir. I, I had things to tend to, so I didn't get your message 'til late. Hopin' I'm not disturbin' you and the missus by appearin' at this hour.'

'It's gone just half eight, Mr Figg, and you are most certainly not disturbing us. I invited you, if you remember.'

'Grateful I am, sir. The boy's taken care of now. I did for him as I promised.'

Pierce James Figg, forty-eight and stocky, eyes red-rimmed from crying, folded his large, gnarled hands in his lap. He was a bare-knuckle prizefighter and boxing instructor whom Charles Dickens, the most prosperous and popular author of his day, the most famous man in England, respected as much as any man he knew.

Dickens threw his head back to clear long brown hair from his face. He sat in the wooden chair he preferred to the overstuffed furniture currently in vogue and now cramming the homes of those Englishmen who could afford it. He thought of the wealth and fame he now enjoyed and sadly shook his head; none of it gave him the power to remove even a portion of Figg's grief. God above, what grief! Figg's son hanged for a crime committed by the same man who had murdered Figg's wife.

Dickens sipped more gin, then stroked his painful throat and eyed the silent prizefighter. Not your delicate piece of porcelain,

Mr Figg, with his bulldog's face and round head which he shaved to prevent ring opponents from grabbing his hair. Scars from forehead to stubborn chin, and nose flatter than paper pasted to a wall. A slight limp in his right leg. No neck. Not the slightest inch of neck on the man. Just a bulldog's head crowning a body shaped like a large boulder, and yet there was a dignity and inner strength to this Mr Figg, whose voice was forever soft because of punches to his throat.

Tonight, Pierce James Figg sat in a black frock-coat borrowed for his son's hanging and burial, a coat which ill fitted his squat body. An awesome sight, dear Mr Figg. Decent, but no man to cross or do the dirty to. Makes his living teaching the use of fist, cudgel, knife and short-sword and no one does it better.

Pierce James Figg, descended from a long line of bare-knuckle prizefighters, was shrewd and plain-speaking, lacking formal education but possessed of an education of a different sort, the kind that came from surviving the brutal prize-ring and life on the edge of the underworld. Dickens knew Figg to be an honest man, something which could not be said for others in prizefighting.

'Your wife, Mrs Dickens. She's well, I trust?'

'Kate's just fine, Mr Figg.' Lord in heaven, thought Dickens, where does he find the strength to be that gracious *now*?

He smiled at Figg. 'She's reading to the children. Helps them to sleep. She says it's better for their health than going on a picnic with me. On occasion, I take my ten-year-old Charley and some of his school chums on picnics down by the river. Jolly, jolly times. We drink champagne. Kate says champagne isn't proper for children, but I tell her it's better than the horrid water spilling from our English taps.'

Dickens stopped. Trivial occurrences in my life, and all less than nothing to this man submerged in more agony than any one human being should be forced to endure. Poor Figg loses his wife and son and I talk of champagne. God in heaven forgive me.

Figg tried to smile and failed. Dickens was relieved. At least Figg hadn't taken offence.

Figg flopped his round shaven head back against the leather chair and spoke to the ceiling. 'Made me boy a promise, I did. He says to me, "Don't let them body-snatchers dig me up and sell me to the anatomists, them bloody doctors who will carve me into little bits. Promise me, dad. Promise me the sack'em-ups won't get me." '

Miserable ghouls, thought Dickens, terrifying us all, because the desecration of a grave was the most hideous of crimes. In a moment of bitter whimsy, someone had also named these criminals *resurrectionists*.

Figg dabbed at his eyes with a large white handkerchief. 'Filled me boy's coffin with quicklime. Done it meself. What's in there now ain't fit for nobody to touch. Won't be nobody dragging Will off for rum money.'

Dickens flinched. He had seven children of his own. *The idea of having to fill their coffins with quicklime . . .*

He remembered seeing a few resurrectionists near the hanging this morning, in the crowded Magpie and Stump tavern, where Figg and Dickens had gone for warm drinks against the wet January cold. Filthy, unshaven men with eyes like dirty coins, and smelling of roast herring and damp clothing, crudely dancing the waltz and polka with slovenly whores to the music of a cornet and fiddle.

To the crowd, the hanging was entertainment and many had waited throughout the night to make certain they were close enough to see it. The resurrectionists saw the hanging as a chance for profit, to perhaps get the boy's body before Figg reached it. But Figg had warned that anyone who touched young Will's body would die for it and no one had tried. The resurrectionists had watched like vultures, none of them with the courage to challenge the boxer.

Dickens finished his gin and lemon, placing the empty glass on a small table beside him. 'Did you talk with Lecky's children once more?'

'Yes, sir. That's also why I'm late. The little ones say police are done with them and don't see no more reason to pursue this matter. The court's judgement is all that's left now.' Figg swallowed and then barely breathed the words. 'Record's goin' to say that my boy Will crushed Mr Lecky's temple with a belt buckle, then put a ball through the head of the little girl what seen him do it.'

Charles Dickens snorted. 'Then sat on the floor dazed until the police came and arrested him. Will did not kill anyone.'

'Yes sir, I know.'

'Jonathan killed the kidsman and he killed the child with Will's pistol. He also hypnotised your lad. That was Will's story and it was the truth.'

'Yes sir.'

'Remember that, Mr Figg.'

The boxer's scarred cheeks were bright with his tears. 'Never goin' to forget it, sir.'

Dickens fingered a small white china monkey which he used as a paperweight and without which he felt he could not write. 'Such swift justice under our gracious Queen Alexandrina Victoria and her beloved Albert. A murder is committed and, one short week later, a boy hangs for it. Wasn't long ago that this country hung a ten-year-old lad and his eight-year-old sister for stealing a lace handkerchief. Why is it that we English are so intent on slaughtering our children? The scaffold or sixteen-hour working days. I wonder which is worse.'

'You've tried to help, sir. Your books, I mean.'

The author looked at his writing desk. *Oliver Twist, Nicholas Nickleby, Barnaby Rudge.* And don't forget the *Daily News,* the newspaper he'd started two years ago. All attempts at some sort of reform, to make the English despise child abuse as much as he did, to make the nation see that it could not continue to brutalise its children without brutalising itself. The children. 'Young lives which . . . had been one horrible endurance of cruelty and neglect.'

But his books, all highly successful, had changed little. England was a paradise for the privileged and a hell for the poor. For too many this nation, under God and Queen, was a place to die an early death, more than likely with an empty belly.

On the other side of the closed study door, the shaggy white terrier Timber Doodle ran in circles as it whined for its master. Dickens turned and smiled in the dog's direction. 'Given to me when I was in America six years ago. A presentation from Mr Mitchell, a popular American comedian.' He turned back to Figg. 'I've spoken to you in the past of my trip to America, and now you are about to embark for that land yourself.'

'To find Jonathan and kill him.'

Dickens crossed his legs and continued to stroke the china monkey. 'You pursue a dangerous quest, my friend. Jonathan's a most deadly adversary, with powers beyond those of mortal men. I'm something of an amateur hypnotist myself, as you know, and have some familiarity with related spiritual matters. I see in Jonathan only the blackest of deeds. And you don't even know what he looks like.'

'I shall kill him, sir.'

'As you must, as you should. Justice has failed you in the matter of your wife and son, so I deeply sympathise with your wish for satisfaction. I intend to assist you in my own fashion.'

'Mr Dickens, you have helped me quite a bit, let me say. I had no money for a solicitor for young Will, and you paid for one out of

16

your own pocket. Your own health's none too good these days, yet you went to the prison with me more than once. I'm deeply grateful.'

Dickens chuckled. 'My health. Ah my dear Figg, let us speak of that. I pen novels, plays, letters, stories, travel books, books for children, and I stand on stage and read from my works to audiences which pay me a pretty penny, by God. I'm quite an actor, they tell me, and the amateur theatricals I wallow in have also been well received. If I am tired, sir, it is my choice. If I have chosen exhaustion over boredom, then so be it. I find myself agreeing with Goethe who, when told he too worked excessively, replied that he had all eternity to rest. Eternity is unavoidable, but until it embraces me I shall keep myself fully consumed with living.'

Dickens stood up and stretched. 'Such days as these should never be as long as they are. I want to help you Mr Figg and I shall. Is it not true that I am very much in your debt?'

Figg squirmed uncomfortably in his chair, thick fingers going to the long, black, scarf-like tie he wore around what little amount of neck he possessed. 'You don't owe me, Mr Dickens, sir. You don't—'

Dickens placed a hand on the prizefighter's shoulder and spoke in a firm, low voice. 'Four years ago, remember? An agonisingly cold December it was, and my two little ones, Charley and Katey, were returning from school. A joyous time for them. Snow on the ground, Christmas to come, and to be young and dreaming of childish pleasures. That's when "the skinners" attacked them.

'You prevented my children from being terrorised and degraded, stripped of their clothes in the cold, Mr Figg. Providence sent you to strike down those men who would have left my Charley and Katey shivering naked in the snow.'

Figg said, 'That's when I met my son.'

Will had been with the skinners as a ten-year-old lookout, a hardened London street orphan who had never known his parents and who survived in the criminal underworld as best he could. Figg's fists had sent the two adult males to the ground, face down and bleeding in the snow, and before young Will could flee, Figg had caught him and slapped his face for being part of the crime.

'I was and still am most grateful,' Dickens said, 'and I shall always be.'

Figg didn't want to talk about what he'd done long ago. 'You've helped me, sir. You've sent people to me academy and I've made a few bob teachin' them. The famous have come to me door because you've told them to. You owe no more.'

Dickens threw back his head and laughed briefly. It hurt his throat to laugh, but he did. 'Send the famous to you? Mr Figg you are acquainted with more notables than I, and I know quite a long list of such fellows. Whom, among the glittering names of our day, have I sent to you? Ah yes. Fellow quill-pushers. Wilkie Collins. Thackeray, Browning, Tennyson. And pray tell, what did they do on arriving at your emporium? Not put on the mufflers, I assure you. Not one glove ever slipped around one ink-stained fist. They stood stock-still and stared with awe. That is what they did and none of it enriched your coffers by much, I'm afraid.'

'Their very presence sir.'

'Does not pay the butcher, Mr Figg. You've taught my young Charley a thing or two. He's had an occasional punch-up with his mates and acquitted himself quite well, thanks to you.'

Figg stared down at his lap. 'Taught young Will. Learnin' fast, he was. On the way to bein' a right-sized man. Had no last name when I met him. After a time, he come to me and he tells me he's takin' mine. My middle name and my last name.'

'The lad loved you. Respected you as well, and that is as it should have been. You took him from the streets, gave him a home and more. With you, there was Christian charity and the discipline a child cannot do without.'

Figg looked at Dickens. 'I think maybe it was me who really killed him.'

'Nonsense. If he spent more time in The Holy Land than he should, well we know the reason, don't we? He had become a changed young man, thanks to you, and that is what he told the unfortunate urchins trapped in that heartbreaking way of life. He wanted them to climb out of that savage squalor to become decent and God-fearing. He tried to give them what you had given him: hope, dignity, a reason for living.'

Figg dropped his chin to his wide chest. 'Shouldna let him keep talkin' to Lecky's children. Now he's got topped. Got hisself hanged.'

'That is hindsight, dear friend. Your son, and he was very much your son, wanted to pull the little ones from a disgusting existence. You have every reason to be proud of Will.'

'Died in my place, he did. I was the one what should have gone for the magician, not him.'

Dickens swallowed to lubricate his sore throat. Figg's guilt seemed to have aged the man. He looked a dozen years older than he had just days ago. 'Like you, Will knew about your wife and Jonathan, which means he also knew the kind of man Jonathan was. When Lecky's children told Will of the particular books they were to steal, books dealing with the spirit world, your son mistakenly thought those books were meant for Jonathan. So Will took it on himself to keep watch over Arthur Lecky.'

'And the magician appears there and me boy dies in me place.' Figg clenched his fingers into a pair of huge, menacing fists. 'Told me he wanted to do for Jonathan because of what the magician done to me and my missus. Smart lad, he was. Brave. Right brave.'

'He wanted to pay you back for taking him off the streets.'

'More than paid me back, he did. Stopped stealin', stopped carryin' a chiv. When I first got him, he used to brag about bein' the best beak hunter in London. Best chicken thief, he used to say he was.' Figg's eyes pleaded with Dickens. 'Sometimes I was thinkin' I was too hard on him, too strict.'

'No such thing, Mr Figg. Children need a most firm hand always. That is how I raise mine, sir. Most firm hand.' Too firm, Kate said. You're not warm enough, Charles, she would say. Dickens ignored her; he was a father, not a simpering country vicar playing up to children to get their attention and boost his own ego. Children needed an iron hand and that was that.

'I suppose you're right,' said Figg.

'It's been proven so. At least you know Jonathan's whereabouts.'

Figg folded his large white handkerchief, placing it neatly on one of his meaty thighs. 'Yes, sir. He was involved with them play actors and now they have all sailed for New York to work for one Phineas Taylor Barnum. I figure as how Jonathan will be there with 'em.'

Play actors. The same theatrical troupe Figg's actress wife had performed with.

Dickens said, 'Is there any chance that Jonathan is still in England?'

'I don't believe so, sir. Lecky's tots helped me some more today. Lecky was a sly one, always wantin' the edge. So after he agrees to do a deal with this American, he had one of his kids follow him just to see what is really and truly occurring in this matter. The little one follows the American to a Harley Street surgeon, he tells me. So when I finish with Will's body today, I pop 'round to see this medical fellow.'

'You have accomplished much today, Mr Figg.'

'Indeed, sir. This medical fellow, he tells me the American is Justin Coltman of New York, and Mr Coltman is dying of cancer. There is not the slightest hope that he will live. At first, mind you, the medical man he don't want to talk to me but he soon decides that I am intent on havin' words with him.'

Dickens smiled. An aroused Pierce James Figg could convince anyone to become suddenly verbal.

'This medical fellow says Mr Coltman wanted to leave for New York as quickly as possible. I have to be thinkin', Mr Dickens, that if Jonathan was involved with Lecky and Lecky was involved with Mr Coltman and these peculiar books, well sir, they must all be somehow involved with each other. I ain't puzzled all of it out yet, but it does seem that way to me.'

'You are thinking wisely, Mr Figg. Perhaps Mr Coltman also seeks Solomon's Throne. We know that Jonathan wants it at any cost.'

'Me wife said so.' Figg's wife. Twenty-two-year-old Althea, with waist-length auburn hair and sad eyes. An actress, whose infatuation with Jonathan had brought a horrible death upon her. When she had learned the truth about him and the acting troupe surrounding him, it was too late.

Figg bowed his round, shaved head. 'My boy weren't really my boy, you understand. I mean I found him, is all.' The tears started again. 'Give me pleasure feelin' he was mine. Sorta liked callin' him that. Late in life for a fella like me, what ain't never had much family to marry a young lady, sir, and have a lad he can call his own. I mean, a man like me cannot hope to rise above his station, and a family was a good thing—'

He broke down and sobbed.

Dickens watched helplessly, both hands now squeezing the tiny white china monkey. Hadn't life already done enough to this man who had survived more than his share of brutality in the prizering? And now it had taken what little family he had and placed them to rot somewhere in the earth. The Greeks are correct: Let no man count himself happy until he is dead. Jonathan. Let Figg find him and kill him.

At his desk, Dickens opened a drawer and pulled out two pale blue envelopes and a man's black leather belt. In the hall, Timber Doodle stopped whining and now began to bark.

Dickens said, 'I promised to help you. Are you certain I cannot offer you spirits or tea?'

'No sir. No stomach for it at the moment, thankin' you.'

'Mr Figg, you have buried three people you loved: a wife, a son, a father-in-law dead of grief. And yet you remain a most considerate gentleman. It is I who should thank you for allowing me to—'

'I have me downy moments, Mr Dickens. Me moments of cunning, sir.'

'As do we all. But here, please take these.' He handed Figg the pair of envelopes and the belt.

Figg held the belt in both hands. It seemed slightly heavy, as though there was some sort of metal under the black leather.

'There's a fold inside,' said Dickens. 'Open it.'

It was a money belt, its inside lined with gold sovereign coins.

Figg frowned, a sight most men would have found upsetting. He looked up at Dickens. 'Sir, I cannot accept this. It is more money than I could ever repay.'

'You can accept it, you shall accept it, and you shall not pay me back.'

'This could do for your lad's boxin' lessons 'til me dyin' day.'

'Call this a payment, a very small one, on the lives of my two children whom you rescued without knowing who they were.'

'Sir, you don't have to—'

'Mr Figg, fortunately I am in the position of being able to do exactly as I choose, thanks to what some say is my materialistic ruthlessness. Now listen to me, for my voice is fast fading and soon I shall be as silent as these walls around us. I have been to America and you, sir, have not. Advantage, mine. That rather crude, uncultured land has no currency. Imagine such a happenstance. No currency.'

Dickens began pacing the study, marching up and down in front of Figg, warming to the task of performing before an audience. 'One barters or pays in gold. Oh, there is *some* paper currency, but it is neither respected nor highly prized. The national government, the governments of local cities, banks, railroads and private citizens, each, sir, issues its own paper funding. One need not be a seer to realise that such an overabundance of financial paper cannot retain excessive value.'

He clapped his hands together once, stopping in place. 'Gold matters in the new world, dear friend, and you now are possessed of a tidy sum. I can well afford to share my good fortune for I have prospered far beyond my wildest dreams, far beyond my worth some would say. I am told and believe that no English author, nay,

21

no author in any language, is as highly paid for his labours as I, for which I thank both providence and my own ability to drive a hard bargain. Publishers—they are the bloodsuckers of our day.

'Now, Mr Figg, you are in my house and I beg you to do me the courtesy of agreeing with me in this matter. The money is yours. I lay no further claim on it and I refuse to entertain the slightest contradiction from you as to whether or not you are going to accept it.'

Figg attempted to interrupt. 'I had planned to sell me academy. There's a person what's interested. Wants to turn it into a hokey-pokey factory. That's a popular sweet at the moment, sir. Americans call it ice-cream.'

'Mr Figg, you also planned to place yourself in the hands of the Jews, did you not?'

Figg nodded. He had talked to the money-lenders.

'Keep your academy, Mr Figg. And keep the sovereigns. They will allow you to travel to America and seek out this man who kills as easily as I sharpen a quill pen. I recommend you sail on Samuel Cunard's steamer *Britannia*, which also was my conveyance to America. Forty guineas passage money, I believe.'

'I have got most of that, sir. Thanks to your generosity, I'll have no trouble with the rest.'

'Good. The journey will take two weeks, possibly less if the sea is smooth. It's a most swift passage, but it has its adventuresome moments. I remember the ship's cook got drunk on my crossing. Captain had him beaten with the fire hose. And we played whist on a day when the sea was in utter turmoil. Had to put the tricks in our pockets.

'Well, Mr Figg, to the matter of these envelopes. One is a letter of introduction to Titus Bootham, an Englishman who is editor and publisher of a small newspaper for Britons living in New York. Call upon him for any assistance in my name. He will gladly extend himself.'

Dickens smiled at the ceiling. 'The other letter. Ah, the other letter.' His throat was worse, the pain was strong but he had to talk now, for he was speaking of—

'Edgar Allan Poe. Remember that name, Mr Figg, for you will find Mr Poe one of the experiences of your lifetime. He is an American writer who is also poet, critic and very much an individual. I met him in Philadelphia during my tour of America six years ago. At that time, let me see, yes he was a journalist. *Graham's Magazine*, I believe. Yes, *Graham's*. Highly intelligent, supremely cultured, though I cannot in truth describe him as the most lovable man on God's earth.'

'Poe, sir?' Figg narrowed his eyes.

'Poe. Little Mr Poe and his black cape. His enemies, of whom he has more than a few, and his friends, of whom he had but a few, have bestowed upon him the nickname "Tomahawk", in tribute to his sharp tongue and aggressive talent for cutting up one and all in print. He can be most murderous when writing of those whom he considers inferior in ability to himself, which I am given to understand is everybody. He is possessed of a rather magnified opinion of himself. He is bitter, he can be amusing, and it is my opinion that he is a man of some literary worth.'

'Poe,' repeated Figg.

'He knows the underbelly of New York. Underworld, theatre, those consumed by the new fad of spiritualism, which I believe to be utter nonsense. He is a man of darkness, our little Mr Poe, but not like Jonathan. Poe's darkness lies in his mind, in his soul and he has effectively placed it on the page. At least that is my opinion. He is far from being a prosperous man and he is bitter because of it.'

Dickens coughed. 'He, I feel, best knows the haunts Jonathan will be drawn to. We have corresponded on occasion and I fear his health is none too good. His wife died a year ago and he still carries that pain. This letter will introduce you and I trust he will be of service.'

'Yes, sir.' Figg had doubts about service from such a man as Mr Poe, but Mr Dickens was trying to help him, so the boxer remained respectful.

'One further matter, Mr Figg. The belt. Can you get it around your waist?'

Figg stood up, taking off his black frock-coat. The belt did surround his waist, barely. Dickens nodded in approval.

Figg said, 'Seems a bit firm near the buckle, I would have to say.'

'It is indeed and not from the added coinage. You'll notice you do not slip the end into the buckle as you do most belts. It fastens on to a catch on the inside, leaving the buckle free. Now do as I say. Grip the buckle, then press that outside stud. Yes. Now pull sharply, Mr Figg.'

Figg did as he was told. The buckle came free and he held a dagger in his hand. The blade was small, but it could kill.

Dickens smiled. 'Assassination has always been a national sport in Italy, which is where I purchased this belt for reasons which elude me to this day. As you have told me, the Italians are experts with knives and stilettos. Should stand you in good stead, I dare say.'

'Thankin' you, sir.'

There was a knock on the study door, and a woman's voice said, 'Charles?'

When the author opened the door, Figg saw a fleshy, large-breasted woman holding the small, white-haired dog in her arms.

'Mr Figg,' she said.

'Mrs Dickens.' Figg quickly slipped the dagger-buckle back into the belt and watched husband and wife whisper.

Then Dickens turned to Figg. 'Mrs Dickens says the dog has been barking at three men who have passed in front of the house more than once tonight. The men have now disappeared into Regent's Park across the street.'

Figg said, 'Jonathan's men.'

'Are you sure?' Dickens walked towards him.

'Mrs Dickens,' said Figg, 'did you 'appen to catch a glance at the men yerself, mum?'

Kate Dickens said, 'I did, Mr Figg, though it is dark and I cannot swear clearly to what I might have seen.'

'Is one carryin' a small lantern, mum?'

'Why, why yes, he is.'

'Is one carryin' a quarterstaff and wearin' a high beaver hat?'

'I did see the staff, yes. The hat I cannot swear to.'

'Jonathan's men,' said Figg. 'Been on me since the hangin'.'

Suddenly Dickens was afraid and Figg knew it.

He said, 'Sorry I am, sir, for bringin' them into your home.'

'Don't be sorry, dear friend. I can rush for the constable if you'll stay here with Kate and the children.' Dickens placed his hands behind his back to keep them from trembling.

Figg picked up his black top hat. 'It is me they will be wantin' and it's me they will be gettin'.'

Kate Dickens said, 'How can you be sure it's—'

'I know, mum. 'Tis my business to know such men.'

Dickens said, 'There's three of them, Mr Figg.'

'Fightin' is me trade, sir.' The boxer placed the black top hat neatly on his shaven head. 'Jonathan would as soon do for me here as have me racin' up his back in America. Perhap I can convince one of the gentlemen in the park to tell me a thing or two. Thankin' you, sir.'

Dickens clutched at Figg's arm. 'Please let me fetch a constable.'

'And what can we officially charge those three out there with, sir?'

Both men stared silently at one another.

'They have come into your home, Mr Dickens. They shouldna done that. I haveta make sure your little ones are safe.'

Dickens took Figg's hand in both of his. 'Godspeed, dear friend.'

'God's been somewhat delayed in helpin' me of late, Mr Dickens, so now I mean to take other measures, if you don't mind.'

'Pray that we meet again, Mr Figg.'

'*You* pray, Mr Dickens. I shall now go out on to the street and deal with my difficulties in more direct manner. Thankin' you once more and good evenin' to you, mum.'

Figg touched the brim of his hat to Kate Dickens.

# CHAPTER THREE

## NEW YORK CITY, February 1848

Hamlet Sproul said of the dead man, whose body he had stolen from its grave two days ago and now held for ransom, 'Let us call him Mr Lazarus, for he too shall rise from the grave when you give us the money we ask.'

'I would like proof that you do indeed possess the body. At present, I have only your word and on that basis, I cannot ask his widow to pay ransom.'

'We could kill you, Mr Poe, and place you beside the decayin' Mr Lazarus. You would then be close enough to ensure yourself that we do own the gentleman in question. You can count on your death at my hands should you play treachery with me.'

'Going into darkness and distance holds no terror for me, sir.'

'Explain, please.'

'Death. I am not afraid of it.'

'Darkness and distance.' Hamlet Sproul aimed his derringer at Poe's forehead. 'The poet's touch.' Sproul squeezed the trigger. *Click.* The hammer fell on an empty chamber.

'One hundred thousand dollars, if you please, dear poet. And cash money. All in eagle coins. Paper money's barely fittin' for pluggin' holes in a man's boot, don't you think?' Sproul's smile was a quick glimpse of crooked yellow teeth surrounded by a blond beard streaked brown with tobacco stains.

Edgar Allan Poe blinked nervously. That filthy bastard Sproul. The pistol was empty. *And Poe had been afraid.* His small hands pushed down hard on the head of his cane, driving its tip deeper in to the sanded floor.

He said, 'You ask a lot in exchange for a dead man.'

Sproul's brogue was slurred by liquor. 'Poet, you must understand the ways of the heart. She'll be lovin' her husband 'til hell freezes over. Actually you both ought to be thankin' me. Instead of her waitin' to go to heaven to meet up with him again, I can deliver her man right here on earth.' Sproul snorted and the two other grave-robbers supported him with sly grins. Poe could have calmly killed all three.

Hamlet Sproul was the leader, a small, bearded man in a red flannel shirt and eyes to match, thought Poe. Sproul's floor-length green overcoat appeared to have been used in cleaning streets, and in addition to the derringer, which he fingered as a nun would beads, Sproul wore a bowie knife on a leather thong around his neck. The blade on the knife was a foot long and as wide as a man's hand.

He was homicidal and almost drunk. Poe watched him drink his fourth *flip*, a sickening concoction of rum, beer, sugar and the touch of a loggerhead, a red hot iron dipped into the brew. Bartenders kept the loggerheads hidden to prevent the drinkers from having at each other with them. Sproul's bloodshot eyes had the brilliance of barely controlled lunacy, thought Poe.

Poe, ill and hating the bitter winter weather, was in a grog shop, a disgusting gin mill in the Five Points slum. In this rum palace, which was no larger than a damp cellar, he sat at a table with the three Irish resurrectionists, who'd stolen the body of the wealthy 'Mr Lazarus' for ransom. At the widow's request, Poe had agreed to arrange an exchange of money for the dead husband. Poe had once been in love with the woman, and loved her still.

'A large sum, poet.' Sproul aimed his empty derringer at a painted, ten-year-old whore who had just entered the grog shop and stood shivering near the door, her thin body wet with snow and unable to stop trembling. 'But word has reached us that the lady is bee-reaved at the removal—'

'Theft.'

Sproul casually looked across the table at Poe and waited long seconds before smiling. 'Heard about your sharp tongue. They say you're a nasty little man of the pen, you are. I say *removal* of her husband's corpus from its final resting place.' His voice dared Poe to challenge him.

'Theft.'

The word was in the air before Poe could stop it. Tonight his courage came not from liquor, but from rage. Yes, he knew these ghouls would as soon spill his blood as spill more whisky. Hamlet Sproul, Tom Lowery, Sylvester Pier. Three of Ireland's worst exports. Paddy at his most loathsome. But in stealing 'Mr Lazarus', they had harmed Rachel.

He said, 'I am not here to agree to your demands unconditionally.'

'You are here as go-between for the weepin' widow, are ye not?'

Poe watched Sproul's eyes dart to the men on either side of him.

Sproul would slaughter butterflies and gouge the eyes from newborn lambs if there was a shilling to be gained from it.

'I am here for proof that you have the body in your possession. Your note indicates that you stole it and indeed someone has, for it is no longer in place.'

'Noticed that, didja?' Tom Lowery sneered, then swallowed more oysters, which at six cents a dozen were among the cheapest of foods. He was a hulking, bearded man in a tattered derby, hobnail boots which he used effectively in fights and a filthy, food-stained white shirt, long minus its collar and studs. Poe found him to be the most stomach-churning of the three ghouls. Lowery was said to have raped his own daughter, then sexually abused the small girl child who had resulted from that rape.

Even now he looked up from his oysters and gin at the child whore who peered through the oil lamp lit darkness for customers. Sproul said, 'None a that, Tom. To business first.'

Sylvester Pier said, 'Paid to notice things, he is, 'cause Mr Poe here is a writer.' The respect in Pier's voice was a mild shock to Poe.

'Read somethin' once,' said Pier.

Once would seem the sum total of your attempts at reading, thought Poe.

'Somethin' of yours, it was. 'Bout a bird.'

'I hates fuckin' birds.' Lowery spoke with his mouth full.

'Mr Poe writes good about birds,' continued Pier. 'This was some sort of poem. 'Bout a raven, I think. Yeah, a raven. Thought it was kinda nice.'

Poe pulled his black cloak tighter around him. Applause from a dullard, from a Hibernian vagabond to whom the picking of his very own nose must be ranked as a metaphysical achievement. Pier was nineteen, youngest of the three, and wore the faded uniform of a commodore in the United States Navy—dark double-breasted frock-coat, blue forage cap, dark blue trousers and a rusted, dull sword minus its scabbard. He was short, stocky, cheerful, and reminded Poe of a hand puppet. Pier's clean-shaven and pleasant face appeared to possess what little decency existed in the three grave-robbers.

Poe, observant, deductive, sensed that Sylvester Pier was a mental defective. How else to explain the youth's choice of trade and companions. Or his eternal, idiotic smile, or his wearing the uniform of an American naval officer and sitting with a grey mongrel dog in his lap. The dog's ears had been sliced off; it was a fighter, to be pitted against other dogs with the owners betting on the outcome. The ears had been removed to prevent them from being chewed off in combat.

'Join us in a glass, Mr Poe.' Sylvester Pier's wide smile seemed nailed in place. It was ear to ear and indicated nothing.

'Thank you, no.' Poe's mouth went suddenly dry and he averted his eyes from the bottle of gin in Pier's hand.

'Come now, sir, you are no son of temperance. That's for sure.'

Poe shook his head in emphatic refusal. Alcohol. *My cup of frenzy.* The smallest amount of liquor was enough to carry him into the arms of personal demons and such an embrace had always proven destructive. He always resisted, always fought the desire to rush to those devils that were his very own, but in the end he always succumbed. Alcohol had not pushed him into sorrow; sorrow had pushed him to drink, a bitter truth understood by few in Poe's life.

He was thirty-nine, his health and creative powers waning after a life of unending poverty and personal hell, and he drank because this was the only way to survive such an existence. He drank because he feared becoming as insane as his sister Rosalie, an adult whose mind had never gone beyond that of a twelve-year-old. He drank because publishers had cheated him during his entire writing career, because critics had insultingly found his work 'learned and mystical', because the American public was moronic and insensitive, a mass of idiots with tobacco juice for brains and the desire to read nothing more complicated than an Indian head penny.

He drank because it made him sick to his stomach to see fortune and praise heaped on talents inferior to his, talents which couldn't draw a straight line in mud with a stick. He drank because he had never made more than $800 for a year's work in his life.

Why did Poe 'sip the juice'? Because his adored wife Virginia had died much too young, as had his beloved mother and his stepmother as well. He drank to forget, and no man had more reason to.

But he could not forget that Rachel trusted him to settle this matter involving her dead husband. Rachel, who even now warmed his heart and gave him some small reason to hope that life held a little joy for him. Again Poe shook his head in refusal of Sylvester Pier's offer of gin. The lower classes called the drink 'Blue Ruin' or 'Strip-and-go-naked'.

'Our little poet musta taken the pledge. He's got a nice big *T* beside his name, I bet.' *T* for total abstinence. Teetotaller. Tom

Lowery didn't like little Mr Poe of the soft voice and precious manners and actin' like a bloody aristocrat and him all in shabby clothes, too. Lowery could squash him like a bug if he had to. Wasn't much to the man. No more than five foot eight, 130 pounds, and pale as the snow fallin' outside.

Lowery bit into a hard-boiled egg without removing the shell. Poe was sickly-looking, like somethin' that belonged under the earth and away from decent people. The poet had brown hair, grey eyes, thin lips and a long nose, too long if you ask Lowery. Shouldn't be puttin' it in other people's business. High, wide forehead you could paint a sign on and a moustache right beneath that long nose of his. Lowery blinked. Poe's unblinking grey eyes were on his.

Lowery annoyed, stopped chewing the boiled egg. Bits of white shell were caught in his beard. ' 'Ere now, what the hell you starin' at? You keep on doin' that and I'm comin' across the table and bite yer goddam nose off.' Gloomy-looking bastard, Lowery thought. Big head on him, too.

Poe's gentle voice had traces of a Southern accent. 'You eat like a Hun, sir.' *Playing with violence as always, aren't you, Eddy?*

Lowery frowned, uncertain, then deciding *yes*, he had been insulted. He grinned. 'Don't know what a Hun is, but I know what a drunk is and that's you, me little man. Seen you in a few rum palaces, drunk as a lord and ravin' at the top of yer lungs and nobody able to understand a goddam word of what you is yellin' about.'

Poe pointed across the table with his walking stick. 'Guard the mongrel well, Mr Pier. Your egg-eating friend may well press his sexual attentions upon it before the evening has ended.' *He enjoyed the danger; even though it terrified him, he enjoyed it.*

An angry Tom Lowery inhaled, his eyes almost closed. Hamlet Sproul placed a small hand against Lowery's chest to keep him seated. 'Stay, Tom. The poet's talent for abuse is well known and far superior to yours. I'm afraid. Words are his cannon and he is well supplied. Don't push Tom too far, Mr Poe. He's a violent man.'

Poe's eyes went to Sproul. 'I demand proof you have the body.'

Sproul petted Pier's grey mongrel. 'Thought you might.' He reached inside his long green coat and took out the brooch. Opening it, he kept it in the palm of his hand, extending his arm across the table to Poe. 'This here was buried with Mr Lazarus. No you can't have it, but you go back and tell the grievin' widow you saw it. She'll know what you are talkin' about, since she was the one who laid it on his breast just before the earth covered him.'

The brooch was gold, trimmed in small white pearls and opened to show tiny black and white daguerreotypes of Rachel and her husband. 'Nice little pictures of Mr and Mrs Lazarus.' A grinning Sproul snapped the brooch closed.

'Got more for you to look at, poet. Under the table. Go on. 'Ere, Tom, take the lamp and hold it down there so's the poet can see what's what.'

Poe shifted on his hard, wooden chair. No gas light in this hell-hole. Five Points had none of the modern conveniences enjoyed by the rest of New York. The grog shop was lit by sperm lamps—lamps filled with whale oil, one to a table and three on the bar. The darkness in here was like that of a mine shaft. The two windows had been whitewashed to prevent prying eyes from seeing inside, and all liquor was served from a plank placed on two empty barrels. The sanded floor was wet from snow-covered boots entering and leaving the grog shop, and the small room smelled of musty dampness, cheap alcohol and smoke from the oil lamps.

Poe watched the child prostitute leave with a burly man large enough to pick her up and carry the tiny whore under his arm.

'You wanted proof, poet. Now, goddam you, *look*!' Sproul's liquored voice was as savage as a meat-axe.

Poe leaned over and looked under the table. Light from the lamp stabbed his eyes and he felt its heat. He flinched at the sight of Lowery's upside-down and leering face, the man's beard shiny with juice from his oysters. ' 'Ere, Mr Poet, you hold the lamp.' A gigantic muddy paw shoved the lamp at Poe, who took it. Poe's mouth was dry and the anxiety he'd always suffered from made it hard to breathe.

Lowery was on his knees, fingers fumbling with a stained, brown sack. 'Feast yer eyes, Mr Poet.'

The ghoul held up the head of Rachel's husband with bits of ice gleaming in its long black hair and on its pale skin. The opened eyes glittered like polished glass and stared at Poe who used every ounce of willpower not to scream.

He sat up in his chair, forcing himself to breathe deeply, to forget the *smell* of the head, the *smell* that the ice could not mask.

Sproul stroked his derringer. 'Gets what you pay for—providin' you pays for it.'

Poe closed his eyes, then opened them and tried to concentrate on coloured prints of George Washington and an American eagle

31

hanging on the grimy wall in semi-darkness behind Tom Lowery. *It had been at his feet all the time.* He wanted to leap from his chair and lay his cane across Sproul's grinning face.

Sproul said, 'Pour a glass for the poet, Mr Pier. I think he needs it.'

Tom Lowery laughed.

Poe had tried, God he had tried. He hadn't had a drink in four days, not since Rachel had contacted him and asked his help. He owed her his best effort and that meant staying sober, staying healthy, staying sane. *But it had been at his feet all the time!*

Poe's trembling hands brought the glass of gin to his lips.

# CHAPTER FOUR

A disgusted Pierce James Figg wanted to kick Mr E. A. Poe in the head and be done with it.

Deep in drunken sleep, Poe lay curled on top of old newspapers in a dark corner of a cold, damp cellar, his slight body just inches from Figg's feet. The boxer was seeing him for the first time, and the man was nothing but a gin-soaked pile of rags. Figg would not piss on Mr Poe if each and every rag was in flames. Figg, squinting in the meagre candlelight, was angry and disappointed. Travelling across an ocean to talk to, God help us, *a lushington with a billy in his hole*, a drunkard with a handkerchief in his mouth, his skinny little body wrapped in black clothing that had seen better days.

Hungry and exhausted, on edge because of the man he was stalking, Figg had come directly from the steamer *Britannia* in New York harbour to the *New York Evening Mirror*, the newspaper which currently employed Mr Poe. In Figg's humble opinion, anyone dumb enough to employ Mr Poe had a pudding for a brain.

It was dawn, still snowing, and in a twenty-five cent cab ride from the docks, Figg had seen and smelled enough of New York to last him a lifetime. A filthy city of wooden houses and muddy streets, with garbage, dead animals and ashes from fireplaces in the streets, and rats and pigs feasting on it all. Gaslight threw beautiful long shadows on the snow, but you forgot that when you passed a slaughterhouse and heard cows and sheep crying out for their lives and you smelled their blood and dried guts, a stench which even the winter cold could not hide. Damn New York. *Find Jonathan quickly, kill him, then leave this city of dirt and ice.*

'What the 'ell was he mutterin' about when I come down them stairs?' Figg spoke to Josiah Rusher, an *Evening Mirror* copyboy and the only other person in the cellar.

'Oh that, sir. "Bird and bug, bird and bug".'

Figg's soft voice took on a sudden harshness. 'I 'eard it. I just wants to know what the 'ell he means by it.' He snapped the words at the boy like a whip, wiping the smile from his face.

'He is speaking of his creative works, sir. Bird is "The Raven", a poem of some magnificence, and bug is "The Gold Bug", a highly unusual work of detection. Public response to both has been most favourable, but I have heard him say that he would rather roast eternally on the devil's spit than be remembered merely for these two achievements.'

'Like to see him stand up, I would. I likes to remember 'im for that.' Poe was a *glock*, a half-wit, and that's all there was to it. Mr Dickens ought to be more particular about choosing his friends.

'Mr Poe is a good man, sir.' Josiah Rusher, seventeen, lean and stoop-shouldered in ink-stained overalls, red flannel shirt and mud-spattered boots, held a candle in one long, bony hand, shielding its flame with the other. Figg was frightening, an ominous-looking bull of a man with a scarred face and limping right leg and he stood between Josiah and the only staircase leading from the newspaper's storeroom. Upstairs, only a handful of people were in the paper at this early hour. But Eddy was his friend, the one person on the newspaper who treated him with kindness.

Josiah used the palm of his right hand to rub candle wax from the back of his left hand. 'Mr Poe is courteous, decisive, with much grace and enthusiasm.'

Figg snorted, then spat. In the candlelight the spit was a silver sliver on Poe's shoe. 'Don't be readin' to me over his bloody coffin, mate. When's his eyes goin' to open, may I ask yer worship?'

Josiah cleared his throat. 'Some-someone put him in a cab and told the driver to bring him here. That was an hour or so ago and I am given to understand that he had been down in Five Points.'

'What is Five Points, if I might make so bold?'

'A terrible slum, sir. Horrible place.' Josiah's eyes widened. 'Filled with Irish and coloureds and almost every soul there involved in the criminal pursuits. A wicked place and not one for a casual stroll.'

'This damn city reeks of Irish.' *So does London, for that matter.*

'Famine, sir, 1846. Over a million died of hunger in Ireland and others left to come—'

'To come to any bleedin' place where they could steal for a livin'.' Figg didn't like the Irish. One had tried to bite Figg's thumb off in a boxing match and Figg had stopped him by gouging out the Irishman's left eye.

'Uh, Mr Figg, if I might say so, he is not well, you know. Eddy is in poor health.'

'Sleeps well enough.'

'The smallest dram of whisky—'

'I can bloody well see that, mate.'

Josiah gripped the candle with both hands to keep it from shaking. Hot wax oozed down on to his fingers. Fear of Figg sent the boy's voice higher. '*Sir*, I mean sir, it is early and perhaps you would be warmed by coffee and brandy. If you come upstairs—'

'I ain't leavin' 'im.'

'He is a sick man, sir. Let him sleep and when he wakes, he will be in better condition to be of service to you.'

Figg, standing just beyond the circle of light from Josiah's candle, looked at the nervous copyboy. Not much older than my Will, and still growing. Within spitting distance of manhood, this one and hair as yellow as the king's gold. Scared of me and tryin' hard not to tremble, him and me bein' alone down here in this flippin' ice-house. Has Will's eyes, he does, eyes as green as England's hills. And he did offer me food and drink.

Brandy. Warms a man and that is a fact. Bit of food might help matters along as well, somethin' simple and not too challengin' to a man's stomach. Figg reached down and picked up the carpetbag containing the few things he had brought with him from London.

'Could use somethin' to eat while I waits. Willin' to pay, I am.' He forced a quick smile which Josiah couldn't see in the darkness.

But the copyboy heard the warmth in the boxer's voice and he considered himself reprieved from the most horrible of unknown fates. His grin was enormous. 'Just up those stairs in back of you, sir. I will place this candle on the packing case here so that Eddy shall have light when he awakens. It will be my pleasure to return and look in on him, and, most assuredly, I shall keep you advised concerning his every move.'

Figg's mumble could scarcely be heard. 'Pin a rose on 'im.'

'Sir?'

'Just sayin' goodbye to Mr Bird and Bug, is all.' Welcome to North America, Pierce James Figg, you frozen, unlucky bugger.

Halfway up the stairs, Figg turned and again looked down at Poe and his mind went back two weeks ago to England where another man lay at Figg's feet, this one having had his throat cut from ear to ear.

By Figg.


*Figg was stomach down in cold, wet grass. He squinted through darkness and falling rain at the three men who had followed him into Regent's Park.*

*The long, black frock-coat he'd worn to his son's hanging earlier today now covered his head and much of his body, allowing him to blend into the night, to become another shadow on the ground, to become an extension of shadows cast by trees near the park zoo. Moonlight gleamed on rain slicked leaves and Figg's right fist tightened around the small belt dagger. Bless you, Mr Dickens, sir. This here little sticker ain't no arsenal, but it is surely some small comfort to me.*

*A chilled rain drummed on his coat, drenching it, making it heavier. Pierce James Figg, master of the noble science of defence, master of the sword and cudgel, planned to use the rain-soaked coat as a weapon. The cold rain didn't bother him; he had been cold and wet before and would be again.*

Three. *Using the dagger point to lift the wet coat up an inch or two, he watched the killers spread out and look around for him. Figg's smile was deadly. Come for my life, have you? Well, step closer me lovelies and we will start the dance, you and I.*

'*He's bloomin' 'ere. Stop fiddle-arsin' around, you two, and find 'im.*' *Figg recognised Rosehearty's voice. Rosehearty was the leader, the one with a lantern and the high beaver hat. Six and a half feet tall, Rosehearty killed by shining the lantern in his victim's face then quickly slashing him across the stomach with a small sword whose blade was keen enough to slice a hair in two.*

'*Ain't with the animals, is he? I mean why the bleedin' 'ell he come to a zoo, say I.*' *That was one-eyed Timothy Buck, who now carried his Boutet flintlock pistol inside his long coat to keep it dry.*

*Rosehearty held the lantern high.* '*Wherever 'e is, we best find 'im. We ain't bein' paid to stand out 'ere in the bloody rain and hold 'ands. We been told to do 'im, and do 'im we will. Stubbs? Stubbs?*'

*Rosehearty called to the albino, a muscular man who carried a quarterstaff across his shoulder as though it was a musket. Stubbs's pure white hair was wet and clinging to a face almost the exact same colour. Figg knew him as a cruel man who robbed judys, those prostitutes who worked without the protection of a ponce. Stubbs enjoyed beating women and had killed three with his hands.*

'*I 'ear you, Master Hearty Rose.*' *Stubbs looked into the darkness towards Figg, as if his pink eyes could see the boxer.*

*Rosehearty pointed towards trees standing to the left of Figg. 'Stroll over there, if you do not mind, and see what you can see. We sees 'im leave Mr Dickens's 'ouse and come in 'ere, but now where the bleedin' 'ell has the bastard gone?'*

*Figg lowered the wet coat an inch, turning his head sideways to watch Stubbs, quarterstaff still on his shoulder, walk away from Rosehearty and Buck.*

'Bloody cold, it is.' Timothy Buck touched his black eyepatch which was soaked, then blew warm air into his cupped hands. He would like it just fine if that limping old bastard Figg would show himself so's Buck could put a ball in his ugly head and then they could all go to a tavern and enjoy life.

'Cold, you say.' Rosehearty's voice was even colder. 'Should we fail to do as Jonathan has ordered, it will grow suddenly warmer and not to our likin', so move your arse, you stupid sod!'

*Rosehearty, shoulder-length grey hair hanging down from under his tall beaver, knew Figg and hated him. Neither man had ever quarrelled; they had never even spoken to one another. But their paths had crossed at sporting events — dog fights, boxing matches, at rat pits where bets were made as to how many rats a fighting dog could slaughter in a given time. Figg knew what Rosehearty was, an assassin for hire and the boxer despised him. Rosehearty hated Figg because Figg was not afraid of him.*

'Buck, for the love of Jesus, will you please walk over there, yes there. Straight ahead. Look for some markin's, somethin' that says he ain't just flapped his wings and gone to heaven. Zoo be the only other place 'round 'ere and them animals is locked up tight, so why should he be 'eaded there.'

*Figg held his breath. Rosehearty was* flummut, *dangerous.*

*Rosehearty looked directly at the hidden Figg and said,* 'Best we not lose him.'

*Buck shivered.* 'What if we do?'

'Then it's a return to the home of the esteemed Master Charles Dickens, where we shall do our best to convince 'im to tell us where we can find Mr Figg. Master Dickens has 'imself several children, so it should be a simple matter to get him to speak up.'

*Figg's eyes narrowed. Dickens's children. Now there was no doubt about what to do. To protect Dickens's family, Figg must kill all three men.*

*Timothy Buck walked towards the trees in front of him, towards Figg.*

*Buck talked to himself through chattering teeth, hugging himself to keep his flintlock pistol from falling from under his coat.* 'Mr Figg, Mr Figg. When I 'ave you, I shall —'

You have me now!

*Figg quickly rose to his knees, the rain soaked coat in his left hand and he tossed it into Timothy Buck's face.*

Buck screamed with fear at the sudden movement, at the attack on his face from the darkness and went back on his heels, arms flailing in the air, trying to stop himself from falling backwards and Figg was up, crouched ready to spring.

'It's 'im! It's 'im! Oh God, oh God!' Buck shrieked like a woman and fell backwards on to the wet grass and Figg was on him, sitting on his chest and pulling the wet coat from Buck's face, then placing the blade of the small dagger hard against the right side of Buck's throat, pushing down and bringing the blade hard, deep and round in one savage stroke.

Then Figg, who had felt the pistol digging into his backside from under Buck's coat, was clawing for it. He looked up, finger still tearing at cloth and buttons, seeing Rosehearty and Stubbs running towards him, with Stubbs the faster, Stubbs with his seven-foot quarterstaff made of firm oak, a weapon that could crush your skull like a grape and smash your kneecaps into jelly. Figg could use one with superb skill. If he had one.

The Boutet flintlock was in his hand and rain was in his eyes, but he fired quickly because the water could easily damage the pistol, wetting the powder and causing it to misfire.

Crack! The ball caught Stubbs in the thigh, making him spin around and throw the quarterstaff in the air. Damn his eyes! Figg had put the ball in Stubbs because he'd wanted that quarterstaff. The wood had reach and that's what Figg wanted against the deadly Rosehearty and his lantern and small sword.

'One ball, Mr Figg. Only one ball!' Rosehearty's voice was triumphant as he raced towards the boxer. One life I got too, thought Figg, and I am not quite ready to part with it.

True, the flintlock fired only one ball but Figg still had use for the pistol. He narrowed his eyes, turning his head to the side, desperate to keep the light from Rosehearty's lantern from blinding him.

He stood and listened, hearing Stubbs moan and curse him and roll around on the wet ground, and he heard Rosehearty rushing towards him, mouth open and breathing loudly, confident of his kill, sure he would kill the boxer whom he hated so intensely.

Figg threw the empty pistol at Rosehearty, then ran towards Stubbs, following the sounds coming from the albino. Behind Figg, Rosehearty crouched, turning his body to protect the lantern, catching the tossed pistol on his right forearm.

'You cannot limp faster than I can run! I shall have you, Figg! I shall!'

Figg, still holding his drenched coat, reached Stubbs who lay on his back, pale, ugly face contorted with pain as he pressed down hard with blood-covered hands on the hole in his left thigh. When he saw Figg, he raised himself to his elbows, eyes searching the darkness for his quarterstaff. 'Kill you, you bloomin'—'

Figg kicked him in the face, snapping Stubbs's head violently to the right. *Bleed and die, mate.*

*The staff. Figg must have it. Where the bloody hell is it? Damn the rain.*

Figg saw it. Long, dark, lying half in moonlight and half in shadow. He limped towards it, widening his eyes to clear them of falling rain. Behind him, Figg heard Rosehearty splashing across the grass with long, loping strides, moving with remarkable swiftness for such a tall man. The staff was in Figg's hand and his back was to Rosehearty who saw an easy kill and continued charging. *The boxer's back and kidneys would bleed as well as his throat, so place the blade where he cannot see it and do as Jonathan ordered.*

Figg, eyes on the ground, saw the yellow pool of light grow larger around him as Rosehearty drew closer, saw his own shadow lengthen, saw Rosehearty's long shadow grow longer, longer ... The rain-soaked boxer waited, his back still to Rosehearty, still keeping the lantern's deadly light directly from his eyes, still on one knee as though tired, fumbling, indecisive.

His eyes never left the ground, never left Rosehearty's growing shadow.

Then he heard Rosehearty, heard the hissing noise as the assassin breathed through tightly clenched teeth, saw the killer's shadow almost on him, and that's when Figg, back still to Rosehearty, savagely drove the end of the quarterstaff into the pit of Rosehearty's stomach.

All of the breath left the tall man in one long, harsh sigh. His eyes bulged and the pressure against his stomach was massive, destructive, and Rosehearty doubled over, his tall beaver hat tumbling from his long, grey head. Figg scampered to his feet and was merciless; in his large hands, the quarterstaff was a blur, a seven-foot length of oak wielded with swift and vicious skill. He thought of his own dead, of what would happen to Dickens's children if Rosehearty was to live. *For Will, for Althea.*

Figg used both ends of the quarterstaff to kill Rosehearty.

A powerful blow broke the tall man's left wrist, sending his lamp to the rain-soaked ground. A second blow crushed his right knee-cap. Rosehearty's scream echoed in the rainy night as the agony

*raced up the right side of his body. And as Rosehearty fell towards
the ground, his arm and leg on fire with pain, Figg delivered the
third blow with his full strength behind it, crushing Rosehearty's
left temple, instantly killing him and driving the tall man into the
wet grass with sickening speed.*

*Figg never again looked at Rosehearty. He knew the man was
dead.*

*Stubbs, face knotted with pain, looked up at the lantern and
small sword in Figg's hands. 'Kill me, you bastard and be done
with it.'*

*Figg listened to the rain, eyes narrowed and on the albino. 'Some
words with you first.'*

*'First? What the bleedin' 'ell is first? You plan to do me, so do
me. You will be gettin' no words from me.' Stubbs closed his eyes
and clenched his teeth, hands pressing hard on his thigh wound.*

*Figg, down on one knee, held the lantern close to Stubbs's face.
'I shall kill you; this is a fact and I shall not deceive you on that
score. But I can kill you quickly or I can make a right bloody mess
of it. You do not have much time in which to consider.'*

*Stubbs frowned. Beads of rain clung to his unshaven chin and
darkened his clothing. 'Dyin' or dyin'. What kind of choice is that?'*

*'Not much. I do not mean for you to have much choice, Stubbs,
and you try my patience. You came for my life and now I mean to
have yours.'*

*'I gots a woman, you know. And kids.'*

*'You are scum, Stubbs. They will be right pleased to be quits of
you. Jonathan sent you to do me. Why?'*

*'Scairt of you. Never says so but we know he is. Says you are a
primitive and terrible force.' The albino used blood-covered fingers
to squeeze rain from his eyes.*

*Figg frowned. Jonathan afraid of him? 'Well paid were you?' he
asked.*

*'A guinea each.'*

*Figg snorted. 'Not very dear, am I?' Money you will spend in
hell, he thought.*

*Stubbs licked rainwater from his lips and tried to sit up. 'You are
cursed. Jonathan has a spell on you.'*

*For the first time that night, Figg felt the cold. 'Curse?'*

*'We saw him. A nail in your footprint. He had us follow you,
then Timothy Buck he runs to get Jonathan and he brings him to
one of your footprints and Jonathan he drives a nail in it, a nail
what comes from a coffin. And he curses you that you be harmed*

*until he pulls the nail from the footprint.'* Stubbs stiffened with pain, falling backwards into a greasy puddle.

'Why is Jonathan goin' to New York?'

Stubbs's lips were pressed tightly together against pain and his eyes were closed and he did not see the quick movement as Figg flicked his wrist and slashed the albino's cheek.

Stubbs squealed, flopping to his right, both hands on the right side of his face. Blood trickled through his fingers to mingle with the falling rain on the backs of his hands.

'I said to you Stubbs that you are lackin' in time. Answer me.'

'The bleedin' bloody throne, he wants. Solomon's Throne.' Stubbs clutched his cheek and moaned.

Solomon's Throne. Justin Coltman and Jonathan now gone to New York in pursuit of it. As Mr Dickens figured. Find Justin Coltman and you find Jonathan.

Stubbs pleaded for his life. 'Ain't never done nothin' to you Figg, afore tonight. Let me live. I promise you I shall never go on the hunt for you again.'

'I think this is correct, Stubbs. You will never hunt me again.'

Figg drove the point of the small sword deep into Stubbs's left side, piercing his heart, and the albino sighed, his eyes turning up in his head.

Figg remained in the park for a further fifteen minutes. He carried Rosehearty's body to a nearby lake, placing it in a rowboat which he then pushed out into the dark, chopping waters. Returning to the scene of the killings, he picked up Stubbs's body and carried it several yards to the zoo, where he threw it into a pile of straw near the elephant's cages. One-eyed Timothy Buck, the smallest, was last; his would be the longest trip.

After retrieving his belt dagger, Figg put on his rain-soaked coat and top hat, slung Timothy Buck over his shoulder and walked deeper into the deserted park. Minutes later, Buck's corpse was shoved under a band-stand in Queen Mary's Gardens. The discovery of three bodies in separate locations would draw less attention than three bodies lying side by side in this park once used by King Henry VIII as a private hunting forest. Little fuss would be made over this trio, Figg knew; they were of the underworld, where a man easily made enemies. Furthermore, the Peelers—the police—would be delighted to have three such vermin removed from this life.

At home, Figg cleaned himself in a hot tub then sipped mulled *wine in front of his fireplace, his mind on what he must do. In the morning he sent a note to Mr Charles Dickens, once more thanking him for his kind help and informing him that the three uninvited guests of last night would not be returning.*

*Three days later Figg was in a closet-sized cabin on the Cunard Steamer* Britannia *using his fingers to gently feed bits of food from his uneaten plate to a thin, grey and white cat smuggled aboard ship under Figg's coat. He watched carefully as the cat leaned its head to the right and chewed.*

*And when the cat did not die, Figg himself ate of the plate, for as he now stalked Jonathan, Jonathan also stalked him, and the life of a cat was a small price to pay for caution.*

Josiah Rusher corked the bottle. Mr Figg had swallowed three cups of coffee and brandy, which appeared to have had no more effect on him than a kiss from a gentle breeze. Josiah said, 'Mr Poe is a most accomplished scholar. He speaks French, Latin, Greek, Spanish and Italian and he is a master of—'

'Sippin' the juice, I suspects.'

Figg bit off a piece of stale bread. At the moment, he would settle for a few words in English from little Mr Poe, never mind all that other posh talk.

'Does not Mr Poe have a home of his own or is it always more convenient for him to lay his head in dark corners?'

Josiah Rusher said, 'He has a small cottage in the country, away from the city. It is in Fordham. He is hard put to meet the yearly rent, I am sorry to say.'

'Which is what amount?'

'One hundred dollars.'

'What is that in English money?'

'Twenty pounds, five dollars to the pound. You will find it to your advantage, Mr Figg, you being newly arrived to our shores, that we here in America still use English currency to some degree. Pounds, shillings, pence. We continue to traffic in them, though I must warn you there is still some ill-feeling against the English people because of the war of eighteen and twelve.'

Figg's soft voice was slightly amused. 'Dear me. Now I will be unable to get me beauty sleep what with this mighty problem weighin' me down.'

'I did not mean sir, that you, that . . . I mean the war was almost forty years ago but people have not forgotten.'

Figg nodded. 'A war can stay on the brain, it can.' He thought of Althea and Will.

From a desk near the front door, Figg looked through a huge plate-glass window out on to the snow-covered street and watched an old, bearded man wrapped in faded blankets stand on tiptoe to put out the flames in nearby gaslights. A cold dawn had streaked the sky a soft blue, gold and grey. A handful of men began arriving at the paper, bearded men bundled in layers of clothing, almost all chewing tobacco and spitting the juice in the general direction of spittoons and not caring if it landed inside or out. The huge ground floor was filled with desks and cubicles, most of which were empty and few of which were located anywhere near the now cold pot-bellied stoves. You could freeze meat in here, thought Figg and the brain of a man as well.

Later today he would pay a visit to Phineas Taylor Barnum's American Museum, to seek out members of Jonathan's acting group. Meanwhile, he would sit and stare at the snow until Mr Poe rose to greet the dawn. From then on, like it or not, the little man with the large forehead and brown hair, who lay wrapped in his own shabby black cloak downstairs, would belong to Pierce James Figg, who, by God, would use him for as long as it suited Figg.

'Josiah, you odious wastrel! Tend the flames before we pull the ice from our beards and stab you in the eyes with it!'

The copyboy flinched, yelling back at the voice. 'Yes, sir. Right quickly, sir.' He smiled weakly at Figg. 'Part of my job, sir. Tend the stoves, clean them, see that there is enough wood.'

'I have your assurance you will keep watch on our friend below?'

'Indeed, sir. As a matter of fact, the wood is stored there so I shall have to watch him, won't I?'

'Seems as much.'

Figg opened his pocket watch. Almost seven in the morning. Could use a lay-down himself, Figg could, but let us first have a nice little heart-to-heart with that dainty rum-pot downstairs. Speaks all of them languages, does he?

Two minutes after leaving Figg, Josiah Rusher returned with a pained look on his face.

'Mr Figg, sir, I—I—'

The boxer was on his feet. He knew.

'Gone.'

'Yes. There is another door, one used for deliveries and—'

Figg, carpetbag in hand, pushed the boy out of his way and ran towards the stairs, his stocky body waddling from side to side. He had not the time for whys and wherefores. That little bastard Poe had moved his arse elsewhere, just when Figg had business with him. Damn his eyes!

Figg disappeared through the door leading to the storeroom and Josiah Rusher shook his head in relief at still being alive.

# CHAPTER FIVE

Poe said, 'Then I take it you do not regard the ransom as excessive?'

'No, Eddy, I do not. I want my husband with me and I shall bear *any* cost of bringing that about. *Any cost.* I am a wealthy woman and would gladly give much more than one hundred thousand dollars to have him—'

Fighting tears, Rachel covered her eyes with a slim hand containing her wedding ring, a thick gold band studded with tiny bluegrey pearls. Poe, who stood looking down at her, waited. In control of herself once more, Rachel looked up at him with violet eyes shimmering behind tears and Poe, who found her one of the most beautiful women he had ever seen, knew he was falling in love with her again. He also sensed that Rachel was hiding something important from him, something involving her dead husband.

'Eddy, please regard this matter with much urgency. I must have him back. I beg you tell them that I accede to all demands.'

'As you wish. I am to place a coded message in the *Evening Mirror* if you agree to their terms. We shall then have to wait until they contact us in the same manner.'

'Wait?' Rachel frowned.

'To be told place and date of the next meeting and I would assume there will be even further delay, for it will be no simple matter to arrange the actual exchange of money for the body of your husband. Those who have him are hardened and suspicious men to whom life is cheap. They are on guard against treachery.' Poe did not tell her about seeing her husband's disembodied head which had caused him to drink and pass out. Nor did he tell her of the resurrectionists' deadly promise: *Betray us in this matter, dainty poet, and we will kill you and sell your remains to a medical school. Be told, poet.*

Poe warmed his cold fingers by bringing them up to his mouth and blowing on them. On the way here from the *Evening Mirror,* Poe had cleaned his face and hands with snow, combing his brown hair with his fingers. Yes, the cold snow had been brutal on his body, which had endured more than enough pain and discomfort in its thirty-nine years on earth, but he was a man who prided himself on a neat appearance. And at the front door of the white marble mansion where Rachel lived on Fifth Avenue, Poe had presented his card to the servant, a card made by himself for he couldn't afford to have them printed. The card was black-bordered and read simply *Edgar A. Poe,* and because Poe had only a few of them, he would have to ask Rachel to return it before he left.

Yes he was poor. He had gone hungry to feed his wife, to give her medicines, and still she had died and there would be no forgiving God for having taken away dearest Virginia, dearest Sissy. To be appreciated you must be read, and in his lifetime Poe had not been read, let us be most precise about that. His poems, his criticism, his short stories, his journalistic endeavours all drew a response best described as negligible. Oh, there was praise, but a stomach cannot fill itself on that; hosannas from Irving, Longfellow, Hawthorne and Dickens put neither logs on the fire nor tea in the cup.

Yes he was poor and he lived in fear of debtors' prison. He'd received as little as $4.94 for a piece of written work and been excessively grateful, for at the time it had been the difference between hunger and survival. Never had he earned more than $800 in a year and even that glorious occasion had occurred only twice in his life. *Twice in thirty-nine years.* He was poor, and therefore limited in everything he wanted to do.

Poverty, rejection. Defeat breeding defeat, and always there was his pride, a most fierce pride. Many called him egomaniac, for had he not said that he could not conceive of any being superior to himself, and did he not believe this to be so even now? Poe didn't regard this observation as mere authorial vanity, for his power to create had been proven by the criticism, poems and short works flowing from his pen in fifteen-hour working days, works which had not been equalled or excelled in that most ignorant land.

America the abominable, rich in stupidity and ruled by the tyrant called Mob. American democracy, 'The most odious and unsupportable despotism . . . upon the face of the earth.' What can one say of a nation whose national anthem is the same tune as the English drinking song 'Anacreon In Heaven'. Poe firmly believed that there was neither education nor culture in America. *Here all think for themselves and they cannot think.*

And Poe had told them so. Told them of their ignorance and in turn, they called him 'Tomahawk', the man who cuts his rivals to shreds with his bitter pen. A destructive man you are, Eddy. *Yes, but only to the aspirations of those untalented and pretentious*

*dolts, who with the intelligence of a squash, reach for heights for-*
*ever beyond them.*

Then you are an honest man, Eddy. *Yes, and I have paid dearly*
*for being so. Aristotle, I beg you to say of me as you said of your-*
*self—I think I have sufficient witness that I speak the truth,*
*namely, my poverty.*

Rachel stood up, turning her back to him and drawing her shawl
tighter around her shoulders. The shawl was lavender, as was her
gown and satin high-heeled shoes, shoes which a servant cleaned
daily with white wine and a piece of muslin. She was an inch
taller than Poe, with long hair that held all of the brown and gold
of autumn, hair combining fire and sun and reaching to her waist.
Poe, with his tremendous capacity for happiness and unhappiness,
had met and loved Rachel a year ago and she had given him both.
At that time she was alone, waiting for her husband to return from
somewhere in the world and Poe's wife was just recently beneath
the earth and he needed to love again.

Their love had not been of the flesh, for Rachel's attachment to
her husband had been firm, deep, unyielding. So Poe, who
worshipped beauty, had worshipped Rachel for it eased the hurt of
losing Virginia.

He had fame and was imaginative, and because women had
warned Rachel against him ('morbid, dangerous, a drunkard,
bitter'), Rachel had found him attractive, as did other women.
They delighted in each other and Poe had drunk deep of her
beauty and lived on hope, that agony of desire.

Then her husband had returned and Rachel left his life. What
remained was pain, something he knew quite well. Now she was in
his life again, in need of his help.

She wanted him to use his contacts as a journalist, as a man of
despair, as a man who knew too much about the underbelly and
dark side of Manhattan, and make contact with the grave-robbers
who had stolen her husband's body.

*But what was Rachel hiding from him?*

She gazed into the fire with eyes that did not blink. On the other
side of the closed door, a maid's laughter faded as she climbed a
staircase. 'Eddy?' Rachel turned to face him. 'Do you ever wish to
see your dearest wife alive, even for one brief moment?'

He twisted his thin mouth into a sad smile. 'I loved her totally,
some would say incoherently. I weep for her not with my tears but
with my heart's blood. My few remaining friends would prefer her
to be alive, for I would drink less and therefore, quarrel less. Were

47

Virginia alive, I would also spend less time in that land which exists between life and death.'

Rachel took one step towards him and stopped. Her eyes locked with his. 'Would it not be worth anything to feel her arms around you once more?'

Poe closed his eyes and shivered. The sickness that now threatened to overtake him was not that caused by drink or ill health. It was an even more cruel sickness, one rooted deep in personal despair. 'Six years ago, a wife whom I loved as no man ever loved before, ruptured a blood-vessel in singing. It was thought she would not live and so I took leave of her forever, undergoing each and every agony of her death. Then she achieved partial recovery and again I clutched at hope.'

Poe opened his eyes and inhaled deeply. 'Once more the vessel broke. And healed. One year later, it happened again and again I had no choice but to suffer with her. Partial recovery again until, until . . .' He blinked tears from his eyes.

'It broke again and again and again, crushing me with unspeakable torment as I watched her die and, yes, I died with her. Her pain only made me love her more dearly, and with all my strength I desperately clung to her life. I am, perhaps, too sensitive and all that concerns me I view with total and extreme seriousness, but this has made me a poet, which I would not change.'

Poe collapsed on to a dark green velvet sofa and spoke to the ceiling high above him. 'I became insane, alternating that hideous state of mind with unfortunate intervals of the most horrible sanity. I drank, God knows how much or how often, and I continued to exist, for one cannot call what I *endured* living. I existed on a pendulum ruthlessly swinging back and forth between despair and hope. Would my dearest one live, would she die? No man, let alone myself, could continue living that way without total loss of reason, and when the deliverance for which I prayed finally came I was no happier. For what cured me of living between despair and hope was the death of my wife. The solution became the problem.'

Poe leaned forward, elbows on his knees. 'My only life died and let me tell you that the one I received in its stead I hurl back at God and curse him for giving it to me.'

He felt Rachel come up behind him and place her hands on his shoulders. 'Eddy, it can be done.'

Poe turned to look at her.

'Eddy, it is possible for the dead to live again.'

He stared at her for long seconds, then said, 'I was correct.'

The tone in his voice made her withdraw her hands.

Poe stood up to face her. He *was* correct. Oversensitive Poe, with his mind buried in tales of terror, revenge and murder, with his soul consumed by death, fantasy, mystery and ratiocination, Poe who never guessed but who analysed carefully and accurately. Poe who was admired, derided, feared, scorned. *Poe knew.*

'Rachel?'

She backed away from him.

'Rachel, who has convinced you that your husband can be brought back to life?'

'I, I—' She folded her arms under the lavender shawl, a barrier against Poe. She aimed her chin at him. She feels anger and fear, he thought, and so do I, for she is now in the hands of those who will harm her if they can.

He shook his head slowly. His Southern voice was softer than usual. 'And so they have you as well.'

She spun round, her back now to him.

Poe hurried around the sofa, a hand reaching out for her. He wanted to protect her. 'Rachel, they are frauds!'

'They are not!'

'Rachel, these newfangled spiritualists are obscene frauds, please believe me. It is a new fad and will soon be exposed for the dangerous nonsense it is. Spiritualists claim they can evoke the dead. Rachel, they cannot. They claim to be able to speak to the dead. They cannot. They claim the dead speak through them and I tell you this is not so. Oh Rachel, do listen, I beg you!'

She covered her face with her hands and Poe took her in his arms, stroking her long hair. 'Rachel, Rachel.'

Poe despised spiritualism because he pursued the truth in all things and this was lies, merely another affront to what little human intelligence could be found in this boorish nation. Money changed hands of course, for as Washington Irving had told him, the almighty dollar reigned in this democratic land. In dark rooms and for large fees, mediums throughout New York City were causing tables to turn and tilt, musical instruments to play through the touch of invisible hands, spirits to 'write' on slates, bells to ring, bodies to levitate in darkness, and even glasses of water to overturn.

And this trickery was growing ever popular in America. In New York spiritualism was an epidemic, a most lucrative one to be sure, with victims prepared to believe over logic and sanity. Spiritualism was on the rise because people like Rachel would do *anything*, pay *anything* to hear that the beloved still lived. These days no one asks after your health, but how does your table turn. *Good, and how is yours, sir?* Spiritualism was fraud for money, a rising fad and one which Poe wanted to see exposed.

She looked at him and he felt her pain.

'Eddy, I love him as much as you loved Virginia. I want him back.'

'You will never see him alive.'

'Eddy, get him back for me. Bring us together again. Please.' Her fingers dug into his arms. Her intensity and determination were unnerving.

'Rachel—'

'He is waiting for me to—'

Poe grabbed her shoulders and shook her, shouting at the top of his voice. 'Not in this world, not in this world! You must understand this. You must! The dead have no place in this life, in this world, not your dead, not my dead, not—'

A fist banged on the door. 'Missus, are you—'

Rachel shouted, 'I am fine, Charles. There is no need for alarm. Please return to your duties, and thank you.'

Poe lowered his voice. 'Do not do this, please! Flee these people. They will only harm—'

'Miles Standish will not harm me!'

'Miles Standish.' Poe's hands dropped from her shoulder. Miles, with his historic name, was the lawyer for Rachel and her husband, a man Poe knew had too much interest in the dead. He was obsessed by the medical profession and spent hours watching the dissection of cadavers. He was wealthy, educated and he would be responsible for arranging for the ransom money to be withdrawn from Rachel's accounts. Poe, who felt that Miles's interest in Rachel was growing more personal than professional, did not like him. It was more than jealousy; on first meeting, Standish had made fun of Poe's threadbare clothes and Poe had retaliated with a cutting remark that had drawn laughter from those present. Poe knew Miles Standish would never forgive him for this public humiliation.

He said, 'Did Miles arrange for you to become involved with—'

'Oh Eddy.' She walked away from him. 'Miles wants me to be happy.' She stood looking through a window out on to Fifth Avenue at a haywagon moving slowly on the cobbled street. 'Hay is expensive, Eddy, did you know that. Thirty dollars a ton.'

'Damn the hay!' He gripped her shoulders and turned her round to face him. 'Rachel!'

Her face was streaked with tears. 'I will die without him, Eddy. Please bring him back to me. Please.'

'Rachel, I—'

'You know how it feels, you know the hurt, the emptiness. You told me.'

Poe bowed his head. 'What do you want me to do?'

'I trust only you, none other. Go to Mr Standish tomorrow. He is away today on business. I shall give you a note. Speak to him about the ransom. Tell him to begin arrangements now, to have the money ready so that, so that . . .'

'I shall.'

'Thank you.' She touched his cheek with one hand. 'Tell him to see me when he has spoken to my bank. I do not want him in this house until he has done as I asked. Please let him understand this.'

'A question.'

'Yes.'

'Who is the spiritualist in whom you have placed your trust?' And your funds, he thought.

She hesitated.

'Rachel, you ask much of me and I do it willingly. But, in turn, you must be honest with me.'

'Paracelsus. He calls himself Paracelsus.'

Poe threw back his head and laughed. 'Paracelsus. To hear this name is worth my trip this morning through the snow. Paracelsus.'

Poe continued to laugh until he again sat down on the green velvet couch. 'I raced from my sleep, such as it was, to arrive here early enough to make my report, and now you tell me that a spiritualist calling himself Paracelsus has promised to reunite you and—'

'I will not have you scorn him!'

Poe quickly stood up. 'My apologies, dearest Rachel. It is just that the name is of such magnitude that I could not help but be impressed. The original Paracelsus was one of the most startling figures in magic. A sixteenth-century Swiss university professor, brilliant, arrogant. He was magician-physician, alchemist, philosopher. It is said he achieved miraculous cures—'

'I do not want to hear more. You mock me.'

'I do not.'

'Then you will do as I ask?'

He nodded slowly.

51

'I thank you, Eddy.'

And even though she stood in front of him, she had closed a door and Poe was no longer able to touch her.

'Rachel—' *He had to make her see that the dead do not return.*

She walked back to the window.

Outside in the February cold, Poe pulled his cloak around him and waited for an omnibus which would take him to a train. From there he'd leave for the country, for his small cottage in Fordham where there was work to do. Mrs Clemm, his mother-in-law, the dearest friend left in his life, lived with him, and it was she who found these horrid and untalented women who paid her a few dollars to have Poe praise and edit their poems. Humiliating labour but it put bread on the table.

More than once, Poe had sat alone on a rock near his tiny cottage and muttered of his 'desire to die and get rid of these literary bores' with their fluttering fans, huge crinolines and handkerchiefs soaked in ether against the odours of dead horses and manure clogging Manhattan streets. He and dear Muddy needed the money, so do it and be done. Then rest, and tomorrow Miles Standish.

Eddy Poe, 'a soul lost', 'a glorious devil' in the eyes of women who collected lost souls, now had less than one dollar in change in his pockets. He turned to see Rachel staring through the window at him, and when she saw him looking back she vanished.


Someone called his name.

Poe quickly brought his head up from his chest. He was awake and listening.

He was in his cold, bare cottage, and seconds ago he'd fallen asleep in the small sitting-room, chin on his chest and slumped on a wooden chair. His sleep was fitful, uneven, a tortuous escape from reading the wretched poetry of women whose hands should be removed to prevent them from ever picking up a pen again. Believe the Talmud when it says—*Who can protest and does not, is an accomplice in the act.* Poe's protest against this drivel had been to slip into uneasy sleep.

*Someone called his name.*

Poe's cloak was around his shoulders, his greatcoat across his knees; he lacked money for firewood. Two cheap candles sputtered and dripped wax on a tiny table covered with sheets of poetry, and though some of the sheets were perfumed, all reeked with the odour of incompetence. Poe was to read, edit and, may God forgive him for doing so, praise these miserable musings.

It was almost midnight, with dear Muddy asleep upstairs, widow's cap covering her snow-white hair, and Poe was now awake and listening. Someone had called his name. Or had he dreamed—

'Eddy! Eddy!'

He heard it clearly. A woman's voice coming from outside the cottage.

'Eddy, come to me! Come to me!'

*Who?*

'Eddy it is I, it is your beloved Sissy!'

*His wife. His dead wife.*

Poe was on his feet, to the door and tearing it open, staring out into the night and seeing her by the snow-covered lilac bushes near the road. His heart was about to shatter; he could barely breathe. The agony was incredibly exciting.

'Eddy, it is I, Virginia. I love you. Come to me!'

He saw the slim, cloaked figure of a woman, her pale thin face made whiter by moonlight and, in Poe's tormented mind, weakened by illness, by sorrow, by unending disappointment, the line between real and unreal disappeared. His heart was seized by well remembered grief and he leaped from the front porch, falling to his knees in snow, screaming her name.

'Sissy! Sissy!'

He crawled towards her, reached for her with trembling hands. He got to his feet, stumbled through knee-high snow, every inch of his body and mind aching to touch her. For one touch, *one touch,* he would give his soul and more. He fell face down in the snow, his eyes now blinded by the icy softness. And when he struggled to his knees, she was gone.

'Sissy!' Her name echoed in the night.

He looked down at the footprints in the snow, saw the blood in them. *His wife had died of a ruptured blood vessel in her throat and that had been one year ago and she died in his arms.*

Still on his knees, Poe pressed handfuls of the blood-stained snow to his lips and cried out his wife's name again and again.

And somewhere in his new-found hell he remembered that Rachel had told him the dead could be made to live once more. He remembered.

# CHAPTER SIX

Sylvester Pier's fingers clawed in vain at the noose drawn tightly around his neck.

He hung from the ceiling, feet just inches from the floor, eyes bulging hideously. The other end of the rope had been passed through a hook embedded in the ceiling of the tenement room, and Jonathan, in controlled rage, now pulled down on it, keeping Sylvester Pier in the air. Pier had betrayed him and would pay for it with his miserable life.

Meanwhile, the childlike grave-robber suffered in his last seconds on earth. Pain and a lack of air had turned his pleasant face blood-red and ugly. He rasped through his open mouth, in a total panic to breathe again, and Jonathan, sensing his agony, pulled harder. The two were alone in a shabby room whose only comforts were a pile of straw for a bed and a tin bucket burning charcoal for light and heat. Sylvester Pier, along with Hamlet Sproul and Tom Lowery, had taken what belonged to Jonathan and, for that, all three would die. The three grave-robbers would be a sacrifice to Asmodeus, to buy Jonathan time in his frenzied attempt to survive the demon.

Brainless Sylvester Pier. Happy when someone else was thinking for him, leaving him free to stroll Manhattan's muddy streets in uniforms stolen from drunken military men.

Pier kicked the air and felt the darkness squeeze his brain tighter and tighter. The noose dug into his neck, making his ears ring and giving him pain that was complete, unrelieved, and his eyes would not stop watering. *Air. For the love of Mary and Joseph, let me breathe.* His grey mongrel dog lay on its side, breathing slowly, for it suffered as well. Jonathan had kicked it several times with a booted foot, crushing ribs on its right side, driving sharp ends of broken bones into the dog's entrails, and the dog had laid down to die.

'I want you to know why you are dying.' Jonathan pulled harder, jerking the young grave-robber higher in the air. 'You are scum, the three of you. I set you an important task and you betrayed me. Here is my answer.'

Jonathan eased his grip on the rope, letting Sylvester Pier's feet barely touch the dusty wooden floor. *Let him think he will live. Let him think that I have been weakened by mercy. Let his agony be prolonged.*

Sylvester Pier, standing on tiptoe, greedily sucked in air. The rusted sword that was part of his uniform slipped from his belt and clattered to the floor. *Air.* He felt as though he'd been without it for a long, long time. He'd come to this decaying, abandoned building because of a message received from Edgar Allan Poe. *Come alone ten tonight. First house, Worth Street. Third floor, corner room. Important we talk. Trust me, your gain. E. A. Poe.*

Your gain. Message and Mr Poe's black-bordered card had been folded around an eagle coin and slipped to Sylvester Pier at a crowded dog fight. After betting the ten dollars and losing, Pier had left to keep his appointment with the little poet, whom he liked.

In full naval officer's uniform and with his dog in his arms, Sylvester Pier had stepped into the dark room and been struck on the head. When he regained consciousness, he was dangling from a rope connected to a ceiling hook where a chandelier had once glittered in days when the slum tenement had been a grand Dutch mansion.

Jonathan jerked hard on the rope, again sending Pier into the air. 'I want you to know why you are dying. You, Sproul and Lowery were hired to do a job for me. Instead you satisfied your own greed and turned from me and I cannot allow that to go unpunished. There will be no disobedience, especially from such as you.'

Caught between an unwillingness to believe what was happening to him and an increasing horror at how near he was to death, Pier tried to say the word *why*.

Jonathan sensed this. He smiled.

'Mr Lazarus,' he said and pulled down on the rope as hard as he could.

When Sylvester Pier was dead, Jonathan released the rope, letting the body fall to the floor. From down in the narrow, muddy street a Hot Corn girl lifted her voice in song.

> 'All you that's got money—
> Poor me that's got none—
> Come buy my lily hot corn—
> And let me go home.'

Jonathan could not go home yet. The sacrifice to Asmodeus must be made, and that meant Sylvester Pier still had a role to play. From under his cloak, Jonathan produced a surgeon's scalpel. Dropping to his knees beside the body, Jonathan pulled open Pier's naval officer's tunic, revealing a red undershirt. With one quick move, the undershirt was slashed, baring the grave-robber's hairless chest.

By the tiny light from the bucket of burning charcoal, Jonathan used the scalpel on Sylvester Pier.

And the Hot Corn girl sang.

# CHAPTER SEVEN

'I shall be blunt, Mr Poe.'

'Which means, Mr Standish, that you are prepared to beat me about the head with unpleasant truths while expecting me to admire your courage in doing so. We despise each other, you and I, and having established that let us proceed.'

Miles Standish, plump, red-bearded and well groomed in a suit of orange and green plaid, continued as though he hadn't heard. 'I shall be blunt, Mr Poe. You have ambitions—'

'A contamination which afflicts you as well.'

'You seek money, sir. A great deal of it. I am referring to your attempts to finance a magazine which you would publish and edit. "The Stylus" I believe you propose to call it, and I ask you now, is it your intention to squeeze money from Rachel—'

'Sir, you are objectionable!' Poe was on his feet, soft Southern voice trembling. The part of him that loved violence wanted to take a whip to this pompous fool and slice him into bleeding strips. Poe's nostrils flared with rage; a vein throbbed on his high pale forehead. He fought for control, forcing himself to speak slowly. 'You are accusing me of using my relationship with a lady for personal profit. That is something I cannot forgive.'

Miles Standish touched his steel-rimmed spectacles with manicured fingers, then hooked his thumbs into the pockets of a green silk waistcoat. Poe was poor, a walking bundle of rags, the writer of unprofitable books. Failure is the only crime, thought Standish, and Poe was guilty of it and therefore should be despised.

Standish said, 'She is a woman quite rich. Need I say that she is also vulnerable at the moment, having lost her husband both in life and in death. I am given to understand that you prefer she not pay the ransom—'

'The money to be snatched from the outstretched palms of the ghouls and pressed into mine. I believe that is your train of thought.'

'It is no secret, Mr Poe, that you have tried for years and failed to get the money to publish your own magazine. Your personal problems are, of course, your concern. But we are discussing my client and she represents a possible upturn in your, let us say, sorry fortunes.'

Standish inhaled snuff from between his thumb and forefinger, sneezed to clear his head, then wiped his nose with an orange silk handkerchief. 'That is, if she agrees to help you, and let me say I shall do all in my power to see that she does not.'

Poe looked down at his worn, snow-wet boots. Battered leather on a spotless, pearl-grey carpet. He and Miles Standish were in the billiard room of the lawyer's Washington Square mansion, a large room with a billiard table, rocking-chairs, huge desk, fireplace, and stained-glass windows alive with the morning sun. The room represented money, something which had eluded Poe all of his life. He didn't need Standish to remind him of this.

Poe stared at a stained-glass window, losing himself in its sensuous beauty, in its bright green, red, purple. He'd always been poor. Practically all of his writing had been short pieces—stories, poems, criticisms, journalism. Quick writing for quick money; he'd never known the luxury of enough cash to attempt longer works. Fast Eddy. Do it in a hurry, collect your few coins and stand ready to do it all over again. Run like a frightened deer. Live from dollar to dollar and watch your wife starve because you couldn't feed her.

His eyes went to the walls covered with red wallpaper, expensive oil paintings and several highly polished gas-jets. No cheap tallow candles for Miles Standish. No oil in a wooden dish with a wick tossed in to furnish the most meagre of lights. He had excellent lighting and now he wanted the best of women. He wanted Rachel and that's why he was attacking Poe. He wanted Poe to know his place. Miles Standish was a fleshy fool who believed himself better than Poe, and Poe, always with a need to prove his superiority, was now going to show Standish that he'd made a mistake with this assumption.

Poe sat down. 'I assume you know what a Barnburner is. If not, allow me to enlighten you. A Barnburner is a member of that fool faction of the Democratic Party who is against slavery. These rather meddlesome fools are quite willing to destroy this country by seeking active conflict with slave interests. They are like the farmer anxious to rid his barn of rats who does so by burning the barn down. So much for the origin of the name.'

Poe steepled his fingers under his chin. 'How much money would it cost you, Mr Standish, if those Southern cotton-growers you represent on Wall Street for high fees were to learn that you, sir, are a

Barnburner, that you contribute money, secretly of course, to anti-slavery causes? Would they be pleased to hear that their New York lawyer is a hypocrite, that he only pretends to favour slavery while secretly doing whatever he can to bring it to an end.'

Standish frowned. Some of the arrogance was gone from his voice. 'And you, sir, are in favour of slavery?'

'Indeed. Now and forever more. I was raised in Virginia where my family owned and sold slaves and I say to you that there is no shame in this. Had God preferred the Negro to be freed, he most certainly would have arranged it before now. Since our darker brethren continue in servitude, it is logical to assume that this is in harmony with divine providence. Negroes represent a danger—'

'Danger?'

'Insurrection, sir. Insurrection. There have been more than a few in the history of the republic and each one has meant hazard to the white man and all that he holds dear. Servitude is preferable to the dangers of insurrection. I might add most slaves are loyal and most masters responsible. I see no reason to damage this acceptable balance.'

'And you now threaten to expose what you refer to as my abolitionist sympathies.'

'I remind you, sir, that I am neither your dog nor the carpet beneath your feet and your attempts at putting me in my place go unheeded.'

Standish, standing near the fireplace, took another pinch of snuff. God above, the man was indeed 'mad, bad and dangerous', which is what they said of Byron, who at least had the decency to be dead these past twenty-four years and consequently was less of a burden than he ordinarily might be. Poe was very much alive, unfortunately. And how did he find out about Standish's anti-slavery activities? *How?*

He said, 'Rachel says you are not pleased about her association with Doctor Paracelsus.'

Poe snorted. 'Spiritualism may be as new as the morning sun but I believe it to be fraud. *Complete—utter—fraud.*' With each word, he slammed his right palm down hard on his knee. 'Your spiritualism, sir, thrives on those possessing open mouth, open eyes, open purse. These parasites, for what else can one call them, present more jeopardy to your *client* than I do.'

'You have not met Doctor Paracelsus.'

'An honour I am prepared to forego.'

Poe sneered, making no attempt to hide his contempt for Miles

Standish. Here stands a lawyer in clothing the colour of carrot and cabbage telling me of his belief in table rattlings and ghostly noises emanating from avaricious charlatans. Said lawyer then draws a breath or two and uses it to push forth freedom for Negroes. Stupidity compounded.

Poe said, 'Are you still entertained by watching the medical profession carve rotting cadavers?'

Standish clenched his fists at his side. He aimed his red-bearded chin at Poe and spoke from behind clenched teeth. 'You morbid little bastard. How dare you? How *dare* you! The world knows you crawl about in the night on your hands and knees baying at the moon like a crazed hound and your own soul is none too stable. You live in a most peculiar world, which is why your writings have failed to fill even *your* belly.'

'Rachel will never love you, Standish. Even supposing you lacked a wife, which you do not, Rachel would not love you.'

Standish fought for control. He snorted, aiming a trembling forefinger at Poe. 'What does a freak like you know of love? Everyone is aware that you bow before every woman you meet, like some whimpering schoolboy. You *adore* them, *worship* them, place no other gods before them. And we men laugh at you. Yes, *laugh*. Behind your back, when you leave the room, when you walk towards us. We laugh, for you are a romantic ass.'

Standish took one step forward. The corners of his mouth were white with saliva. His eyes gleamed with menace. 'You married your first cousin did you not?'

Poe blinked.

Standish whispered, 'She was twelve years old, a fact concealed from authorities at the time. And you, you were twenty-six, and her own mother consented to this bizarre arrangement. Bizarre, I say, for it is known that the two of you never lay together as man and wife should. You are not a man to lay with any woman so do not talk to me of *love*.'

Poe, rigid with rage, gripped the arms of the dark brown leather chair he sat in. 'From this day, you have made of me a most unforgiving enemy.'

Miles Standish smiled and bowed from the waist. 'An honour I am prepared to accept.'

Poe said, 'And are you still involved with prostitution?'

Standish quickly straightened up.

Poe, dangerously angry at what Standish had said about his relationship with Sissy, showed no mercy. 'You seem to know an extraordinary amount about me. Can I do less for you? You, sir, are paying church deacons to purchase property which is then turned over to you. Using your legalistic abilities, you make sure that the property remains in the name of clergymen but the real owners are whoremongers, flesh peddlers, men and women engaged in the most loathsome trade of prostitution. Thanks to men such as yourself, this diabolical business does not lack a roof over its head.'

Standish shrieked, 'Leave! Leave my home immediately!'

Poe's grey eyes were bright with triumph. 'And what shall I tell Rachel concerning my abrupt dismissal from your presence this morning?'

Standish, hands over his ears, looked up at the ceiling and blinked tears from his eyes. He wanted to kill Poe. *It was true, all of it was true.*

Quickly running to his desk, the lawyer opened a drawer and removed a bottle of brandy. Uncorking it, he drank from the bottle, gripping it with trembling hands. Poe dug his nails into the leather of the chair. I shall never forgive nor forget what he said about Sissy and me. He desecrates her name with his foul mouth, and he stands before me to support freedom for black flesh and slavery for white. I condemn him for his pitiful judgement and lack of mercy.

Standish wiped his mouth with the back of his hand. 'We were to discuss my client's difficulty.'

'She wants the ransom paid and I will not oppose that. It is her belief, as you know, that this Doctor Paracelsus can be of some aid and comfort to her. She desires the body of her husband to be returned and I shall do all possible to see that it is. She claims that the dead can live—' Poe thought of last night and Virginia. Had he seen his wife? Had he dreamed it?

Poe continued, 'She claims the dead can be made to live but I do not subscribe to this and you may inform Doctor Paracelsus of my conclusion. The dead cannot be reached in this life. They exist in an uncharted world which as yet can only be imagined and this, sir, is how I feel on the matter. I do not believe.'

Miles Standish, still shocked by what Poe knew of his business dealings, turned his back to the writer. Damn him, damn him to hell. *He knew.* But how? Did he truly have mystical powers or was he merely a snoop who knew too much about too many things? Why had he been brought into this matter of Rachel's husband? Because Rachel trusted him, because like so many other women she was drawn by the image of self-destructive poet. Standish had never hated anyone in his life as much as he hated Poe.

The lawyer spoke with his back to Poe. His voice was hoarse and that of a beaten man. 'You will be made to believe. You will be forced to believe.'

Poe, remembering last night, shivered. *His dead wife had appeared and called to him. But hadn't that been a dream?*

He stood up. 'What did you say?'

Standish turned quickly to face him. 'I, I said one is forced to *grieve*. I meant that life and circumstances leave one no choice but to grieve when death strikes. Uh, Rachel and her husband, her sadness at his death. I, I must leave you. Please excuse me, I shall return shortly.'

Poe watched Miles Standish, still clutching the bottle of brandy, hurry across the carpet. When the door to the billiard room slammed behind the lawyer, Poe was alone and still wondering if he had heard Standish correctly. *Believe. Grieve.* As the eternal fear of insanity came down on him once more, he went suddenly cold. He would never stop fearing it. Insanity. Where one laughed but smiled no more.

He walked to the red-papered wall in front of him, to stand before three paintings by Pieter Bruegel the Elder, a sixteenth-century Dutch artist in oils. Bruegel was vigorous, earthy, with strong, bold colours and figures. You could smell his peasants and barnyard animals, you could touch their clothing and skin. There was power in Bruegel, a vulgarity that was overwhelming and stunning.

The first painting showed peasants shearing sheep in front of a thatched cottage. The second showed three men in coloured doublets and thigh-boots, hands tied behind their backs and hanging from a gibbet. Their heads hung at an angle possible only in dead men. The third painting was the most striking. It was a Renaissance carnival blended with a nightmare. There were dwarfs holding snakes and death-heads, whores soliciting customers, a juggler, sword-swallower, knife-thrower, and, off to the side, horned demons lay in wait for anyone foolish enough to enter the carnival. The painting was a powerful portrayal of a sinister world and time. It was alive with an intimidating energy.

Poe blinked his eyes several times. He was dizzy, sweating, and it was hard to draw breath. Warm, too warm in the room, and he heard noises, laughter, but he was alone, wasn't he? He opened his eyes wide, closed them again and tried not to be sick to his stomach. What was happening to him?

He staggered backwards, coughing, his hands pressed against his throat and his eyes closed. He smelled incense and he heard a harp. *There was a harpist in the carnival painting.*

Poe opened his eyes *and saw two dwarfs standing in front of him.* Living dwarfs. Both were dressed exactly as the dwarfs in the painting and each held a death's head, a grinning skull. One shrieked, hurling his skull at Poe, who backed into the billiard table. The skull bounced off his knee.

Both dwarfs rushed him and, as an unseen harpist played, Poe screamed and kicked at the dwarfs, driving them back. He turned to his right to see a woman dressed as one of the whores in the painting walk slowly towards him, snakes entwined around her neck and both wrists. She was wet-lipped and open-mouthed.

*The painting had come to life!*

A dizzy Poe edged away from the whore, one hand behind him and on the billiard table. He was in hell. At last his mind had betrayed him.

'Noooooo!' Poe's scream filled the room.

A sound made him turn in time to see the knife-thrower, two hands around the handle of his knife, bring it down towards Poe's face. Poe's left hand went up quickly and the knife slashed him across the palm. He screamed, falling to one knee, hands clinging to the billiard table, his blood smearing the polished wooden edge. *The pain was real. The blood was real.*

'Nooooo! I am not insane! I am not mad!'

Driven by a frenzy to survive, Poe grabbed a cue from the billiard table and swung with all his strength, breaking the cue against the knife-thrower's face. The man, thin, bearded with a flat nose, staggered backwards and fell. A crazed Poe, no longer sure of real and unreal, used the remaining part of the cue stick as a short spear and jabbed down at the dwarfs pulling on his legs. *He was not mad, he was not mad.*

A dwarf squealed, both hands going to an eye, and the other dwarf spun round, hands covering a slash running from his ear and down the side of his neck. Poe was living a nightmare and could do nothing but lash out at the world. His head was light and his heart threatened to tear itself loose from its strings. The harpist sent gentle notes of music into the room, and Poe fought to breathe. He heard the whore laugh and, when he turned to face her, she threw snakes at him and laughed louder.

He felt the cold, wet body of a snake against his face, and Poe couldn't stop screaming. He was on his knees, hands pulling the long, green snake from his face. His head was filled with the noise of his own shrieks and, when it seemed certain that he would never breathe again, Poe fell forward on his face, into a blessed darkness that alternated with a pain redder than the sun. The last thing he remembered was two horned demons reaching out for him.

He awoke lying flat on his back and gazing up at a tall, thin woman with a small, round head and black hair parted in the middle. She wore all black and no rouge on her unsmiling face and she clutched a Bible to her bosomless chest. She was Miles Standish's wife.

'I shall read over you, Mr Poe, for the word of the Lord has power—'

Poe sat up. 'The painting. It was alive.'

'I shall read over you, Mr Poe.' She opened the Bible.

Behind Poe, Miles Standish's voice was again calm and sure.

'Nonsense from a quill-pusher who survives by lecturing on the metaphysical. Conclusions springing from whisky. Sound and fury signifying nothing.'

Mrs Standish read from the Book of Revelations, and Poe, clutching the billiard table, raised himself to his knees. 'It *was* alive.'

He was on his feet, breathing heavily through his mouth. 'It was alive.'

Miles Standish stared down at the backs of his own hands. 'I believe in being blunt, sir. You are a drunkard, a man with a known mystical turn of mind. You reek of alcohol—'

Poe sniffed the air, touched his clothes. He *did* reek of whisky. His shirt and coat were wet with it. A half-empty bottle and a glass stood on the side of the billiard table. *Was he losing his mind?*

A Negro servant held out Poe's cloak, hat, walking stick. 'I suggest you consult a physician,' said Standish. 'I know of several. Perhaps Doctor Paracelsus would consent to—'

Poe shoved his left arm at Miles Standish causing the lawyer to lean away. 'Demons stretched out their hands for me and I say to you, this is blood, *my blood!*'

Poe showed his slashed left palm.

Both of Standish's eyebrows crept slowly up his forehead. 'I would agree. And do try not to break any more cue sticks. They are handmade and expensive. His eyes went to the floor and Poe followed his gaze. A broken, bloodstained cue lay on the grey carpet.

A silent, stunned Poe left the billiard room with the sound of Mrs

Standish's Bible-reading following him into the hall and out into the cold. He heard Miles Standish say that all arrangements for the ransom would be made, but Poe paid no attention. He clenched his left fist to stop the bleeding and he wondered how much longer he would be able to function before his mind snapped and he joined his brother and sister in that world of permanent horror known only to the hopelessly insane.

# CHAPTER EIGHT

Jonathan slashed Tom Lowery's throat so that when the burly grave-robber opened his mouth to scream, no sound came out. Lowery, fighting to free himself from a drugged sleep, willed himself to sit up, to rise from the straw mattress and destroy the man who had done this terrible thing to him. But his powerful body would no longer obey him.

Lowery's eyes were wide with horror, and blood gushed from severed arteries under both ears as he watched Jonathan use the scalpel on his naked body with terrifying efficiency. When the pain became excruciating, Lowery passed out and never knew that he, like Sylvester Pier, was both the victim of Jonathan's revenge as well as an offering to Asmodeus, king of demons.

# CHAPTER NINE

In a narrow, windswept alley between two rundown wooden buildings, several children crawled on their hands and knees in mud. None of the children spoke. Each crawled silently and slowly through the dark brown ooze. Figg, standing beside Titus Bootham, said, 'Odd sort of game, that. Tots frolickin' in mud on a day what's cold as this.'

The English journalist said, 'They are not frolicking, my friend. They are trying to eat.'

'Eat mud?' Figg's frown, as usual, made him appear ferocious.

'No, not actually eat it. They are searching through the mud for dead animals. Rats, cats, birds, dogs, anything. When they find what they are looking for, the children will take these rotting carcasses to meat dealers, who use the carcasses to feed pigs. The pigs, in turn, will be slaughtered for pork, a large part of the American diet. Not my diet, let me assure you. The children earn a few pennies for this deadly work. What one earns by eating pork I dare not say.'

'Ain't there no other way for them to eat?'

'Some collect *chips* from the street. Dried manure. Pays four pennies to the bucket. Some become prostitutes; they sell their little bodies. More than some, sad to say. Others become thieves, beggars, the pedlars of paper flowers, dried apples, two-a-penny matches. Ten thousand homeless children roaming the streets of New York and, I assure you, not all of them are acolytes in church.'

Figg and Bootham were across the street from Phineas Taylor Barnum's American Museum, a mammoth five-storey marble building on the corner of lower Broadway and Ann Street. At eleven o'clock in the morning, traffic in the area was extremely heavy. Never in Figg's life had he seen such a crush of people, horses and anything that moved on wheels, foot, hoof all in one place, at one time. Stagecoaches, painted, with glorious names embossed on each side; wagons and handcarts piled high with merchandise; private carriages with uniformed drivers; an unending stream of cabs; high-stepping horses with breath turning to steam in the cold. *Noises.* Drivers cursing and snapping their whips in the air like so many pistol shots; iron horseshoes striking cobblestones where snow had melted or been worn away; men, women, children talking, shouting and no one pausing for breath; bells jingling on the reins of horse-drawn sleighs. *People.* Young, pink-faced messenger-boys darting through crowds and risking their lives in traffic; tall men in tall hats, capes, long coats, greased side-whiskers and thick beards, their mouths filled with cigars or tobacco juice; women in fur and silks, their hands warmed by muffs; a parade of women in a rainbow of bonnets, plumed hats, with lace and diamonds at their throats and each woman stepping daintily into ankle-deep mud, lifting a skirt to show leather boots which buttoned on the side.

The sight and sound of it all was splendid and frightening. Nothing in London—not Piccadilly and Oxford Circuses, not the Strand or Oxford Street—could compare to what Figg was seeing on the Broadway of New York.

The number of shops was unending and the buildings, mostly wooden and none over five storeys tall, seemed to draw people by the thousands.

Power, energy, riches. This was New York and Figg was intimidated by such a city. But he saw other things, too. There were gutters packed with garbage and trash, and there were side streets jammed with empty barrels, boxes and battered buckets filled with coal ashes. There were ugly pigs roaming the streets, brown pigs with long thin legs and sickening black blotches on their backs. They rooted noisily in the trash and garbage, oblivious to blocking the sidewalk, forcing pedestrians to either push through them or walk around them into ankle-deep mud.

Titus Bootham, wrapped in a shaggy coat of black bear fur, was a short, gentle, 55-year-old with the lined face of an old woman who had endured much without knowing why. He was awed by Figg. Awed, impressed, pleased to be in his company. Like all Englishmen, Bootham saw boxing as being an exact metaphor for all of life, the chance for a man to show maximum courage and doggedness, the chance to give and receive pain, persisting in this ideal like the British bulldog who hung on once he laid his teeth into a thing. The prize-ring was John Bull, Englishman, at his finest, and for Bootham the opportunity to associate himself with Pierce James Figg was equal to drinking ale with the Prince of Wales.

Bootham said, 'Twenty odd years ago it was. You and Hazlitt at Hinkley Downs. Magnificent it was. Fifty-two rounds in the sun until you picked him up and slammed him down on the boards. I was never so excited in my life. What became of Hazlitt?'

'Still in the game.'

'You're joking. He must be over sixty.'

'That he is. Still catchin' punches with his face, he is. Blind in one eye and the other none too good. But he can't do anything' else. What time does Mr Barnum open his establishment?'

'Around noon I believe. I saw Tom Spring and Jack Langan fight for the heavyweight championship. Eighteen and twenty-four, I believe. Seventy-seven rounds. Spring won. Thirty thousand people from all over England saw that one. God, what a thrill it was! Whatever happened to Spring?'

'Him and Langan fought again. Six months later, I think. Spring did a right neat job on Langan. Bloodied him from noon to Sunday, but Spring's hands they got botched and he never fought no more. He's now an innkeeper, he is. Langan opened a hotel in Liverpool. He died two years ago. What's Mr P. T. Barnum got in his museum that's so special?'

'Six hundred thousand different attractions, some of them pure humbug and hokum, some quite interesting. Americans are rather prudish and they believe theatre and such entertainments to be the devil's work and a sure road to hell. Master Barnum is a sly one. He shrewdly calls his emporium a museum, pretending to offer education for the family instead of time-wasting amusement and entertainment. Thus the public feels virtuous when they pay twenty-five cents admission to watch dancing girls or some cross-eyed Italian balance a bayoneted rifle on his long nose. And is it true that you are descended from *the* James Figg?'

From the respect in Titus Bootham's voice, Figg would have thought the question was: Are you related to Moses? Figg looked at him and nodded. He thought Titus Bootham would swoon with delight. 'Direct descendant,' said Figg. 'Me great-great-grand-father. All of us Figgs took to the trade.'

*The* James Figg. In 1719 he became the first recorded heavy-weight boxing champion in England's history and from that date boxing, as the world was to know it, began. Father of boxing and first to openly promote the teaching of the sport. Master swords-man, expert fencer and even more skilled in the use of the cudgel. Patronised by nobles and bluebloods. *The* James Figg. William Hogarth gladly painted his portrait and designed his calling card. Jonathan Swift and Alexander Pope were just two of the import-ant men and women who sought his friendship and now Titus

Bootham was standing beside his great-great-grandson, a man of note in his own right. Even in February cold the excitement caused Titus Bootham to perspire.

Bootham said, 'When you see Mr Dickens, please convey my gratitude at singling me out to be of service to you. The pleasure and the honour is indeed mine.'

'Not yours entirely.'

'Ah yes, there is Mr Poe.' Bootham sighed. 'A most peculiar man. He views existence as does a man without sight. All darkness.'

Figg said, 'Come to think of it, he weren't seein' much when I met him.'

Titus Bootham adjusted a scarf to protect the bottom half of his face against the cold. 'One wonders at the sort of mind which conceives his particular prose, though let me add he *has* earned a reputation in literary circles. This has not made him one of our Yankee millionaires, of which we do have a few. Mr Poe can be a nasty little piece of baggage, especially when in his cups. Did Mr Dickens tell you that Mr Poe once asked employment of him?'

'No.'

'Happened when Mr Dickens began his London newspaper a couple of years ago. Mr Poe wrote and asked to be made the American correspondent. He never got the job. Have no idea why, actually.'

Figg eyed Mr Barnum's American Museum. Oh it was a sight, it was. The outside of the marble building was a collection of colour and oddities that would make a dead man sit up and take notice. Around each of the building's top four storeys were oval oil paintings of beasts, birds and much stranger animals, a few of them springing from Mr Barnum's imagination. Two dozen flags flew from the rooftop and snapped in the cold February wind, with a monstrous American red, white and blue towering over all. Other flags flew from a second-storey balcony, where uniformed musicians began to fit themselves into chairs. There were posters and banners on the ground floor and Figg had to admit that merely to gaze upon Mr Barnum's handiwork was to view a wonder. The building was a mass of colours. To Figg it looked as though drunken gypsies had been given paint and cloth and told to indulge themselves beyond all reason and at Mr Barnum's expense. The boxer had toured Britain with many a carnival and knew the importance of pulling in a crowd as skilfully as possible. Mr Barnum seemed to be the man who could do it.

*And here is where Figg would find those actors involved with Jonathan.*

*Here is where he would begin his revenge on those who had killed his wife and son.*

'What think you of Mr Barnum's painted box?' asked Titus Bootham.

'Trips you up, it does. Makes you stop. That is what a man in his postition must do. Has himself a little band, I notice.'

'If you call thirty or forty musicians little, yes. But wait until you hear them. Mr Figg, I assure you that no more horrendous sound has ever reached your ears. Barnum has deliberately hired the worst musicians money can buy. Deliberately, I say.'

'American custom?'

'American greed. A crowd always gathers to listen and when this awful music comes down upon them, many seek refuge inside the museum, at an entrance fee of course.'

Figg nodded. 'Right smart. Yes sir, right smart.'

'Mr Figg?'

'Yes, Mr Bootham?'

'I have no wish to pry into your business, but please regard me as a friend. I deem it an honour to assist you in any way possible and not merely because Mr Dickens has asked me to do so.'

'Much appreciated, Mr—' Figg stopped talking.

'Mr Figg, what's wrong?'

Figg waited until a wagon piled high with boxes had passed in front of the museum. When he spoke, his voice was ice. 'Those two men there, the ones talking to that lady who just stepped from the black carriage.'

Titus Bootham squinted behind steel-rimmed spectacles. 'Yes, yes, I see them.'

'Them is two who I come here to see.'

Titus Bootham felt the menace in Figg's voice and suddenly he was glad that Figg hadn't come to see *him* in such fashion. He said, 'The woman, yes I know her. Yes.'

'Who is she?'

'Mrs Coltman. Mrs Rachel Coltman.'

Figg looked at Bootham. 'Husband named Justin?'

'He's dead now, God rest his soul. Died of cancer a few weeks ago. Shortly after returning from England, I believe. Quite a wealthy man. We gave him a rather large obituary. She is—'

'Your carriage.' Figg took Bootham by the elbow, pushing him forward.

'Where? Where? I thought you wanted to—'

Figg, hand still tightly gripping Bootham's elbow, reached the journalist's carriage tied up at a nearby hitching rail, now crowded with single horses. At the hitching rack, two young boys pulled feathers from a pair of geese and threw the feathers at pigs nosing about in the mud and snow.

Figg's soft voice was steely. 'Mrs Coltman has finished her little chat and she's leavin' and I would like to see where she is about to take herself.' *Find Justin Coltman and you find Jonathan.*

'Your friends at the museum—'

'Ain't my friends. Besides, I know where to get my hands on that lot. It is the lady what interests me now.' *Jonathan has to be near her, he has to be. Her husband was about to find the Throne of Solomon.*

Titus Bootham slowly manoeuvred his horse-drawn carriage through the growing tangle of wagons, horses, people.

An impatient Figg said, 'Do not lose sight of her.'

'I suspect she might be returning home.'

'And where might that be?'

'Fifth Avenue. It is the correct place for the wealthy to reside these days. Ironic, since not too long ago that area was a swamp fit only for poor Irish and herds of wild pigs. Do you know Mrs Coltman?'

'We have things to touch upon.'

Figg looked at the traffic hemming them in left, right, back and front. The noise attacked his ears and he didn't see how a man could live with it without going balmy. He felt the thrill of the hunt, the excitement of a satisfaction soon to be his. Rachel Coltman would lead him to Jonathan, and Figg would kill him, then leave this bedlam of a city, with its mud, foul smells and children who had to collect dead animals in order to get a crust of bread.

Let little Mr Poe keep New York. The city was as mad as he was.

Figg snatched the whip from Titus Bootham's hand, stood up in the carriage and began to flay the horse. *Jonathan.*

'Mr Figg, Mr Figg, please I beg of you don't—'

Figg stopped.

Bootham had tears in his eyes. 'She is not a young horse, sir and she has served me well. I beg you.'

Burning with shame, Figg sat down, unable to look Titus Bootham in the face and tell him that he hadn't been whipping the horse; he'd been whipping the man who'd killed his wife and son.

The two men followed Rachel Coltman's carriage in silence.

# CHAPTER TEN

'Believe,' said Paracelsus.

'I do.'

*'Believe!'* The word was a command.

'I do believe, sir. Oh I do, with all my heart.'

'Then I can bring your wife to you once again, but only for an instant. It is not easy to control the spirits of those who have gone on ahead. They are now free, you must understand this. Free from all worlds, all restraints—'

Lorenzo Ballou leaped from his chair, voice breaking with pain. 'Dear God, anything! I will do anything you ask, pay any amount. Only bring her to me once more, I beg you!'

Paracelsus gently lifted a white-gloved hand from the table, pointed it at Ballou, then lowered the hand to the table once more. As if by magic, Ballou sat down.

'Mr Ballou, I do not seek your money. I require only that you place your faith in me without reservation, for without your complete commitment there is little I can achieve.'

Ballou, 250 pounds and five-foot four, wiped his perspiring forehead with one of his dead wife's lace handkerchiefs. He was jowly, with pink flesh from his face and neck dripping over an expensive collar and silk cravat. His puffy and grey mutton-chop whiskers smelled of his wife's perfume, which he watered in order not to run out of it. Ballou, fifty-five, was rich from crooked real-estate dealings; two months ago his nineteen-year-old wife had died in a fall from a new horse he'd purchased for her.

'Doctor Paracelsus, you have given me more than any man ever has. Twice you have united my dearest Martha and me, and I cannot convey how much this has meant to me.'

'I understand.'

'You tell me things about Martha and me, things no mortal man could possibly know and, oh, how reassuring it is to hear them once more.'

Paracelsus nodded. Lorenzo Ballou was a toy, something to mould into a believer who would open his wallet willingly. Paracelsus, a large man with shoulder-length white hair that appeared to glow in the dark candle-lit room, touched a white beard that

73

reached his chest and knew that today Mr Ballou would be most generous. The spiritualist, himself a ghostly-looking figure in a floor-length white robe, could sense when a survivor's gratitude was about to overflow. Mr Ballou's certainly would, especially after the little tableau Paracelsus was about to unfold for the widower's private viewing. This would be a most successful and lucrative seance.

The two men were alone in a totally dark room lit only by five black candles on a table of black marble. Paracelsus had made Martha Ballou *appear* on two occasions. And now once again it was time for the grieving Mr Ballou to view the dear departed.

'Extend your hands, Mr Ballou. Both hands. Yes. Keep them flat on the table and extend your fingers until they touch mine. Yes, yes.'

The fat man did as ordered, his eyes on Paracelsus' face. The spiritualist had a majestic nose, large but far from comical. It belonged on a king, thought Ballou, on a man used to ruling others. And his eyes. A burning green. Yes that was it. A burning green, eyes of green fire. And behind those eyes was a power to bring dear Martha back to this world again. Ballou's heart was about to burst with joy, fear, anticipation.

And then he felt something brush his face. The fat man looked up at the ceiling to see rose petals falling down on him.

'Her favourite flower!' Ballou's shout filled the small room. 'How did you know?'

Paracelsus, eyes closed, placed his hands on top of Ballou's and pressed down hard. 'You must not move. You must not disturb the spirits or they will retreat.'

'Yes, yes. Oh please don't let her go away. I—'

Ballou listened.

Then—'That song. It's one she used to sing on the stage.' He turned around in his chair and saw a trumpet floating in the air. The trumpet glowed in the dark, a shade of green almost as bright as Paracelsus' eyes.

'Who is there? Who is playing?' Ballou tried to leave his chair, but the spiritualist, using surprising strength, pressed down harder on his hands, keeping the fat man in place.

When Ballou turned to face Paracelsus again, he looked down at the table and suddenly inhaled. Jerking both hands free, he picked up the pearl necklace. 'But, but this is at home in my safe! It belonged to Martha and no one has the combination to the safe but me. Where—'

74

'Lorenzo. Lorenzo!'

The fat man snapped his head towards the woman's voice and when he saw her, his eyes widened and he whimpered like a puppy—exactly like a puppy, thought Paracelsus.

'Martha' oh Martha dearest!' Ballou wept, his corpulent body shaking, his jowls shiny with his tears.

*He is mine,* thought Paracelsus. *I have him now.*

The ghost was in a doorway behind a curtain of yellow gauze. A slim woman, dark-haired and pretty in a pale blue robe with a hood that hid half of her face. She stood with her right profile to Lorenzo Ballou and had both hands folded in prayer.

'I come to you, dear Lorenzo, for only a moment. Only a moment.'

He stood up. 'M-Martha.'

Paracelsus spoke swiftly. 'If you go towards her, she will disappear. Obey me or she—'

He didn't have to finish. Ballou sat down, his tear-stained face still on the ghost behind the yellow gauze curtain. A wet whale, thought Paracelsus, but a rich one and that is what concerns me.

'M-Martha. M-M-Martha.' All Ballou could do was sit and weep. They had so little time together before her death. Three months married, then—

'Lorenzo, dearest, you should not have killed Zachery and Beau. You should not have done that.'

The colour left the fat man's face and his breathing stopped. Zachery was the name of the horse Ballou had given her and Beau was the Negro groom who had saddled it for her. The day after his wife's death, Lorenzo Ballou had taken both horse and groom deep into a wood and killed them both. The fat man, crazed with grief, had been *alone* when he'd done the killings.

'Martha, I—'

Her voice was gentle. 'It was not the fault of the horse nor of dear, faithful Beau. They did not deserve to die, Lorenzo, but I forgive you. That is why I have come, to tell you not to have further nightmares about what you have done.' The ghost maintained the prayerful pose.

A stunned Ballou looked at Paracelsus. 'I did not, I, I—'

Paracelsus lifted his white-gloved hands shoulder-high, as if in a blessing. 'I am not your judge. So long as you believe in me, no harm can come to you.'

'Yes, yes.' Ballou licked his fat lips and wiped more perspiration from his face. A nigger and a horse. Both were his property, to do with as he wished, and neither had been missed. Ballou's story was that the horse had been stolen and the nigger had run away, probably *ridden* away on the back of the stolen horse, who had been named Zachery after General Zachery Taylor, victorious general in the recent American war against Mexico.

'Martha?' Ballou looked at her. 'Are you happy? Is all well with you?'

'I am supremely happy, Lorenzo.' The trumpet floated across the room, still playing the tune Martha had been singing when Ballou had first seen her, the tune she frequently sang around their lovely home. The tune, the ghost, the necklace and the dark room and Paracelsus' green eyes. Lorenzo Ballou now had no will of his own, no mind but the mind that Paracelsus wanted him to have. The fat man *wanted* to believe, wanted to hear the voice of his wife and his own mind was as much Paracelsus' ally as any deception the spiritualist could devise.

'I miss you, Lorenzo, dearest. I think of you and hope you think of me.'

'Oh, I do, I do. Every day of my life, my love.' The tears would not stop flowing.

'Perhaps I can come to you again. The power lies with Doctor Paracelsus. If he can continue his work, if he can—'

More rose petals fell and the smell of Martha Ballou's perfume was now stronger than ever in the room. A mother-of-pearl comb fell from the ceiling. *Hers.* It clattered on the black marble table and Ballou recoiled from it as though the comb was a snake. Again he looked up at the ceiling, at falling rose petals and the flying green trumpet which continued to play *that song*, and when he again turned towards the ghost, she'd vanished.

He screamed her name, leaping from his chair and waddling across the room with all the speed in his fat, squat body. Reaching the doorway, he jerked the yellow gauze curtain left, right, all the while still whimpering like a puppy abandoned by its mother.

When he looked at Paracelsus, Lorenzo Ballou was a broken man.

'You must bring her back, you must!'

'My work is not my own. I am controlled by forces beyond my knowledge. Soon I must go, I must leave this place.'

'G-go? I do not understand.'

'I only serve.' Paracelsus bowed his head. 'I follow my calling wherever it leads—'

'S-stay.' Lorenzo Ballou was on his knees, clutching the hem of

Paracelsus' white robe, then touching it to his lips. 'I will give you any amount of money if you will only stay.'

'I cannot.'

'I beg you stay.' Ballou touched his forehead to the floor, his fat body shaking as he sobbed 'Ask-ask anything of m-me, anything and I shall do it. Only do-do not go. S-stay and b-bring Martha back to m-me.'

After Lorenzo Ballou left, Paracelsus locked the front door of his home, leaned back against it and sighed, nodded his head several times in complete satisfaction with all that he had achieved concerning the fat man, then returned upstairs to the seance room.

In his absence, gas-jets had been lit and a beautiful woman with dark brown hair parted in the middle, and a beauty mark to the left of her small mouth, sat with booted feet on the black marble table. Her shapely body was naked under an organdie negligée. She drank claret from a handcut crystal glass and smoked a tiny black cigar. Her name was Sarah Clannon and she lifted the glass to the spiritualist who ignored the gesture and walked directly to a full-length mirror, turning his back to her and taking off the long white wig. Dropping it to the floor, he pulled off his white robe, then removed shoulder and stomach padding, also letting this material fall at his feet. Since all around him did his bidding, it was just as easy for them to pick up after him as well. When he'd removed his false nose, he used the hem of the robe to wipe most of the makeup from his face.

Now he looked slim, handsome, thirty years younger. His face and body were perfect. Still wearing the white gloves, he stood nude before the mirror, gazing into his own hypnotic green eyes, and when he smiled at his reflection, his eyes remained detached from any movement of his lips.

Sarah Clannon, eyes on the naked man, brought the small cigar to her lips. 'How much?'

'Fifteen thousand. In gold. Personally delivered tomorrow by Mr Ballou and his banker. And more to come.'

Her smile was dazzling, as pleased with him as it was with the money that would be hers tomorrow. She was an extremely sensual woman with eyes that lured and mocked, except that the naked man she now stared at with deep interest was someone she would never mock. She said, 'Have someone oil that trap-door. It almost stuck and had that happened, I would still be folded under this rather musty floor.' She blew a perfect pale blue smoke ring at his back.

He seemed entranced with his own eyes. 'Laertes must be informed that his trumpet playing should coincide with the speed of the second trumpet as it flies overhead. One must do a thing perfectly.'

'I failed to notice, being preoccupied with my ethereal state. I thought I was an excellent dead wife.'

He turned to her and, when he smiled, the effect on her was amazing. Her heart speeded up and she actually felt weak in the stomach. Only he, of the many men in her life, had that power over her. She neither knew, nor cared why. That he possessed it was enough. That she responded to it was everything.

He said, 'Dead wives, dead wives. Last night Mrs Edgar Allan Poe—'

'And damn cold it was in all that snow. I thought he would scream himself to death.'

'And this afternoon, Mrs Lorenzo Ballou—'

'A whore fortunate enough to marry a wealthy thief. A whore who died while riding to meet her lover. What would Mr Ballou say were he to learn that his wife was a slut who met her death because she was unfaithful.'

He said, 'It would kill him and therefore impoverish us. Did you send Charles—'

'On the swiftest horse possible to the home of Mr Ballou, where Charles will see that the pearl necklace and comb are placed back into the safe before Mr Ballou arrives. You amaze me.'

'How so?'

'I would have thought Mr Ballou would have clutched that necklace to his ample bosom and never turned it loose. But you accurately predicted that the combined effect of music, roses and the sight of me, his dear dead spouse, would so cloud his mind that he would not even remember his name. And so it did.'

He nodded. 'And so it did.'

'With help from your eyes, my love. You rule us all with but a single gaze.' Her tone was mocking, but only gently. She believed in his power over all who were around him. She feared that power and because she feared it, she was drawn to him. He was a challenge, a man whom she could never control and therefore had to have.

He began to peel off the white gloves. 'I wish you to handle any remaining monies owed to Mr Ballou's servants.'

'And to his lawyer?'

'And to his lawyer. All those who gave us needed information should be paid as soon as possible. Which brings me to Martha's fellow whores—'

'Done,' she said. 'Paid in full yesterday.'

'Excellent. Come bathe me.' He walked towards the onyx bathtub which had been placed in the room near the black marble table.

She stood up, ready to obey him. As always. 'What of Mr Poe?'

He eased down into the warm water. 'Ah, yes. Mr Poe. Twice we have presented him with visions of our choosing and twice he has found cause to doubt his own senses. Let us see if there is any change in him, if he is now more inclined to see other worlds as more real than this one.'

'And if he does not choose to believe as we wish him to believe?'

His eyes were closed. 'I shall destroy him.'

She nodded, giving no more thought to Poe's fate that she did to the floor beneath her. She was on her knees at the side of the tub, her hands slowly rubbing the warm water into his flesh and when she reached down into the tub, she took one of his hands and brought it to her lips, kissing it.

The little finger was missing. As it was on the other.

Jonathan, his eyes still closed, thought of the Throne of Solomon. And of Asmodeus.

# CHAPTER ELEVEN

Carefully placing his booted foot at the base of Poe's spine, Hamlet Sproul savagely pushed the writer, sending him rushing forward, arms flailing the air for balance.

At the same time, Chopback, who carried an axe behind his neck and across both shoulders—the axe to be used on Mr E. A. Poe—stuck his foot out, tripping Poe. The writer dived into the air, landing painfully on his left side, then slowly rolling over until he was face down, right arm outstretched, fingers digging into the stable's straw-covered dirt floor. Last night, the *vision* of his dead wife. This morning, a sixteenth-century painting had come to life and attacked him. And now this.

Sproul, Isaac Bard and Chopback had dragged Poe off the street and into a nearby Fifth Avenue stable to make the little poet pay for his treachery. Pay with his rum-soaked life. Hamlet Sproul unbuttoned his long green overcoat, then jerked on the leather thong around his neck until the bowie knife that hung down between his shoulder blades was in front of him. He was going to draw blood from Mr E. A. Poe which should surely make a good Christian of this sorry excuse for a man, and when Sproul finished, Chopback could use his axe to end the little poet's days of betrayal.

Mr Poe, author of numerous unsuccessful mystical works, would die this afternoon, die among horses standing quietly in stalls, among broken carriage-wheels, bales of hay, dusty horse-collars and yards of reins and bridles hanging from nails in the wall.

Poe, on his knees, pressed both hands against his aching spine.

'I would like to know—'

Hamlet Sproul grabbed a handful of Poe's hair, snapped the writer's head back on his shoulders and twisted the hair so that Mr Poe felt pain. Sproul leaned over until he was nose to nose with this man he hated so much.

'You wants to know and so you shall, my poetic friend. And so you shall, you snivellin' little Judas! Yes, *Judas*! Know this: As the Bible proclaims, "man's days are short and full of woe" and I say unto you, Mr Poe, your days are down to one. Today is your last on God's green earth.'

*They intend to kill me.* Poe, living still another nightmare, knew immediately that this one was real. He had been only a half block from Rachel Coltman's Fifth Avenue mansion, on his way to talk to her about his meeting with Miles Standish, when Hamlet Sproul and two sinister friends had leaped from a parked carriage to drag him roughly across the street and into this stable.

Poe's spine ached and his neck would be out of line *if he lived,* for Sproul's grip on his hair was vicious. The cut on the palm of his hand from this morning's attack by the painting was forgotten. Poe managed to croak one word.

'Why?'

Sproul's answer was to spit tobacco juice into his eyes, blinding him; and even as Poe dug his fingertips into the corners of his eyes to stop the burning, he felt pain explode in his left temple from Sproul's fist. Poe fell to his right, hands still over his eyes but he was now staring into the red eye of the sun. *His brain was on fire.*

Sproul's voice came to him from far away. 'We agreed, you and I, that there would be no treachery on your part. I dealt with you, sir, as one Christian gentleman to another, and you repay me with death.'

Poe stared up at Sproul. 'Death?'

'Sylvester Pier is dead. Tom Lowery is dead. Someone hired you to deal with us for the corpus of Justin Coltman, but you had no intention of being honourable. Not you Mr Poe. You were the stalking horse, the pathfinder, the lighthouse that lit the way. He used you to find us and when he found us, he slaughtered my treasured companions.'

'Who hired me? I do not understand.'

'I could pull out your lyin' tongue and eat it meself.'

'*Who?*'

Very well, then. I shall play your little game for a while longer. Not that much longer, poet. Jonathan hired you to find us. He followed you and when he learned our whereabouts he struck.'

Sproul frowned, tongue nervously licking his lips. Jonathan was no human agency, no normal man. But Sproul would triumph over both him and his snot of a servant, E. A. Poe.

Poe said, 'I know of no Jonathan.'

'You lie. And do not leave your knees. Stay exactly as you now are. Any attempts at gettin' to your feet will bring punishment down on you all the sooner. Master Chopback, that gentleman with the axe, he is here to assist and would welcome the chance to apply that instrument in removin' most of your spine. His name came from lovingly usin' his axe on the backs of his enemies. Include yourself as an enemy, Mr Poe. Chopback and Sylvester Pier were cousins of a sort. Both were lads in County Cork, chasin' virgins and anxious to avoid dyin' of starvation, so they came here and now Sylvester no longer has to concern hisself with virgins or a full belly, thanks to you. Chopback is anxious to get his own back, Mr Poe and that means you are a man facin' difficulty.'

Hamlet Sproul's eyes were as hard as buttons, and as empty of feeling. The lunacy in the bearded grave-robber was about to manifest itself and the result would be Poe's death. *Poe did not want to die.*

He said, 'I tell you I know of no Jonathan.'

'Your story smells rather tall.' Sproul's finger's stroked the sheathed bowie knife.

'Tell me why I am to die.'

'You expect me to believe you don't know. Yes, it is written all over your bloodless face. Very well, poet. We talk, then I shall have your life and laugh about it as a hyena laughs over a dead nigger. Sylvester Pier was topped. Hung until he died but that was not all. His heart was cut out and so was his liver and they was both set fire to. Made a neat little pile of ashes and burned flesh beside his bleedin' body. Your card was found in the room.'

'*My* card?'

'None other. The same happened to Tom Lowery, with a difference or two. Poisoned whisky helped it along, but his heart and liver was removed and burned as well. Throat cut ear to ear and your card was found in his pocket. *Your card!*'

Sproul's shout filled the stable. 'There never was any hope of us collectin' ransom, was there? You and Jonathan weaved your little web and you lets us stroll into it. He follows you to us and we die. Well, poet, today *you* die. We shall pay your respects to your lady friend, that one you was on your way to see.'

Poe pleaded. 'I swear to you I had no hand in the death of your two friends. I am not capable of such deeds.'

'I leave it to you to make your apologies when you join them in the next world. Yours may not have been the hand on the knife that done 'em, but yours was the callin' card found near their mortal remains. And let it be noted that Sylvester Pier and Tom Lowery was breathin' 'til comin' upon you. I allow that the actual blood-lettin' is Jonathan's handiwork, for I know only too well that he has his little ways about him.'

Sproul pointed a forefinger at Poe who was still on his knees. 'But I charge you with leadin' Jonathan to the killin' ground, and now our talk is done.' He drew the bowie knife from its worn, leather sheath and stepped twards Poe.

Poe leaned back, eyes on the foot-long blade. *And the fever called living is conquered at last.* But he didn't want to die. He had found Rachel again and he didn't want to die. To love a beautiful woman was to be *alive* and Poe loved this beautiful woman.

He saw everything around him in precise detail: the tarnished buttons on Sproul's coat, a glint of sunlight on the bowie knife's blade, a pitchfork leaning against a horse's stall, a saddle resting on a bale of hay, and he thought that eternity, which he had so often both longed for and dreaded, should not be as ugly as it now appeared to him. *Death should not be this ugly.*

Sproul, eyes wide, began to feel sick from fear of Jonathan and somewhere in his mind he wished that he had not attempted to cheat him by stealing Justin Coltman's body, but the die had been cast, the arrow shot and there was no turning back. Kill Poe. Then run to ground again and pray that Jonathan would not find him as he had found the others.

'*Stand!* Everybody as you are, if you please! First man what moves a bleedin' hair gets a ball for his trouble!'

Figg crouched at the top of a ladder leading from the hayloft down to the ground floor, two pocket pistols pointed at Sproul, Chopback and the third man, Isaac Bard.

Poe's eyes quickly went to his deliverer. He saw a small mountain of a man in black top hat, long black coat and boots, with the face of a monstrous and surly bulldog. The face belonged to someone who ate raw meat with the run still in it. But this specimen of prehistoric man had just pulled Poe back from that greatest of unknowns and Poe accepted his deliverance from death gladly.

He stood up and watched Figg start down the ladder, moving carefully, eyes on the men below him. Figg had never seen a knife like Sproul's before; the blade was large enough to be melted down for cannon, if a man had a mind to. The one called Chopback had his axe, and the third man showed no weapon, which was not a reason for Figg to play him cheap. The boxer knew that staying alive in the world meant treating all men as capable of removing you from it.

Poe used the sleeve of his greatcoat to wipe the remainder of the tobacco juice from his face. He'd never seen Bulldog Face before and, in so far as he could remember, he had never done him a good turn. So why was he racing to Poe's rescue?

Sproul continued to chew his tobacco, never taking his eyes from

Figg as the boxer slowly made his way down the ladder. 'You ain't the stable-boy, I'm thinkin'.'

'Ain't your Aunt Nelly neither. You would be doin' yourself a favour if you were to drop that cuttin' tool you are holdin'. Must be a most heavy burden for such a slight fella as yourself.'

'Does what I tell it.'

'Tell it to lie on the ground. I will not be askin' you agin.'

Sproul opened his fingers, dropping the huge knife to the ground.

Stopping his descent, Figg said, 'Mr Poe, there is a stable door in front of you direct. Use it, if you please. Outside you will find a worried-lookin' gentleman in a carriage pulled by a rather sad-lookin' bay horse. Introduce yourself and be tellin' him I sent you.'

Poe bent over to pick up his hat and stick. Removing himself from this society of homicidal imbeciles would be his pleasure; let them devour one another. Let them bathe in each other's blood.

Chopback made his move. No one was going to cheat him out of what he'd come here for. He was a small, black-bearded man with the widely-spaced pop-eyes of a frog, and using his axe on those he hated made made him feel as tall as anyone walking the earth. Chopback, who had swung the blade of his axe into the backs of a tidy number of men, thought of his dead cousin Sylvester Pier and the ugly death that had been his, thanks to Mr Poe, and Chopback lifted his short-handled axe high over his head.

Figg extended one arm and fired.

Smoke appeared from beneath the hammer and from the barrel of his six-inch pocket pistol and, two seconds later, there was a neat, round hole over Chopback's left eyebrow. Dead on his feet, the frog-eyed little man dropped the axe behind him, falling backwards and on top of it.

That same shot almost killed Pierce James Figg.

The four horses in the stable—like all horses of that time—were not trained to accept gunfire. These horses whinnied, shied, kicked against the stalls, and one pulled his bridle free and backed out in a panic; his movements increased the fear and uncertainty among the other three and all crashed against their stalls. It was the first one, a black with a shiny coat and white, thunderbolt-like streak running from eyes to nose, who backed out of his stall and into the ladder Figg stood on, sending the boxer flying, causing him to drop both pistols.

Poe's heart sank as Figg hit the ground, but the boxer leaped to his feet empty handed—and sidestepped the frightened horse.

All of the horses now backed out of their stalls and milled around the centre of the stable where Poe, his would-be killers and would-be rescuer were. To avoid being trampled to death, Poe ducked into an empty stall. There was no back door to the stable, and between Poe and the front door were three dangerous men and four terrified horses. It was necessary to absent himself from this precarious ground, but how? On his knees, he peeked out of a stall and saw Hamlet Sproul snatch up his bowie knife, then leap backwards to avoid a galloping horse. He saw Isaac Bard pull the axe from under the dead Chopback and he saw the two of them direct their full attentions to Poe's deliverer, the man with the bulldog's face.

Isaac Bard was a grey, squat fifty-year-old who was trying to hang on in the dangerous underworld of Five Points and the Bowery, an underworld controlled by the tough young Irish. Bard was a member of 'The Dead Rabbits', the most vicious Irish gang in Five Points, a gang that wore a red stripe down the side of their pants and carried a dead rabbit into battle stuck on a pike. Isaac Bard hired himself out as often as he could; for a dollar he had agreed to be Hamlet Sproul's man for as long as it took to deal with Master E. A. Poe. Bard could neither read nor write, so the fact that Master Poe was a man of letters was lost on him. The scribbler was only a day's work; that work meant taking his life.

Poe's throat was tight with fear. His rescuer was trapped between a panicked, whinnying horse and two armed men, each holding cold steel. The bulldog had only empty hands, not enough to keep both him and Poe alive.

Poe saw the bulldog quickly crouch, pick up the ladder he'd just fallen from and, gripping it tightly in both hands, charge Sproul and Bard, hitting both men simultaneously, driving them back, back. Both men went down and Figg dropped the ladder on top of them.

Poe watched the violence with total concentration, fascinated by it, attaching himself to it completely and losing himself in it so that he became one with all three men. Violence had always lured him and now he succumbed to it, on his feet so that they could better view the life and death drama being played solely for him. *For him.*

He watched Isaac Bard die.

Bard, flat on his back, kept his grip on the axe but he was slower than Figg, whose life had been a study of combat. Isaac Bard rolled to his left side, one hand gripping the axe, the other against the ground to push himself to his feet.

His head was waist-high when Figg, standing in front of him, placed both hands behind Bard's head and pulled it down hard into his raised knee. Poe heard Bard sigh as though drifting into sleep. Bard, his nose crushed, panicked at the horrible hurt exploding in his face; he panicked because he could no longer breathe. Poe saw the axe fall, but he also saw that Figg didn't let go of Bard's head.

With his left hand on the top of the grey-haired man's head, Figg cupped the man's chin with his right hand and savagely twisted the head as though turning a wheel. Figg snapped Isaac Bard's neck, killing him. To Poe, what he had just seen had the beauty and grace of dance. He watched with fascination as Figg dropped Bard's limp body, and Poe wondered what it would be like to lay your bare hands on a man and kill him with such arrogant ease.

Poe cringed, recoiling as Sproul, keeping the bowie knife low, inched towards Figg. *If the bulldog perishes, then my own life is forfeit.*

A horse reared up on its hind legs. Poe's eyes went to it, to the closed stable door. To get out of the stable he had to pass Hamlet Sproul and the bulldog, who no longer wore his tall black hat. Bulldog's head, crudely shorn of whatever hair nature had seen fit to bless it with, was visible and of no beauty worth mentioning. His face was enough to scare the whole of purgatory. But he did not back up as Sproul slithered towards him like some stalking lizard. Bulldog had courage. Grant him that before he died.

The stable door slid open and sunlight entered suddenly, forcing Poe to close his eyes. When he opened them, the horses had fled out on to Fifth Avenue, where they kicked up snow as they ran. There was a silhouette in the doorway and Poe narrowed his eyes and focused on it.

'Mr Figg! Mr Figg, are you safe, sir! I heard a shot and there was an awful noise from the horses throwing themselves against the door.' In the doorway Titus Bootham shaded his eyes and looked into the stable.

Hamlet Sproul stopped, both hands on the bowie knife, arms extended in front of him. His voice broke with fear. 'Jonathan sent you.'

Figg shook his head.

86

Sproul shrieked, 'You lie! You are here to kill me!' He began backing away from Figg. 'You will not burn my heart or nothin' else that is inside of me. You will not burn—'

He turned and ran.

Poe watched him flee through the wide open stable door, not pausing to even glance at the short man who stood there in steel-rimmed spectacles and a black bear-fur coat. *Jonathan.* Why did Sproul, a man feared by the underworld, fear *Jonathan*? Did this hairless and monstrous bulldog, who now bent over to pick up his two pocket pistols and tall black hat, work for Jonathan, this Jonathan whom Sproul claimed had killed Pier and Lowery and *burned their hearts and liver*?

Poe closed his eyes and his body shook. He was cold with fear, suddenly aware of a massive evil in his life, of being caught in a quicksand of events over which he had no control. *All that we see or seem/Is but a dream within a dream.*

*Jonathan.* Without knowing why, Poe sensed that Jonathan was very much a danger to him and could destroy him unless that danger was eliminated. The darkness that Jonathan carried with him was not that unleashed by Poe on the printed page. It was something real and never too far away, and all of this Poe sensed in the seconds he stood in the stable with closed eyes.

When he opened his eyes, the bulldog and his short friend in the bear coat stood before him.

Poe's eyes met Figg's. The writer said softly, 'Are you from Jonathan?'

Figg said, 'I come to kill him.'

Poe nodded. He was not surprised.

He watched Figg slip the two pistols into the outside pockets of his long black coat.

There was no need for Poe to remain here any longer. 'I thank you for saving my life. I wish there was something further I could do—'

'There is.'

'I am in your debt, Mr—'

'Figg. Pierce James Figg. I seek your aid in finding Jonathan. I have here in my possession a letter of introduction from—'

Poe close his eyes and shook his head. 'I fear you mistake me for someone else.'

'You are Edgar Allan Poe and I have here in my possession, a letter—'

Fear brought on Poe's anger. 'I have some small curiosity, Mr

Figg, as to how you made my acquaintance without my having made yours.'

'We ain't been introduced if that is where you are placin' your words.'

Titus Bootham plucked at Figg's sleeve. 'May I suggest we continue this conversation elsewhere, as I am afraid we may soon draw servants seeking an explanation regarding the disappearance of four excellent horses. Oh, Mr Figg, dare I ask? Are those two men—' he pointed to Isaac Bard and Chopback, 'are they—'

Figg kept staring at Poe. 'They are. Mr Poe—'

Poe feared the unseen Jonathan and he wanted nothing to do with this Figg who hunted him. 'I have no interest in your letter of introduction even were it signed by Aristotle and witnessed by Shakespeare and the Prophet John. I seek no further involvement in this business—'

He thought of Rachel Coltman. 'I seek no further involvement than I have already incurred and that is nothing I care to discuss with you.'

Why hadn't this Figg rushed out into the wintery gusts like the other animals?

Figg took one step towards him and Poe stepped back. Figg made him uneasy.

'You *will* help me, Mr Poe. You *will*.'

'I have refused you, sir.'

'I have just killed two men.'

'Are you threatening me?'

Figg's voice was that of a man with a dusty throat. Figg's smile was the size of a sixpenny piece and lasted no longer than a drop of water in the fires of hell. 'Threatenin' *you* Mr Poe. Go on. Now why would I indulge in such practices?—me an Englishman and all.'

'You have threatened me, sir. I know it.'

'Then know that I mean to have your help, Mr Poe. And consider us joined by God until I completes me business, or until God puts us asunder.'

'You mean until you kill whom you seek or until he kills us both?'

Figg placed an army around Poe's small shoulders, forcing him to walk with him towards the front door of the stable. 'I am newly arrived in your country and I am sure you *will* be of some small assistance to me.'

Poe watched Figg reach inside his long black coat. 'I have here in me possession a letter of introduction—'

Poe felt Figg's fingers dig into his shoulder, keeping the two of them joined and in step.

*Deep into that darkness peering, long I stood there wondering, fearing/Doubting, dreaming dreams no mortal ever dared to dream before.*

# CHAPTER TWELVE

Figg cleaned his two pistols while speaking.

'Me and Mr Bootham here, we was followin' you, Mrs Coltman, us havin' come upon you at the American Museum of Master Phineas Taylor Barnum. We comes near yer 'ouse and we spies Mr Poe a-strollin' 'bout his business and we sees three gents leave a carriage and drag him from public view. These gents did not seem to be clergymen. I finds me way into the stable and—'

Figg stopped talking but kept working on the pistols. He sat behind the large oak desk in Rachel Coltman's library. Mrs Coltman, Titus Bootham and Poe sat in front of him; Figg could feel the little poet's hostility towards him, not that it mattered a rat's ass. Figg was going to squeeze assistance from Edgar Allan if he had to knuckle him a time or two to put him in a warmer frame of mind.

He looked up to see Poe glaring at him. Figg returned to his guns.

Poe's soft Southern voice dripped malice. He hadn't forgotten Figg's implied threat if Poe didn't help him to find this Jonathan. 'Were you busy with cleaning-rags when you first made the acquaintance of Charles Dickens?'

Figg didn't look up. 'Mr Poe, had these pistols failed to perform properly, you would now resemble a gutted hog danglin' from a slaughterhouse hook. I takes care of me firearms and they takes care of me.'

Poe crossed his legs, then turned his head so that he stared at Figg from the corner of his left eye. 'You seem to have a way of convincing people, no matter how reluctant they may be, to do your bidding. Why not converse with the pistols and make them aware of the consequences of disobeying you.'

'Mr Poe, allow me to tell you a wee bit about these particular pistols. They were handmade especially for me by the Reverend Alexander John Forsyth.'

Titus Bootham sat up in his chair, impressed. 'Oh, I say! Were they really?'

Figg placed both pistols in a flat black wooden box containing bullet mould, powder flask, rammer and other accessories. Closing the top of the box, he set it to one side and folded his hands. 'Reverend Forsyth had the cure of souls in Aberdeenshire, which task did not prevent him from bein' a right fine chemist and huntsman. In usin' flintlocks, he learned that the powder flashed in the pan seconds before the weapon actually fired. This gave the birds and other game a right amount of time to escape. It was the Reverend Forsyth who designed a different sort of magazine and powder which stopped the flame from goin' outside. He made the flame go directly down *into* the weapon.'

Poe rolled his eyes up to the ceiling.

Figg said, 'The Reverend Forsyth became very famous in England for his work with firearms. Napoleon Bonaparte offered him twenty thousand pounds for the secret of his special gunpowder but the Reverend bein' a good Englishman, he said no to the Frenchie. Now the Frenchie, he does not take no for an answer. He lets out that he was goin' to have Forsyth's secret one way or the other, this bein' more than twenty years ago and the war bein' on. So the Duke of Wellington, he comes to me dad and he asks him to be protector for the Reverend Forsyth, to be his bodyguard. Me dad agrees, me dad bein' in the trade like I am now, and he stays with the Reverend.'

Figg stroked a scar that divided his left eyebrow. 'Some Frenchies come for the Reverend one night, but me dad was a good man in a fight so he kills three of 'em and drives off the rest.'

Poe covered his mouth with a small, white hand. 'Did he trample the roses as well?'

'Sad to say, me dad took a ball in the leg that night and he died of gangrene.' He looked at Poe. 'The Reverend, he made me these here pistols out of gratitude. His grace the Duke of Wellington, he taught me how to use 'em.'

Titus Bootham's eyes were misty behind his steel-rimmed glasses. 'Oh I say, jolly good. Jolly, jolly good.'

Poe, eyes on the carpet, combed his forehead with his fingers. He wasn't going to apologise for what he'd just said, but he *did* feel uncomfortable. 'I still desire to know why you followed Mrs Coltman through the streets. There is nothing in Mr Dickens's letter of introduction encouraging you to do such a thing.'

'Granted. I was at the museum of Mr Barnum in order to locate some of Jonathan's associates who'd come here from England. I saw Mrs Coltman havin' a chat with one or two of them and—'

Rachel pulled nervously on a small, lace handkerchief. 'Mr Figg, I too would like to know your role in my life.'

'Yes, mum. A month ago Jonathan killed my wife, Althea. She was young, mum, pretty like yourself, and she had no experience of the world. Maybe I was too old for her, but she and I, we had some little happiness until—'

Figg closed his eyes, then opened them. 'She was an actress and that went against the teachin's of her father, the Archbishop Claridge. When she went upon the stage, he asked her to leave his home and she had no place to go. I give her a home, and, in time, we married. In a church I'm proud to say. But the people she was play-actin' with, they was bad people, odd people, and Jonathan was their leader. He and Althea soon became, they became . . .'

Rachel flushed. 'I understand, Mr Figg.'

'Thankin' you, mum. It is a hurtin' thing to speak of, so I thank you for understandin'. Now Jonathan, he is a man what worships demons. He has given himself to the powers of darkness. Oh he is clever, I will allow that. But he is more, mum. Special powers he has, and all of them given him by evil bein's. For years he has been searchin' for the Throne of Solomon—'

Rachel inhaled sharply, both hands going to her mouth.

Figg noticed, but made no comment. 'Althea told me of these things. Towards the end, she had to talk to someone. She said this here throne, it has got a special magic it does. Can make a man wealthy and more powerful than Satan himself. Jonathan has been after it for a long time.'

Figg looked at Rachel Coltman. 'Same as yer husband, mum. Mr Justin wanted that throne, did he not?'

He saw her nod, then pull hard on the handkerchief as if trying to shred it. Figg didn't want to upset the lady but the truth had to be told. 'Mum, if you have anythin' to do with Jonathan, I beg you do no more deals from this day on. He will destroy you and all who tries to prevent him from gettin' that throne. Althea said that Jonathan had to get the throne or one of those demons he bows down to would get him.'

Poe leaned forward in his chair, more interested in Figg than he had been seconds ago. 'And you believe your wife spoke the truth when she told you this?'

'Yes, Mr Poe, I do. Jonathan tried to use her father, even though he was a man of God. Jonathan had some Greek and Latin writin's which he thought would lead him to the throne. He wanted help translatin' them, so he comes to Althea's father, the Archbishop, who was a scholar in these matters. That was his plan all along, to use my wife to get to her father. But the Archbishop, he says no. He curses Joanthan. Jonathan then took his revenge.'

Figg blinked tears down his scarred cheeks. Poor Althea. Dead while scum like Jonathan still lived. Somewhere in the house, Figg heard a grandfather clock strike the hour. He said, 'Mr Poe, you are one with some knowledge of Greek subjects. Jonathan brought down the punishment of Tantalus on me wife and the Archbishop. I wants you to remember this when I asks yer help.'

Poe frowned, again combing the furrows in his forehead with a small hand. 'Tantalus, Tantalus. Ah yes. Son of Zeus and a most disgusting son at that. Admitted to the circle of gods on Mount Olympus, but eventually he proved so foul that he was punished by being tied to the bough of a fruit tree which hung over a pool of water. Whenever he bent down to drink the water, it receded. When he would reach for the fruit, it would pull away from him. Thus we get the word tantalise—'

'I do not refer to that, Mr Poe.'

Poe narrowed his grey eyes. A horrible thought was worming its way into his mind. Suddenly, his mouth dropped open. 'Good Lord, man! Are you saying—'

Figg exhaled, dropping his chin to his chest. 'The books say that Tantalus killed his very own son and served his flesh to the gods, and then Tantalus told the gods that since they was all-knowin' they should know what they was eatin'. That was the reason for Tantalus' punishment, Mr Poe. Jonathan killed my wife Althea and he had her flesh served to her own father. *And to me.* We didn't know, we didn't know . . .'

Titus Bootham whispered, 'My God!'

Rachel Coltman's mouth was open; her eyes unblinking.

Poe couldn't take his eyes from Pierce James Figg. There was no mystery as to why Figg wanted Jonathan's life. Every man his own hell, wrote Byron. Figg was living in hell every day. *He had eaten the flesh of his own dead wife.* But there was more to this matter than what Poe had heard here. Much more. He looked at Rachel Coltman.

Her eyes were on Figg. Clearing her throat, she called the boxer's name in a tiny voice. 'Mr Figg, you said my late husband sought the Throne of Solomon. This is true. He believed it would cure him of a most horrid disease but he died before, before . . .'

She used the lace handkerchief to blot tears from her eyes. 'My husband did not find the throne before passing on. I can guarantee this. Myself, I have no belief in such an item. But my husband did,

93

and since I wanted him to live, I supported anything that would help him to. If this Jonathan is indeed seeking the throne, there is little he can expect from me, save some of my husband's books on demons, witchcraft—'

Poe was on his feet. His was a freed subconscious, a mind that analysed, that ruthlessly pursued truth. What he was about to do was painful but necessary. He *had* to know the truth, especially in light of what had happened to him last night at his Fordham cottage. Or this morning in Miles Standish's office. Or minutes ago at the stable across the street.

He spoke slowly, sadly. 'Rachel, you have been false with me. You have used me most foully and I am deeply grieved by it.'

She turned quickly to face him and he saw her prepare to lie, then decide against it.

'Eddy, I—'

'I forgive you, dearest Rachel. But I must ask that you speak to me from the heart and in no other manner. Early on Mr Figg said that he was at the museum of Barnum in order to seek out Jonathan's henchmen. When he saw them, they were talking to you. Rachel, you are involved in a most sordid matter and I fear you have involved me as well. Why?'

Her eyes pleaded with him not to ask her, but he stared at her until she spoke. Her eyes were filled with tears and never had she looked so beautiful to him as she did now. 'Eddy, the dead body of my husband was indeed removed from its final resting place, but with my knowledge and permission.'

Poe was stunned. 'You mean the resurrectionists did your bidding?'

She nodded, hands folded in her lap and twisting the handkerchief. 'I followed his order.'

'Whose orders?'

'Doctor Paracelsus. He told me that he could bring my husband back to life if he could obtain the body. I was to have no guards at the grave and the mausoleum door was to be unlocked. I loved Justin, you must know that. So I willingly did as Doctor Paracelsus requested.'

Poe was angry and hurt at being used. 'I suppose the esteemed Doctor Paracelsus demanded a pretty penny for this giving of life?'

'I paid him, yes.' Rachel was defensive now. Figg watched her and Poe as he would two fighters, either one of whom he would fight in the future. Both Mrs Coltman and Mr Poe were nearer to Jonathan than either knew, which suited Figg just fine. The poet or the woman could be *his* Judas goat and lead him to the demon-man.

Poe extended his arms towards Rachel. He's hurtin', thought Figg. He's too much into that woman and she has hurt 'im. And I know Jonathan is the cause.

Poe said, 'Rachel, this man Paracelsus is a fraud.'

She turned from him.

'Rachel, the dead do not return to live with us. He has humbugged you. Shall I tell you what he plans once he obtains the body of your husband?'

She looked at him again, her face set against whatever he would say to her. 'I suppose I cannot stop you.'

'He will indulge in *necromancy*, the blackest of all the black arts. He will use Justin for purposes of divination. The art can be traced back to the ancient Greeks, who believed that the dead, having passed from the earthly limitations of space, time and causation, are able to predict the future, to reveal the whereabouts of hidden treasure. Through necromancy, a magician like Jonathan controls demons, devils.'

Figg watched Poe kneel at the woman's side and continue talking. 'Rachel, this sinister business is a hazard to the conjurer for he may attract demons and evil to the scene and be unable to control them. If you are near when—'

She stood up quickly, her back to him. Poe stayed on his knees, his face unable to conceal his torment, his fear for her safety. 'For nine days the conjurer prepares. He steeps himself in death, dressing in gruesome clothing torn from corpses, and he will wear this clothing until the ceremony is completed. He will eat the flesh of a dog and bread that is black, unleavened and without salt, for salt preserves and the conjurer is drawn only to decay. He will drink grape juice that is unfermented, for it symbolises the absence of life. He will sit within a consecrated circle and meditate on death and there are frightening incantations which must be chanted—'

She swung around to face him. 'I do not care what you say! Doctor Paracelsus *will* bring Justin back to me. I shall not turn on him. I have his promise—'

Figg stood up. 'Here now, just who is this Doctor Paracelsus?'

Poe, his face streaked with tears, shouted at him: 'He is whom you seek! He is Jonathan! He is the man who killed your wife! He killed Sylvester Pier and Tom Lowery! Jonathannnnn!'

Figg ran to him, shook his shoulders and slapped him twice.

As Poe sobbed, Figg held him in his arms, looking over Poe's shoulder at Rachel Coltman. This beautiful red-headed woman would be seeing a lot of Figg before this matter was settled.

When Poe had calmed down and was again sitting, Figg stood over him and said, 'How do you know this Paracelsus is Jonathan? Mr Dickens tells me you write things that involve a mysterious turn of mind.'

'Mystery stories.' Poe could barely be heard.

'And stories about a detective, a Frenchie called—'

'C. Auguste Dupin.'

'Yeah. Does this sort of writin' make you any smarter than the ordinary fella what is walkin' around?'

Poe sighed, leaning back and closing in his eyes. He kept them closed as he spoke. 'Deductive reasoning. That is the process, sir. Example: Doctor Paracelsus wants the body of Justin Coltman. According to Hamlet Sproul, who is the sole survivor of your handiwork in the stable, Jonathan has also put in a claim for the deceased. Sproul has the body and there is evidence of but a single set of ghouls. Conclusion: Paracelsus and Jonathan are one and the same.'

Rachel's voice was firm. 'No! I cannot accept that, Eddy. Paracelsus saved my life. I wanted to be with Justin badly enough to kill myself and he prevented that. I cannot believe such a man would—'

Poe opened his eyes. 'Rachel, you used me and I forgive you for that. But I cannot live my life without truth and I demand truth even from you. Approach this matter with me logically. Hamlet Sproul was going to kill me, therefore he had no reason to resort to deception of any sort. He was quite forward on Jonathan having instigated the desecration of your husband's final resting place. Next, you are seen talking to men Mr Figg indentifies as associates of Jonathan.'

'Eddy, these people at the museum are connected with Doctor Paracelsus. I cannot go to him when I wish. I must meet with go-betweens and give them messages—'

'Dear Rachel, you are refusing to reason. The same men who serve Jonathan serve Paracelsus. Both Jonathan and Paracelsus deal in matters beyond this world. I now ask you, when did you first encounter Paracelsus?'

'Immediately upon the death of Justin. I had no need for him prior to that.'

'Barely three weeks ago. Mr Figg, when did Jonathan flee England?'

'The same time, it was. Right after he saw to it that my son got hanged for a crime what Jonathan had done.'

Poe leaned forward. 'My profound sorrow upon your losses, sir. And now, I shall tell you both what has occurred in this matter. I shall do it with intuitive perception. Such analytical power shall indicate the true state of affairs. Imaginative you may call me, but I challenge you to prove me wrong. Jonathan fled England not merely to avoid retribution from Mr Figg. He fled to be nearer Coltman, who through his wealth and interest in the occult was obviously closer to the Throne of Solomon than was Jonathan.'

Poe stood up. 'Upon learning Justin had died, he attempted to seize the body, having first insinuated himself in your life, Rachel, as Doctor Paracelsus. This gave him information and access to all matters pertaining to your Justin. By that I mean access to your servants, friends, associates. He then engaged resurrectionists to remove the corpse, which they did. However, instead of turning the corpse over to Jonathan as arranged, the resurrectionists kept it for themselves and sought a handsome fee for its return. This can easily be deduced from the terror evident in Hamlet Sproul as well as from certain remarks he let slip before taking himself elsewhere.'

'Rachel, your association with those at the museum of Barnum led Mr Figg to my rescue. Mr Figg, fortunately, had come upon me at the newspaper, where, at the time of our meeting, I was unable to reciprocate his greeting with one of my own. I surmise, too, dear Rachel, that Paracelsus has told into your private ear certain facts about your life that you thought were unknown to all except you and Justin.'

She nodded, less on guard now. 'He has. I have repaid him for his help to me by introducing him to my friends who have also lost a loved one and wish to contact—'

Poe said, 'I assume these friends are wealthy.'

'Eddy, this part of my life does not concern you. If you have ever cared for me, I beg you to remember this.'

'Rachel, you and I are pawns. Because of me, two men are dead. Was it not Paracelsus who told you to engage *me* as go-between? Did he not say that it would be better for *me* to come to terms with the resurrectionists, rather than seek someone else for this dangerous task?'

'No! You were my choice because I felt you cared for me and would be certain to handle this matter most carefully. Paracelsus was against using you. He said your reputation as "Mr Toma-hawk" would make you difficult to control. He said you were too analytical, too piercing in your judgements, too obsessed by your mania for the truth.'

Poe let his arms flop to his side. 'Left-handed compliments. Accepted nonetheless. What he got was a man at home with the scum of our day, a position for which I am most qualified. I am at ease in grog shops, rum palaces and gutters from the Battery to the farmland beyond 42nd Street. Hamlet Sproul deduced I was the Judas goat and so I was. Sproul said their hearts and livers were cut out and burned. Rachel, this is a demon rite going back thousands of years. It is an offering to Asmodeus, king of all demons, he who triumphed over Solomon, wisest of Christian rulers.'

Rachel shook her head. 'I shall *never* betray Paracelsus, Eddy. Never.'

'He has killed men, Rachel. He could well kill you.'

'Eddy, I do not believe this.'

'The man who butchered Sylvester Pier and Tom Lowery, in this frightening ritual, is a man who will stop at nothing to get what he wants. Had he felt Paracelsus was in his way, he would have murdered him as well. I can only deduce that the continued existence of Paracelsus, with his interest in the body of Justin, means that Jonathan does not want Paracelsus dead. Progressing further, it means both men are one and the same. The fiend who slaughtered those two ghouls is not a man to accept interference or competition. That Paracelsus continues to live means he is Jonathan or, at the least, totally serves him.'

She found the strength to be cruel to him. 'This sounds like one of your better tales, Eddy. I would pay a penny to read it, which is twice what it is worth.'

'Rachel, do not—'

'Is it true that you fall asleep at night only with the aid of an opium pipe?'

'Rachel, I beg you, do not hurt me this way!'

She angrily turned on Figg. 'And you, sir, this business of eating the flesh of your dead wife. I would wager that the Archbishop would find it amusing, were he to hear it.'

'He's dead, mum.' Figg looked down at the carpet. 'He, after he had eaten, he, uh, he became disturbed in the head, mum, and he cursed God. He could no longer believe in a god what could let somethin' like this happen, so he killed himself. Hung himself from a church bell-tower.'

She broke down, sobbing behind her hands. Figg watched Poe go to her and take her in his arms. Maybe she didn't mean them things she just said about little Mr Poe, thought Figg, but she was still much in favour of this Paracelsus, who Mr Poe says is one and the same as Jonathan. That bein' the case, the weepin' widow was just the one to lead Figg to the good doctor.

Figg said, 'Beggin' your pardon, mum, but what does this Doctor Paracelsus look like?'

She lifted her head from Poe's shoulder. Even in tears, Rachel Coltman was never less than lovely. 'He is old, grey in hair and beard, and he is large in the chest, a most impressive man. I do not see how he could possibly be your Jonathan.'

Figg frowned. He'd seen Jonathan, but in the dark of night and from a distance, and even then he had not seen Jonathan's face. Still, what he'd seen had been a slim, young man who moved quickly and gracefully. Nothing like this Paracelsus.

Figg said, 'Jonathan is a much younger man, Mr Poe.'

Poe kept his back to Figg and his arms around Rachel Coltman. 'Mr Figg, did you not yourself tell us that Jonathan was involved with travelling players?'

'That I did.'

'So, does it surprise you that his appearance can vary at will?'

'No, it does not, Mr Poe. Leastwise since you have pointed it out. And I thank you.' Mr Dickens was correct. Our little friend in the black clothing has his uses.

Rachel pushed Poe away from her. 'I cannot help you, Eddy. I cannot. I will help neither you nor Mr Figg to harm Doctor Paracelsus.'

'Rachel, twice within hours someone has attempted to destroy my mind, to shatter my sanity with illusions.' He opened his hand to show her the cut. 'Something designed to make me doubt my reason occurred at the home of Miles Standish. A similar and most cruel occasion was visited upon me last night, and as yet I do not know why.' *Virginia, my dearest, dearest, do not leave me.*

'Rachel, it is my belief that Paracelsus, or Jonathan, wants to harm me in a manner that could be my utter ruin. Can you tell me why?'

Her hand reached out to touch his cheek. 'Oh Eddy, oh darling Eddy. Ask anything of me, but do not ask me to deprive myself of Doctor Paracelsus. I will do all that you say in the matter except betray *him*.'

Figg said, 'Tell us when Jonathan or Paracelsus contacts you again. Tell us when he asks you to arrange a meetin' with some of your friends.'

'A seance,' said Poe. 'It is termed a seance, Mr Figg.'

Rachel shook her head. 'I will not.'

Poe gripped her hands. 'You must!'

'No!'

'You are in danger. I swear it!'

'Eddy, I must leave now. Miles sent a message earlier regarding the ransom and I must meet him to sign papers releasing the money. That is my sole concern at the moment. I am counting on your assistance in recovering the body of my husband.'

Figg saw Poe nod. Figg himself bowed when Rachel Coltman said, 'Mr Figg, Mr Bootham,' then left the room, shutting the door behind her.

Mr Bootham's long, loud sigh was the only sound. He cleared his throat. 'I, I . . . is there any assistance I can render, Mr Figg?'

Figg kept his eyes on the closed door. 'You can forget what you just 'eard 'ere today, Mr Bootham. Your life is forfeit if you don't. Jonathan would do you as easily as peelin' a banana.'

'I understand, sir. You can rely on me. It is all quite upsetting, quite upsetting. I came to this New York as a war correspondent over thirty-five years ago and I cannot get used to its unending violence. This city, dear Jesus, this city. It is alive and savage with its mind-boggling extremes of wealth and poverty. It is the largest city in a half-civilised land, a city of widespread crime and heart-breaking destitution and slums more heinous than any found in Europe.' The little journalist shook his head. 'It is a city of cholera, yellow fever and smallpox, but none of these plagues pose the danger of this man Jonathan.'

'Paracelsus,' said Poe, walking over to a decanter of brandy.

When he reached for it, Figg's hand gripped his wrist. 'None a that, squire. I need you.'

Poe sneered. 'I have needs of my own, sir.'

'Satisfy 'em when our business is concluded.' Figg tightened his grip on Poe's wrist. Let the poet know early on whose hand was on the whip.

Poe tried to pull away, but couldn't. 'I come from a fine family, sir, and we lived like quality, in quality surroundings, in a quality home. Had you laid hands on me then, I would have had you horsewhipped.'

Figg jerked, pulling Poe to him. 'I was born on straw, Mr Poe. I ain't got no ancestral home. A cow ate it. You and me is goin' to find me a place to live, then we are goin' forth to seek Jonathan. I dare say he will soon be aware that you have been doin' some thinkin' on your own, so he might just be seekin' you out as well. Caution should be the watchword, I would think.'

Poe pulled and pulled, trying to free himself from Figg's grip on his wrist. 'Sir, you cannot force me to accompany you.'

Figg smiled, releasing the wrist. 'You are correct in that assumption, squire. I cannot force you to walk either behind or in front of me. That is somethin' you are goin' to do of your own free will.'

Poe, rubbing his wrist, shook his head—no. The bulldog did not have that power over him. Poe was going to drink until he could not remember anything, and the last thing he wanted to do was follow Figg.

Figg said, 'I cannot force you to walk, as I said. All I can do is see that you do not walk at all. If you do not come with me, squire, I shall put a ball in your knee and you will not be walkin' much at all, I'm thinkin'.'

Poe stopped rubbing his pained wrist.

Titus Bootham plucked at Figg's sleeve. 'Mr Figg, you wouldn't—'

Figg turned to him and smiled coldly.

Titus Bootham said, 'You *would*.'

Figg's smile broadened.

Seconds later, the three men left Rachel Coltman's mansion.

Five minutes later a coloured servant, bundled against the cold, left the mansion, crossed the street and peered into the stable. After staring at the dead bodies of Isaac Bard and Chopback for a few seconds, the coloured servant closed the stable door and hurried through the snow to make his report to Jonathan.

# CHAPTER THIRTEEN

Jonathan said, 'Poe *is* dangerous, yes. I am more aware of this than you are.'

'Then why do you refuse to have him killed?'

'Because, my dear Miles Standish, the fact that he punctured your ego is no reason for me to alter my plans.'

'He did not—'

Jonathan held up a hand. 'Please, please. You are not pleading your case before the usual corrupt and venal New York judge, so spare me your turgid denials. I know what happened today between you and Edgar Allan Poe, I mean in addition to that little tableau we arranged for him. Our "Tomahawk" made mention of matters you prefer kept secret, and he appeared to have poured a pitcher of warm spit over those fantasies in which you imagine yourself to be Rachel Coltman's lover.'

'He is an untalented, miserable little blackguard!'

'Hardly. He happens to be a most capable writer, though impoverished, which is more the shame of this nation than it is dear Poe's. Bad taste is essential in both writer and reader if there is to be any literary success. Americans have always wallowed in bad taste and show no signs of reversing this trend. Unfortunately, Poe *does* have taste and therein lies his hard life in this hard land. He is a man out of time, out of step, far in advance of any of your colonials putting pen to paper today. I rather enjoy his morbid musings.'

Miles Standish, determined to have Poe murdered, leaned forward on to the black marble table in Jonathan's seance room. Standish's pride was his weak point, thought Jonathan. That and his lust for beautiful women. Because of pride and lust, Miles Standish ended up playing the fool. The lawyer angrily said, 'Are you spying on me in my own home? You seem so well informed about my personal affairs. Which of my servants have you bribed? You are so good at that, you know!'

Jonathan ignored the outburst. 'Poe is needed. He will help me find the body of Justin Coltman. That is why Poe is alive; that is the sole reason. The reason is functional; it is one of utility, not whim, not weakness. Rachel Coltman has more than a small degree of faith in our Edgar, especially in his ability to survive among the dregs, and I refer to Hamlet Sproul, our one and only link to the body of Justin Coltman.

'Now, dear Miles, whether it delights you or not, the lady trusts Poe. She seeks his advice, she believes him to be wise. Oh, I grant you they are not in harmony all of the time, but Poe, ever the romantic, ever the swain in waiting, will not desert Mrs Coltman in her hour of need. He reminds me of what is said about the Germans: they are either at your throat or at your feet. Count on Edgar the lovelorn to stay involved, to resume his role as go-between in the matter of exchanging Justin Coltman, deceased, for hard cash, American. The reason we are tampering with Edgar's sanity is to make him more of a believer in the spirit world and less of a believer in not paying ransoms. We want him to believe in us, so that he will not attempt to dissuade Mrs Coltman from unloosening her purse.'

Miles Standish stroked his thick red beard. 'I want him dead.'

'No. The things he said about you were true. Accept the truth and it will cease to bother you.'

'You have spies everywhere, not merely in my home and Mrs Coltman's. Why can't you locate Hamlet Sproul without the aid of that detestable rumpot?'

Jonathan's mind flashed to Asmodeus, then pushed thoughts of the demon aside. 'Because I do not have the time. I need Justin Coltman's body as soon as possible.'

'And you cannot achieve the throne without him? You cannot do it alone?'

'No. Would that I could. Coltman had the necessary books and they are now missing—and have been since his death. The combined knowledge in those books will give me what I have sought for years, but only Coltman has either that knowledge or knows the whereabouts of those books. He made no arrangement with other magicians or sorcerers before he died. Of this I am certain. I must get Justin Coltman to speak, to tell me what he knows of the throne or where I can obtain those books. *Then* I will have it. *Then* the throne will be mine.' Jonathan's clenched fists rested on the marble table and he breathed deeply, loudly.

Miles Standish had a goal, too. He wanted Poe dead. 'He can expose all of us. I am talking about *Poe.* Yes, he *exposed* me, if you must know. But his very long nose can probe into corners affecting us all, and I include you.'

'Let me worry about that.'

'I am saying you are not the only one who will worry. What about the others, those with the fat and ready purses. The monies you receive from these quarters might well evaporate when it is learned that a meddlesome busybody like Poe is applying his bizarre talents to pry into their lives. Men like Volney Gunning and Hugh Larney, to name two, are not disposed to having their connection with you become public knowledge. I tell you that this could well be the result should Poe continue to live.'

Jonathan's hands were palms down on the black marble table, his eyes closed. Standish and his asinine pride. Did he wish the world to stop revolving while he exacted his revenge on an impoverished writer whose offence had been to be more attractive to a beautiful widow than was a prosperous and pompous attorney? As for Volney Gunning and Hugh Larney, Jonathan admitted they had their uses.

Gunning and Larney were wealthy men who gave him money or saw that he obtained it in large amounts from their friends and acquaintances. Jonathan needed information on the Throne of Solomon, on the rich and their dead relatives. Meaning he needed spies and spies had to be paid.

Spies. Servants, maids, friends of friends, thieves who stole purses, wallets, personal papers, artifacts and who broke into safes without leaving a trace of having been there. Lawyers, police, judges, relatives, business associates, doctors and others around the world whom Jonathan enlisted to do his bidding. All had to be paid, resulting in an unending need for money. Bribes, payoffs, expenses; they were all constant. The information thus purchased made Jonathan appear supernatural, powerful, all-knowing.

Being ominiscient did not come cheap.

Jonathan opened his eyes. His voice was hard, different in pitch, a sound minus all warmth. Miles Standish flinched. 'This ends the matter, Miles. Poe will live until I feel his living is a detriment to me. As for those who give us money, they received adequate compensation.'

Standish knew what that compensation was. Some of the wealthy enjoyed attending seances, while others enjoyed black rites, all of which Jonathan staged for their pleasure. Men like Volney Gunning and Hugh Lorney had other preferences; Volney was a homosexual and Hugh Larney preferred to lie with young girls who had not reached the age of consent. Jonathan saw to it that each man satisfied his particular lust in the fashion craved, in a manner giving pleasure beyond anything imaginable. Miles Standish also had cravings.

The woman that Jonathan called Sarah, dearest God in heaven! Miles's mouth watered at the thought of her. In bed she denied him nothing and gave him everything. She submitted, giving her body as demanded, matching Miles's lust with hers, and always at the end she would surpass him in knowledge of what the body could sexually achieve. But that was at the end. First she would submit, allowing him to use her. Her triumph, her need for sexual supremacy was not allowed to intrude on his dominance. Miles wanted her now.

Black magic, fear, lust, murder, money, blackmail. Jonathan binds us to him, thought Miles. And we let him do it. We let him climb to heights of evil over our souls and bodies which we stack ever so neatly for him. He throws us a bone of our choosing and we let him do with us as he wills.

Miles Standish was a man of position and property in New York and he did not want a failure like Poe shouting his secrets to the four winds. Soon Poe would know all about the other men of position and property who supported Jonathan, and *that*, friends, would be a hive of bees turned loose in a crowded room. To wait until one was up to one's hips in alligators before draining the swamp was not prudent. Not prudent at all. Poe must die.

As though reading his mind, Jonathan said, 'He lives, Miles. A day, an hour, for as long as it suits me, he lives.'

'Yes, yes. Of course, Jonathan. As you wish.'

Later, Jonathan and Sarah stood at the third-floor window looking down at the street. They watched Miles Standish's carriage pull away.

Sarah took Jonathan's arm and leaned against his shoulder. 'Shall I sleep with him?'

Jonathan shook his head, letting the curtain fall into place. 'That will not cure him of his exalted opinion of himself. "Whom the gods would destroy, they first make proud." As true now as it was when first uttered in ancient Greece.'

She kissed his bare shoulder. 'Are you going to destroy Miles Standish?' Her tone was seductive and aimed at Jonathan; the words conveyed no sympathy for the plump, well-groomed lawyer.

'After.'

'After what?'

'After he commits his mistake of hubris. I feel strongly that

Miles Standish, unlike his historical predecessor, will soon be speaking for himself and not for the rest of us. After he commits this nonsense—'

'What nonsense?'

'Attempting to kill Poe.'

'You told him Poe was to live.'

'Miles is alone in his enthusiasm for what passes for his mental processes. I fear he has to learn by direct experience. The newly-arrived Mr Figg is possibly more of a problem than the poet. Come bathe me.'

# CHAPTER FOURTEEN

Poe eyed Figg with all the hatred he could muster. 'I shall see you dead, sir. On my honour, I shall see you dead.'

Figg held his nose and gently shaved under it with an ivory-handled straight razor, making his voice, when he spoke, oddly nasal. 'Dear me, I think it's complainin'.'

Poe, oversensitive and unstable at the best of times, was ready to scream, to claw a hole in the hotel wall and crawl through. Never had he been so humiliated in his life. 'I am walking through that door. You may shoot me if you choose, but I cannot stay in your company any longer, not after what you have done to me.'

Figg, face half covered with shaving soap, turned to look at him. 'Oh, you means my tying your wrists together, then stickin' a towel in yer yap and forcin' you at the point of a gun to get on the floor and me tyin' you to the bed and tellin' you if you woke me up I was gonna punch a hole in yer skull. Is that what you are referrin' to, squire?'

Poe burned with rage.

Figg said, 'Go. Turn the knob and walk. Done had me three-hour rest and I feels shiny as a new penny. Go on, I ain't gonna put a ball in yer knee. Not now. Ain't gonna knuckle you either.' Figg grinned, a hideous sight that reminded Poe of gargoyles perched on top of medieval French cathedrals.

Poe gripped the end of the brass bed. The shame of being tied like a calf on the way to a slaughterhouse. Damn it all to hell! 'I shall leave, sir, and when I return I shall not be alone. The police—'

'Oh dear, oh dear, oh dear.' Figg turned back to the mirror and resumed shaving.

'Now, squire, first let us jaw about the police of this fair city. Mr Bootham tells me they do not do a good job, that they ain't the best when it comes to solvin' crimes or protecting honest citizens like yours truly. Mr Bootham says the police of New York are corrupt, incompetent and leave much to be desired. Says they get knuckled muchly by your local footpads and thugs, sorry to say. Fact is, your police have such a tough time of it that they no longer wear them nice new shiny uniforms with nice new shiny brass buttons. Tried that a while back and your very own criminal classes thought it was quite comical and they attacked your police. So now, your New York police dress up like you and me so as not to get too heavily damaged, and I hear they wears a copper shield so's somebody will know they are police.'

Poe, curious as to the direction of Figg's ramblings, looked into the mirror to see Figg grinning back at him. If only he'd slice his throat, then Poe would grin as well.

'Oh, I should say that with your reputation as a man known to down a dram or two, it is bloody unlikely that anythin' you tell a copper, see I know the word, anythin' you tell a copper will be taken too seriously. It will be your word against mine about what I done, and I'm thinkin' your word ain't comin' directly from the New Testament.'

Poe watched Figg put down the razor, bend over the washbasin and bring large hands cupped with water to his face. 'Hot water. The miracle of progress. This here is some palace. Beg pardon. Hotel, you Americans call it. John Jacob Astor's House, who Mr Bootham says got too old and sick to walk about, so his servants would toss him up and down in a blanket to get his circulation goin'. Mr Bootham says John Jacob is dyin' and when he goes, he will leave behind him some twenty millions of dollars, seein' as how he owns half of Manhattan.'

Figg began towelling his face. 'Now squire, allow me to tell you why you ain't gonna leave my side and of your own free will, I might add. Allow me to say why you will not set foot in that hall without me. You and me is wed, little friend.'

Poe sneered. 'A consummation is devoutly not to be hoped for.'

'Don't know what all that means, seein' as how I am a plain man and cannot hope to match your lordship's way with words. But this I do know: during the three hours I was sleepin', Jonathan has had an opportunity to make a few plans concernin' the two of us. His spies are everywhere, which is the reason I do not plan to spend more than one or two nights in any one place. Jonathan and that Hamlet Sproul fella you mentioned, both are probably on the hunt for you. Lookin' for me too, I might add. There is the matter of two dead men in a stable, which might also be tied up to you, but what I think is that if you go walkin' 'round New York town on your lonesome, somebody just might do you a bit of harm. I can also do me best to see that no harm comes to your lady Rachel, knowing how much you care about her an'all. This is a sticky business we are about and Mrs Coltman is in what I would call extreme danger from Jonathan. If you care about her, you will give me your aid.'

Poe immediately knew the boxer was right. And that only made him hate Figg more. 'And you, I suppose, plan to protect us with all your might and main.'

'That I do, squire, that I do. That is, so long as you are of some use to me.'

Poe sat down on the edge of the bed. This wasn't the way he wanted to visit the Astor House, Manhattan's largest and most spectacular hotel. A pet dog had more freedom and dignity than Poe had at the moment, but Figg's assumption about his immediate future had more than a ring of casual truth to it. It was night and the streets of Manhattan were normally dangerous, and worth your life to stroll upon. Somewhere out there in the darkness Jonathan, Hamlet Sproul and god knows who else were indeed on the hunt for Poe. *Jonathan, who removed hearts and livers and burned them as offerings to the demon god, Asmodeus.*

To keep Rachel alive, Poe was now forced to help Figg. There was no choice but to associate with this most wretched man.

Figg sat on the bed, pulling on his boots. He was disgustingly cheerful, whistling tonelessly through cracked teeth, pushing air through them as though it was a Bach cantata. He also acted as though Poe had already agreed to stick by him. *You and me is wed, little friend.*

'Oh Mr Poe, I have a query. When we was comin' in this room, I sees all them holes in the door, sort of near the lock. Can you explain please?'

Poe dropped his shoulders and sighed. 'Those guests unused to gaslight would blow out the flame, not knowing they were leaving the gas on. Gas is without colour and can also be without odour. Inhaled in large doses it can be fatal, and since the ignorant blew out the flame upon retiring, they lay in bed and eventually died of asphyxiation.'

'As what?'

'Call it a form of strangulation. Strangulation by chemicals.'

'Oh dear, oh dear. Go on, squire.'

'Those holes in the door, plugged up now as you can see, represent previous locks. The locks were pulled out to allow the police in to remove the bodies.

Figg smiled. 'I'll be keepin' that in mind. Are you acquainted with Mr Barnum?'

Poe, who still wanted to scream, nodded his head.

' 'Ere now,' said Figg, 'that's nice to 'ear. You seem to have made the acquaintance of quite a few people in your time, Mr Poe. Must be nice to be a writer and have so many folks come up to you and say how much they likes what you write. Very convenient, the hotel bein' across the street from Mr Barnum's American Museum. Some people over there we gots to talk with.'

Poe shook his head, chin on his chest. Figg was stupid, insensitive, with no more culture than you would find in a tree stump, and he reeked of a horrible cologne that smelled like cornbread and kerosene. When would these nightmares end?

Figg finished wrapping his long tie around his neck. 'Tell you what, squire. Why don't we go downstairs and have ourselves somethin' to eat, then go across the street and jaw with Master Barnum. You and him can talk about old times and I can have a look around for some of them play-actors what my wife was involved with. I could eat me a whole goose, feathers and all.'

Poe snorted, mumbling almost to himself. 'Try an entire ox and do keep the hooves on.'

'What was that, squire?'

'I would like to leave the room now,' Poe hesitated. 'In your company, of course.'

'Squire, them's me thoughts exactly. You do look a little peaked and the night air would do you good, I expects.' Figg tucked the two pistols in the pockets of his long black coat. When he saw Poe looking at him, Figg frowned. 'You don't expects me to go 'round naked, does you?'

Poe turned his back to him and walked to the door. 'Why not? This *is* our wedding night, I am told.'

Figg laughed and continued to laugh as the two men walked down the hall, the boxer with an arm around Poe's shoulders. 'Say, squire, did I tell you that Mr Dickens stayed at this hotel when he comes over in eighteen and forty-two? Says to me, he says, "Mr Figg. Do make sure you guard your ears against that awful gong the Americans use to summon guests to the dining-room. It horribly disturbs us nervous foreigners," he says.'

And you nervous foreigners, thought Poe, irritated by the weight of Figg's right arm across his shoulders, horribly disturb us native Americans, which seems to concern no one quite the way it concerns your obedient servant, E. A. Poe.

# CHAPTER FIFTEEN

Ordinarily, Miles Standish found it easy to dismiss Hugh Larney as useless, no more worth listening to than a crow cawing over a bit of rotten fruit. Larney talked too much and was a nouveau riche social climber with pretensions to culture; Standish cringed when Larney affected a British accent in a falsetto voice. Like others, he laughed behind Larney's back when Larney lavishly spent his newly acquired riches in a desperate attempt to make friends among those he called 'Manhattan's quality elite'.

But as water finds its own level, so did Hugh Larney find his. He was a gambler, preferring the sporting world of horse racing, dog fights and pugilists. He was a sensualist, preferring the company of child prostitutes, little girls procured especially for him by a blind Dutch pimp named Wade Bruenhausen. None of the wealth gained from selling impure food to thousands could hide the fact that Hugh Larney was weak and self-indulgent.

This noon, however, Miles Standish hung on every word coming from Larney's dime-sized mouth. Larney was telling him about a bizarre duel to the death about to be fought several feet from where the two men stood in ankle-deep snow under a huge oak tree. Larney, thirty-five, little and dapper in customed British tailoring, with a clean-shaven face of angles – long nose, pointed chin, thin triangle of blond hair for eyebrows—talked while sipping chilled champagne from a blue-purple goblet.

'A most unusual confrontation, dear Miles. Each duellist naked to the waist, clothed merely in trousers and boots, and seated inside of that coach yonder, the one with abominable brown paint peeling from its side. Once inside the coach, left arms to be bound at the wrist and forearm and each man to be armed with a stiletto, honed steel I might add. Steel sharp enough to slice the wind and make it bleed. The morning cries out for a keen blade. 'Tis such a bore to watch grown men merely scratch each other like playful kittens.'

' 'Tis indeed,' mumbled Standish, eyes on the brown coach, surprised at being so fascinated by what was to take place. A duel to the death in a coach. Why?

As Larney became more excited, his voice became more British.

New York was still strongly English in matters from fashions to table manners, and this some seventy odd years after the war of independence. Snobs like Larney could keep that influence alive for another hundred years, thought Standish.

Larney sipped champagne, his long nose dipping into the goblet. 'Ummm, scrumptious stuff, this. Now, dear Miles, do listen most carefully. The coach will travel twice around this rather dreary little race-track, giving the two men inside ample time to kill one another. There is some snow as you can see, but the way is not impassable. We are having some of it cleared, hence the wait. Twice around, matter of minutes wouldn't you say? Survivor of the journey to win twenty dollars in gold, said purse proffered by me. Oh, do allow me to tell you how I conceived the idea.'

He swallowed champagne, patted himself gently on the chest with a hand covered by a doeskin glove. 'I tell a lie. The idea is not mine. Occurred in Paris, actually. Twelve years or so ago. Two French army officers selected this method of settling differences. Right in the heart of Paris, can you imagine? Twice around a great square and, to be expected, one officer suffered mortal wounds. Perished, poor fellow. The other was also seriously damaged. Close quarters, you see. Nowhere to run, each man in constant contact with the other. The beautiful part of this, Miles, is that no one can actually see what occurs in the coach. You watch, you wonder, your mind soars, your imagination races and perhaps, perhaps you hear a scream, a cry of pain, a plea for mercy and then the coach speeds by you and your heart pounds and you wait for the journey to end. Some of us here have placed a wager or two. Would you care to indulge?'

Miles Standish, repelled and attracted by the upcoming duel, shook his head. 'I rode out into this godforsaken wilderness to talk with you and Volney Gunning about removing Poe.'

'Yes, yes. I know. Bear with me, please. Let us not speak of that wretch until the duel is completed.' Hugh Larney took a perfumed handkerchief from his sleeve and gently touched his long nose with it. A puny little fop, thought Standish. Serves him right if Poe is the instrument to topple him from his precarious perch.

'Hugh, you sound like the Prince of Wales, for God's sake. By the way, do you mind telling me how you were able to find two men willing to die for twenty dollars and the amusement of your guests?'

Larney smiled, reaching down into the snow for the almost empty bottle of champagne. 'In my travels, dear Miles—'

'Slumming, dear Hugh.'

'Slumming. Encountered two men, one Mr Brown Boole and one Mr Oliver van Meter. They were in front of that rather colourful dance hall, the Louvre—'

'A hellhole of thieves, whores, cut throats.'

'It amuses me and my friends. They had never seen such a place and, as I am well known in all colourful quarters of Gotham, I escorted them there. In front of the place, Mr Boole and Mr van Meter were arguing over the proceeds of a recent robbery in which they had been participants. The argument was over the division of eighteen cents they had removed from the victim and they were about to kill one another over this small yield. I had always wanted to see the Parisian duel, having heard so much about it from friends who have been to Paris. So I simply arranged it. I offered each man five dollars then and there to stop fighting, which they most eagerly accepted. Then I made arrangements for them to remain at peace with one another until I could arrange this duel, and here they are today prepared to annihilate one another for more money than either man has ever seen in his life.'

Standish nodded, drawing his greatcoat tighter around his neck. Just the sort of thing one would expect from Hugh Larney and the type of people he attracted. Standish looked around at the dozen or so men who stood in small groups near carriages and sleighs, eating Hugh Larney's food and drinking his champagne while waiting for the duel to begin. The small, private racetrack, located on an abandoned horse farm owned by Larney, was nothing more than a section of land crudely cleared of trees and stumps. The farm was several miles beyond New York City limits, which ended at 42nd Street. Beyond 42nd Street lay the two-thirds of Manhattan that still comprised farmland, woods, swamps and mountains.

On the property was a modest-sized wooden house, barn and two small shacks, all empty, gutted and stripped of anything useable, all crumbling, decayed and weather-destroyed. Hugh Larney, who also made money in real estate speculation, had decided to stop breeding horses on this hundred acres and wait until Manhattan inevitably expanded northward, thus greatly increasing the value of his farmland.

Miles Standish glanced at Hugh Larney's carriage, catching a glimpse though an open door of Dearborn Lapham, the incredibly beautiful child prostitute Larney had brought to the duel as his guest. Dearborn's expensive clothing was all paid for by Larney, who would occasionally allow her to keep one or two of the articles.

Bruenhasen, the blind Dutch pimp, invariably sold the clothing pocketing the money. In the carriage Dearborn Lapham poured iced champagne and dispensed food to Larney's male guests, accepting their smiles, playful taunts, soft-spoken lust. Standish knew that Larney was parading the girl in front of the men, showing her off for those who appreciated the charms of little girls.

Leaning against the carriage and never too far from Larney was another piece of flesh the food merchant owned and was proud of: Thor, twenty-five, a Negro boxer, six foot seven inches, and Hugh Larney's muscular bodyguard, driver and private man, a man who did as ordered and never asked questions. Miles Standish, despite abolitionist sympathies, found the confident Thor, with his controlled arrogance, to be annoying and intimidating. Thor's grin and politeness were traits supposedly proper to his station as a coloured, traits indicating that he knew his place.

But Standish found the Negro's grin to be sly, his politeness to be sardonic. Hugh Larney won money matching Thor against other boxers, black and white, all of whom the Negro had easily and brutally defeated. There were rumours that Thor killed men at Larney's request. It was no rumour that Thor had waited in darkness to give a bloody beating to anyone who had somehow irked Larney—which is why few dared to laugh at Larney's pretensions to his face. Standish, like others, had no wish to receive a night visit from the terrifying Thor.

Police and other authorities had yet to investigate a complaint regarding Thor's massive fists. Thor's arrogance and immunity were firmly rooted in Larney's money.

Hugh Larney wiped his dripping nose with his silk handkerchief, then pointed with his goblet of champagne to a tall man who walked through the snow towards Larney's carriage. 'Ah yes, dear Volney has returned. One wonders what masterful cash deal he has perpetrated while sitting in Prosper Benjamin's carriage for these past few minutes.'

Miles Standish watched his own breath turn to steam in the cold air. Prosper Benjamin was a thief and a rascal and so was Volney Gunning. Prosper Benjamin owned ships which were faulty and deadly to sail in, sailing them out of European ports, filling them with immigrants desperate to come to America, crowding men, women and children into dark, narrow berths on board these 'coffin ships'.

Those who survived the journey fell into the hands of such men as Volney Gunning. He built slum tenements in Manhattan, charging the immigrants disgraceful rents to live there. Gunning, fifty, reed-thin with watery blue eyes which could not stop blinking, spent much of his time at Scotch Ann's, a Manhattan brothel where the beautiful women were actually young men in expensive gowns, wigs, and the loveliest of women's names.

Miles Standish stepped carefully through the snow. 'Has Volney given up the idea of making Thor his concubine?'

Hugh Larney stopped, threw his head back and roared. 'Oh dear, oh dear, oh dear. You are a delight, dear Miles. Of course you are cross with Volney for having ignored your hasty warning about the dangers posed by Poe. I dare say you are probably cross with me as well.'

Miles blew into cupped hands. 'I have travelled a long way to settle this business, only to find the both of you preoccupied with other matters.'

'Matters that suit *me* at the moment, dear Miles.'

'Are you forgetting that Poe has swung his tomahawk in your direction on previous occasions?'

Larney again stopped walking and when Miles Standish looked at his face, the lawyer grew frightened. Larney was angry, which could well mean Thor. There was no false British accent now, just hard words from a man who was cruel because he was too weak not to be. 'I remember all too well, dear counsellor. *"Mr Larney, for profit and no small amount of gain, has pulled down the curtain on this city by stealing oil."* Stinging words from our "Tomahawk". He accused me of taking the oil that the city was to use for street lights along Third Avenue.'

You did indeed steal it, thought Standish, who kept quiet.

'Yes, dear Miles, I have never forgotten. Thank you for reminding me.' He quickly smiled. 'Now on to other prospects. I have seen to the authenticity of today's business. In Paris it is traditional for a duellist to have his last breakfast at Tortini's restaurant. Today, from my carriage, I offer the same food: iced champagne, broiled kidneys, a cornucopia of patés for your palate, and there is fish and game. Paris awaits in my carriage.'

'Hugh, if Poe is not killed he can and will expose us all. I fear that man, for he is loose and unsound. All of us—you, me, Gunning—are men of substance, and if our connection with Jonathan was known—'

Hugh Larney frowned, nodding his head. 'Why did you not say this to me earlier, instead of telling me of the danger to the widow Coltman and by extension yourself?'

'You did not allow me the opportunity.'

Larney looked down at the empty goblet which he twirled between his fingers. 'A crazed one, our Poe. Well, dear Miles, you have presented the problem less frantically and with less self interest. So we are forced to give it more thought. First, we confer with Volney, who I see is again attempting to ingratiate himself with Thor. Volney! Dear Volney! To me! Please to me, dear fellow!'

Miles Standish noticed fleeting smirks on the faces of men standing in the snow, smirks directed at Hugh Larney's way of talking. But the smirks faded quickly.

When Miles had finished speaking of Poe's danger to the three of them, Volney Gunning closed his eyes and nodded in agreement. Gunning's voice was surprisingly deep. 'The danger does exist. We can only benefit from the absence of E. A. Poe and it is doubtful if the world will miss him.'

Gunning wore a fawn-coloured top hat and an ankle-length coat of red lynx fur. Standish wondered if Gunning's pinched cheeks and thin lips were red with the cold or, as rumoured, red with rouge.

Standish chose his next words carefully. 'Jonathan is a most careful man, as you both know. He is grateful for your financial support. He has no wish to see it stop.'

Gunning coughed and bowed his head. 'We are pleased that he appreciates our aid.'

And pleased with the peculiar drugs he procures for you from all over the world, thought Standish. And pleased you should be with his taste in beautiful boys, which so coincides with yours.

Standish said, 'Jonathan is involved in a most important quest, which we need not go into.'

'Yes, the throne,' hissed Larney, eyes as bright as the beautiful empty goblet in his fingers. 'Oh, the magic of it, the wonder—'

'Shhh.' Miles cautioned the food merchant. Standish knew how skilfully Jonathan played upon their weaknesses, giving each the pleasure most wanted, encouraging each to believe that once the Throne of Solomon was made to materialise, all of their wishes and desires would be fulfilled. Standish had reminded Larney and Gunning of this.

He said, 'Poe is determined to have his own magazine. He lives with the dream of being his own man, and to secure financing he will do anything. Should he reach Mrs Coltman's private ear, then her funds would be diverted from Jonathan to Poe's most needful purse. This, of course, would place a greater financial burden on the rest of us, since we all know how determined Jonathan is.' He paused. 'And always in need of money.'

Volney Gunning narrowed his watery blue eyes. 'So we would each be liable for additional funds, should Jonathan request.'

Standish's smile was as cold as the snow beneath his feet. 'A request from Jonathan is never to be taken lightly.'

And in the silence that followed, Standish knew they would agree with him to kill Poe. Whether to continue their pleasures, or to save money, Larney and Gunning would help him to murder Poe. *And Rachel would belong to Miles Standish.*

Gunning said, 'You saw Jonathan?'

'Yesterday.'

'And Jonathan wants Poe dead?'

Miles cleared his throat, looked down at the snow. He said nothing.

Larney tapped his small mouth with a gloved finger. 'So be it. We must survive, must we not? Why should men as we be shamed and disgraced by the rantings of such as Poe?'

When Volney Gunning nodded his head in agreement his eyes were blinking at the massive Thor, as though sending him a heart-felt invitation.

'Listen!' Hugh Larney smiled, pointing to his carriage where three well-dressed men with cigars and goblets of champagne looked inside the open door while listening to Dearborn Lapham sing.

Larney threw his goblet high into the air. 'Dear me, a hymn! One I do so adore: "There is Rest For The Weary". I paid an ancient and toothless whore to teach it to the child. It is my favourite. Mother and I would often sing it together, my little head on her knee.'

Miles Standish coughed behind his hand, biting his lip to keep from laughing out loud. The drivel one had to tolerate in order to arrange the killing of something as useless as Poe.

The little girl's reedy voice carried across the snow-covered field. Now all the men, wherever they were, stopped to listen.

"There is rest for the weary,
There is rest for you,
On the other side of Jordan,

In the sweet fields of Eden,
Where the Tree of Life is blooming,
There is rest for you.'

As scattered applause echoed in the frozen air, Miles Standish watched a sweating Negro bundled in winter clothing and boots rush up to Hugh Larney and whisper into his ear.

Larney threw his head back. 'Ahhh. We commence. Some difficulty securing a horse without a damaged hoof, and we had to clear away snow somewhat, though not entirely.'

He placed his hands to his mouth and yelled. 'Gentlemen! Gentlemen, please! Make final your wagers! Those who wish to challenge me, I am going with Mr Brown Boole and will accept all bets to the contrary, even money! Gentlemen, your wagers please!'

Larney, eyes shining with thoughts of the excitement to come, whispered from the corner of his mouth, 'Boole's your man, Miles. Large in the chest and strong teeth.'

'Strong teeth?'

He has torn off many an ear in a punch-up with those teeth of his. Care to—'

'No thank you.'

'Then watch, my good fellow. Good sport, this. Much good sport. We have a physician on hand and I am sure we will have need of him. Combat at such close quarters. Oh Miles, dear Miles, does not your heart lift at such a thought?'

It did, which bothered Miles. But it didn't bother him enough to leave. He watched the two duellists, bare-chested and unsmiling, step into the brown coach. Two Negroes, bodies stocky with heavy clothing, their black faces impassive, entered the coach after the duellists. One Negro held the pair of stilettos in his hand and sunlight glittered from the keen blades.

Larney said, 'When the men are connected, my boys will drive the coach twice around.'

Standish asked, 'What is to stop the duellists from killing each other immediately, I mean before the duel officially begins?'

'One of my boys will be on top with the driver. He will have a pistol, two pistols actually, with orders to put a ball into whoever violates the spirit of today's glorious festivities.'

Standish couldn't take his eyes away from the brown coach. After long minutes, the two Negroes came out of the coach and one immediately climbed up to the driver's seat, pulled back a small panel and taking a pistol from his belt, poked it into the opening. The other Negro waved his arms in a signal to Hugh Larney.

'Oh my, oh my!' cried Larney. 'We are ready. Come, Miles, come and watch me give the signal!'

Now all of the spectators, all male, drew closer to one another, groping near the brown coach, cigars, champagne and food now forgotten. Standish watched Thor lift little Dearborn Lapham from the snow-covered ground up to the driver's seat of Larney's coach so that she could watch the duel. By God, that little girl was pretty, so very pretty! Standish, who had never been with a child whore, found himself staring at her. Then he shook his head. Child whores. And men about to slash each other with knives for the amusement of others. Today in these surroundings he knew he could easily end up wanting the child whore and he knew for certain that he was not going to leave this place until the duel was over.

Yes it was Hugh Larney who had arranged the duel, but it was Jonathan who had taught Miles Standish to choose excitement over shame.

Larney's voice was shrill with anticipation. 'Amos, are you ready?' The Negro driver touched the reins to his cap. His companion on top of the coach kept his pistol pointed down inside, never taking his eyes from the duellists.

Larney's small mouth was open, his eyes wide and bright as he quickly looked at his guests standing in the snow and staring back at him. He shouted, 'Hail Caesar! We who are about to die salute thee! Let the games commence!'

Larney, arm outstreched, dropped his white silk handkerchief in the snow.

'Eeeeeah!' Amos yelled at the team of four horses, snapped his whip and the cracking noise of it echoed across the flat and frozen land. Miles Standish shivered with excitement as he watched the brown carriage fight for traction in the snow, slide left then right, roll forward and pick up speed. Again the whip cracked and now the coach rolled faster, pulling away from the starting point, picking up speed, its iron-rimmed wooden wheels spraying snow to either side of the road.

As the silent men and child whore watched, a man screamed inside the coach.

As if this was a signal, a few spectators ran after the coach, shouting, encouraging one man to kill, the other to die; and Miles Standish, so excited that the cold no longer bothered him, imagined that the man screaming was Poe.

When the coach neared a turn in the crude snow-covered race-track, the screaming suddenly stopped. Then the whip cracked over the horses' flanks and when the scream started again, Miles's breathing was almost orgasmic, for in his mind the screaming man in the coach *was* Poe. *Rachel Coltman now belonged to Miles Standish.*

# CHAPTER SIXTEEN

*A terrified Poe couldn't breathe.*

*Paralysed by panic, he stood on the edge of a dark abyss, in a cold wind that whipped his brown hair around his face. He was in a night without end, unable to pull his eyes away from the interminable blackness at his feet, knowing he was doomed to tumble into it, to disappear down into its unending horror. The abyss was deep, bottomless. He was frightened of anything deep—the ocean, a pit, crater, the grave. He desperately wanted to flee this place but his feet were imbedded on the edge. The cold wind howled and shrieked, knifing into his bare flesh and still he couldn't run, couldn't leave the edge of the abyss. He had no control over himself; he teetered forward, leaning into the blackness.*

*And suddenly he was in a coffin, deep within a grave, buried alive beneath damp earth, chest rising and falling as he fought for air. He pounded the inside of the coffin lid, fists wet with his own blood, knuckles pained and smashed, his cries of terror filling his ears. Buried alive! All of his life he'd lived with this fear and now it was real. Buried alive!*

*Death had been Poe's obsession, a companion ever since it had claimed his mother, stepmother, wife, those he'd loved above all others. Death, that most awesome of forces, had crept into his mind and lay in wait until called forth in his writings. But Death had warned Poe, warned him that it wanted more than merely his recognition of its existence; Death wanted Poe's soul and now Death had claimed it, holding him in its clammy grip.*

*Poe yielded to the terror of the grave; he punched the coffin until all feeling left his bloodied fists. 'Air! For God's sake, air! I beg you, someone help me! I am buried alive! Aliiiiiiiive!'*

'All right, squire, all right. It's all right now. Come on, wakey, wakey. Mr Poe! Mr Poe! It's me, Figg. Let's see both yer eyes. Open wide. That's it, that's it.'

Poe looked up from his bed to see Figg sitting on the edge, a worried look on his bulldog face. Figg handed him a towel. 'You been nightmarin', squire. Tossin', turnin', yellin' yer fool 'ead off.

'Ere, dry yerself. You're wet, all in a lather like some race horse whats done its best. Woke me up, you did, and probably the rest of the bleedin' unfortunates in this bleedin' hotel. You always carry on like this when you're 'spose to be sleepin'?'

Poe, bare-chested, heart racing much too fast, quickly sat up. *Nightmare*. He pressed the palms of both hands against the sides of his head. 'Need a drink. Rum, whisky, anything.'

'Nay to that, squire. Alcohol puts you too much sleepy bye, from what I can gather, and I can't 'ave that, no sir. Got some water in the basin over there and I can open the window and bring you a handful of snow. But you ain't touchin' spirits whilst you and me is associated.'

Poe hung his head and inhaled deeply. 'The thought, sir, of continued association with you is most unpleasant.'

'Awww now, squire, that don't come from the heart. You and me is on the same quest. Ain't it me what's woke you up? You were carryin' on like a man possessed.'

'I am indeed a man possessed. I need drink, sir. I need stimulants. I also have need for stimulating and intoxicating conversation and again you offer me abstinence, forced abstinence, since you, sir, are an exceedingly unphilosophical man.'

Poe, tensed face shiny with perspiration, let his eyes get used to the dim gaslight. A look at the curtained window told him it was still dark outside and that he was still in a room at the Hotel Astor with Pierce James Figg. He took a deep breath, held it, then exhaled. He was calmer now, but he didn't want to go back to sleep. Not just yet.

There were always nights like this, nights when his fears mounted a deadly attack on his sanity. Poe feared everything: a hostile world that had rejected and impoverished him; the insanity that had already laid deadly hands on members of his family and could well reach out for him. He feared the demons lurking in his tortured mind, that spewed forth the incredible imaginings no American writer had ever produced. He feared loneliness, he feared dying without ever having been recognised for being an original talent. He feared being buried alive.

But he did not fear Figg. Not any more. Figg was beneath Poe, a brute masquerading as a man, something barely animate that smelled of sweat and cheap food, a thing that lacked intelligence and culture and whose thick skull contained a barren void posing as a mind.

He glared at the boxer. 'I need relief, sir, from myself, from you.'

Figg grinned. 'Now that's all of us what's in the room, ain't it. Mr Poe is displeased by what he sees in God's universe and would the rest of us in the world kindly leave and allow Mr Poe to carry on by his lonesome.'

Figg stood up, yawned, stretching his arms towards the ceiling. 'Dear me, ain't life hard. Mind what I said: your lady friend, Mrs Coltman, can stand a bit of lookin' after, 'cause if Doctor Par-rididdle—'

'Paracelsus.'

'Yeah, him. If him and Jonathan is one and the same, well your lady is close enough to this particular fire to get more than her pretty little fingers burned. I know you ain't happy with a common man like me tellin' a scholarly gent like yerself what he should be doin' and all, but you just give some thought to Jonathan carvin' on the widow Coltman. Heart cut out, liver cut out, oh me, oh my!'

Poe snorted. *'Aut Caesar, aut nihil.'*

'Beg pardon?'

'Latin. Uttered by Cesare Borgia. "Either Caesar or nothing." To modernise it, "Follow Figg or travel not at all." '

'Yes sir, I can see where you would say that. I ain't askin' you to grieve for my dead. All I wants is for you to help me somewhat and I will be puttin' things right meself. But you, Mr Poe? You be a most proud man, now that's a fact. Ain't nobody goin' to tell you what to do or order you about. No sir. Been that way all yer life, I bet.'

'You seem to disapprove, not that I give a damn about your opinion.'

'Tell you a little story. Back in the days when I was likely to shake a loose leg, meanin' I did a bit of travellin', I was with this fair that went up north of England. Small towns we played, puttin' on a good show for the folks. Tumblers, acrobats, fat ladies, horse racin' and gypsies what could tell yer future for a bit of silver.'

Figg nodded, remembering. Poe watched the boxer's right hand go to his bare chest, the back of his hand stroking three six-inch scars on the right side of his rib-cage, scars that were now a faded white. In the flickering gaslight, Poe found the scars on Figg's face, chest and arms repugnant as well as fascinating. For brief seconds he empathised with the pain the man had obviously endured in his miserable existence. But he forced that small bit of compassion from his mind and resumed listening indifferently to what Figg was telling him.

'Now this here fair I was with was nothin' like the elaborate establishment of Master Phineas Taylor Barnum, which we visited tonight. Master Barnum has done himself most splendid, but let me tell me own tale—'

'I am all agog.'

'Now I had me a little booth, see, just like me father and his father and his father before him. Nothing different. I charge a few pennies to teach a man the use of knife, cudgel, broadsword, and towards the end, see, I puts up a pound or two as prize money and I says that any man in the crowd what feels he is able, let him come forward and challenge me in boxin'. Two rounds, no more. Usually there is some local boy what thinks he is good with his fists and his friends encourage him to try his luck. But the lad don't last long 'cause it ain't just what you do with your body, see.' Figg tapped his forehead with a thick finger. 'Man got to use his mind in the ring.'

Poe said, 'For the present, I shall take your word that anyone stepping into a prize ring is possessed of a mind. Do continue. I find this account of your past life most entertaining.'

I crave drink, thought Poe, and instead I get a pugilist reeking of sentiment. So desperately did he crave alcohol, that Poe would gladly have downed a cup of New Jersey Champagne, that putrid concoction of turnip juice, brandy and sugar. A disgusting blend enjoyed by those with puny purses and little pride in what they swallowed.

Still sitting up in the bed Poe clenched both fists under the sheet and wondered what harm he had ever done to Charles Dickens to deserve such fate as Pierce James Figg.

'Now, Mr Poe, I am comin' to the point of this story. There was a very important man in England, or so he believed himself to be. This important man owned a huge circus and oft times our small little fair would be in competition with him. It was always a race to see who would get to a town first, him or us. Whoever got there first, naturally got the customers' money first.'

'I am impressed by your logic. Do go on.'

'Well, one day we gets to a town up north near Manchester and we makes our pitch, we sets up camp. We got a good spot but it is a spot that this important man wants for his very own circus. So what does he do? He sends his wagons speedin' down a hill and crashin' into ours, damagin' our goods, our property, not to mention our very lives.'

'Not to mention.'

'So what do we do to this most important man what has got a lot of pride?'

'Ah, now I see. The story of a proud man brought to heel.'

'Indeed, Mr Poe. What do we do? Now you gots to understand that the travellin' life ain't for the timid soul. It is a hard existence and them what takes it up ain't your everyday petunia-pickers. What we do is we get some clubs, some tools and we sneaks up behind the wagons belongin' to this most important man and we gets to openin' them. We starts to let his animals loose. Lions, leopards, elephants, we opens a few locks and before you know it, this most important man is weepin' and wailin', not to mention bein' somewhat terrified 'cause now some of these very valuable and I might add very hungry animals, is strollin' about the country-side.'

Poe found himself smiling.

'Now Mr Poe, this very important man, him and his henchmen are forced to stop whatever they is doin' and set to work recoverin' all these very valuable—'

Poe chuckled in spite of himself. 'And hungry—'

'Indeed, sir. And hungry animals. Need I say we never had any more trouble with that most important man, leastwise whilst I was with the fair.'

'Those scars on your rib-cage, were they—'

'Ah Mr Poe, Master Charles Dickens was correct, sir. You are a most observant gent. These here scars decoratin' me body was a present from a lion what I turned loose that day and by way of thankin' me he waved a cheery bye. Except he has got these claws, see, and each one is as sharp as a Jew's nose for money, and I failed to remove meself from his way of passage at the precise moment the lion would have preferred I so move.'

Poe fell back on the bed and roared. He cackled, he shrieked. Figg's silly story released the tension caused by bad dreams and fear, tension over concern for Rachel Coltman, tension from a growing fear of the mysterious and deadly Jonathan.

Pierce James Figg and his lion.

Phineas Taylor Barnum and his bald eagle.

Leaving the Astor Hotel earlier tonight, Poe and Figg had plunged into the Broadway crowds, joining them in making a pre-carious trek across muddy Broadway jammed with horses, sleighs, carriages. Humans and vehicles all seemed to be heading to Barn-um's brightly lit American Museum which shone in the darkness like a five-storey jewel. Here Figg hoped to find those associates of

Jonathan he had pursued from London. Poe, who had a slight acquaintance with Barnum, was to make the introductions.

Phineas Taylor Barnum, the man who had made the American Museum the number-one entertainment attraction in all of America, as well as one of the wonders of the world, agreed to meet the two men. But he insisted that business not stop because of mere conversation. Barnum, America's first and most bombastic showman, worked seven days a week promoting both his exhibits and his ego, an ego Poe found too large to be contained by the huge museum, which Barnum claimed housed over six hundred thousand examples of the freakish and outlandish.

Barnum was an amiable fraud, a champion hoaxer and humbug specialist who always managed to entertain and therefore offended no one. He took your twenty-five cents at the door and delivered illusions, jokes, songs, dances and the most interesting nonsense available. He had created what he called 'the show business', none of it as impressive as Phineas Taylor Barnum himself, a man who had made self-advertising an art form. He was world-famous, wealthy and a believer in his own maxim that 'There is a sucker born every minute'. He should have added, thought Poe, that there is also a Barnum waiting outside of the womb to fleece the newborn fool.

The 37-year-old, highly successful showman was six foot two, fleshy and running to fat, with a nose the size of a potato, blue eyes, full mouth and fast disappearing curly hair. Tonight he wore a suit of bright pink squares outlined in dark green, a frilly yellow shirt, red cravat, and his squeaky voice hit Poe's ears like an icicle, particularly when the squeak was intense, as it was at this particular moment.

'The goat is shitting!' Barnum's heated squeak was aimed at a pockmarked blond youth who cringed in the doorway of the small basement room. 'I know goddam well the goat is shitting! What I summoned you down here to learn, most callow youth, is *why* the goat is shitting and what is being done to stem this particular tide.'

'Mr Barnum, we have tried everything imaginable to get the goat to stop—'

'Dear Homer. Tonight on the five storeys of these very premises are thousands of Americans, a goodly portion of whom will undoubtedly repair to the lecture hall where they will expect our goat to tap out a lively though simple tune on a toy piano. Now get upstairs and do not reappear in my presence until you are able to assure me that the goat will not fail those Americans who have come to expect P. T. Barnum to deliver in full.'

As the young man turned and fled up the stairs, Poe watched Barnum give his attention to a pair of Negro men who sat at a long wooden table stuffing a dead bald eagle. The smell was horrible; the stench from the dead bird along with the elements used to preserve his carcass threatened to mangle Poe's nostrils and leave him prostrate on the floor. Neither of the coloureds, each of whom wore a handkerchief over his nose and mouth, impressed Poe as being speedy at his task, which is what Barnum was exhorting them to be.

'Hannibal and Job, may I be allowed to inform you pair of stone-fingered Africans that you are faced with *one* eagle, not a flock of same. Cease handling the deceased as though it was made of porcelain. Stuff, then sew. Stuff, then sew. And you will both receive your reward in heaven, if not on this earth.'

Barnum touched a handkerchief to his nostrils. 'Damn bird is more offensive in death than he ever was in life. I pay these darkies four dollars a week and it's rare I get as much as twelve hours a day out of them, let alone more.'

He looked at Poe and Figg. 'Upstairs I have on exhibition such eye-catching marvels as the wooden leg of Santa Ana, a bearded woman who stands nine feet tall and weighs four hundred and twenty pounds, and I have fleas in my employ, sir, fleas who do the most astounding things. Upstairs there are jugglers, a family of pig-faced humans, lecturers on every topic known to human reason, ventriloquists, and the one and only General Tom Thumb, that thirty inches of marvellous man, a midget born but a giant among giants. But tonight, tonight I am cursed with a goat who gives every indication of shitting forty days and forty nights and two fumble-fingered Ethiopians on the verge of being defeated by a dead eagle. Gentlemen, I find the odour in this room taxing. Let us retire to the stairs where we can converse and I can gaze down upon these two slackers as they rob me of a week's salary.'

From the bottom step Barnum watched the two Negroes prepare the bald eagle for exhibition; Poe and Figg stood a few steps above him, with Figg doing most of the talking, his husky voice telling Barnum in plain words of his murdered wife, of Jonathan, and of the men he had followed from London to Barnum's American Museum. Poe noticed that no mention was made of the brutal way in which Althea Figg had died.

A frowning Barnum turned to look at Figg. 'My deepest sympathies on the death of your wife, sir. I can only imagine your sorrow, though I know that should such a fate befall my darling

Charity, I would be crushed. I can tell you that such men as you describe are with me now and, yes, the Renaissance Players you refer to did recently join me from London, at my express invitation. Their arrival does coincide with the time you claim they departed England. I encountered them during my final year in Europe. Some four years ago I first visited your country, dividing my time between England and the Continent for more than three years.'

Poe was astounded when Figg said, 'I was at Buckingham Palace the night of yer first command performance before our gracious Queen.'

Barnum's eyebrows quickly climbed to the top of his round face. 'You were present on that momentous occasion?'

'I was indeed.'

'Ah, let me say that this was a night for the ages. Charlie—that is what I call General Tom Thumb, for Charles S. Stratton is his Christian name—Charlie and I dressed for the occasion, him in brown silk and velvet, the both of us in knee-britches. Two Yankees in the court of courts. Your indeed gracious Queen, sir, was instrumental in making my fortune, for after having been received at court, the world then became my oyster and since then I have dined well.'

A curious Poe asked Figg the reason for his being at Buckingham Palace.

'I was the guest of the Duke of Wellington and Prince Albert hisself. There was some talk about me teachin' the Prince of Wales the use of his fists, as every gentleman should know somethin' of this art. But the Prince he was only three at the time and it was decided that he was too young.'

Barnum said, 'Mr Poe mentioned earlier that you are acquainted with Mr Charles Dickens, whom I also met in London. Mr Dickens is a most successful author, a man expert at generating large sums of money for his work.'

Poe shifted uncomfortably on the steps. He saw Figg look at him, then look at Barnum and say, ' 'E's 'ad 'is hard times, Mr Dickens has. 'E's been cheated more than once and some of his friends ain't really his friends, if you know what I mean.'

Barnum nodded, silently encouraging Figg to continue.

Figg said, 'Indeed Mr Dickens is quite successful, sir—'

'His cash register rings,' said Barnum. It was a sound dear to the showman's ear, Poe noted.

'Here now,' said Figg. 'It ain't all that simple. You gets to be high and mighty and other people always resent it. They don't want you lookin' down on them. Mr Dickens ain't no different. He's got those what envy him and are more than jealous besides. Mr William Thackeray, 'e's jealous. Mr Thomas Carlyle, 'e says Mr Dickens ain't nothin' but an entertainer, and both these gents, Thackeray and Carlyle, they are 'spose to be friends of Mr Dickens. Mr Alfred Tennyson is a friend, leastwise I think 'e is, but with that long face he carries 'round with him, one can never tell. I know for a fact that Mr Dickens has been betrayed and hurt on more than one occasion, and I don't mean just in regards to his purse. The world will harm you if it can, I figure.'

For a few seconds, Poe had the feeling that Figg was showing him some tiny bit of sympathy. But the writer quickly rejected the idea. How could someone as close to a Neanderthal as Figg was be blessed with even a modicum of sensitivity. Yet Figg had been in the company of some of the most creative men in the English language and, what's more, he seemed to have a speck of insight into their real attitude towards Charles Dickens. Either that or perhaps Figg was given to lying, which Poe didn't believe he was.

Figg said, 'That night in the palace, we was all pleased with your little Tom Thumb. Like a pretty little doll he was, leapin' about and him no bigger than tot's toy. Dancin', singin', tellin' jokes.'

Poe found the idea of a midget like Tom Thumb having such a hold on the public to be abominable. People had no desire to think. Divert, entertain, bamboozle and deceive them as did Barnum, and you had free and easy access to their purses and brains forever.

Barnum squeaked at the two Negroes stuffing the eagle. 'For God's sake, do not damage his eyes! And I want both wings wired, *both*.' He turned back to his guests. 'Please forgive me. The darker brother must be consistently guided down life's more thorny paths. You were saying Mr Figg?'

'Yes. I was sayin' how pleased we all was with Tom Thumb, him bein' so little and so capable and all.'

'I never let on his real age,' said Barnum. 'He was five when I found him in Connecticut with his family but I told the world he was eleven. These days I forget how old Charlie really is.'

'That night at the palace you and him was backin' out down a long gallery. The lord-in-waitin', he was bowin' out behind you, showin' you the way, he was.'

Barnum grinned. 'Protocol.'

'Well, you and the lord was doin' just fine. But Tom Thumb, his

legs was too small to back up as fast as you two so he kept turnin'
and runnin' after you, then he went back to backin' out. Then he'd
turn and run some more and back out some more.'

Barnum's roar exploded in the narrow stairway.

'And somethin' else, Mr Barnum. Whilst you two was backin'
out, the Queen's little poodle, it runs and attacks Tom Thumb who
is now fightin' for 'is life. He 'ad this little cane, Thumb did, and
he uses it like a tiny sword and he's really goin' at it with this
poodle and we was all laughin' 'til the tears come to our eyes.'

Barnum wiped the tears of laughter from *his* eyes. 'I remember.
Oh how I remember.'

'Then Mr Barnum, I runs to the window and I sees you and Tom
Thumb outside, and I sees the two of you smilin' at each other. I
sees you bow to each other, then you picks up Tom Thumb and
you puts him in your carriage and the two of you drive off.'

'My fortune was made that night, sir. With my command appearance at the palace of your 25-year-old Queen, my fortune was
made. From that moment on I have stood in a shower of gold.'

Poe didn't look at Barnum when he spoke. 'You have done well,
particularly when it comes to advertising yourself.'

'I have sir, I have. Advertising is to a genuine article what
manure is to land—it largely increases the product.'

Poe didn't mean to criticise Barnum, but the poet's sharp tongue
had been the habit of a lifetime. 'Is it not a fact that your articles
are not always genuine? I am referring to your luring people to see
your embalmed "Feejee Mermaid" who turned out to be a concoction of half fish, half monkey and no mermaid at all. Or what
about "The Great Model of Niagara Falls", which was only eighteen inches high. You were not advertising the genuine article
when you told the world about these attractions.'

Barnum chuckled. 'No sir, I was not. I have been called charlatan, hoaxer, deceiver and deceptor deluxe. I have been called
controversial but never have I been called dull. It may be said
that I occasionally trick the people of this young republic but I
invariably give them a good show. I understand and cater to the
common man, the average man and therein lies my success and, I
might add, my acceptability by one and all. You and I, Mr Poe,
are paddlers in the same canoe. We have this hoaxing business in
common.'

Poe sneered. 'Do we? I write truthfully, sir. Not merely for
money but for truth.'

He didn't like the grin that eased its way across Barnum's wide mouth. 'Mr Poe, you are not always truthful. Four years ago you published a story in the New York *Sun* newspaper about eight people who crossed the Atlantic Ocean in a passenger balloon, a trip your story claimed took a mere three days.'

Poe held his breath, pressing his lips together tightly. Then forcing himself to smile, he said, 'I was newly arrived in the city and in desperate need of money to support my sick wife and aged mother-in-law.'

'It was a hoax, sir.'

'It was.'

'And a most effective one. All copies of that newspaper were purchased.'

'Not too much later I did better with my pen, though not exceedingly better financially.'

Barnum nodded. 'I am well aware. "The Raven", it was called. A poem to strike terror in the hearts of all who read it. Ah, I think these two darkies are beginning to triumph over that dead fowl. Well, Mr Figg, I must ask you the question, one I have avoided these past few minutes. You do not intend to discuss the matter of your wife's death with the authorities?'

'No sir, I do not. I have been told by Mr Dickens and others that the police in this here city are not the finest.'

'Hmmmm. They do have their lapses, yes. And so you intend to seek out those members of the Renaissance Players who have offended you and deal with them in your own fashion.'

'Yes sir, I do.'

Barnum scratched his bulbous nose. 'I want no part of this, allow me to state at the outset. I have only your word as to what occurred, though I have read your letters of introduction from Mr Charles Dickens to Mr Poe and Mr Titus Bootham. Granted they could be forgeries, though I doubt it. In any case, I cannot condone the slaughter of those in my employ. So allow me to say this: I ask only that you not shed blood in my museum, sir. It is my life's work and there are women and children gathered here at all times in anticipation of merriment and the finest of informative entertainment.'

Boxer, beware the manure, thought Poe.

Barnum cleared his throat. 'Mr Figg, please give me your word that you will not secure your revenge anywhere on my property. Naturally I have no control over what you do elsewhere.'

'You have me word, Mr Barnum.'

'Excellent. Then I shall tell you that the Renaissance Players are staying at the second boarding house two blocks west of the Hotel

Astor. But, before you can race off for a confrontation, know that they are on loan for a day. There is a dying man over in Brooklyn who all his life had wished to see travelling players, clowns and such. He is the father of a youngster in my employ. I sent the Renaissance Players and others to this man's farm, where they are giving a private performance for him and his family.'

Figg nodded gravely. 'Decent of you, Mr Barnum.'

Surprisingly so, thought Poe. But then again, not so surprising since Barnum was known to commit an impulsive act of kindness when not promoting himself with all-out vigour.

'They are due back sometime on the morrow. But I do have your promise that nothing will happen inside these walls?'

'You do, sir.'

There were footsteps behind Poe and Figg, who turned to see the blond youth coming down the stairs at top speed. 'Mr. Barnum, Mr Barnum, the goat has stopped shitting! The goat has stopped shitting!'

Barnum pushed his way between Poe and Figg and towards the boy. 'Praise be. What is wrong, boy? You seem troubled.'

'We have caught a pickpocket upstairs, sir, and no one knows what to do with him.'

The showman shook his rough head. 'Pickpockets are trouble. But catch one and shut him up and tell all that a live pickpocket may be seen for a quarter, you will draw fools and some who are not.' To Poe and Figg—'Gentlemen, please excuse me' and he was gone, pushing the blond boy ahead of him, leaving Poe and Figg behind with the odour of the dead bald eagle.

' 'E's a man on fire, that one,' said Figg. 'Seems to whirl about like a spinnin' top.'

Poe started slowly walking up the stairs. 'He makes money because people want to know if what he sells is real or humbug. First he tricks them and then they pay to hear him tell how he did it. Barnum could swindle a man out of twenty dollars and the man would give a quarter to hear Barnum tell of it. I have an intense desire to avoid all eagles in the future, living or dead. Tomorrow the Renaissance Players, I assume.'

'You assume correct.'

'Forgive me if I do not join the slaughter.'

Poe would always remember Figg's soft, husky voice. 'There will be no forgiveness for me until I do what has to be done.'

Poe, hearing the determination to destroy in the boxer's voice, continued climbing the stairs, keeping his thoughts to himself.

That had been hours ago.

Now Poe, staring up at the ceiling, felt Figg nudge him.

'Ain't sleepin', is you?'

'With my eyes open? Hardly!'

'You was so quiet, like you was driftin' off or somethin'.'

'Thinking about Barnum, our meeting with him earlier tonight. I know you have those travelling players on your mind, but tomorrow I intend to visit the newspaper where I am employed, to see if Rachel Coltman has left a message for me. She has no idea where I am.'

Figg nodded. 'Anything to keep you happy, squire. We do that first thing, then we got to see the play actors. It's them what I seen in front of the museum talkin' with Mrs Coltman and one other gent. They are gonna tell me how to find Jonathan. After that they won't be needin' to travel anywhere. I saw you tryin' to write a bit before we went to sleep, but you hid your papers like you was afraid I was goin' to eat them for me supper.'

'It is my habit when writing. I desire no audience until a completed work is achieved.'

'How long it take you to write a poem?'

'As long as it takes. Which is usually not long. I prefer short works of art, since I am in constant need of money and the quicker I finish, the quicker I can begin the obscene practice of begging people to buy my work.'

Figg nodded, his head cocked far to the right. He looked down at Poe, studying him carefully. Poe ignored the boxer, his mind on other matters. Rachel. My dearest Rachel.

Figg said, 'She know you love her?'

Poe eyed him and said nothing. He didn't want any intimacy with Figg, but at times Poe had the feeling that he had grossly underestimated the boxer's mind. Still, he continued to push him away. 'My private life is none of your business.'

'Tell her, squire. Tell her before it is too late.'

'My very own cupid. Did you not promise me you would keep her alive if I aided you in your search for vengeance?'

'I did promise. But I am only a man, squire, and there is the chance I might fail, might even lose me own life. This Jonathan, he is a man but more than a man. Don't know if I am makin' meself clear. I could die in this cold country of yours, so you best make yer peace with Mrs Coltman and tell her you love her and see what she says.'

'How do I tell her that she is my last hope, my last chance to be a man, to live and love, and, yes, to obtain money enough to start my own magazine.' Poe sat up quickly in his bed. 'Is that what you wanted to hear? Did you want me to bare my soul to you? Well I have, and now please cease to torment me with your questions. If it is no bother to you, and since I cannot sleep, I would like to continue using hotel pen and paper and make some attempt at putting down a few lines in this story which will not leave my head any more than you will leave my side.'

Figg brightened. 'You are really goin' to work on a story while I watch? Never seen a real writer write before. Always wondered how it was done. What is the story about, squire?'

'It is a story of revenge and I shall call it "Hop-Frog". It is a tale of a man abused who strikes back at his enemies, destroying all of them.'

'Sounds like somethin' you would like to do, eh squire?'

Which is why I am writing it, thought Poe. And this brute quickly perceives the truth, that I apply to paper, and with bitter precision, all of my darkest fantasies and daydreams, that I write of the life I ofttimes wish was mine. He perceives this.

Poe swung off the bed, turned up the gaslight and walked away from Figg. Seated at the desk, he began to write as though he was alone in the room. Once he was able to write fifteen hours a day almost without stopping. Now he no longer had heart nor energy to do that. So he wrote when he could, and now he wanted to.

Hop-Frog.

Yes, Hop-Frog is a dwarf, a jester, a man laughed at and scorned, one whose very life is in the world only so that others may exploit him. But the jester will have his pound of flesh. Hop-Frog will have his revenge. On paper.

And Poe will become Hop-Frog, getting back at a world which has given him nothing but pain and failure. Poe will have his revenge. On paper.

He wrote.

And Figg lay silently on the bed and watched him, awed and mystified at actually seeing a man *write*.

# CHAPTER SEVENTEEN

Jonathan chanted in Latin.

'*Noscere, audere, velle, tacere.*'

Naked and face down, he lay inside the magic circle on the wooden floor, his slim body beaded with perspiration and rigid with concentration. Both legs were wide apart, his arms straight out from his sides; head, hands and feet formed the five points of a star. Neither gaslight from the street below nor moonlight penetrated the humid darkness of the room in which the only light came from four black candles just outside the magic circle. The circle was composed of powdered human and animal bone sprinkled on the floor.

'*Noscere, audere, velle, tacere*'

To know, to dare, to will, to be silent.

Four powers of the magician. Qualities needed for the successful practice of any magic. All four must be present, each balancing the other.

Knowledge without daring was useless, as useless as daring without knowledge. And while the will engendered persistence, persistence was useless unless the magician possessed the daring to begin.

The fourth power—silence—was the most important of all. To tell others your thoughts and plans was to weaken the force behind all you wished to attain. To violate the power of silence was to betray yourself; your lack of discretion was a warning to your enemies.

'*Noscere, audere, velle, tacere.*'

Jonathan chanted. He concentrated.

The ritual was for the demon Asmodeus, to let him know that tonight would bring three more blood sacrifices in appeasement, three more deaths to buy Jonathan time in his search for the Throne of Solomon. Tonight, Jonathan was going to kill Hamlet Sproul's woman and two children. Like Lucifer, Jonathan had courage and cunning, wisdom and insight, along with an implacable and incurable hatred towards the human race. Hamlet Sproul's betrayal in keeping Justin Coltman's body must be met with an all-consuming vengeance.

The ritual murders of the grave-robber's woman and children were part of that revenge; it would bring pain to Hamlet Sproul for the rest of his days, weakening his mind and soul, turning him into a shaken adversary. Most important of all, these murders would satisfy Asmodeus for a time. Not for long, just for a time.

Incense floated from four corners of the dark room. The four black candles, placed north, east, south and west at points on the compass, sent small black shadows dancing across Jonathan's sweating, naked body like so many tiny bats. Written in dog's blood on the floor near each candle was the name of four other demons.

Zimmar, who ruled the north.

Gorson, who ruled the south.

Amayan, who ruled the east.

Goap, who ruled the west.

The dog's blood was in homage to Hecate, goddess of witches, magicians, and ruler of the world of darkness, who was always accompanied by howling dogs, long considered symbols of death.

By remaining within the circle, Jonathan protected himself from Asmodeus and those demons he might raise but be unable to control. The circle also kept in the magical energy produced during the ritual; being naked allowed Jonathan's energy and power to flow unobstructed.

Jonathan chanted.

He chanted incantations long forgotten by almost all of mankind, incantations first spoken by the ancient Egyptians, then by the Magi, those priests of old Persia, who served Zoroaster and who gave their name to magic and magicians and who worshipped on tops of mountains, sacrificing to the sun, moon, earth, fire and winds long before and after the birth of Christ.

He chanted incantations from ancient Greece and from the Moors who carried *wicca*, craft of the wise, from north Africa to western Europe where it became witchcraft.

Jonathan's body was now totally rigid on the floor as he forced his mind deeper into that world of darkness which had belonged to the universe for as long as time.

Through clenched teeth, he whispered the nine mystic names in words combining Greek and Hebrew: *'Shaddai, Elohim Tzabaoth, El Adonai Tzabaoth, Eloah V a-Daath, Iod, Eheieh, Tetragrammaton Elohim, El, Elohim Gibor.'*

Suddenly he heard a rush of wind in the closed room, felt its blood-freezing chill sweep across his body, and still he lay face down, chanting, chanting, chanting.

Within the room Jonathan heard moans, shrieks from souls lost and still wandering in darkness, souls of men and women desperate to find their way back to this world. They were a danger to Jonathan, for if they could, these souls would enter his body to spare themselves further torment in the world of darkness.

He concentrated with all of his mind, clenched fists vibrating with tension. The moans and shrieks stopped. Jonathan had defeated all attempts to possess him.

Silence.

Jonathan, weak with the strain of performing the ritual, did not leave the circle. He waited. To leave the circle now was to die. Asmodeus was in the room.

The smell of the demon king was horrible, beyond even the stench of burning human flesh, which Jonathan had smelled before. The odour was paralysing, unearthly, a burning beyond all burnings, and with it came the terrible sounds—the roar of a dragon, of a bull, the raw sound from the throat of a ram, and the sound of a man screaming in maniacal rage.

Jonathan, fighting an awesome fear, lifted his head inches from the floor and saw the demon king.

The sight, sound and smell of him lasted brief seconds but it was terrifying. Jonathan trembled, forcing himself not to run, to stay within the protective magic circle.

The demon king filled the room with his image and presence, seeming to be everywhere at once, beside Jonathan, then hovering over him, taunting, threatening, tempting him to leave the magic circle. Asmodeus' face changed swiftly into different faces, each more terrible than the last, and the demon's three heads blended into one, then separated before blending into one again. Colours surrounding him came and went, shifting from the red of an open wound, to a black that blended purple with blue then became the deepest black once more. For terrible seconds Jonathan feared he'd lost control, that for the first time he'd raised forces which he could not control. But the demon king did not enter the circle and Jonathan sent his thoughts out of him, telling Asmodeus of the blood sacrifice that was to be his, of the woman and children who would soon die to give Jonathan more time to locate the Throne of Solomon.

Would Asmodeus accept this sacrifice as he had accepted the others?

The dragon roared, the cold wind blew, and Asmodeus opened the mouths on his three heads to show teeth glistening with spit and blood.

Then the colours faded and the cold wind disappeared, and soon the demon king was gone. Asmodeus *would* accept the sacrifice. Jonathan had bought himself more time. Now there was no chance of him showing mercy to the woman and children; only if they died could Jonathan live.

When Jonathan sensed that the room was empty, he stood and left the circle, stepping near the black candle facing north and into the blood-scrawled name of the demon Zimmar. Later, Jonathan would smile at the thought of demons being beneath his feet.

# CHAPTER EIGHTEEN

Rachel Coltman noticed that Eddy Poe was very much the polite and courtly Southerner towards the beautiful child Dearborn Lapham, who had arrived at Rachel's Fifth Avenue home this afternoon with Hugh Larney and Miles Standish. The Eddy who was talking to little Dearborn was not the Eddy who used words with bitter precision. This Eddy Poe had the aristocratic charm of the Virginia in which he'd been raised; Rachel delighted in seeing his pleasantries to this lovely child, whom Hugh Larney had introduced as his niece.

Dearborn, in an ankle-length dress of green taffeta, her golden curls reaching to her waist, stirred her tea with a delicate silver spoon gripped between thumb and forefinger, the other three fingers of her right hand pointing up at the ceiling.

'I shall be an actress, you know. One day I shall.'

Poe, sitting across from her, nodded with a half smile. 'A laudable profession, Miss Lapham, one in which my mother excelled.'

The child whore looked at him for several seconds. Her smile came after some small reflection, mildly surprising Rachel who found such poise intimidating in a child. Was it Rachel's imagination or had Miles Standish actually smirked behind his hand when Hugh Larney had introduced Dearborn as his niece?

Dearborn said, 'Did your mother love the stage, sir?'

'I am told she did. She died when I was but a child, just days short of my third birthday. Yes, she loved the stage. She performed some two hundred different roles, this in addition to her chorus and singing work.'

'Your parents were travelling players, sir?'

Poe smiled. 'I am the son of an actress, Miss Lapham. It is my boast.'

Dearborn sipped tea, gently placing the cup back on the saucer she held in her left hand. 'I have never known my parents, sir.'

Hugh Larney, sitting beside her on a small leather sofa near the fireplace, smiled into his half-filled glass of brandy. 'She has a Dutch uncle who sees that her hands are never idle. I myself arrange excursions for our little Dearborn which take her far from this teeming metropolis. Why, today she accompanied me to the country where we had a rousing good time, did we not, Dearborn?'

The child looked down at her snow-wet boots. 'Yes, sir. We did see some things indeed, sir.'

She looked at Poe. 'You are from the South, sir?'

His smile was gentle. 'Yes and no. I was born in Boston—'

'That is far north, is it not, sir?'

'Massachusetts. And not too far north. Then I spent some time in Virginia—'

'Oh, I see, sir.'

'Then it was to England, where my family and I lived five years.'

'Is England far, sir? Is it near Virginia?'

'No, my dear. It is indeed far, a long way across the ocean.'

*She reminds me of Sissy, my dearest wife. She has the beauty and gentleness of darling Sissy, and she is around the age Sissy was when we married.*

But Dearborn Lapham was a child whore, one seen in the company of Hugh Larney on more than one occasion, one known to belong to Wade Bruenhausen, the blind, Bible-reading Dutch procurer. In the child's company Poe had noticed the startling resemblance to his wife and first cousin, a resemblance that had overshadowed what he knew of Dearborn's life. To think of her as a whore was to resent Hugh Larney more than usual, something Poe didn't want to do this afternoon, for Rachel's sake.

Rachel said, 'I am glad you received my message, Eddy. I cannot tell you how ashamed I am of my behaviour to you yesterday.'

'Rachel please—'

'No Eddy, it must be said.'

'It has been said, dearest Rachel.'

'I shall say it again. You are a most treasured friend and one I shall never again deceive or disgrace. I shall follow your advice in this personal matter, I give you my word.'

Except, thought Poe, when it comes to renouncing any and all allegiance to Doctor Paracelsus. You will be guided by me in the matter of the ransom, providing we hear again from Hamlet Sproul. But, in truth, you will also be guided by Paracelsus, whom I truly suspect as being more deadly than his appearance conveys.

Miles Standish said, 'We assumed you would be in touch with Mrs Coltman, which is why we are here. I would like to know if you are still in touch with Sproul?'

'No.' Poe's eyes were on Dearborn Lapham.

Pierce James Figg, sitting near a window, took his gaze from Poe to look out on to the street at the huge black man who stood near

Larney's carriage talking to a tall white man in a top hat and ankle-length red fur coat. Then Figg looked back at Poe. Little Mr Poe has a sudden interest in the tiny dolly-mop, thought the boxer, but I don't think it's got anything to do with havin' a go at her. That's what the little dandy fella is doin' what brought her here, the fella with the pointed chin and the look about him of a man who'll steal shit from a parrot's cage and sell it to you as mayonnaise. Figg did not trust a man with a mouth as small as Larney's.

Standish stood with his back to the fire. Rachel noticed that he treated Eddy as though Eddy was a wild beast about to strike unless spoken to in soft tones. Standish said, 'Mr Poe, I would like to know if you feel that the recent attack upon you signals an end to any communication with the ghouls.'

With an effort Poe took his gaze away from Dearborn. 'I have no answer for that Mr Standish. When time has elapsed and I hear nothing, I will then assume you are correct. The timely intervention of Mr Figg has reduced the criminal population by two, but I have yet to learn if it has reduced my chances of recovering Justin Coltman.'

Standish coughed into his fist. 'I shall assume you will be in contact with me.'

'And Rachel.'

Standish coughed again. 'Yes. Of course. I can leave a message for you—'

'With Rachel or the *Evening Mirror*.' Poe turned his attention back to Dearborn.

Rachel saw Eddy frown as he observed Hugh Larney reach out and pat the child's knee. Eddy and Hugh Larney had not said much to each other, giving Rachel the distinct impression of mutual hostility. She found Larney weak, offering only surface charm and the self-serving efforts of the devoted social climber. If he and Eddy disliked each other, it was because Eddy was the more honest man. Or was it because of Dearborn Lapham? Dear God, what a horrible thought! Both men somehow involved with this beautiful child, this child who appeared far more knowing than her years warranted. No, such a thing was unimaginable. Eddy would not—

Eddy. She'd sent a note to him at the *Evening Mirror*, apologising for the horrid things she'd said to him yesterday, inviting him to call upon her as soon as possible. He had done so, still in the company of the stern-looking Mr Figg. She had been deeply sorry for what she'd done and Eddy, dear Eddy, he had been a gentle, forgiving man, making her feel as though nothing had occurred, telling her she was ever on his mind, in his thoughts. Dear Eddy. He was the only man since Justin that she had wanted to be with, talk to, had looked forward to seeing.

If he disliked Hugh Larney, so be it. Rachel watched Hugh Larney cross his legs, fingers toying with Dearborn's waist-length blonde hair. Larney's niece. Rachel wasn't so sure about that.

She saw Poe's brow furrow and she knew he did not like the idea of Larney touching the child. Larney smiled as though Poe's displeasure had been his goal all along.

The food merchant, never one to miss an opportunity to parade his possessions, leaned his head back, staring at Poe through slitted eyes. 'Mr Poe, I ask you: do you believe Dearborn has a chance of becoming a successful performer? I myself have a rather personal view of how well she performs but I wonder how you feel about her chances to succeed in a field you seem to know so much about.'

Figg thought: he's baiting you, mate. Catch it early on and handle it. But you won't, will you? You'll let him set fire to you, which is what he's tryin' to do.

Poe said nothing. He looked down at his black coat, stroking its lapels with his thumbs.

Larney said, 'You are a critic, sir. Surely you can venture an opinion in this matter?'

Standish stepped away from the fire. 'I think we should be leaving, Hugh. We have learned what we came here to learn, which is that there has been no contact between—'

'Mr Poe.' Larney smirked, a hand kneading Dearborn's neck. 'Give us your opinion, sir.'

Poe, chin on his chest, looked across at Larney with brooding grey eyes that penetrated anything in their path. Rachel held her breath, fearful of what was to come.

Fool, thought Standish. We came here to learn how to reach him so that we could kill him, and you, Larney, have to challenge him. Dolt. Ninny. Baboon. There are not words enough for you, Larney. Standish, with Thor on his mind, kept silent.

Larney said, 'Mr Poe, you are usually a gentleman of no hesitancy when it comes to revealing your impressions of the world around you. Yet now you hesitate and methinks you are in awe of Dearborn's . . . oh, let us call them possibilities.'

Poe's drawl was soft and deadly. 'You sand your sugar, you sell tea composed of wood shavings and dried leaves—'

Larney's hand froze on Dearborn's neck.

Poe said, 'The butter you sell is rag pulp and lard. One could make a towel from it.'

Larney's voice was soft, too. 'I have taken all I intend to from you. I shall go to the door and when I have called Thor—'

Figg said, 'That would be your manservant, the one what's in the cold talkin' to the gent in the fancy red fur.'

Larney said nothing.

Figg stood up. 'Leave him be, Mr Larney. Let him enjoy the fresh air.'

Standish stepped between the two men. 'Gentlemen, please remember where you are!'

Larney swivelled around on the leather couch until he could see Figg. 'Sir, are you addressing me?'

Figg said, 'I don't wants no trouble 'ere. But you call your man into this 'ouse to harm Mr Poe and the first thing I shall do is to deal with you, Mr Larney.'

Larney inhaled, exhaled, not moving a muscle. When he stood up, his back was to Figg. 'Mrs Coltman. Miles, we shall wait for you in the carriage. Do not bother to show me out.'

Rachel, her face tense, walked over to him. 'I shall have a servant give you your coat and the child's wrap.'

As Larney turned to leave the room, Poe said, 'You seek recognition, sir. It is the talk of Gotham, your courting of your betters. Your search for accommodation among the respectful is tantamount to sprinkling rose petals on a dung heap.'

Larney stopped, his back to everyone in the room. He held both of Dearborn's hands. Then he continued walking until he'd closed the study door behind him.

Rachel looked at Poe. 'Oh Eddy. Did you have to do that?'

'I did. And I shall live with it.' He looked at Figg, then looked away.

Miles Standish coughed. 'I must go.' Poe deserved killing. Larney would only reaffirm that now, and Miles was glad. For once he was glad that Poe had opened his insulting mouth. He'd just dug his grave with it. Larney would never forgive these insults.

As Rachel stood alone in front of the fireplace, hugging herself, Poe and Figg stood at the window looking out at Larney, Volney Gunning and Miles Standish as they leaned close together and talked in the cold, sending steamed breath into each other's face.

Poe spoke in a small, sad whisper while he stared at them. 'That lovely child is Larney's whore, Mr Figg, a most lamentable business. Once or twice I have seen the two of them from a distance. However, to be in her company magnifies greatly my discomfort regarding any claim of Larney upon her.'

'You has men in the world, Mr Poe, what fancies little girls. Never seen the appeal in it meself.'

'This little girl is a startling reminder of my late wife when she was that same age.'

Figg scratched his bulldog chin with the back of a blackened thumbnail. 'Wondered why you was diggin' at that little fop, Larney. He seems to place great store by that huge blackamoor what drives him around. I know the look of men who do bodily harm and the big black fits into that selection. Anyway, you best keep your mind on things at hand. We gots to look up them Renaissance Players—'

'*You* do, Mr Figg. I shall point you in the right direction, but the business of slaying I leave to you.' Poe watched Miles Standish climb into his carriage and reach for the reins.

'Fair enough, Mr Poe. Sun comes up, sun goes down, and what happens in between ain't usually worth what you scrape off the bottom of yer boot. Things is bad in the world, always has been. Change 'em and you only make 'em worse. I know you worries over women like a mother hen, but I have the feelin' that this little girl what's with Larney can handle herself.'

'I do not want Larney to have her.'

'From where I sits he already does.'

A vein throbbed on Poe's high, wide forehead. Figg watched the writer and slowly shook his head. Little Mr Poe getting himself all worked up over a tiny *judy*. You'd have thought God died and left him in charge of the welfare of all the ladies in the world. Beatin' his breast, sobbin', gettin' a lump in his throat every time a petticoat and laced boots come strollin' by. Hope the rest of the bleedin' men in bleedin' New York ain't like this.

When Hugh Larney's carriage, with the huge Thor sitting up top on the driver's seat, pulled away on to snow-covered Fifth Avenue, Poe let the green curtain fall into place and turned to look at Figg.

'I know of her so-called Dutch uncle, one Wade Bruenhausen, who is a flesh peddler with foul habits and more than a casual share of nature's cruelty. He is possessed of formidable hypocrisy.

'Sounds darlin', he does.'

'Prior to sending forth the children to steal and whore, Mr Bruenhausen stirs their tiny hearts with a reading from the Bible and occasionally a hymn into the bargain.'

'Right peculiar sort, ain't he?'

'Paracelsus, Miles Standish, Bruenhausen and now Hugh Larney. Such men make me ill. They use women and I find such men despicable.'

Figg watched Poe's thin mouth quiver under the writer's moustache. Lord high protector, thought the boxer. Never got the chance to protect his mum and 'e can't protect his wife now 'cause she's in the ground, so he's got to find some lady what needs him. Or *he* thinks needs him.

'You best face facts, Mr Poe—'

'Facts!' Poe threw both hands up in the air.

Over by the fireplace, Rachel Coltman flinched at the sudden loudness of his voice. She'd stayed away from their conversation at the window. Somehow she'd sensed that Poe and Figg were talking about the child Dearborn in a manner that no nineteenth-century lady should overhear. Modesty was much in fashion and there were things between men that the ears of no self-respecting woman should encounter.

She watched an angry Eddy stalk away from Mr Figg. In the centre of the book-lined study, Poe stopped, his glittering eyes boring first into Rachel then into Figg. It was at times like these that he frightened and attracted her. She found herself breathing faster, drawn to him despite a tiny voice of caution within her.

'Facts?' snapped Poe again. 'Heed me now, sir. You think me a buffoon around women?'

Figg sat down on the leather couch. 'I minds me manners in front of a lady. I do not recall sayin'—'

'I am about to demonstrate a clarity of mind which you surmise I lack. I shall prove to you now, sir—'

Figg reached for a cup half filled with cold tea, dwarfing it between his huge hands. He mumbled, his wide mouth hidden by the cup, 'Mr Dickens says you have the cravin' to prove your superiority over one and all.'

'Speak up, sir! We are all of us here fluent in the mother tongue.'

Rachel walked over to Poe, placing an arm around his shoulders. 'Dear Eddy, calm yourself.'

Poe patted the back of her hand. 'Thank you, beloved friend, but be at ease. I am not the maniacal and dangerous fellow my enemies have created from their own ignorance. Sit and listen, for I shall now say more of this business of Paracelsus, of Jonathan and the grave-robbers. Both you and Mr Figg shall listen and observe that my intelligence functions most incisively. Yes, the sorrow of my

145

existence has forced me to live in constant disappointment and discomfort. Mine has been a life of poverty and depression, but—'

He aimed a forefinger at Figg. 'But, sir, I never *guess* at anything. I analyse most intelligently. Facts, you say. Well hear me. Let me tell you of the original Doctor Paracelsus, the original—'

Figg, with a two-handed grip on the fragile tea cup, paused in his drinking. 'You sayin' there is two of 'em?'

'The original Paracelsus was Swiss, born in the fifteenth century to a poor nobleman. Christencd Theopharastus Bombastus von Hohenheim, the son studied medicine and became a doctor while also possessing psychic skills. These talents allowed him to perform unusual cures which soon brought him fame as well as appointment as professor of medicine at the University of Basel. Von Hohenheim took the name of Celsus, that famed physician of ancient Rome, adding *Para* which means "beyond" in Greek. It follows from all of this that von Hohenheim ranked himself as greater than Celsus.'

Ain't got a patch on you, mate, thought Figg. You and him both thinks you can walk on water.

'As Paracelsus,' Poe continued, 'our fifteenth-century man of medicine was also a sorcerer, magician, a sensitive believed to have the power to read the future as well as the minds of men. He became egocentric, a man of extraordinary vanity. He began to drink too much and he developed a violent temper, as well as a strong belief in his self-created legend. He ordered his students to burn the books of those men who disagreed with him, and he made numerous enemies. He imagined many plots against him and in truth there *were* plots against him. When his enemies grew larger in numbers, Paracelsus was forced to flee the university, thereafter wandering Europe for fourteen years, becoming even more violent and abusive. He saw a world filled with enemies and he was both correct and in error in his thinking. Some were his foes, some were not. The death of Paracelsus only increased the mystery of the man.'

Poe walked over to the fireplace, extending the palms of his hands towards the warmth of the flames. 'Some say he was poisoned; others say he became drunk, rolled down a hill and died as a result of injuries. In death he gained even more fame. Today those who follow the dark science consider Paracelsus a patron saint, an icon to be worshipped and imitated. It is safe to call the man both an adept and a charlatan, for in truth he did possess the power of healing as well as a talent for deception. On occasion, yes, he could call up from deep within himself those strange powers which have eternally baffled man. But Paracelsus was boastful, proud and often dangerous.'

Poe turned to face Rachel and Figg. 'As is the Paracelsus now within our midst. I have given you the history of one man so that you might understand the history of the other. Mark them as one, except that there is more evil in that Paracelsus who walks among us. I am referring to the manner in which the grave-robbers were killed.'

Rachel said, 'Eddy, you did not tell me—'

'I tell you now, dear Rachel, for it is my opinion that Jonathan is no human agency. Yes, he is a man of flesh and blood but he is a terrifying force in servitude to demons. The grave-robbers who took Justin's body had their hearts and livers removed, then the organs were burned. This is a sacrifice to Asmodeus, king of demons, who in Hebrew mythology was forced by Solomon to build the Temple in Jerusalem. The smoke from the burning heart and liver is said to drive Asmodeus away.'

Rachel shook her head. 'Eddy, Doctor Paracelsus would never do such a thing. He is helping me—'

'By promising to bring your husband back from the dead.' Poe held up his left hand, the slashed palm towards Rachel, who winced when she saw it.

He said, 'This is the result of a visit yesterday to the home of Miles Standish, where a brief, violent tableau was staged for my benefit.'

Rachel's hand was in front of her mouth. 'Miles did that?'

'He had it done. A painting supposedly came to life and attacked me.'

Once more, Figg stopped sipping cold tea. 'It what?'

'Attacked me. I first had to be drugged, which was accomplished by gas through the jets, gas mixed with incense.'

Figg frowned. 'You didn't tell me any of this, squire.'

'I said to you, Mr Figg, that I do deal in facts, that my mind is occupied with more than the welfare of the female portion of mankind. My intelligence functions in its own manner; it is a process that has baffled, amused, tormented and upset various segments of the American public, not to mention critics, of whom the less said the better. Because I do not choose to tell you all that I am concerned with, Mr Figg, does not in any way indicate I am concerned with nothing at all.'

Figg sneered. 'You are a delight, you are.'

'Eddy, are you saying that Miles—'

'He is involved in this attempt to obtain ransom, as well as the body of your husband. He is in league with Jonathan, or, if you will, in league with Paracelsus.'

Rachel shook her head. No. Eddy was once again off on a flight of fancy. He had to be. Miles would never harm her. Never.

'Eddy, how can you say this about Miles?'

'Because Miles does not want me in your life, because he wants you for himself, because it appears to me to be of some benefit to him as well as Jonathan if I doubt my sanity, question myself and not question any attempts of extorting ransom from you. In that matter, I was to ask no questions, formulate no opposition. I can only surmise that it is felt I have some small degree of influence with you.'

Rachel felt the tears slide down her face. 'You do, Eddy. Oh, indeed you do. But of Miles, how can you say he betrays me?'

He moved to her side, taking one of her hands in his. 'Paracelsus needs spies, he functions on the information they bring him. If anyone knows what you can afford to pay in ransom, it is Miles. If anyone would render me helpless, because of his desire for you and a desire to eliminate all opposition to the ransom, it is Miles. That my alleged hallucination occurred in his home, and nowhere else, is proof of this. I would also wager that some of your servants and friends are passing on to Jonathan/Paracelsus certain confidences about you, for omniscience is not impossible to attain if one knows how.'

Figg stood up. 'A question, squire, since you seem brimmin' over with *facts*. Does the Throne of Solomon really exist?'

Poe, down on one knee beside Rachel, turned to look up at him. 'Jews and ancient Persians and Arabs say it does. A legend in old Persia claims that the throne or great chair is carved from solid rock on the border of India and Afghanistan. According to the Koran, the holy book of the Arab, Solomon had the power to ride the wind while seated on his throne. Evil spirits were subject to him and brought him wealth and did his bidding. There are said to be several books of magic hidden under the throne, books purporting to reveal the ways in which Solomon maintained power over spirits, men, the winds.'

Poe stood up. 'It is *said* to exist, Mr Figg, as it is *said* to contain power that can be used for much and great evil. In truth, I cannot say yea or nay as to whether I myself believe it real or apparition.'

'Then, squire you are sayin' it could be true as well as not.'

'I am saying so, yes.'

'Then if Jonathan gets it, he wins.'

'And the world loses. Providing there *is* such a thing as the Throne of Solomon, Mr Figg.'

'Man like Jonathan, he ain't one to fritter away the hours.'

'I would imagine that to be true. I have not seen him but I feel him to be someone who—Rachel, Rachel!'

She ran from the room, hands covering her tear-stained face. 'Please, please forgive me. I must leave.'

The door slammed behind her. Poe stared at it, then said, 'Mr Figg, you are here to kill, are you not?'

'You know it to be true.'

'Then kill Jonathan quickly, for I fear if you do not, he will be the cause of harm to her. I shall not involve myself in any of your other planned homicides, but in the matter of Jonathan, count on me to aid you in disposing of him in any way you deem feasible.'

'For the sake of the woman.'

'For the same reason, Mr Figg, *you* seek the death of Jonathan. For a woman.'

Suddenly, Figg placed a thick finger to his wide mouth, motioning Poe into silence. Seconds later, Figg had tiptoed to the door and cupped the knob in his huge fist. After a quick look at Poe, Figg yanked the door open.

The brown-carpeted hallway, lined with oil paintings and dotted with busts of Roman emperors, was empty.

' 'Eard somebody out 'ere.' Figg, his eyes narrowed and alert, looked left, then right.

Poe walked quickly towards him. 'Perhaps Rachel.'

Figg closed the door. 'No, squire. She's the missus 'ere, so she has no call to go skulkin' around. Anyway she was already inside, hearin' it all so why should she creep about. Someone else, it was. One of them spies you been carryin' on about, I dare say. Best you and me get hoppin'. Get to the boardin' 'ouse where the Renaissance Players lays their little 'eads. After that, I ain't too sure what we does.'

'I am. Sproul.'

'Why 'im?'

'To remove the body of Justin Coltman from his clutches.'

'Now why should we want to do that?'

'So that Jonathan will come to claim it. So that you, Mr Figg, can then kill him. The safety of Mrs Coltman is important to me and I am convinced she is in danger so long as Jonathan lives.'

'Squire, you are a devious little fellow. 'Ere I'm thinkin' I'm leadin' you and now all of a sudden it's you what's leadin' me. Mind tellin' me why we don't just attach ourselves to Mr Miles Standish and let him lead us to Jonathan.'

'For the same reason we do not follow Hugh Larney or others my intelligence tells me are a part of this foul business. We do not know *when* Miles Standish will contact Jonathan/Paracelsus. Were we to attach ourselves to Mr Standish we might have a long wait until he reveals himself and, more important, I prefer that we do not merely drift into matters, if at all possible. Sproul is our next move.'

Figg grinned as he placed his tall top hat on his shaven head. 'Ah, Mr Poe. You has the makin's of a right foxy gent, you does.'

Poe, licking his lips, stared at several bottles of alcohol on a sideboard near a bookcase. He wanted . . .

Then he tore his eyes away focusing on Figg. 'We have work before us, Mr Figg, for which a clear head is most desirable. Let us be gone from here and God be with us, for we will both have need of Him before this matter is resolved.'

# CHAPTER NINETEEN

Manhattan is a thin island thirteen miles long and no more than two and a half miles at its widest point. By 1840 this finger-shaped piece of land contained the world's worst slum—Five Points—which surpassed the urban horrors to be found in London, Paris or Calcutta. Located at the base of Manhattan and within walking distance of City Hall, Five Points was the name given to the area where five streets—Cross, Anthony, Little Water, Orange and Mulberry—met. By 1848, names and sizes of the streets had changed, but Five Points remained. Now it was the most dangerous place in New York City.

At the beginning of the nineteenth century, Five Points did not exist. The area had been swamp and marshland until Manhattan's increasing population, with its resultant demand for living space, forced New York City to drain that land and fill it with earth. Five Points then enjoyed a brief respectability. But because the swamps and marshes had been poorly drained, the tenements above began to slide and collapse into the ground below, and those families who could afford to move did so quickly.

Those remaining or now entering Five Points were people who had been destined to exist in terrible poverty. Crime as a means of survival was inevitable and the Irish, who formed the majority, were the most visible as murderers, thieves, gamblers and purveyors of the casual violence which became a part of New York City early in its history.

Irish gangs ruled the streets and vice of Five Points under names such as the Kerryonians (from County Kerry), Shirt Tails, Roach Guards, Plug Uglies, Black Birds, Chichesters. In five-storey tenements of old and rotting wood, Irish and Negroes lived without heat, gaslight or running water, in buildings on the verge of tumbling into the streets where the mud was knee-deep when not covered by garbage or packs of wild pigs.

The decaying structures were connected by tunnels which were the site of horrible crimes, in addition to being escape routes for those slum-dwellers who had murdered and robbed, thereby bringing down unwanted attention on themselves. Within the tenements, behind windows patched with rags, lived starving men, women and children who endured their miserable existence by staying drunk as often as possible. They fought rats and each other to stay alive in buildings with names like 'Bucket of Blood', 'Dead Man's Place', 'Gates of Hell', 'Knife In The Throat'. They survived by any means imaginable and at the expense of each other.

Along with grinding poverty, vice was everywhere in Five Points. There were brothels, dance halls, rum shops, gambling rooms and 'green groceries', supposedly selling vegetables but actually selling homemade whisky that was as much a health hazard as a stroll through the streets of Five Points alone on a dark night.

Dominating Five Points was the Old Brewery, called Coulter's Brewery when built in 1792. By 1837 the huge five-storey wooden building was ugly and decrepit, surrounded by the horror of Five Points and occupied by more than a thousand Irish and Negro men, women and children who lived in constant danger. The danger came not only from the surrounding slum but from the inhabitants of the brewery, who had no qualms about preying on one another. It was a population of murderers, prostitutes, thieves, and beggars all desperate enough to do anything, all living in shocking sexual licentiousness and decay.

Though it was said for many years that one person was murdered daily inside of the Old Brewery, the crime invariably went unpunished, for police avoided the building out of fear for their own lives. If on rare occasions police did enter the mammoth, foul-smelling structure, it was always in force, with almost no chance of capturing an offender well acquainted with the hidden tunnels and passageways.

Jonathan had come to the Old Brewery to kill Hamlet Sproul's woman, Ida Sairs, and the two children she'd borne the grave-robber. The slum held no terror for Jonathan, for he had completed the ritual. *He* dared anything.

In the night Jonathan was a noiseless shadow, travelling as silently as smoke, bringing death to those he had marked for sacrifice, for revenge.

*For you, Asmodeus. Their deaths I lay at your feet. Grant me time, demon king, to find the throne, to make the dead Justin Coltman speak.*

Ida Sairs, small, with red hair parted and pulled tightly back into a bun, her pale, thin face spotted with freckles, knelt on the floor of her room in front of a bucket of burning charcoal, using a foot-long wooden stick to poke at a piece of blackened pork which was to feed herself and the two boys, aged two and three. When the meat was done, she would heat what was left of the coffee, which would taste of roast peas and chicory, and for a sweet there would be hard, stale bread covered in molasses. Not a feast for a king but at least it was something in the belly. She would have liked a pail of beer, but there was not a coin to waste on something like that. Be patient, Hamlet had said. His fortune would soon change and there would be beer to bathe in. Yes, there would be that indeed.

She looked over at the boys. They sat on the bare floor watching the burnt pork and bright red charcoal beneath it, their faces slack-jawed with hunger, their eyes gleaming as do the eyes of starving children anywhere in the world. Ida was eighteen, barefoot in a ragged blue dress, with a half of a tattered blanket around her shoulders for warmth in the unheated room. No fireplace, two buckets in the corner for slops and waste; and water has to be fetched upstairs three flights in two more buckets. Be patient, Hamlet had said. Be patient, dearest Ida, for you have my love and shall soon have me money and plenty of it. Dearest Hamlet. He was one of too many men she had been with since she was nine, but he alone didn't beat her. He alone loved her and she desperately loved him in return.

Ida Sairs stood up, turned and swallowed a scream as she saw the cloaked figure reach out for her.

Jonathan slashed her throat, choking off any sound.

She fell to her knees, hands at her pained throat, hands wet with her own blood. The pain in her neck savagely attacked her skull and she knew she was in hell, with no idea as to how it had happened. Her mouth was open and in vain she willed herself to scream that no harm should come to her children.

Jonathan, sensing what she was trying to say, shook his head.

'Their lives are forfeit,' he whispered. 'Their lives have been promised to him who threatens mine.'

Ida Sairs, wide-eyed and dying, fell to the floor and Jonathan stepped over her bleeding body, his blood-red scalpel pointing towards the two dirty-faced boys who had not taken their eyes from the pork blackening over the bucket of burning charcoal.


Later that night, a nervous Rachel whispered, 'I beg of you, Doctor Paracelsus, the truth. You have pledged to me that my husband lives. Does he?'

Jonathan closed his eyes, white-gloved hands palms down on the black marble-topped table between him and the anxious woman.

'Justin Coltman lives. I, Paracelsus, tell you that he exists, but in a world not of this world; he lives unseen among the unseen. You have never questioned me before, Mrs Coltman. Why do you doubt me now?'

'I—I am here to, to—'

She hesitated. *Order me to believe in you. Remove my doubts.* Paracelsus, a huge figure in white, sat across from her in the dark room, quietly waiting for her to speak, and for the first time Rachel felt unsure of him.

'I—I have spoken of you to my friend, Mr Poe—'

'Ah yes, Mr Poe. The writer and critic. A man of savage wit and bloodcurdling pronouncements. His fame grows daily, though the public continues to deny him financial success, which is the same as declaring Mr Poe's philosophy useless. Mrs Coltman, in no way do I wish to defame your friend who has suffered a most tormented life. I merely wish to define the limits of his effectiveness. And it is he, I assume, who tells you that the dead cannot live again.'

'He, yes he has said this.'

'He has also told you that lack of life in the departed indicates total cessation of life for all time to come.'

Rachel Coltman, feeling that Doctor Paracelsus could see almost to her bare skin, pulled the blue lace shawl tighter around her shoulders, then pushed both hands deeper into the muff of blue fitch fur which hung from her neck on a long, thin silver chain.

'My friend Mr Poe has said all of these things and more.'

'He accuses me of being a demon man, of having committed the most heinous crimes because of my link with the world of dark spirits.'

'Why, why yes, yes he has. How did you—'

'I am gifted with second sight, Mrs Coltman, which allows me to see as few men in the universe can.'

She watched him open his eyes and at that exact instant, she heard the soft, eerie sound of a flute. And there was the odour of incense, sweet, sweet incense. She quickly glanced around the dark room, seeing nothing but tiny orange flames of gaslight flickering high on the four walls.

Rachel Coltman was given no time to be afraid. There was the trill of the flute, apparently coming from several directions at once, and there was Paracelsus' voice, mesmerising and soothing, seeming to stroke her temples and forehead while gently coaxing her eyes to close, to close, to close . . .

She snapped her head back, stiffened in her chair, forcing herself to stay awake, to stare at Paracelsus. Inside of the muff, she dug her fingernails into the palms of her hands.

'Mrs Coltman, did not your husband speak to you about life beyond the grave?'

'He did. But Eddy, I mean Mr Poe—' She stopped. Suddenly she didn't want Paracelsus to read her mind, to discover her feelings about Eddy.

'You are attracted to Mr Poe, are you not?'

She wanted to lie, but it was as though Paracelsus was controlling her every word, her every thought. 'I—I do find him pleasant. Yes *pleasant*.'

More than pleasant, thought Jonathan, studying Rachel Coltman through narrowed eyes. Behold the triumph of the sad and sickly poet. Blame it on the late George Gordon, Lord Byron, among the first to use his goose-quill and precarious health to disturb the hearts and sanity of females who otherwise pride themselves upon possessing balanced minds.

Association, dear Rachel, breeds attachment, and continued association with dear Eddy will surely increase your attachment to him. Meaning that Eddy's opposition to me may eventually convince you to deny me both your husband's corpse and his money.

Yet Jonathan saw no reason to kill Poe. Poe could still serve as a contact for Hamlet Sproul, the momentary possessor of Justin Coltman's decaying flesh. And because Poe was an extreme romantic in matters of women, he would make it his business to do as Rachel Coltman demanded regarding her dead husband. No, Jonathan would allow Poe to live for a while longer, until Jonathan had Justin Coltman's body in his possession. After that, it would be time enough to dispose of the sad and sickly poet.

Meanwhile, Jonathan would toy with Poe, tilt the balance of the poet's sanity, play a game with this man who was so proud of his intelligence, so puffed with the sense of his own ego. He *was* an unusual man, dear Eddy, and undoubtedly history would be kinder to him than America had been up until now. Jonathan sensed that Poe was a man in advance of his time, far ahead of all thought around him, but acceptance for Poe's achievements would come to him only long after he was dead.

And that is why Jonathan found it a challenge to manipulate Poe *now*. For if Poe was eventually to achieve greatness, was not Jonathan, in using him, even greater? Did not the power and intelligence of the magician surpass that of anyone born of woman?

Jonathan said, 'Men deny the existence of those things they are unable to comprehend. All earthly intelligence is limited, for man and all he touches is bound down by time, space and causation. I offer that the mind of man is unstable; the world reveals this to be so. It is public knowledge that the mind of Mr Poe has long been unstable, a fact perhaps owing to his lifelong mourning for his mother, his stepmother, his wife. I would advise against your reliance upon Mr Poe's judgment.'

'Yes, it is true that he has endured the pain of bereavement longer than most.'

'More intensely than most as well. Had he believed in a life hereafter, he would have been spared continual suffering. There would have been comfort in the knowledge that his loved ones now live on another plane of existence.'

'Doctor Paracelsus, I—I do not mean to doubt you but I see nothing except the life around me. How can there possibly be another plane of existence?'

'Mrs Coltman, the stars come out at night and shine most brightly. During the day they are unseen, but where have they gone? Nowhere, Mrs Coltman. Nowhere at all. They are still present but we cannot see them. Would you say the stars and moon have disappeared merely because they go unseen at high noon?'

'I—I, no, Doctor Paracelsus. I—I understand. But Eddy is a most brilliant man. Surely he has his reasons for believing as he does.'

Jonathan lifted a hand from the table. The music stopped. After long seconds of silence, he again placed his hand down on the table and the flute was heard once more.

'Reason. Mrs Coltman, I shall tell you of reason. The oldest civilisation on earth is to be found in Sumer, where 6,500 years ago animals were sacrificed and buried with dead men and women, to continue serving them in a world far beyond this one. The dead kings of Egypt were buried in elaborate pyramids with servants, chariots and jewels to please them in the afterlife. The Shang Dynasty of China buried its rulers with the bodies of wives, servants, concubines killed for similar reasons as did the Viking warriors. Christian, Jew, Mohammedan, all preach of a heaven awaiting the faithful.'

Jonathan again lifted a hand from the table, stopping the music.

'Reason, Mrs Coltman, this is reason, and I tell you only what is known by all of humanity. There *is* life after death, there is an existence invisible to our eyes, and your husband is there. I can call him back to this plane, but I shall need his body. Will you pay the ransom?'

156

'If—if you say I must.'

'You must.'

She *is* beautiful, thought Jonathan. Long auburn hair flowing down her back and the pale complexion of one who by suffering always draws men to her. How correct the French are in saying that when God creates a beautiful woman, he also provides a fool to keep her. Rachel Coltman will always have her share of fools.

'Doctor Paracelsus, I—I—'

'Speak.'

'Eddy, Mr Poe, says you are someone else. He says—'

'That I am Jonathan, a sorcerer and killer.'

'Yes.'

Jonathan thrust both hands up the sleeves of his flowing white robe. 'Did he also tell you that a painting came to life and tried to kill him?'

She nodded.

He smiled with a corner of his mouth. 'One seems as likely as the other, wouldn't you say?'

Her smile was quick, disappearing the instant it flashed across her lips.

Suddenly, the flute hit an extraordinarily high note directly overhead and Rachel Coltman quickly looked up at the ceiling. When she looked back at Jonathan, he was pointing to —

She saw it and inhaled sharply.

'Justin's snuff-box.' She picked up the tiny silver box in both hands, handling it as though it was fragile porcelain.

'Open it, Mrs Coltman.'

She did and her jaw dropped.

'Where—'

'A most lovely ring, Mrs Coltman. Your husband had it made for you on your first trip to England together. It is modelled after the ring Queen Elizabeth gave to Lord Essex, it is not?'

Rachel could only nod her head. Her eyes shimmered behind tears. 'I thought I lost them both forever.'

Stolen and kept until needed, thought Jonathan. They are needed now. His hands were still in his sleeves. The hands of a master magician. From his sleeve and across the table in an infinitesimal fraction of a second. And she believed it was a miracle.

'A miracle,' she whispered. 'A miracle. How did you—'

'Mrs Coltman, do you believe in me?'

'Yes, oh yes.'

'I want you to tell me more about Jonathan.' This is a most enjoyable game, he thought.

Tears slid down her pale cheeks. Jonathan found her one of the few women who could weep and still remain beautiful. He watched her squeeze the snuff-box in a hand covered by a blue velvet glove. She still *wanted* to believe.

'A miracle,' she whispered, looking around the room and seeing no one but the magician.

'There are indeed other worlds, Mr Coltman, other planes.' And servants who steal.

'My deepest gratitude, Doctor Paracelsus.'

'Do you believe me to be who I say I am?'

'Yes, yes I do.'

'Tell me more about this Jonathan.'

'Eddy and his friend, Mr Figg, are searching for him. Mr Figg intends to kill Jonathan, but first the two of them are going to a boarding house on Ann Street to seek a group of travelling actors.'

Jonathan's hands slowly clenched and unclenched. Figg. A primitive force capable of destroying him. An ordinary man made extraordinary by the intensity of the revenge he craved. If there was one thing Jonathan understood it was the power of revenge. Figg was definitely dangerous, and not one to toy with as was Poe; the boxer stalked Jonathan with the intention of spilling his blood, nothing less. Figg would have to be dealt with immediately.

But first—

'The Renaissance Players,' said Rachel Coltman. 'Mr Figg claims two of their members are somehow involved in the death of his wife.'

She looked across the table. 'Joseph Barian and Bernard Leddy. They—'

Jonathan interrupted. 'You are about to say they have acted as go-betweens for you and myself. This is true. But they are no longer associated with me. On the day you spoke to Mr Barian and Mr Leddy in front of Barnum's American Museum, I had released them from my employ, and this you may tell Mr Poe and Mr Figg. Barian and Leddy misused my kindness by keeping hidden from me the account of their criminal pastimes which I was just informed is on file at New York Police headquarters. They sought my aid in contacting departed loved ones and, even though both men lacked funds, gave of myself and my services for my heart does ache at the sight of another's pain. Instead of money, each man begged me to allow him to serve me as best he could and I agreed. But as you have learned tonight, you can now contact me through Miss Sarah Clannon.'

Rachel nodded, hanging on his every word. Jonathan controlled her once more and gloried in that knowledge.

He said, 'I could not continue to have around me such men of deceit as Mr Barian and Mr Leddy. Their very lives poison the atmosphere, though I would rather suffer from excessive kindness than to deny one human being any peace of soul my efforts can make possible.'

She believed him. Jonathan sensed it and forced himself not to smile.

He said, 'When do Mr Poe and Mr Figg plan to visit this boarding house on Ann Street?'

'As soon as possible.'


'As soon as possible,' Jonathan said to Sarah Clannon minutes after Rachel Coltman had left him. 'Send Laertes and Charles to me. They shall do the task.'

Sarah Clannon drew on a thin cigar. 'Adieu to Mr Barian and Mr Leddy.'

'Exactly. I want their throats cut to eliminate even the slightest possibility of conversation with passing strangers. Then I want the boarding house to be set afire, with particular attention to the room of Barian and Leddy. With even the smallest of good fortune, their bodies will be consumed by flames and the entire event will be viewed merely as an accidental fire. Laertes and Charles are to execute this matter with utmost speed, for I do not wish Poe and Figg to exchange words with either man.'

Sarah Clannon licked the tip of her forefinger, touched a small packet of rouge and then the nipple of her bare breast. 'Lovely colour, this. I take it our Mr Figg is only aware of Barian and Leddy and not of your connection with others of the Renaissance Players?'

Jonathan kissed the back of her neck. 'Possibly.'

'When the boarding house catches fire, innocent people may die.'

'God will know his own. Now dress yourself and find Laertes and Charles. And bring me fresh fruit. I am famished.'

# CHAPTER TWENTY

'A rat,' said Poe.

Figg raised one scarred eyebrow. 'You take me for a bloody fool? Damn thing was big as me leg.'

The rat, bright-eyed and a filthy grey, had sped across the muddy street, disappearing into a pile of garbage in front of a nearby church.

Poe glanced in the rat's direction, then, when their cab started up again he leaned back against the seat, sinking deeper into his greatcoat. 'Now it dines with the blessings of Mother Church and a most economical meal it shall be too. A present from the citizens of Manhattan.'

'Bleedin' rats,' muttered Figg, turning to look back at the pile of garbage. New York was crawling with rats, rats bigger than any he'd seen in English waterfront towns, and those that sat by England's waters were sometimes the size of a man's boot. To Figg, American rats were big enough to pull carts behind them, and they were everywhere, according to little Mr Poe. Rats in mansions, tenements, churches, department stores and in City Hall.

New York stank like an aging French whore. Damn city had no sanitation, no sewers, and all the waste and trash from a half million people was tossed out into the bleeding street where the pigs and rats gathered to fill their bellies. New York town smelled like the biggest pile of shit God had ever created and Figg's *hooter*—his nose—was going to be in a sorry state when this visit to America was over.

Earlier he and Poe had gone to the Ann Street boarding house only to learn that the Renaissance Players had not returned from their charity performance in the country; it was felt that the delay was due to snow-covered roads. So now it was take a cab to Five Points to see a gent called Johnnie Bill Baker, who Mr Poe said was a dance-hall keeper and member of a gang of thieves called 'The Daybreak Boys'.

'They strike at that hour when sleep is deepest,' said Poe. 'Hence the name. At break of day, as the mind lies in blessed repose, Mr Baker and cohorts enter the homes of those living in the country-side, preferring to loot those victims existing in isolation. In swift fashion, the thieves remove any and all articles of value then vanish. If a householder exhibits untimely pluck, he is slain, but that is in the nature of such a business.'

Poe's head was against the seat as he looked up at the back of the cab-driver sitting in front of him. So long as Figg was paying, Poe was willing to ride. 'Occasionally a victim is held for ransom, and thus does Mr Baker add to the monies he makes from the Louvre.'

'Loo? Loo is a place where a man pisses.'

Poe sneered. Figg the thickheaded. '*Louvre*, not loo. Louvre is the name of his licentious and lively dance-hall, to which we are being carted by this most slow pair of horses. A famed Paris museum has some prior claim to that title, but no matter. Mr Baker is a lively, Irish—'

'Thief. All the bloody thieves in this 'ere city is Irish.'

'A thesis not worth contesting. Take care you do not mock Mr Baker.'

As the wooden cab wheels bounced over a poorly cobbled street, Figg jerked upright in his seat. 'Now why would I want a giggle at Mr Baker's expense? Ain't 'e the one whats goin' to place us in contact with Mr Hamlet Sproul?'

'Mr Baker is pleasant-looking, though unfortunately cursed with crossed eyes. He is said to have killed men who find this deformity a laughing matter.'

Figg turned up his coat collar at the cold night air. 'I will remember that. Take care not to laugh at a man what's lookin' at both sides of 'is nose at the same time. My gawd, the smell!' Figg held his nose with fingers Poe thought were the size of bananas.

'Slaughterhouses, stables, buildings where liquors are made and the mountains of garbage. Like the poor, Mr Figg, these odours are everywhere.'

Ahead of them, Figg watched the gaslights that brightened the streets and shop windows on either side of Broadway. Wagons, coaches, sleighs all carried burning lanterns on the back and Figg had never seen so many people clogging a street at night.

So many lights. Like polished jewels. And people. Weren't any of them bothered by the smells?

More bonfires. Almost on every street corner. Figg asked why.

'Epidemics, Mr Figg. Cholera and yellow fever strike this filthy city every year, and it is the belief of some that a burning fire will clean the air of such plagues. Look at your boots.'

Figg did, squinting in the darkness. 'Stuff on 'em. What—'

'Coal dust mixed with quicklime. Spread throughout the streets also in the belief that it will prevent disease.'

Figg frowned, a sight Poe would never regard as reassuring. ' 'Ere now, I don't want to be catchin' no plague, you understand.'

'I am not the one to speak to about that. Considering your eating habits, you may expire of kitchen excess long before the plague succeeds—'

Figg growled, 'What's so displeasin' about me eatin' habits, squire, if I might make so bold?'

Poe leaned right as the cab turned sharply, its back wheels sliding on snow-covered cobbles. Figg had eaten three omelettes, four dishes of chocolate ice cream and an entire loaf of bread, washed down with two pots of coffee and all of it swallowed in record time. The man ate like a Hun.

' Your eating habits,' said Poe, 'are Paleolithic.'

'What's that 'spose to mean?'

'It means you approach food with an enthusiasm unseen since man first learned to walk upright.'

'I gets the impression you are being sarcastic.'

Poe turned to him. 'Bravo. It gets impressions. Fan that tiny flame of sensitivity and eventually it will grow into a veritable blaze of mediocrity,' Poe sneered.

Figg's smile was slow and he kept it in place for a short time before speaking. 'Squire, if I didn't need you, I would give some thought to punchin' yer big 'ead down deep 'twixt yer shoulders.'

'Am I to assume that this represents your mind functioning at its subtle best?'

'Squire, assume that you are still livin' and that you are a most fortunate gent.'

' "Let there be light! said God, and there was light! Let there be blood! says man, and there's a sea." ' Poe snorted. 'Before you ask, it is a quote from Lord Byron, a poet of some note.'

Figg removed his top hat, running a thick hand over his shaven skull. 'Fancied hisself a boxer, Bryon did. Never saw a gent what pulled the ladies. Everytime I meets him, he has three or four ladies—'

Poe's voice was barely a whisper. 'You *met* Byron?'

Figg looked out of his side of the cab at the strolling night-time crowds. 'Tried teachin' him a wee bit of boxin', but he had that club foot and he was always eating' boiled potatoes drowned in vinegar to give him that pale complexion he thought the ladies all loved, so he didn't have the strength to—'

'You met *Byron*?' The English poet, dead for twenty-four years, had been the most dashing and romantic figure in his time, the most controversial poet to emerge from England in this century, and he had been a major influence on Poe.

'I see you are impressed, squire. Yes, I met him and a right sorry lot he was, too. Him and me was both young men but he was throwin' away his life chasin' the ladies or lettin' them chase him, and he owed money and he gets hisself into some kind of scandal concernin' his half-sister.' Figg shook his head sadly. 'Wasted life, if you ask me. Dies in Greece fightin' somebody else's war. Damn stupid, I say.'

'A glorious way to die,' said Poe, eyes on Figg.

'Squire, we all are goin' to end up as food for the worms but I think it's better to die fightin' for somethin' that's your own, get me meanin'?'

Poe nodded. This ape sitting beside him with the bulldog face had actually *met* Byron. And Dickens. Thackeray. Carlyle. Tennyson. And damn little of it had rubbed off, it appeared. He was still rude, crude and not one to take to the palace. Change that. He *had* been to the palace. Poe shook his head.

'Mr Figg? Mr Figg?'

But Figg had slumped down in his seat, top hat covering his face.

'Gots to gets me beauty nap when I can, squire, when I can. Long night in front. From the Irishman it's back to them Renaissance travellin' players. Wake me when we gets where we're goin'.'

Poe wanted to talk about Byron, and Figg wanted to sleep. The poet sighed. The ape sleeps in ignorance of the greatness around him. He absorbs it not. Surely God is a buffoon to have created so many buffoons in his image.

Poe, shivering in his greatcoat, licked his lips and thought of the taste of gin. And rum. And wine. He hadn't had a drink in almost two days. Forty-eight hours. His mouth tasted of ashes yet his head felt clear and he was functioning. But he was writing little and giving no thought to his job at the *Evening Mirror*, or the fifty cents a page he earned there for scribbling anything that came to mind. He smiled. No money, no liquor, which was not unusual. Rachel. The thought of her was enough. He smiled again.

The cab-driver flicked the whip and both horses strained against their harnesses. Poe breathed in the cool night air and thought of Jonathan, demons and Dearborn Lapham. And the very dead, still immersed in ice somewhere on this stinking island, Justin Coltman.

# CHAPTER TWENTY-ONE

Hamlet Sproul sat on the floor, Ida Sairs's cold hand pressed against his cheek. He had never known such terrible sorrow in all his life. He wept, moaned, rocked back and forth and he vowed revenge.

Jonathan. Mr Poe. Yes, even the Englishman with the ugly bull-dog face, who had climbed down the ladder to kill Chopback and Isaac Bard. He, too. They would all die for what had happened here this night. Hamlet Sproul would have his revenge for the killing of his boys and Ida. Dear little Ida, who had hurt no man and who had been hurt by all men. Ida, who had brought a wel-comed sweetness into the hard life of Hamlet Sproul.

He screamed at the top of his voice, a wordless cry torn deep from his pained soul.

What kind of beast would carve the heart and liver from small boys and a gentle woman? *And burn them.*

*Jonathan.* With help from that bastard Poe. This was *his* vengeance for trying to kill him in the stable. To do this to a woman—

Woman. Poe had a woman. Yes, that was it! Let *him* feel this same unholy agony that was tearing apart Hamlet Sproul. Let Poe weep and shriek for *his* dead woman. Oh yes, Poe would die and so would Mr Ugly Bulldog. And Jonathan. *That* would not be easy, but anything could be done if a man put his whole self on it, and Hamlet Sproul had every reason in the world to put his whole self on killing Jonathan.

He squeezed Ida Sair's cold hand again, kissing it and tasting the salt of his own tears. On her dead head and that of his two sons, he vowed to kill Rachel Coltman as soon as possible. And her death would be most unpleasant.

# CHAPTER TWENTY-TWO

Five Points.

Figg doubted that the devil himself would have the nerve to show his horned head in this bit of hell. The cab-driver, strong on self-preservation, had stopped on the edge of the slum, refusing to go further. So it was step down into mud shoe-top high and, with Poe as guide, trek through narrow streets and alleys lacking all gaslight. There was light, if you could call it that. A stub of a candle flickering in a window lacking all glass. A lantern in the hands of passing, hard-faced strangers. A burning end of a cigar in the mouth of a filthy whore calling from a doorway. Small bonfires of trash in the streets where adults and children in rags warmed their hands, their dirty faces blank with despair. The cold night couldn't hide the stink; nothing but foul air everywhere. Figg walked past rotting tenements worse than anything to be found in London's Seven Dials slum or even 'The Holy Land'. He and Poe brushed past men, women and children wrapped in dirt-encrusted rags, most of them drunk and surly, cursing each other and anyone unfortunate enough to be near them. Children fought each other over the last few drops in a whisky bottle. There was less hope here than in the breast of a man standing on a scaffold with a rope around his neck.

And Figg knew that a man's life wasn't worth a farthing in Five Points. Keep your eyes open and your powder dry. Figg's hands were in his pockets around the butts of his two pocket flintlocks. Lord bless and keep the gunsmith.

He and Poe reached the Louvre.

Inside the smell of oil from lamps attached to wagon wheels hanging from the ceiling was heavy in the air. Figg smelled whisky and sweat from the crowd of people packed on the dance floor and sitting on long wooden benches against the wall. The dance-hall resembled a dark tunnel filled with men and women clutching each other and dancing crude polkas and waltzes, the men bearded and chewing tobacco, the women with pinched, sombre faces and bad teeth.

Harp, drum and trumpet furnished the music. A tiny woman with a sad face gently plucked the harp strings, her eyes closed as though imagining herself to be somewhere else. The trumpet-player was a lad who Figg guessed to be no older than fourteen. From the sounds of him, he hadn't had the instrument to his lips more than a few times in his life. The drummer was old, small, bald and had only one arm. Pounds that bleedin' drum like he was shoeing a horse, thought Figg, hands still in his pockets.

He and Poe found a seat on the bench, the wall to their backs, which Figg preferred. He turned to Poe. Ain't no tables 'ere.'

'One comes here to dance rather than converse.'

'And drink, from the looks of it.'

'The waiter girls will indulge your every whim, be it alcoholic or more intimate.'

'Figured more than rum was for sale down 'ere.' Figg looked at the waiter girls. Young ones, some of them. Babies. Maybe fourteen, fifteen years old and the oldest not much over twenty. Short black dresses, black net stockings and red knee boots with tassels and bells. Waiter girls. Whores for a few coins.

Johnnie Bill Baker of the crossed eyes was not a man to spend much on inside light. Figg could see that and damn little else in the darkness around him. Whale-oil lamps hanging from the ceiling, some tallow candles on the wall and behind the long plank-on-barrels bar, but other than that a man needed good eyes and good luck in order to see his hand in front of his face.

Cheap dresses on the women. No crinoline, no puffy skirts with ten petticoats underneath. Just faded cloth with unwashed flesh underneath. Dark clothes and shirts without collars and cuffs for the men. Worn boots on a dance floor sanded to give boots a better grip. The usual tobacco-spitting going on, with more juice hitting the floor than the inside of a spittoon. And an air that reeked of people who didn't bathe and didn't care one way or another about it.

Poe stood up to stop a waiter girl, whispered in her ear, then sat down. 'She will bring Johnnie Bill Baker to us.'

'You knows the gent, you say?'

'I have encountered him during my travels in the lower depths of our republic.'

'What kind of man is he, besides what you been tellin' me?'

'Shrewd. A killer. Concerned with himself and all that concerns him. If you are not already aware of it, this place does not welcome strangers, and the people who populate it are quick to prey on the unwary.'

Figg unbuttoned one button on his black frock-coat. 'I will bear that in mind, Mr Poe.'

166

The young waiter girl returned. She was bone thin, looked younger than her fourteen years and had eyes that were much older. She spoke with a slight lisp. 'Mr Baker annountheth that he ain't in the habit of talkin' to people what geth drunk and patheth out in the rat pit on his premitheth.'

Figg looked at Poe, who mumbled. 'There is a rat pit in the back and I did—' He stopped, then raised his voice. 'Please announce to Mr Baker that our business with him is urgent and—'

'Little girl,' said Figg behind an unfriendly grin as he grabbed her wrist. 'Announce to Mr Baker for me that it would be best for the peace of 'is premises if 'e were to come 'ere and talk with us. Otherwise I shall get up from where I now sits and seek 'im out. Announce that, if you will be so kind.'

The frightened girl backed away rubbing her sore wrist, then turned and disappeared into the crowd of shuffling dancers. Figg looked at Poe. 'You passed out in a rat pit?'

A rat pit was a circle six feet in diameter and surrounded by a wooden fence four feet high. Several dozen rats were turned loose inside it, along with a starved dog. Bets were then placed on how many rats the dog would kill in a given period of time. Ratting, as it was called, was popular in both England and America.

Poe said, 'I had succumbed to my intemperate habits while in this establishment and I passed out. When I came to, I was in the rat pit and Johnnie Bill Baker, along with some of his acquaintances, were keeping amused by tossing dead rats on to me.'

'My God!'

'And you have challenged this man in his own lair.'

'So long as he comes to us, squire.'

'He shall and with an attitude of belligerence. Nor will he arrive alone.'

Figg took a hand from his pocket to adjust his black top hat, then put the hand back into his pocket again. 'So long as he arrives mate. From 'im to Sproul to Jonathan. Ain't that your plan?'

'My plan includes survival.'

'You let me do the worryin' about that, squire. You jes' think up some more quotes. I finds them fascinatin'.'

Johnnie Bill Baker stood in front of them.

And he wasn't alone.

A path had cleared for him on the dance floor, then the path had closed behind him and two men plus a woman the likes of which Figg had never seen in life or in picture books. The woman was

167

black, gigantic, with dyed yellow hair and fists as big as Pierce James Figg's. She wore a shiny green silk dress, with a stiletto sticking from the top of a man's boot (feet as big as Figg's, too!) and a slung shot—a leather thong with an egg-sized lump of iron tied at one end—dangled from her wrist. The woman was frightening to look at and Figg, who knew the look of people who could kill, knew that this huge Negro woman was a killer.

Johnnie Bill Baker, legs apart, fists on his hips, looked down at Poe. 'You can't be the bucko who talks in such a hard manner. Nor are ye the ugly one the little girl spoke of so—'

He looked at Figg. 'It must be you, friend. And I do so want to hear your story, which is why me friends and I have travelled so far. Make it a good one. The last story should always be a good one.'

Figg, hat low on his forehead, stared at him. Handsome, he was, with a face as clean as a baby's bottom and clothes that cost a pretty penny. Grey suit, grey waistcoat and grey silk ascot, with a fancy white shirt and lace cuffs. Red hair parted in the middle. Diamond rings on both hands. Johnny the Gent. And damn me if he *didn't* have crossed eyes. Not too tall, slim, and the kind to set a maid's heart to flutter, but he was as cross-eyed as somebody's idiot child.

Two men just behind him. Irish thugs by the looks of 'em, with pistols in the belt and both itching for a punch-up. The kind who gouge out your eyes, bite off your ear and put the boot into your temple, then go to church on Sunday. And don't forget the black woman. Dark as the inside of a mine shaft. Probably more of a hard case than either of the men backing Johnny the Gent.

One of the Irish thugs, a squat, unshaven man with eyebrows that met over the bridge of his nose, spat on Figg's outstretched leg. The thug said, 'It don't talk much, Johnnie. Sits there like a bleedin' Buddha. Think I'll write home and tell me mother it's ugly enough to curdle milk.'

Baker said, 'You have a name, ugly man. Let's hear it before we apply ourselves to dealin' with your forward ways.'

'Figg. Pierce James Figg.'

Baker frowned, stroking the side of his nose with a slim finger. 'Figg. Figg. Name strikes a response.'

'Figg is a delicate fruit,' said the squat thug. 'By the sounds of it, it's English, though it don't look too delicate to me. Stand up when you come among the Irish, English swine. We don't care to be summoned by the likes of you.'

He lifted his booted foot high, preparing to bring it down on Figg's ankle.

Bloomin' amateurs, thought Figg.

The squat thug's foot was on the way down, when Figg slid off the bench and brought his ankle up into the thug's crotch with all his strength. The thug folded in half, jaw slack, eyes entirely whites. Then Figg was on his feet, moving into the thug whose hands were folded across his crotch in a vain attempt to stop the pain.

The punch was a short, vicious left hook; it didn't travel far but it had most of Figg's power behind it. The punch crashed into the thug's right temple, lifting him from the floor and sending him flying backwards and into the crowd of dancers. Immediately a space cleared around him.

When Figg took the one step which brought him belly to belly with Johnnie Bill Baker, both of the boxer's hands were again in his pockets and he spoke through clenched teeth. 'Mr Baker, we are needin' to talk with you. Please accommodate us.'

Baker felt the pressure against his gut. When the other thug and the huge black woman started towards Figg, Baker lifted up both hands to halt them in place. The Irish thief's smile was forced.

'Suddenly I feel the need to talk with Mr Figg. And with you too, Mr Poe, of course. Would you be tellin' what make of persuasion you have hard against me, Mr Figg?'

'From this distance, it don't matter, do it Mr Baker?'

'You have a silver tongue, Mr Figg. Figg.' Baker snapped his fingers. 'Of course! The boxer. Pierce James Figg.'

Baker's manner changed. He relaxed and seemed genuinely pleased to meet Figg. He clasped both of the boxer's shoulders. 'Twenty-five years ago in England, it was. I was a lad of ten and me dad took me to see you fight Ned Painter. Fifty-two rounds and you lost because of a broken arm and by God, man, you were winnin'. Winnin'!'

He turned to the crowd. 'Keep on dancin', folks. Meself and me friends here is talkin' over old toimes.'

Baker said to the man and large black woman behind him: 'Give yer greetin's to Mr Pierce James Figg, one of the best who ever put a foot in a prize ring.'

'Figg,' muttered the other thug. He blinked, flinched. ' 'Eard of 'im.'

'Heard of 'im, now have ya?' Baker placed his face almost nose to nose with the thug. ' 'E's the best, 'e is, and you were fixin' to die young by bracin' the man.' The thug took one step backwards, licking his lips.

Baker said, 'Mr Figg, this here lady is Black Turtle. As you can see, she is ample and black as a hangman's heart. But I loves her, yes I do. She's my lieutenant of sorts, keepin' the girls in line and seein' that peace and harmony reign over these here premises. Fights like a wounded tiger, she does, and she's put a few men under the earth. No man in Five Points dares stand up to her unless, of course, he has provided in advance for his widow.'

Baker's smile was easy, filled with white teeth. 'I see, Mr Figg, that you are in the company of that known man of letters, Mr E. Poe, and I say welcome to ye both. Yes sir, welcome to ye both.'

Poe said nothing.

Baker placed an arm around Figg's shoulders. The boxer sniffed twice at the Irishman's heavy cologne which smelled of cinnamon and gin.

'Figg, me bucko, it is indeed an honour and a privilege to have a warrior like yourself in me place. Yes it is, sir. Your name is legend among those who follow "The Fancy". You have carved your name high atop the mountain crest of pugilism, sir. Saw you fight twice, *twice,* and a thrill it was. Bested Jem Ward, you did. Year was '26. And him goin' on to become heavyweight champion of Britain. Good fighter he was, but I heard stories about him.'

Figg's eyes were on the huge black woman who looked as though she wanted to kill him. The other thug was dragging away the man that Figg had knocked out. Figg said, 'Ward had the skill, true enough. But he was a disgrace to the prize ring. He gambled too much. Bet on 'isself to lose and he usually made sure he did.'

'You beat him fair and square, if remember.'

'I did. He come into the ring that afternoon to kill me, so we had a go at it, 'im and me.'

Baker produced another wide, sincere smile. 'I was twelve then but by God, I did love "The Fancy". Lived for the prize ring, I did. The smell of it, the sounds, sights, the blood. All of it. Excitin' world to a little fella. To a big fella too, let me tell ya. We have our boxers over here, some of 'em pretty good. But ahh, those from me days as a snot-nosed little mick brat, they were the best, I tell ya. Me dad never had a job long enough to tie his shoes but he always had a coin to bet on a prizefight. Tell me, has the game in England gone down as low as I hear?'

Figg nodded once. 'It has. Gamblin's taken its toll. Crooked fights, poisoned water to the fighters 'twixt rounds, hooligans hired to break up a match if the wrong man's winnin'. It's gone wrong, true enough.'

Baker hung his head. 'Sad. Very sad. Well now, how may I serve ye?'

Figg's hands still did not leave his pockets. 'Hamlet Sproul. Wants you should arrange a meetin' with 'im.'

'Hamlet Sproul, Hamlet Sproul.' Baker's handsome and cross-eyed face turned thoughtful.

Poe, impatient with Baker's hypocrisy, stood up. 'Sproul has bragged about accompanying you and the Daybreak Boys on un-scheduled visits to country homes.'

Baker's eyes narrowed. Figg had seen that look before. The mick was measuring Poe's neck for a blade, but then Baker smiled. 'Yes, yes. Now it comes to me. Ham-a-let Sprou-well. I understand he is in the business of removals, of a sort.'

Behind him, Black Turtle snorted.

'Mortal remains and all that,' said Baker, hooking his thumbs in the pockets of his grey silk waistcoat. 'And what would you two citizens be wantin' with such a man?'

Figg's hoarse voice was even. The harp's plink-plink and the shuffle of boots on sand were a musical counterpart to his words. 'We will discuss that with Hamlet Sproul. We prefer you get word to him that Mr Poe and Mr Figg wants a face-to-face with 'im as soon as possible. Tell 'im it would be to 'is advantage to do so. Tell 'im it could very well save 'is life.'

Baker nodded slowly, gravely. Cross eyes do indeed make him look funny, thought Figg. He's slicker than egg-white on a tile floor. Johnnie the Gent would kick a nun in the head when she's down, then charge her sixpence to help her off the floor.

'Save his life,' said Johnnie Bill Baker. 'Now that ought to get his attention, eh Black Turtle me darlin'.'

She'd stepped away from him. A fight. Not too far away from where they stood. Without hesitating, Black Turtle waded in swinging her slung shot, scattering men and women before her as though they were driven by a strong wind.

Two men didn't run. Sailors by the look of 'em, thought Figg, and they want to try her. They're not the type to bow to a woman, so now she's being put to the test.

Johnnie Bill Baker smiled, gently nudging Figg with his elbow. 'Behold, Mr Figg. You are about to witness a remarkable per-formance which shall include the education of two gentlemen unacquainted with our ways.'

Now there was a space on the dance floor. The music trailed off and people watched. Two sailors, angered at being hit by the Negro woman, the both of them unfamiliar with her, were ready. They wanted to fight. So did Black Turtle.

'Nigger bitch,' grunted one. 'Nigger bitch.' He charged her and Black Turtle kicked him in the knee with her booted foot, spinning him around and to the floor. The other sailor, smaller but as mean, was almost on her when she turned, hooking her right fist deep into his stomach. As he doubled up, she jammed her left thumb into his eye. He squealed, both hands quickly covering the eye.

Figg, who'd seen fighters in his time, was fascinated. She was the equal of any man and better than most, and she wasn't finished, not by a long shot. The woman fought without heat, without passion, saying nothing and showing no expression, and Figg hadn't seen many with that kind of control or love of bloodsport inside 'em. Black Turtle was that rare one, a fighter empty of all feeling or compassion. Expect no mercy from her, for it was none you'd get.

Bending over, she came up with the stiletto from her boot top. Quick hands, thought Figg. Decisive. No hesitating with this one. The blade was against the temple of the sailor whose eye she'd just tried to put out. Then with one savage stroke, she brought the blade down, removing the ear. He screamed, spun around, spraying those near him with his blood.

Now the unlucky one on the floor had her attention. Black Turtle took her time walking over to him, which was just as well because he wasn't going anywhere. Couldn't stand. Figg watched the Negro woman raise her arm, then bring down the slung shot on the man, whipping him brutally, bouncing the egg-shaped piece of metal off his arms, thighs, head, stomach, hitting him again and again. Those watching laughed, pointed, howled, applauded. There was no mercy in Five Points. There were victors and victims and nothing in between.

Baker turned to Figg and Poe with his biggest grin of the night. Stands there like a proud parent, thought Figg, on the day his first-born has finally learned to walk without daddy holding her up.

'Devoted to me, she is,' said Baker. 'Ain't nothin' on two legs or four that can beat her.'

He stepped between Figg and Poe, an arm around each man's shoulders. 'Gents, tonight you will be drinkin' the finest and it is on Johnnie Bill Baker, none other. Now sit you down and a waiter gal will bring you a small libation—'

'None for me,' said Figg. He hesitated, then, 'And Mr Poe is on temperance.'

Baker's eyebrows crawled up his forehead in mock shock. 'Oh dear, oh dear, oh dear. Well, Mr Poe, I do hope the distilleries of Manhattan refuse to panic at this sudden news. And all this time I thought the most wondrous sight of all would be that of a camel sashayin' through the eye of a needle. I offer me finest spirits and I am refused. Well, no matter. Take a pew the both of you, and I will have Mr Sproul summoned and your business with him can be concluded. Johnnie Bill Baker knows how to treat a guest. Yes sir, that he does.'

From where they had originally been sitting, Figg and Poe watched Baker, Black Turtle and two men talk out of earshot several feet away. A dancing couple came between both groups, then moved on.

Figg, both hands still in his pockets, wished the lad with the trumpet would lay it down and go milk cows. The lad was a sorry mess and had no more music in him than a pig could fly. The lady harpist knew what she was doing and the one-armed drummer appeared to have gotten drunk and passed out. As Figg shifted his eyes to Baker's group, a hideous-looking old woman, tiny and dry as a dead sparrow, crossed the dance floor, miraculously managing to avoid dancing couples. Her hair was sparse and white and she barely had a handful of teeth in her tiny head. She'd been somewhere in the darkness behind Baker.

Standing in front of Figg and Poe, the old woman began speaking softly in French.

Figg whispered from the corner of his mouth. 'A nutter, she is. Balmy and around the bend. You takin' charge of 'er life, too?'

Poe answered her in French. Ain't that nice, thought Figg. The two of 'em carrying on like they was in Paree. French ain't no language for a grown man. All them foreign words in it and you speak it from your nose.

The little old woman swayed, smiled at Figg, then continued speaking in French to Poe. Looney, moonstruck old biddy. They only come to the little poet when they are crippled in some manner. Cripples. They're drawn to him like flies to rotting meat.

Poe's Southern drawl was respectful. 'Mr Figg, have you a coin to spare?'

'For this one? Give me a good reason why I should.'

'She has just warned us. Baker plans to betray you and me. No, do not stand, do not move. Stay as you are and listen.'

Poe sighed. 'This dear woman is called Montaigne, though it is not her real name. It is the name of a sixteenth-century French philosopher. Her own name? A mystery to us, perhaps even to her, for her mind has been ravaged by alcohol and drugs. The sorrow that brought this on was great. She is French and once she was tutor to the children of the King of France. How she came to fall this low is another tale for another time. Life has treated her with contempt and disdain, and to most she is only a pile of rags in a doorway or under a bar, something to be ignored and discounted. Which is what happened tonight. Baker and others ignored her and she heard him plan our destruction. Baker knows where Sproul is, but will not lead us to him.'

'Did she learn why Baker is against us?'

'Does it matter?'

'No it don't.'

Figg took a hand from his pocket and stuck it inside his coat. When he brought the hand out, it held a gold sovereign.

Poe said, 'A suggestion, Mr Figg. If you give her the gold coin, there is the chance that someone in here will see it and cut her throat for it. In Five Points, children are stabbed for their pennies. I suggest you buy her two or three bottles of liquor. She would be most appreciative, I am certain.'

'Ask her.'

'She understands English, Mr Figg.'

'Yeah, I guess she does.' Figg tipped his hat to her. 'You will 'ave it, miss. And I am thankin' yew muchly.'

She smiled. Her eyes were too bright, Figg thought. She's addled, but thank dear Jesus, she ain't too addled. 'Mr Poe, please find us a waiter gal for Missus Montaigne.'

The old woman spoke in French to Figg.

Poe said. ' "Sit we upon the world's highest throne, sit we upon our own asses". It is from her namesake, her way of telling us that we have no right to look down upon her, for all of us are mortal and ordinary and none too elevated, despite our vanity.'

Figg nodded to her. She nodded back.

Poe leaned closer to the boxer. 'We could leave now, Mr Figg. Flee before plans are finalised for our destruction.'

'If we do not find Mr Sproul, your lady friend is that much longer in the clutches of Jonathan.'

Poe sighed. 'Too true. Then what are you suggesting we do, sir?'

'Continue sittin' on this 'ere bench and listenin' to that sorry lad with the horn in his mouth.'

'We shall die if we remain, sir!' Poe leaned away from Figg.

'Mr Poe, get one of them waiter galls so's we can get Missus Montaigne her just desserts. If we flee, we learn nothin'. And about dyin', well, I got me own thoughts on that. Yes, squire, indeed I do.'

# CHAPTER TWENTY-THREE

Ten minutes past midnight. For the second time tonight, Poe watched fire bring death to someone.

An hour ago in Five Points, he'd been near enough to feel the heat from flames that had killed Johnnie Bill Baker. He'd been sick to his stomach at watching the Irishman die. But there was that part of him always drawn by violence and the dark side of life, so he'd fought hard against admitting to himself the fascination he'd felt witnessing Baker shriek as fire crawled all over him. Fascination, then guilt.

Now Poe and Figg stood with the crowd looking at the Ann Street boarding house go up in flames. Witnesses said that some of the Renaissance Players had got out alive. Some hadn't. The three who'd survived were not those Figg had been searching for.

The disappointed boxer's whisper came from the corner of his mouth 'Convenient little business, this. Now it appears there will be nobody to converse with.'

'You wanted them dead. Circumstance appears to have spared you the labour involved.'

' 'Nother road leadin' nowhere, squire. If I coulda got me 'ands round the neck of one of them players, it wouldna been long before me 'ands were around Jonathan's neck as well.'

Damn them, thought Poe of the chattering crowd around him. They conduct themselves as if this was a sporting event. Mothers hold babes up to see the terrible beauty that is fire and men share their bottles with strangers, a sudden harmony engendered by gazing upon the misery of others. Coloured stableboys point at the disaster, then jabber to each other as though they still swung from trees by their tails. Children crawl from warm beds for such an event as this, for it is a promise of more momentous occasions to come, a false promise I could tell them, for too soon misery will be theirs to embrace and others will stare at *them* and point.

'You are silent, Mr Poe.'

'Tonight, sir,' I have seen too much of such things as this.' He desperately craved alcohol. The guilt was now mingled with disgust.

'No sense dwellin' on Mr Baker. It was 'im or us. Don't the Bible say that 'im what digs a hole for others gets to fall in it imself?'

Two small boys ran out of the night and at Figg, throwing themselves to the ground just in front of him, then turning to watch the fire.

Figg gave the boys a half smile. 'When I was their age, would 'ave given a king's ransom for such a fire as this. I—'

He looked around.

*Poe was gone.*

Damn his eyes! Figg angrily pushed through the crowd, looking left, right. That sneaky little bastard. What the bleedin' hell was upsetting his tender soul—seeing Johnny the Gent turn into a cozy fireplace in front of his eyes? Seeing the boarding house get toasted to a crisp? That was it. Too much burnin' for the little man.

Maybe he was back at the Astor Hotel. Maybe. But not bloody likely. Little Mr Poe of the sad grey eyes was probably indulging himself in strong beverage and weepin' like some old woman. Well, maybe he's got a right to his tears. Ain't every day you see a man burn to death, and you close enough to spit on him.

*They were beneath the Louvre in a dark, damp storeroom dug from the earth. Around them were opened barrels of homemade whisky, along with stacks of dark green unlabelled bottles in which to put it. The air was musty, breathing was an effort. Rats squeaked and ran in terror and twice bats had flown low over their heads, flapping their wings, then disappearing into the black tunnel straight in front of the four people who'd just entered the storeroom. Poe held the only light, two cheap whale-oil lanterns.*

*Figg shoved the muzzle of the flintlock into the ear of Johnnie Bill Baker, who faced an earthen wall, leaning forward on tip toe and touching the wall with just his index fingers. Black Turtle, beside him, did the same. Seconds ago, Baker had followed Figg's order and climbed into—then out of—a barrel of whisky, submerging himself in it up to the neck. Now he reeked of alcohol, his expensive clothing drenched and ruined.*

*'Speak softly, Johnny Gent,' said Figg. 'How many's up ahead waitin' fer us?'*

*'Three. They are waitin' in a tiny room at tunnel's end.'*

*'I would like to inquire why you was plannin' to kill Mr Poe and meself?'*

*'Mr Figg, now who said anythin' about killin'.' The Irishman, clinging to his courage and charm, attempted to turn around*

slowly. Figg pressed the flintlock harder against his ear, his other pistol still aimed at Black Turtle.

'Ah, Mr Figg, I get your point. Very well, me bucko, I shall remain in this most uncomfortable position, though I must admit the smell of me own whisky is not as pleasin' as I once thought. Now I had not planned for you and Mr Poe to die. Hamlet Sproul wants you to die, but not me. You have me word on that.'

Poe coughed. The dampness down here sent a chill deep in to his bones. 'Why does Sproul require your assistance to kill us?'

'He blames you and Mr Figg here for the deaths of his woman and two sons. Asked me 'elp in gettin' him a few good boys to accompany him in some little scheme he's got to get back at you. When I sees you both, I figured no sense turnin' you over to him. I'd turn ye over to Captain Collect and make a shillin' or two for meself. I'd let them crimp you, then tell Sproul I killed ye both meself and he'd have to live with that. He doesn't know you're here.'

Poe's anger made his hands shake and the light from the two lanterns sent jiggling shadows across the backs of Baker and Black Turtle. 'Crimping means drugging and kidnapping men to serve at sea. The life of a sailor is miserable and Captain Collect is the most brutal sea captain of all. His real name is Z. C. Leap and men die on every voyage he makes on his whaler. No one sails with him willingly, so he 'collects' them by crimping. Mr Baker was going to sell us to him, Mr Figg.'

Figg was quiet.

Baker, trembling from the effort of balancing himself on his toes and two fingers, closed his eyes tightly. He was less sure of himself now. 'A re-regrettable error, Mr Figg, one which I prefer to drown upstairs in champagne, if you would be so kind. Let us all retire into me dance-hall.'

Poe's anger had only grown. 'I do not trust him, Mr Figg. Upstairs or down, we are at his mercy.'

Baker grinned at the wall. 'The man is correct, Mr Figg. You are at me mercy. Fire your pistol and those men up ahead will hear it and come runnin'. Try going back upstairs and me boyos will come down on ye like the wrath of heaven. God, this whisky of mine is an abomination, it is. Must do somethin' about it. Well Mr Figg, what is it to be? Hand me those pistols and I promise—'

Slipping one pistol under his arm, Figg hooked his left fist into Baker's side, driving him into Black Turtle. Both of them fell to the ground. The huge black woman was quick to get up, snarling like an animal, her mouth flecked with spit. Baker rolled left and right in agony. When she'd helped him to his feet, his crossed eyes bore into Figg with as much hatred as the boxer had ever seen.

'Black Turtle will not—' he winced at the pain in his ribs. 'She will kill you, Mr Figg. Bet on that. Nobody harms her Johnnie, no-nobody. Down-down here in this dust and cobwebs or-or in an alley. She will find you and kill you for what you have done to me this night.'

He jerked, eyes closed. Black Turtle held him up, keeping him from collapsing.

Figg said, 'Now Mr Baker, I shall tell you why you are wearin' yer own whisky. Slip open the panel on one a them lamps, Mr Poe.'

Poe did.

'Now, Johnny Gent, you see that tiny flame. Well, the minute you get to be too much for me to handle, I am going to toss that tiny flame on you and you, me bucko, are goin' to become one big flame.'

Baker frowned.

Figg said, 'Tell yer blackamoor to walk easy. One false move from her and you get a touch of the fire. Ever seen fire mix with whisky? Ain't a pleasant thing to watch. Now you and yer lady friend move on ahead of us. You gets them inside to open the door in a nice manner. When that happens, you and the blackamoor step in then stand aside. Hear me well on this: play me cheap the both of you and I will have your lives.'

The walk to the tiny room was short. And a nightmare to Poe. Squeaking rats. Low-flying bats. Cobwebs. Water dripping from the dirt ceiling down on to Poe's neck. The darkness. Deep, deep darkness and only the flames from two cheap lanterns to give some little light. And the excitement. What lay in wait for them on the other side of the door? Poe wanted to turn and run. He wanted to continue. He was terrified and he was irresistibly drawn towards that door.

They stood in front of it.

Baker turned to look at Figg, who nodded at him, while sticking one pistol into his belt and taking a lantern from Poe.

Baker knocked on the door. 'It's me, Johnnie.'

The door opened.

Poe saw more darkness. A stub of a candle in a dish on the table. Another lantern in the hand of someone beckoning them inside. Poe's heart leaped within him and he bit his lip to avoid crying out.

Figg whispered to him, 'Stay behind and don't get in me way!'

Baker and Black Turtle stepped inside the room and Poe watched Figg stiff arm them violently aside and shoot the man holding the lantern.

Baker screamed, 'Kill him! Kill him! He's on to you! Kill him!'

Poe wanted to run and couldn't. He stepped inside the room, shaking hands holding the lantern.

'Kill him!' Baker was hysterical. There was another shot and from a dark corner of the room, a man screamed.

Poe saw Black Turtle and another man rush Figg.

But, before they reached him, Figg quickly swung his lantern into Baker's stomach.

The Irishman ignited as quickly as a torch dipped in oil, shrieking as his whisky-drenched clothes went up in flames. He spun around and ran into an earthen wall, clawing at it, then spinning and running into another wall.

Figg was on the ground, Black Turtle and the last remaining man from Captain Collect punching, clawing at him!

But it was Johnnie Bill Baker who kept Poe transfixed in the open doorway. Johnnie Bill Baker who lit up the room with his dying and filled with his screams. 'Sweet Jesus, help me! Help meee!' He bounced from wall to wall, running blindly, filling the tiny room with a horrible light and the sickening smell of his burning flesh. This is a nightmare, thought Poe. Not real. But it is real and I am watching it happen.

On the floor, Figg fought for his life. Struggling to his knees, he smashed his left elbow into the face of Captain Collect's man, crushing his nose, driving him back to the dirt floor. But there was a sharp pain in Figg's eye. The black bitch. She'd stuck her fingers in his eyes and was digging, digging . . .

Pulling his head back, Figg opened his mouth and sunk his teeth deep into her fingers. She clawed at his throat. Pushing her hand away he rose, bringing his knee up under her chin at the same time. She flew backwards, rolled over and began getting to her feet. She was hurt, but still ready to fight. She was as tough as any man Figg had ever faced and she would not stop until she had his life.

Black Turtle charged, head down. Figg side-stepped and she hit the table behind him, going down to the floor with it. Shaking her head, she jammed a foot down on the table, gripped one of its legs with her hands and tore it loose.

And me without a pistol, thought Figg. Behind her he could see Johnnie Bill Baker's body on the floor, wrapped in orange, yellow and blue flames, the body curling up and the man within the

180

*flames crying out no more. And the big black woman who served him was going to kill Figg if she could.*

*Poe watched.*

*She edged towards the boxer; he covered his belt buckle with his hand. She didn't notice him removing the tiny knife and it would have made no difference, Figg knew. Nothing would have stopped her. Besides, she had the better weapon. A long, heavy piece of wood against a tiny blade. The reach was hers. And she had the stomach for killing.*

*Figg had the knowledge.*

*She charged, the wood lifted high over her head.*

*Figg waited, timing his move perfectly.*

*The technique was called the Boar's Thrust, one of the most famous moves in combat fencing, the invention of Donald McBane, the great professional swordsman of the late seventeenth and early eighteenth centuries. McBane, who taught the finest sword-play from his string of establishments combining fencing schools and brothels.*

*When Black Turtle was almost on him, Figg dropped his right knee and left hand to the ground as though genuflecting in church. But the position had a much more deadly intent. As soon as he touched the ground, he thrust his right hand up and forward, driving the tiny knife deep into Black Turtle's stomach. On one knee with Mr Dickens's little knife, Figg became the deadly boar with a horn that killed.*

*She staggered backwards, stopped, eyes protruding, hand still gripping the table leg. Then she stumbled towards him, a dark stain growing across her shiny green dress. She said the first and only word Figg had ever heard come from her mouth. 'Johnnie . . .'*

*Figg took a step backwards. Black Turtle stopped, her large bosom rising and falling as her breathing became more laboured and the pain increased. The table leg slipped from her hands, which went down to the stain and pressed against it. Turning her back to Figg, she staggered towards Baker's burning body, and that's when Poe felt Figg grab his wrist.*

*As Figg dragged him towards a small door at the back of the earthen room, Poe looked back to see Black Turtle fall forward across Johnnie Bill Baker's burning body.*

Poe, on his knees, head on his chest, looked up and smiled at nothing and nobody, for the Hotel Astor hallway was empty, to be expected at almost three o'clock in the morning. He was drunk, indeed, and to hell with worrying about it. Two glasses of wine. No more, no less. Never did have much capacity for spirits, did you Eddy. Takes little of that dreaded water to make you sick, drunk, quarrelsome and a wild man. The mere smell of it is enough to set you off, is it not? Well stand up, Eddy, and stagger down the hall to the hotel room you share with Figg.

If he's asleep, wake him. Perhaps he'll give you a few coins to take a train back to Fordham. You have just spent your last money on the cheapest wine available and now you are stuck with Figg's company. Figg the man-burner. Johnnie Bill Baker has been fricasséed and there is one less paddy to break the law in Gotham.

But do not blame Figg, for Baker and his coloured female behemoth would have killed us both. Indeed, indeed.

Poe was on his feet, both hands on the wall and he walked, slowly, most unsteadily, and now he was at the door of the room he shared with Figg. An odd one, our Figg. Skilled in the ways of destruction but a man who has seen important personages. If he has not achieved the culture and breeding of a Socrates, he has at least learned to function in this not so best of all possible worlds.

In front of the door, Poe stopped, frowned, sniffed. He smelled something. Something. Gas. He smelled *gas*. Why was there gas coming from the room? Poe closed his eyes, opened them wide, blinked. *Gas*. He banged on the door.

'Figg, you ninny. Why is there gas in there? I demand to know why, sir.'

Poe leaned backwards, then forward, finally getting his key out of his pocket. *Gas*. And then Poe knew. The alcohol controlled most of him but not all of him. Something was wrong inside, something quite wrong. He dropped the key, bent over and after reaching for it several times, gripped it tightly, then fumbled at the keyhole, finally opening the door.

The gas smell was overpowering. The room was filled with it.

Poe staggered forward, grabbed the washbasin and hurled it through the window. Cold air hit him with force, a most welcome force. He coughed, his eyes watered and he saw everything in the dark room as though viewing it all through a pinhole. His lungs burned and he yearned for air. *Air*.

Poe flopped across Figg's bed. 'Get up, damn you, get up! He tugged at the boxer, pulled his arm. Figg didn't move. *Violence*. This you'll understand. Poe slapped Figg's face and fell to the floor himself. On his knees, he slapped Figg's face again, again, and lifting his arm to do so was the hardest thing Poe had ever done in his life. His arm seemed to weigh a ton and the hand came down in slow motion, as if this was all a dream.

Figg groaned.

'Damn you, get up!'

Poe pulled at him. Figg moved.

Now they were both on the floor. Figg had fallen out of bed.

Poe sat on the floor, mouth open, his lungs burning, his brain whirling and threatening to disintegrate as he gripped Figg's upper arm and pulled. The open door was behind him, light from the hallway beckoning them to safety.

He pulled. Figg inched himself forward towards the light, towards the sound of Poe's voice. To the boxer, the voice seemed to be life itself, warning him away from death, pulling him back from something hideous, something horrible and unknown.

Poe shouted, not knowing what he shouted, and he pulled at Figg and he scraped himself towards the door, towards light, towards air, towards life.

Both men collapsed in the hallway, Poe on his back and feeling himself sink into that blackness which always seemed to be reaching out for him. He heard footsteps running towards him and then he could hear no more.

# CHAPTER TWENTY-FOUR

Jonathan, dressed in the white robe and beard of Paracelsus, handed Mrs Viola Sontag a highly polished piece of steel exactly the size of a saucer.

'The mirror of Solomon,' he said to the horse-faced woman, who wore a black veil to hide skin pitted by smallpox. 'With it you can divine the future.'

She took it from him gently, using both hands, inhaling softly and seeing her reflection in it with brown eyes kept fashionably bright by squeezing orange juice into them nightly before going to bed. This beauty custom, long favoured by Spanish women, was now popular among certain wealthy and well-travelled New York women. Jonathan found it idiotic, since the juice burned the eyes and stained the pillowcase. But then, so much about the widow Sontag was idiotic.

Caught up in the enthusiasm for spiritualism now sweeping New York, and also to amuse her friends during dinner parties, Mrs Sontag, forty-nine and as rich as she was thin and ugly, wanted to learn to read the future. Jonathan had agreed to accept her for a series of sittings, all of which had been lucrative for him while filling Mrs Sontag's boring life with something of interest. She was his first sitting this morning and, as usual, paid in gold, in advance.

Jonathan slowly placed his white-gloved hands down on the back marble table. 'You must slice the throat of a white pigeon and with its blood write the names Jehovah, Adonay, Metatron and Eloym at the four corners of the mirror.'

'Yessss.' Mrs Sontag hissed through loose false teeth, as pleased with the piece of steel as if it had been a new Christmas toy.

'Keep it in a clean white cloth.'

'Oh yessss. Yessss.'

'Daily gaze upon the sky the first hour after sunset and when you see a new moon, repeat the chant I have written out for you. It commands the spirits to obey and aid you in reading the future from the mirror you now hold.'

He could see her large teeth through the veil like marble columns dimly visible in the night. The woman was hideous, insisting upon wearing crinolines everywhere, those corded petticoats lined with horsehair and reinforced with straw. From her servants Jonathan had learned that she also wore several muslin petticoats over that, meaning from the hips down she was several yards wide. Fortunately Jonathan's home had large doors. During the sitting, Mrs Sontag sat alone on a couch, covering it with her tentlike skirt and petticoats.

She clutched the steel mirror to her flat chest. 'Oh Doctor Paracelsus, I cannot tell you the excitement that I feel! I cannot wait to follow your instructions.'

'Follow them carefully. The prayer, the perfume I have given you—'

'To be sprinkled upon burning coals as I say the prayer, yesss?'

'Yes. Then breathe upon the mirror, uttering that name you are never to reveal but are to speak only as so instructed.'

'Yesssss.'

'Make the sign of the cross upon the mirror for the next forty-five days without missing a single day.'

'Oh yesss. Will Solomon himself appear to me?'

*He has not as yet appeared to me, you brainless bitch. Why should be reveal himself to you?* Jonathan folded his hands and closed his eyes. 'Who can say.'

'May I continue my sittings with you during those forty-five days?'

He nodded. *And keep the gold flowing from your bony hands.*

Later, Jonathan spoke to Sarah Clannon. 'Five hundred in gold for aiding that ridiculous woman to become even more of a fool than she is. Well, to business. You will not appear to Lorenzo Ballou in a dream tonight. He is to be denied your body, which so far he has lustfully accepted as that of his sluttish dead wife. I want you to become Virginia Poe once more. Dear Eddy needs another jab from the sharp needle of personal agony.'

Sarah Clannon spooned strawberries and champagne into her small, sensuous mouth. She had no questions. If Jonathan felt she should know the reason for the change, he would tell her.

He did. 'Rachel Coltman is more drawn to Mr E. A. Poe than she is willing to admit.'

'Love?'

'Perhaps the dawn of it. Perhaps not. Her feelings for her dead husband reflect as much guilt as affection. Survivors often feel guilty at merely being alive when a loved one has died. Guilt or imagined love, both are enough to create a state of mind in which she sees herself as passionately involved with her dead husband when in truth she is not. It would not take too much prodding from Mr Poe to get Rachel to place herself more in his camp than mine. Neither of them know this. However I know and I cannot afford to have it happen. Find Mr Poe and appear to him as darling Sissy. Let it be one more reason for him to believe that the dead do indeed live. Damage his mind a little more so that he aids me in obtaining the Throne of Solomon.'

Sarah Clannon, in black corset, black stockings and lace boots, bit a strawberry in half. 'It is enjoyable to disturb the mind of Poe. It is such an easy task.'

Jonathan stood naked in front of a long mirror, shaving with a straight razor but without soap or water. 'His life has not been a joy. Father deserted the family when Poe was a babe. Odd man, dear pater. Lawyer turned actor. Bad lawyer, worse actor. Could never accept criticism, much of which was deservedly negative. Always threatening violence to his critics, a trait continued somewhat in dear Eddy.'

Jonathan shaved gently under his nose. 'Mother dies when Edgar is two. Then there was brother William Henry, eventually to become an alcoholic and die of it, while sister Rosalie still exists in the prison of insanity, a fear our Poe is never without. When mother dies, he is sent to the household of John Allan, a rather cold and penny-pinching foster-father. Eddie and John will not like each other, and throughout his life Eddy will avoid using the name Allan, preferring the initial A.'

Jonathan leaned back to admire himself, running a hand over his smooth cheeks. 'John Allan, businessman, wanted to be a writer. No talent. Possibly jealous of Edgar who did have talent and intelligence. Takes Edgar to England for five years, where the lad is exposed to culture, history, aesthetics of one sort or another. Back in America, dear Eddy with high opinion of himself, attends school in Richmond, Virginia, where he has to defend himself against Southern aristocrats who insult him upon learning his natural parents were travelling players.'

Jonathan snapped his razor shut and continued to stare at himself in the miror. 'Death, desertion, snobbery, criticism, a stone-hearted Scotsman for a foster-father and a brother and sister who were of questionable mental health. His sadness started early. Allan beat the boy once or twice, never an endearing trait in a parent, and I speak from experience.'

He walked across the room, kissed Sarah Clannon, removing a champagne-soaked strawberry from her mouth. 'Poe was born sad, has lived most sadly. He has appeared on stage himself, you know. Fairly skilled. He has fought a duel, been buried alive, that by mistake and it is a most horrid story which I shall tell you at another time. In college he gambled, lost, and father Allan refused to pay his debts. For that reason Poe left college and existed in the army as Edgar A. Perry. Made sergeant-major. Was good.'

Jonathan picked up a strawberry with his fingers. 'He is something of a liar, sad to say. Lied about going to Europe to fight in the Greek revolution. On occasion, he has stolen the work of other men and used it in his own, and one can only look with narrowed eyes upon his having married his first cousin Virginia when she was merely twelve and he twenty-six. But for all of that he is a hard-working poet, newspaperman, critic and writer of highly imaginative short pieces. He is ever in need of love and sympathy and his drunkenness is easily caused by as little as a half glass of spirits. His reputation as a guzzler is undeserved. I am familiar with him because he is important to me in my quest for the Throne of Solomon. I also find him interesting in a bizarre way.

'He has failed, primarily because he is a man out of time. This is a barbaric, uncultured nation with no use for talent such as Poe's. He has fought the good fight, as the Bible says, with nothing to show for it except monumental bitterness. Rachel is in his last chance and I fear that once she becomes fully aware of this, she may succumb to pity which, when combined with her growing affection, would give Poe total power over her and I must assume this would mean the end of my securing Justin Coltman's body.'

Sarah Clannon licked a strawberry, then placed it in Jonathan's mouth. 'I shall touch his mind once more. Virginia will come to him tonight.'

'Always in darkness, my love. Always, always in darkness. Meagre light aids mystery and prevents precise identification. I killed my father in darkness, you know.'

'Yes.' She'd heard the story before, but no matter. Let Jonathan tell it once more. At times he told it so intensely that he frightened her.

Jonathan sat down, his eyes staring at nothing. 'He was a travelling player, merely passing through Rouen on his way to Cherbourg and the ship that would take him from France to his native England. My father. A magician, a sorcerer, a madman. He raped my mother and went away. She was only fifteen.'

He opened the razor, gently laying the flat of the blade against his throat. 'Raped her and went away. I was ten when I finally found him, and he never knew who I was. For three years I travelled Europe with him, learning the black arts from him, finally surpassing him as I was destined to do. It pleased me that he was aware of my knowing more about the world of darkness than did he. My mother. When he, when he . . .'

Jonathan looked at Sarah Clannon. 'He had destroyed her mind, though he never knew it. His pleasure was all that mattered, nothing more. Once we spoke of France and of Rouen and he told me that it was the town in which Joan of Arc was burned at the stake for witchcraft. An illiterate mystic who died for the political ends of men more mad than she could ever have become.

'In my mother's madness, she knew me. Knew me. And she was all I ever loved and I killed my father because of her. In darkness. Killed him in darkness and I never told him that my mother, in her insanity, had also burned to death in Rouen, as had Joan the mystic maid.'

Sarah Clannon took his hands in hers, as he said, 'I have travelled the world over and I have done more than the mind of man can imagine or dread, but I have not shed tears since that dark night when I killed him.'

He held up his hands. 'Not even when these were cut off as offerings.'

She looked at the spaces where his little fingers should have been.

Quickly, he grabbed her wrists, jerking her closer to him. His grip was painful and she was frightened.

'I did not weep for him, you know. I wept for her, for my mother.'

Sarah Clannon nodded.

Jonathan said, 'Evil be thou my good.' His eyes pleaded with her. 'I have nothing else in my life now but evil.'

She took him in her arms. Jonathan her obsession. Jonathan, be thou my good, my all.

She held him close to her and they stayed that way for a time.

# CHAPTER TWENTY-FIVE

'I had intended to contact the police, Mr Figg, regarding your mission here in New York and what occurred at the boarding house last night. But in the light of what I now know, I offer you my apologies for summoning you here this morning and I extend my hand to you, sir. I would feel honoured if you accept it.'

Figg shook hands with Phineas Taylor Barnum, who was dressed in a pale lavender suit, yellow silk waistcoat and brown cravat. The squeaky-voiced showman looked as though he'd selected his wardrobe in the dark with his eyes closed.

'Mr Barnum, sir, I pledge to you that I 'ad nothin' to do with settin' no fire. Ain't never set no fire in me life.'

'I concur, sir. To begin with, two men were seen fleeing the premises shortly after the blaze got under way and there is the matter of the landlady having seen late-night visitors, also two men, walk past her open door and go upstairs. May I add that those Europeans in my employ tell me you are known in England as an honest prizefighter and friend to nobility. I am told that Pierce James Figg stands for respect and fair play, something I admire much in the English.'

Figg, top hat in his hands, looked down at the floor. 'Does me best, sir.'

'Sir, you are too modest, a virtue I do not covet but admire from afar. I seem to remember the other day that you did possess a letter of introduction from Charles Dickens.'

'Yes sir. To Mr Poe.' Little Mr Poe who saved me life. Comes back drunk as a lord, he does, and heaves a washbasin through the windows to give me air to breathe and he slaps me bleedin' face to wake me up. And somehow the little man gets me out of bed and into the bleedin' hallway. Somebody turned on the gas last night. Damn thing was shut off before I closed me eyes. Jonathan. Who else wants to kill me?

Except Figg wasn't so sure it was Jonathan. Jonathan preferred blood sacrifices. Offerings to his demons. But if it wasn't him, then who the bloody hell was it? What's more, Figg's leg ached from being kicked last night by Black Turtle.

Barnum, eyes still on Figg, fingered a new poster on his desk.

He and Figg were in Barnum's office at the American Museum, a room bright with posters from past attractions. People rushed by in the hall and from everywhere Figg heard the sounds of crowds. Not much past eleven in the morning and Mr Barnum's place of business was packed.

'Mr Poe,' said Barnum. 'Is he—'

'Waitin' outside in a cab. A bit under the weather, 'e is.'

'Yes. I understand.'

You sure as bloody hell don't, thought Figg, suddenly feeling defensive about the man who'd saved his life. He ain't drunk. He's sick from two glasses of wine and from seeing people burn to death and from swallowing gas while trying to save my hide.

Figg said, 'Takin' 'im home to Fordham, which 'e's asked me to do. He wants to rest, get some air.' Owe him that much, I do. Who the hell is dear Muddy he keeps on about? He ain't but half alive now, sitting out there wrapped in a blanket I nicked from John Jacob Astor's fine hotel. Mr Astor won't miss it. Mr Bootham says Mr Astor is almost eighty-five years old and dying and so blind that a coloured stands behind his chair and guides the spoon to 'is mouth. What's Mr Astor goin' to do with his twenty million dollars now and him owning half of the land in stinkin' New York City.

'I take it, Mr Figg, that Mr Poe has been of some assistance to you.'

'You might say so, yes.'

'Peculiar man, Mr Poe. Has his problems in getting along with people. One hears stories of his bad temper, constant arguments, his unwillingness to compromise.'

'Probably thinks 'e's correct in some things, sir. Like you do, I would imagine.'

Barnum grinned. 'Point well taken, Mr Figg.'

Figg shifted. He wanted to leave. Get Poe out in the country, then back to New York to continue the hunt. 'Well, Mr Barnum, I won't be takin' up any more of yer time, sir. You must be a most busy man.'

Barnum smiled, picking up the poster from his desk. 'A sensational new act, Mr Figg, and I invite you and Mr Poe to enjoy it as my guests. Ethiopian Delineators, sir. Black minstrels. The most popular entertainment on the modern scene. White men in blackface singing the catchiest of darky tunes and, by God, your toe will be tapping from the moment they strike that first note. These are "The Dixie Melodeers", whom I expect to draw joyous crowds for me, and well they should for what I am paying them.'

Barnum beamed at the poster. 'Banjos twanging, tambourines, the clackety-clack of the bones. Total pleasure, sir. Total pleasure.'

The poster—'The Dixie Melodeers In Melodies For You'— showed drawings of five men in black faces, battered top hats and ragged clothes each one seated and grinning while holding either a banjo, fiddle, tambourine or dry bones. Each man's name was beneath the drawing. Further down was a full-length drawing of each man standing erect, well dressed and minus burnt cork, wigs, rags. Barnum wanted to make sure his audiences knew that the Dixie Melodeers were actually white men.

Barnum said, 'A new composer, Stephen Foster, has written some of the tunes the Dixie Melodeers will perform. Young Foster is a bookkeeper, but I feel he has talent and the ability to capture the true darky spirit. I tell you, Mr Figg, the minstrel show is the American national opera and has many long years ahead of it. I cannot convey to you how heated is the craze for this sort of show at the moment.'

He laid down the poster. 'Well, I am sure you have interests of your own. Do you still seek this Jonathan?'

'I do.'

'Forgive me for ever doubting when you first mentioned him to me. A man such as yourself, sir, the associate of nobles and the great, is a man to be trusted and admired.' Barnum responded to important people and he now considered Figg important.

Figg knew this, but said nothing. The world is full of them what is climbing somewheres and Mr Barnum is a climber of the highest order and easily impressed. Best leave before he wants to hug and kiss me. 'Me and Mr Poe's got to be goin', sir. Thankin' you fer yer kind offer of assistance.'

Barnum hurried from around the desk, taking Figg's hand in both of his. 'Remember, sir, the word of Barnum is money in the bank. Come, let me escort you to the entrance.'

The halls, rooms, exhibits, of the museum were jammed with people. Barnum's appearance drew a rush of attention from patrons and staff members. Figg was pushed, jostled, squashed in the mob. Barnum loved the excitement, greeting all who came near him in his squeaky voice.

Turning to Figg, he said. 'They are pleased with *whatever* I do for them, Mr Figg. Watch this!' Barnum raised his voice. 'Everyone, please listen! Follow me to the Egress! To the Egress!'

Others took up the cry and Figg found himself pushed in the human tide. What the bloody 'ell was a flippin' egress? Figg couldn't do anything but head in that general direction. And then he saw the sign over a door: *To The Egress.*

The crowd pushed harder, faster. Now Figg and Barnum were to one side of the door and the crowd poured through, some of them shouting 'Let us see the egress! The egress!'

When most of the crowd had poured through the door, Barnum closed it signalling a uniformed employee to stand guard and let no one in or out.

Figg frowned. Hell he was this close, why couldn't *he* have seen the damn thing.

Barnum laid a hand on his shoulder. 'An egress, Mr Figg, is an exit, the way out of a building, nothing more. I was faced with having crowds inside, who while they had paid their quarter to enter, were preventing the crowds outside from doing the same. Rather than give up that money waiting for me on the pavement, I devised this scheme to empty my museum, and while it smacks of deceit, I prefer to think of it as charming humbug. People take it in good stride.'

Figg nodded. Right clever bloke, this Barnum. Ain't no egress 'ere 'cept a door what gets you outside.

The showman took him past a lecture hall, called such by Barnum rather than the theatre it actually was. Theatre was thought to be immoral. On stage the Dixie Melodeers, in exaggerated Negro dialect, were singing 'Nigger Put Down Dat Jug' to a huge, delighted audience. Barnum and Figg stopped to listen. Right entertaining, thought Figg. Lively chaps on stage flappin' their arms, liftin' their knees, rollin' their eyes and all that black stuff on their faces. Right pleasant. Figg wished he could stay and see more, but . . .

At the entrance, Barnum, surrounded by patrons, again clasped Figg's hand with his. 'Do return, Mr Figg, and my regards to Mr Poe. Remember, sir, I am your friend.'

Figg smiled. 'Thankin' you, Mr Barnum. Pleased to have seen the egress.'

Barnum grinned.

A bearded man with an eyepatch tugged at Barnum's sleeve. 'Look here, commodore. What is an egress?'

'Egress?' Barnum's squeaky voice carried over the din. 'My friend, do I detect the sad misfortune on your part indicating that you have never viewed the egress?'

The man's jaw dropped.

'Follow me,' said Barnum. 'To the egress it is, sir!'

'Egress, egress.' The cry was taken up and the crowd followed Barnum.

For the first time since arriving in New York several days ago, Figg laughed out loud.


Hugh Larney would lay with her in the coffin. He would carry Dearborn in his arms to this small room on the top floor of his white marble Fifth Avenue mansion, a room far in the back and away from everyone. Not even the servants were allowed inside, and Dearborn had once seen Hugh Larney curse and kick a teenage Irish maid for having entered here. The girl had been driven limping and weeping from the house on the spot, to survive in New York as best she could.

Dearborn, naked and alone in the room, lay in a silver-handled coffin; its white satin was cool against her bare flesh. She shivered and tried to listen to the conversation going on out in the hall. Miles Standish had pounded on the door, demanding that Hugh Larney come out. It was important that they talk immediately. The servants had been unable to prevent Miles Standish from coming upstairs. He'd simply lashed out with his cane until they had stepped aside for him.

Dearborn sat up. Miles was shouting. *'It failed, it failed,'* he said. *'Poe lives.'* Hugh Larney tried to get him to lower his voice but Miles refused. 'Poe lives. His friend lives. The gas did not—'

Silence.

Dearborn sat up in the coffin, looking around at the human skulls on shelves filled with books, at the circle on the floor, a circle of white paint that surrounded the coffin. Mr Larney had a strong interest in the devil, for she'd heard him talk of it to Mr Standish and a few others. Once or twice he'd even spoken of the devil to Dearborn, but there was little she could tell him. She only knew that the devil was bad and would come for her if she did anything wrong. What she did with men was not wrong, for she only did as they ordered her.

She left the coffin and tiptoed to the door, a thin child with golden hair and a face of heartbreaking beauty. The talk was all whispers.

'The gas did not work,' whispered Standish. 'I should not have let you talk me into it.'

'Calm yourself, Miles.'

'Poe must die!'

'Agreed, agreed.'

'We must be direct this time. Nothing subtle. And nothing to link the matter with us.'

'Yes, yes, Miles.'

'You look the fool standing there naked as Adam.'

'You sound the fool. Come away from the door. Is Volney—'

'He is still with us.'

A frightened Dearborn scampered back to the coffin, climbed in and closed her eyes.

She heard the door to the room open.

Larney whispered, 'I gave her wine. She seems to be sound asleep. Exquisite thing, is she not?'

'Yes, yes. Now about Poe—'

'Oh, how your loins do ache for Rachel.'

Larney chuckled softly, closed the door and Dearborn heard the two men move away and down the hall. Poor Mr Poe. He was such a nice man, talking sweetly to her of his mother and of her being an actress. A gentle voice he had and a most pleasing manner. Why did Hugh Larney and the others want to kill him? Well, it was not for Dearborn to worry or question such things, for women and girls were on earth to obey and not to raise their heads or eyes unless a man so beckoned. That is how the world is made.

She yawned. The wine *had* made her sleepy and without Hugh Larney beside her and touching her, she could rest. She drew her knees up to her chin, and shivered and closed her eyes. Seconds later she was asleep.

Glass shattered. A woman screamed. Rachel looked up from the book she was trying to read. Outside in the hallway footsteps hurried past the closed study door. It had just gone noon and Rachel, without an appetite, was alone trying to read without success. Too much on her mind. Doctor Paracelsus and his miracles. Justin. She wore his ring again, the one modelled on that given to Lord Essex by Queen Elizabeth.

And she thought of Eddy. Always Eddy.

'Not up here, she ain't!' A man's gruff voice came from the top of the stairs.

'Then find the bloody bitch you stupid bugger! Find her!' The voice of a man not too far from the study door. Neither man was one of her servants. None of them would talk in such disgusting fashion.

She put the book down on the arm of her chair, crossed the study and opened the door.

Hamlet Sproul looked at her. Spitting tobacco juice on the rug, he brought his right arm up, gigantic bowie knife in his fist, then placed the arm around Rachel's neck, yanking her close to him. She cringed, too paralysed with fear to scream. 'You-you are hurting me!'

'I mean to.' She felt his beard scrape her face and she smelled tobacco and the stink of him and from the corner of her eye she saw the wildness in his bloodshot green eyes.

Sproul whispered. 'You cannot give me back what I have lost, so I take what you have—and that is your life.'

Rachel heard them looting the house, terrorising the servants.

Sproul leaned back his head and shouted, 'I have her! I have her! Let us be gone from here!'

To Rachel, he said, 'Resist and you die here. At best I promise you a little more life, but that is all you shall get from Hamlet Sproul, miss.'

Rachel tried to pull away from him. He slapped her hard, driving her into the wall. Then he shoved her ahead of him and she tripped over a body in her way, falling to the floor. When she pushed herself into a sitting position, her hands were wet and sticky with blood. She screamed and Hamlet Sproul laughed.

'And so it begins, dear lady. But you do not die that easily, not until I have had me time with you. Then death will come as a mercy and you will be grateful for it, I assure you.'

He yanked her to her feet. Throughout the house his men looted swiftly, taking the spoils they had been promised. Sproul had his, now let them get theirs, and then it was back to Five Points where no man dare enter, not the police, not the goddam army. Poe's lady friend would be taken there and never leave—which was her problem. Sproul's men had only the problem of taking as much loot as they could carry.

# CHAPTER TWENTY-SIX

Poe rubbed his unshaven chin. 'The practice of magic, Mr Figg, of sorcery, witchcraft, devil worship and related occult sciences, begins with the caveman. It is as old as time. When dinosaurs roamed the earth and men ate their meat raw, blood red and steaming from the carcasses of beasts no longer present in nature's order, humanity believed in magic, in what has been described as hidden knowledge. You say to me that Jonathan is missing the little fingers on both hands.'

'That 'e is.'

'On the walls of caves in France and Africa have been found imprints of mutilated hands, imprints dating back to the Pleistocene period, a pause between two ice ages.'

'Older than me gran lived to be.'

Poe's smile was weak. 'I dare say. The hands had first been dipped in some coloured substance, then pressed against the cave wall. Joints from fingers, even entire fingers were missing. These mutilations, performed with a stone knife, were offerings to prevent death and keep away evil. We know the truth of this for the custom is still with us in these modern times. Such imprints are to be found in the mosques of Mohammedans in India. The removal of fingers as a method of keeping away both death and disease is also a custom among the Bushman tribes of South Africa, Australia and certain tribes of North American Indians.'

Figg, a half filled bowl of soup in two hands, paused with the bowl in front of his face. 'You sayin' that Jonathan ain't got 'is little fingers 'cause he gave 'em away to some demon?'

'That is correct.'

Mrs Marie Clemm, Poe's mother-in-law, inhaled sharply, eyebrows going up, jaw dropping down. 'Oh my! Eddy, this is unpleasant to hear.'

However, Poe noticed that she made no move to leave the dinner table.

Tonight in Poe cottage there was a guest—Pierce James Figg, who drank his soup from a bowl—and Mrs Clemm wanted to enjoy his company.

'Yes, dear Muddy, most unpleasant.' Poe reached across the

196

table to gently pat her large hand. Dearest Muddy. Now *she* was the mother he needed, the companion and true friend he depended on for sympathy and encouragement. At sixty years old, she was still strong, tall with white hair and a face as plain as unvarnished wood. She wore her one dress, a threadbare, black garment always kept clean and presentable, a minor miracle. It was Poe's shame and disappointment that he was too poor to give her a better life; it was his good fortune that she was loyal to him and believed in his writing ability.

Poe said, 'Please excuse our sad table, Mr Figg. My fortunes are at their usual low ebb and I cannot afford to dine any better than the lowliest immigrant.'

Figg put down his bowl. 'Mr Poe, the worms would be dinin' on me tonight, if you had not saved me life. This 'ere soup and bread tastes just fine, thankin' you much.'

Poe nodded. 'You have performed a similar service for me, sir.' Ironic, he thought, thinking back to the stable where he'd first seen Figg. He'd come down from above, looking more like a gargoyle than an angel, and he delivered me from the hands of mine enemies. Last night, while only a millimetre short of being paralytic drunk, I delivered *him*. And now for the first time since meeting we speak to one another as men, not as antagonist and opponent.

Poe, having saved Figg's life, sensed the boxer's increasing respect for him. No more naked and undisguised contempt between the two men; contempt seemed to have slipped from their manner with almost miraculous ease. Figg, Poe noticed, was independent as opposed to surly, a man lacking pretence and pomposity. The boxer was a man of morals and principles, at home with thieves and kings, yet retaining his own integrity and sense of worth. Figg, like Poe, was his own man.

True, Figg was no formal scholar and if he could read, he undoubtedly did so by moving his lips and drawing his finger slowly across the page. Yet despite remaining areas of disagreement between the two men (there were more than a few), Poe reluctantly admitted to himself—he dared not admit it to others—that he was pleased and gratified by Figg's silent, unspoken respect; this same Figg whom, not too long ago, Poe had considered as monumentally stupid and bordering on the sub-human.

Poe had told Muddy that the gas which had almost killed Figg last night at the Hotel Astor had also made Poe ill to the point of collapse. Neither he nor Figg had added that two glasses of wine prior to inhaling the gas had almost destroyed Poe's ability to think, walk, speak and function in any capacity whatsoever. How he'd managed to save Figg's life eluded him.

Neither gas nor cheap wine were a boost to the health of a man whose thirty-nine years on earth had consisted of bad health in both body and mind, who had been engaged in a lifelong and savage struggle for bread and had thus been doomed to soul-destroying poverty, along with lacerations of the mind, heart and soul. Poe needed a day's rest in his small Fordham cottage, and Figg had taken him there on a train which had sped dangerously across ill-laid tracks, somehow managing to avoid an accident, a miracle considering the poor safety record on nineteenth-century American trains.

Poe had slept, a sleep not entirely free from personal demons but it was badly needed rest, and the smell and taste of gas had eventually left him. At Muddy's insistence, he'd eaten a handful or two of food, not enough to cover his protruding ribs with flesh, but he'd eaten. Then it was sleep once more, and when he'd awakened Figg had been looking down at him; the boxer seemed surprised that Poe was still lingering in this world instead of floating somewhere in the next.

Poe felt he'd be strong enough to return to the city tomorrow, and once again a surprise; Figg had nodded, saying tomorrow was time enough for his own return as well and with Poe's permission he'd be pleased to spend the night in the tiny, heatless cottage. And as Muddy prepared food on a little stove, the two men had quietly talked of their lives, with Figg slowly, carefully, cleaning and reloading his two pistols.

Now over their meagre supper there was conversation, with Poe doing most of the talking. Figg and Mrs Clemm listened intently.

'To understand the tradition of the occult is to understand the mind of Jonathan and those sources upon which he draws his knowledge and strength. Ancient Egyptians, Babylonians, Greeks, Romans, Semite civilisations and those societies of early Europe all had systems of magic as part of their religion and priestcraft. Thus magic was endowed with an official, state-approved status. It is with the advent of Christianity that the attitude towards magic undergoes a change, for the church condemned it, denied it, branded it as being against the spirit of Jesus Christ.

'It is not surprising that this pronouncement in effect created two camps: Christianity on one side, black arts on the other. Magic and sorcery were driven underground where they elevated demons and devils to positions of adoration. If magic was to be in opposition to Mother Church, then it would exist with opposite effects to call its own. So it is here that we get the black mass, the anti-Christ, the bowing down to evil and to forces of destruction.'

Poe closed his eyes, breathing deeply to rid himself of the smell of gas suddenly returning to his nostrils. 'The Church's opposition was in vain, for people had been too long involved with what was now branded pagan rituals or the occult. I submit that with these influences still very much in the world today, it is easy to understand how a man like Jonathan can so deeply submerge himself in such a philosophy. It is all around him.'

Poe smiled at Figg. 'I see a scepticism written upon your face, sir. You doubt my thesis?'

Figg put his soup bowl down on the table. 'Now I knows you to be a right bright agent, I do, so I say maybe you knows what yer goin' on about. But I wonder how much you can really tell me about Jonathan, what with yer never havin' met 'im and all. I sees him once or twice, real quick like and then 'e's gone like smoke blown before the wind. Understand I am a guest in yer home and I listens politely, but—'

'Oh Mr Figg,' Mrs Clemm reached over to touch his arm. 'Eddy is most astute and possessed of deductive powers unequalled by anyone.'

'Yes, mum.' Figg wasn't going to argue with the old lady. Not in her house, such as it was. Not much of a cottage, with three little rooms on the ground floor and upstairs an attic divided into two rooms not much bigger than closets. Wasn't much furniture about but the place was as neat as a pin, with floors scrubbed white as new flour. Not a bit of heat, though.

Figg was staying tonight because he wanted to make sure little Mr Poe was alive and kicking. He was owed that much. Couldn't stop Poe from talking, though to be fair he did talk pretty good, almost as good as Mr Dickens.

Convinced of his superiority, Poe rarely ignored an opportunity to convince others. Now he swelled with pride, grey eyes boring into Figg.

'It was in Philadelphia some eight years ago. I edited a magazine for William Burton, though I was given neither credit nor responsibility as editor, and in the end Burton and I quarrelled, but no matter. It was here that I issued a challenge to the reading public: to send me cryptograms—coded epigrams—in French, Italian, Spanish, German, Latin, Greek, and I would solve them. I received one hundred replies in these languages and I solved ninety-nine of them. Ninety-nine, Mr Figg. The hundredth was inaccurate to begin with, thus a false challenge and so I discarded it.

'Now, on to more serious challenges met and accomplished. A little over six years ago, there was a murder in this fair city of most interesting proportions. A beautiful and graceful girl, Mary Cecilia Rogers, who toiled as a tobacconist at the Hotel Astor, was murdered and the newspapers blazoned the story day after day. This foul deed attracted the interest of everyone, for Mary was known throughout the city for her beauty and many a man had tried his charm upon her. I used only the information available to me in the newspapers and with that and only that, I wrote a work of fiction, of make-believe, changing names but solving the murder, Mr Figg. Solving the murder.'

'Months after my story, "The Mystery of Marie Rorget", was published, the actual murder was solved. Those confessing to it were the people I had fictionally described, and they had done this deed in those ways I had indicated. I have written other such tales of detection and, for all of the praise given me as the inventor of deductive policemen, I have yet to prosper from this genre. I, the father of detective stories, have apparently suffered one more literary stillbirth. Yes, Mr Figg, I know whereof I reason. It may appear guesswork, but it is not, sir. My mind never guesses, it only reasons. I serve logic, sir, not the whims of prevailing fashions no matter how acceptable they may be to the world around me. I serve truth with reckless abandon and such truthfulness, sir, has cost me acceptance, prosperity and I fear some portion of my sanity.'

Figg nodded, impressed but still watchful. Poe didn't work hard at being likeable, but he wasn't a dull lot and he had saved Figg's life.

Poe sank back in his chair, eyes on a spoon he rolled between thumb and forefinger. 'Some say magic is superstition, the god of savages, a hidden force beyond the limits of those few exact sciences we now toy with and call ourselves informed. Magic and sorcery touch on philosophy, religion and much that is taboo, and its believers talk of its hidden wisdom.'

Poe dropped the spoon. 'I too consider the existence of more things than we now know but I am concerned with the imagination, with the depths of the mind, with examining the fullest extent of the human spirit. Though my way sometimes seems dark, it is destructive only to me if to anyone, for I have lived with the demons of suffering and frustration found in this world and in desperation I turned inward, exploring, ever exploring. For someone like me there is no remaining challenge in a world such as this save that to be found in the world of the imagination. In this particular world, I find my own magic. In the world within, I rely on ... I am not yet sure what I rely on. I live from hour to hour and I hope that I do not go insane.'

Reaching to touch his hand, Mrs Clemm said softly, 'Oh, dearest Eddy—'

In silent gratitude he smiled sadly at her.

Poe turned to Figg, 'You have mentioned that Jonathan fears you, a fact told to you by the assassins who attacked you in London.'

'That is correct.'

'Has it occurred to you, Mr Figg, that Jonathan sees in you a primitive force perhaps equal to or surpassing his own?'

'I don't see how, Mr Poe. I ain't but a normal man. Nothin' special 'bout me, 'ceptin' I plan to kill Jonathan. Beggin' your pardon, missus.'

Mrs Clemm nodded, fascinated at hearing one man actually say he planned to kill another. But this Jonathan had tried to harm her Eddy, so he must be detestable. Let Mr Figg indeed take Mr Jonathan's life.

'Mr Figg,' said Poe, 'I assume you know nothing of witchcraft.'

' 'Ere now, what do you take me for? I ain't no witch.'

'And yet I heard you make a reference to "scoring above the breath", did I not?'

'Me wife Althea said that. She 'eard it from Jonathan, but yeah, I know what it means. Every Englishman knows that it means you kill a witch by slicing her 'cross the forehead, by spillin' her blood above her nose. 'Er power is in 'er blood. That's the way to do 'er.'

'Did I not see you eat a hard-boiled egg, then turn the shell upside down?'

'Every child in England does it. Keeps witches away. Just a habit, that's all. Did it without thinkin'. You sayin' I'm some kinda demon meself?'

'No, Mr Figg. I am saying you and others know more about the black arts than you are aware of, and perhaps you, in other lives, in another existence—'

Figg smiled, waving Poe away. 'Go on, now, squire. I ain't been alive but once. This 'ere life is it. I knows that much, I do.'

'I will not press the question, sir. I merely state that you could be more of a supernatural force than you recognise, and Jonathan, having trained his intelligence along certain lines, can see things in you that no one else does. It is a fact, Mr Figg, that your English ancestors, the Celts, the Angles, the Saxons, yes even that most dangerous priesthood the Druids, worshipped strange gods and conceived peculiar rituals, many of which still exist throughout England today. Is it not possible that some of these ancient forces, in a benign, decent way, are manifest in you?'

Figg chuckled. 'You likes to carry on, squire. Now you have 'ad your little joke—'

'Mr Figg, tell me of the legend of the magpie as it is believed in the British Isles.'

Figg frowned. 'I knows you spent some time in England but—'

'Please tell me.'

'Well, as lads we was told that the magpie did not mourn properly when Christ he was on the cross, so we look on it as an evil bird and it is supposed to carry a drop of the devil's blood under its tongue.'

'And is it not traditional that English lads still hunt and kill the wren, the king of birds, and on December 26, which is called Boxing Day in your country, is it not traditional for the boys to carry the dead bodies of freshly murdered wrens from house to house, collecting coins?'

Figg nodded grimly.

'Mr Figg, is it not true that in England people refuse to talk near cats, believing cats to be witches in disguise, and thus it is feared that witches, through cats, will learn your secrets? Do you believe this to be true?'

Figg shrugged, admitting nothing. He wondered if Poe was making fun of him, trying to show him as a stupid man filled with superstitions. He decided no, Poe wasn't doing that. There was no venom in the writer's voice, no poison in his tone.

Figg said, 'Hares are supposed to turn themselves into witches, too. And we was told that dogs can see ghosts, but nobody really takes that twaddle seriously. Leastwise I don't.'

'But you are aware of it, Mr Figg, and of more as well. Have you not heard, for example, that the Celts believe the souls of the dead travel on horse to that land where the dead go and do not return, and that witches in England are still said to "hag ride" a horse during the night, bringing him back to his owner at dawn sweated and exhausted.'

Figg nodded. 'As boys we 'eard it, but I ain't never seen it.'

Poe's voice was very soft. 'Jonathan fears you, Mr Figg. Whatever the forces within you, he fears you, and that places you in mortal danger. Jonathan follows "the left-handed path", for such is the name given to black magic.'

Figg looked into his empty coffee cup. 'You claims to be a logical man, a man what thinks and who don't believe in such things as spiritualism and the black arts.'

'Ah Mr Figg, but I do. I believe in such thoughts for those who believe in such thoughts. If a man believes that eating mud will give him a presentable face and an extra toe on each foot, it is entirely possible that he will indeed become more presentable and have twelve toes, but it is for *him* that such a thing is possible. My belief is limited to that of an observer. I feel that such an outlook is functional for those with such faith and such needs. I do not believe, Mr Figg. Others do, and let them. I remain unconvinced, though my mind will deal with it as a matter of scholarship, nothing else.'

'Tell you the truth, Mr Poe, I have me own thoughts. I don't want to believe in such things but Jonathan ain't normal. 'E's got somethin' beyond . . . well all I can say is so long as I keep on hatin' 'im I have the backbone to seek 'im out. I jes' want to complete me business with 'im before I gets to fearin' 'im more than I do. And, between you and me, I fears 'im a little.'

'Mr Figg, whether or not I believe in a thing has little to do with its existence, for truth is that which is true under all circumstances. Truth is that which does not take into consideration the opinions of anyone. In performing necromancy, Jonathan must deal with the dead and he must control them, bringing them from beyond in spite of their wish to remain there. He has offended Asmodeus, King of Demons, or he feels he has, and so he kills to stay alive. He sacrifices his own flesh, his little fingers, to stay alive. Jonathan will call on powerful spirits to aid him, any and all of which could destroy him if the ritual is performed incorrectly. I say this to you, Mr Figg: should you come upon Jonathan during this ritual, it is possible that you, sir, will suffer grievous injury of some kind. Kill him, yes, but *before* he begins the ceremony. *Before*.'

Figg said, 'You claim it takes nine days to perform, once he gets the body.'

' *"The dead rise and come to me"* begins the ceremony which is performed at night, always at night and in such places as a graveyard, a forest, a crossroads, a crypt. There are circles of power drawn on the ground and he must remain in them, for this is a terribly dangerous ceremony. And there is the danger, real or imagined of Asmodeus. Jonathan will cut himself off from the world for nine days. He will dress in a shroud, sleep by day and move by night. He will eat only at midnight and then it will be the flesh of dogs, unfermented wine and unleavened bread, these last two foods lacking life. The dog serves Hecate, goddess of death.'

Figg sighed. 'So we must find Jonathan before the ceremony.'

Poe nodded. 'Before the ceremony, certainly before the ninth day, for by then he will charge and command the spirit of the dead to come forth. He will offer worship to all four points of the compass, ending with the north. Only one group of people in the world venerate the north as a holy point: the dreaded Yezidi of south Asia, who worship the devil in all his evil. Most of humanity regards the north as black, the home of Satan, the abode of freezing wind and death.'

Poe rubbed the back of his neck, then scratched his high, wide forehead. 'Christians have long feared the north, reserving the north side of a churchyard for suicides, those unfortunates who cannot be buried in consecrated ground. Though I do not directly concern myself with these matters, save on the printed page, I tell you, Mr Figg, that Jonathan has such faith in what he pursues that he is capable of unleashing a horror which could bring down a hell upon us all. Kill him swiftly, for all our sakes.'

Figg said, 'If I do not claim his life, Mr Poe, it will be because he has first succeeded in claiming mine. Is there more you can detect about Jonathan and his business?'

'Yes. He is European. The cult worship of Asmodeus has existed in that section of the world for years, even among members of royal houses. He is obviously a scholar, for merely to familiarise himself with occult writings requires intelligence, possibly linguistic abilities since many of the books and scrolls are written in Latin, Hebrew, Greek, old French and old German. And, as we have learned by his use of Althea and her father, he is careful to seek help if something is obscure. He is young, physically strong, and trained in medicine—for he is able to remove body organs under primitive conditions and apparently fairly quickly.'

Poe looked up at the ceiling. 'He is travelled; his association with the Renaissance Players indicates the need for a passport to get him easily from one country to another. Since I claim he is also Paracelsus, I submit Jonathan is an actor, skilled in stage technique and make-up. He is meticulous, thorough. This can be seen in how much he knows about the lives of those who seek him out as spiritualist. To deceive them, he must know everything about them, so our Jonathan is a planner, a schemer, a man who looks ahead, who is able to convince one man to betray another by fair means or foul. He must be capable of inspiring some degree of loyalty, for it is not possible to purchase the hearts and minds of everyone in the universe.

'Jonathan is vengeful, unforgiving. Witness the death of Sproul's associates. I sense in him a strong ego, a love of power, the strong need to dominate, to have all bow to his will without question. He sees himself the equal of the gods, for he has challenged Asmodeus as evidenced by that barbaric ritual involving the slaughter of several people. He will stop at nothing to get what he wants, and there are no barriers to his evil. Witness, Mr Figg, what he did to your wife. Jonathan defies God and Satan and he wants to rank beside them, never beneath them. He dreams grand dreams, does Jonathan, and he undoubtedly is the most intelligent, determined and deadly individual any of us have ever encountered.'

Poe leaned across the table. 'And, Mr Figg, *he* did not attempt to kill you last night.'

'Go on now, you bloomin' well know he did. Who else wants me under the earth save 'im?'

'Jonathan lives in darkness, Mr Figg. His awareness of the Throne of Solomon and his single-mindedness in pursuing it, indicates a deep and abiding interest in magic. His slaying of your wife, his slaying of Sproul's cohorts, his attempts at clouding my mind—all of these things were committed by a magician, a sorcerer. By comparison, the attempt at destroying you with gas seems crude, unimaginative, hasty and above all, absent from the realm of the supernatural. Even his bringing a painting to life at the home of Miles Standish—'

Poe stopped. He frowned. 'Miles Standish. Miles Standish.' He looked at Figg, then smiled quickly. 'Well sir, let us talk of lighter things for my Muddy is sitting between us stunned and made silent by these sombre matters.'

She playfully slapped his hand. 'Oh Eddy, do not make me out to be such a fossil.'

Figg wanted to ask more questions, but no sense in pushing Poe. Later he would get dear Eddy to talk some more. Did Poe believe Miles Standish to be behind that business with the gas? Well, no more talk of killing; ain't the business of a man to speak these things in front of a woman.

Figg grinned. 'Riddle me, riddle me ree.'

'Oh Eddy, a riddle. I do so love them.' Mrs Clemm's plain face broke out in a smile as she clapped her hands.

Poe smiled as Figg's husky voice assumed the singsong rhythm of a child's verse. 'Little Nancy Etticoat/With a white petticoat/and a red nose/She has no feet or hands/the longer she stands/the shorter she grows.'

Poe was quick. 'A candle.'

'Right you are, squire. Now try this 'ere one. A house full, a hole full/You cannot gather a bowlful.'

Poe closed his eyes, then opened them. 'Smoke. Perhaps, perhaps mist.'

All three laughed.

Figg tried several more and no matter how obscure they were, Poe guessed them all. The silliness of the game delighted him more than anything had in a long time. Muddy was pleased and if Poe had not brought her money or food this time, he'd brought her the surprising Pierce James Figg, pugilist and reciter of English children's riddles.

And, for a short time, that was something for both of them to be warmed by in an existence where there was so little to be warmed by.


Upstairs, Mrs Clemm stood in the tiny, cold attic room where Figg was to spend the night. The cold numbed his fingers, toes, and he'd have to sleep with his clothes and boots on.

The yellow stub of a candle in her long fingers was the only light. 'We have straw for you, Mr Figg and I shall bring you the blanket from my room.'

'No, mum. Ain't takin' a blanket away from no lady, thankin' you muchly just the same. Straw is fine, for I was born on it and it's been me bed more than once in me life.'

'You are our guest, sir. I can do no less than give you—'

'No, mum. Now if you go and do such a thing, bring me *your* blanket I mean, then I will just wait until you fall asleep, and come into your room and cover you. It ain't correct for a gentleman to enter a lady's chamber in such fashion, so do not place me in such a predicament.'

Lord help us, he thought. If I was to go in for a bit of night crawlin', with all due respect Mrs Clemm wouldn't be what I'd care to see at the end of me creepin'.

She blushed. 'I appreciate your good manners, Mr Figg. Now allow me to give you all of the disturbing news at once. Eddy is downstairs attempting to write, so I am unable to leave you with even this small bit of candle. We cannot afford to purchase even the cheapest tallow. What light we have is necessary for his work. I—' She was too embarrassed to speak.

Figg said, 'Mum, seein' as how I shall be lyin' 'ere with me eyes shut tight, a candle does not appear to be needed.'

'Thank you, Mr Figg. Eddy has not been in good health of late and since the death one year ago of my daughter, his wife, he has written little. Two poems and a book review, plus what journalistic work he can obtain at only pennies a page. So whenever he feels the urge to write, I must encourage him. It is no secret that he is perhaps in the twilight of his life, though I hope and pray with all my heart that this is not so. Well, Mr Figg, I bid you good ni—'

'Noooooooooo! Do not do this, I beg you!'

Poe. From downstairs where he was writing.

Quickly Figg found his flat, black wooden case and grabbed the two pistols. Pushing his way past Mrs Clemm, he limped forward into darkness as fast as he could, stumbling down the stairs, pistols held high.

Behind him, Mrs Clemm shouted, 'Eddy! Eddy!'


Poe and Figg stood side by side on the cottage porch, looking into the night. Then Poe pointed. 'There! Near the trees! There! I heard her call to me and she said she was Virginia, but I know this to be false!'

Figg saw her in the moonlight, a cloaked figure running across the snow, towards trees leading down to the road. Jonathan's wench. The one Poe said tried to drive him batty.

Figg leaped from the porch, landing in snow. He ran. The figure ahead of him would reach the trees soon. Jonathan's wench. Figg stopped and fired. The flintlock cracked once, sending a small puff of smoke from its chamber, the shot echoing across the countryside.

The figure disappeared into the trees.

Figg and Poe gave chase in the snow. In front of the trees, Poe dropped to one knee. 'Blood on the snow, Mr Figg. That is how they deceived me the last time. False blood. Mr Figg? Mr Figg?'

'Over 'ere, squire.'

Poe ran to him. Just inside the grove of trees, Figg held a woman's cloak that had caught on to a snow-covered bush. He fingered a hole in the back made by the flintlock's ball. There was dampness around the small hole.

'No deceivin' this time, squire. Whoever the lady is, she's got a ball in her. Come, let us see if we can find a trace of her.'

Figg looked up at the sky. 'Moon's full. We 'ave the light.' He limped forward in a crouch, eyes on the snow, the cloak over his shoulder. The empty flintlock was jammed down into his belt. The other was in his hand and if he had to use it on the woman again, so be it. She was Jonathan's wench and Figg would kill her as easily as he sipped ale.

In the cold, moonlit night he and Poe kept their eyes down and looked for blood in the soft, beautiful snow.

# CHAPTER TWENTY-SEVEN

'Hugh Larney, do not turn around. Stay as you are.'

The soft voice was Jonathan's and it came from behind Larney. The food merchant's blood turned cold; he held his breath. Jonathan had managed to enter Larney's home unseen and was now upstairs in the special room, the room with the silver-handled coffin and the books on black magic and witchcraft. A servant had reported the door to the room slightly ajar and a fire burning in the fireplace. An enraged Larney had rushed upstairs, a poker in his hand.

Jonathan.

Larney's hands shook; he dropped the poker.

'Listen, and listen well. I said do not turn around. The sight of your stupid face might force me to kill you here. Last night you and Miles attempted to murder Poe against my orders. Why?'

'M-Miles said you wanted him dead.'

'Miles lied. And you believed him.'

'He said—said you wanted Poe dead and yes, yes I believed him.'

'Miles does not think, he reacts. And I shall kill him for it.'

Larney throught he heard a cat meow. Or, in his fear, had he imagined it? A cat?

'Jonathan, I would not—'

'But you have. You, Miles and Volney Gunning. What shall I do with the three of you, Hugh? Tell me. I have already told you what I intend to do with Miles.'

A cat meowed again. Larney wanted to turn around; he wanted to run. But he wanted to live and so he did nothing. 'Jonathan, I have—have to tell you something.'

'You, Miles and Volney have mounted one more attack on the life of Poe.'

'Ye-yes.'

'Your intelligence is transparent. Do you wish to die?'

'N-no. Oh please, oh—'

'You can buy your life.'

'I will give you anything, anything.'

'You cannot buy it with money. You can buy it with blood, both you and Volney must purchase your lives in blood.'

'We shall, we will.'

'You both are to kill Miles Standish. First let me say if your second attack on Poe's life succeeds, all three of you will die by my hand and most painfully. Should Poe survive this attack, leave him alone until I tell you differently.'

'Yes. I understand.'

'I knew you would. Again, you and Volney Gunning are to kill Miles Standish.'

'W-when?'

'As soon as it can be arranged, and Larney—'

'Yes, Jonathan?'

'Succeed in this task.'

'I shall, Jonathan. I shall. You have my word—'

Larney heard the cat meow again, heard the movement of Jonathan's arm as he brought the small piece of metal down against the back of Larney's head.

The blow was painful, but not hard. It wasn't meant to be. Larney dropped to the floor on his knees and hands. Blackness squeezed his brain, then released it and he shook his head to clear it, forcing his eyes open, forcing them to focus.

The shrieking came from the fireplace and it was horrible, shredding Larney's nerves, shocking him into full awakeness. Jonathan had tossed a sack of live cats into the fireplace and now the sack jerked, twisted and took on a terrified life of its own as the burning cats struggled to get out.

*Jonathan's warning. A hellish ritual from a time long forgotten.*

The cats howled and their cries pierced Larney's brain like shards of cold steel. Still on his knees, he closed his eyes, hands over his ears to drown out the sound of the burning cats. Now the smell of the tortured animals reached his nose and Larney screamed.

Servants pounded on the locked door and still Larney screamed.

Later, when he had left the room, he asked the servants if they had seen anyone in the house who didn't belong there. A frightened Larney was not surprised when they told him *no*, no one had entered or left the house for the past few hours.

With Jonathan's threat very much on his mind and the sound and smell of the burning cats still with him, Hugh Larney quickly left his home to seek out Volney Gunning. Miles Standish would die before the setting of the sun.

# CHAPTER TWENTY-EIGHT

Figg pushed the last of his custard and hard-boiled egg into his mouth, chewing while staring through the window of the speeding train at the snow-covered ground and trees. The train was carrying him and Poe from Fordham back to New York. 'This 'ere thing moves right along. Ain't no trains in England what speeds like this one.'

Poe, seated across from him, nibbled on a slice of ham. 'A speeding train, such as this one, is a dangerous business, sir.'

'It's *what*?'

'An American train, Mr Figg, is as poorly constructed as the track upon which it rolls. Curves are sharp, grades steep and the consideration given to passenger safety can best be described as fleeting. America is being speedily erected. It rises overnight from a wilderness, and under such circumstances there is little time to waste upon being precise. Our Republic worships the obsolete; it builds nothing that will last, and it seems the citizenry, in its blissful ignorance, prefers this state of affairs. American trains undergo accidents at an astounding rate, a brutal truth we accept as we do political promises and heavy-handed dentists. Unpleasantries to be endured and survived, the process to be repeated much too frequently.'

Figg grunted. 'Nothin' built to last, you say.'

Poe nodded.

'Then why build a bloody thing at all? I mean in your New York you have people buildin' one thing or another everywhere you turn. A man cannot stroll about your fair city without he gets the dust of cement and plaster in 'is nostrils.'

Poe fingered the woman's cloak found last night near his cottage. It lay across his knees warming him. 'We call that the spirit of "go-ahead", Mr Figg. The "go-aheads" tear down the beautiful old Dutch housing and churches of this city, to replace them with the ugly, cramped wooden tenements needed to house a growing immigrant population, that welcomed source of cheap labour for a growing nation. New York feeds on progress. Mr Figg, and progress feeds on destruction.'

Poe's finger found the hole in the cloak made by the ball from

Figg's flintlock. ' "Go-ahead". "Self-improvement". These words sound better than greed. Well, let us trust to the almighty that we reach New York without mishap, where we shall continue our search for Hamlet Sproul.'

Figg patted the flat, black wooden box on the seat next to him, the box that held his two flintlocks. 'And we has a chat with Miles Standish, for if 'e's the one what turned on the gas, I would like to know why. If 'e ain't, it's time he led us to Jonathan.'

He looked at the unfinished piece of ham Poe held in his lap. ' 'Ere now, if you ain't gonna eat the rest of that, give it 'ere. Leastwise we eat on yer American trains. Fella what comes up and down the aisle has enough food on 'im to feed a bleedin' army.'

Poe blinked at the noon sun, then closed his eyes against the glare.

'Have you noticed something, Mr Figg?'

'Noticed that ham you ain't eatin'.'

Poe smiled and handed it to him. 'Look around you.'

Figg did so, fingers of one hand pushing the ham into his mouth. Nothing much to see. A long, empty train car with seats covered in faded brown leather. Floors stained by tobacco juice. Heavy oil lamps on the walls above every two seats.

Figg spoke with a mouth full of ham. 'Nothin' much to notice, squire.'

'Precisely,' said Poe. He leaned forward until his knees almost touched Figg's knees. 'Nothing to notice. This car is empty, Mr Figg, save for you and me.'

'What is so out of the way about that?'

'Why should two passengers be blessed with a separate car? Mr Figg, we have made three stops, taking on passengers at each station, and no one has entered this car. Twice I have noticed passengers attempting to enter what seems to have become our private domain and twice the conductor has prevented them from doing so. The rear door'—Poe pointed—'is locked, for persons have attempted to enter it without success. It *is* the custom, yes, to have separate cars on American trains.'

Poe leaned closer. 'There is a separate car for Negroes, there is one for women and one for men. But I have never heard of such a distinction being accorded a poet and a pugilist.'

Poe watched Figg's bulldog face knot with the effort of sudden thought. 'You are sayin', squire, that all is not correct on our journey.'

At the far end of the car, the door opened and slammed shut loudly. Both men stood up, looked and saw nothing. They sat down. Poe's grey eyes were almost closed. 'Odd,' he whispered, fingering the cloak on his lap. 'A locked door slams shut. Yet apparently no one enters or leaves. Odd.'

Figg started to say something and Poe hushed him. 'Shhhhh, Silence, Mr Figg.'

' 'Ere now, ain't nobody in 'ere but you and me.'

Poe's whisper was barely audible. 'That is the question. *Are* we alone—'

*The assassins struck.*

Screaming, they leaped over the seats at Poe and Figg, two men dressed in the ragged clothes, burnt-cork make-up and woolly wigs of black minstrels. Each assassin carried a straight razor. At the front end of the coach, the door crashed open and a third razor-carrying minstrel ran down the aisle towards them.

Figg leaped from his seat, arms extended to grab the head of the minstrel nearest him and with both hands behind the man's neck, Figg pulled with all his strength. The minstrel's face smashed into the boxer's shaven skull. *The Liverpool Kiss:* a fighting technique named for that English port city where those who entered its waterfront taverns left as either the lucky or the dead.

No time for Figg to open his black wooden box, to remove and cock a flintlock. Poe was down in the aisle, both hands pushing the woman's cloak at the minstrel who slashed it once, twice, the razor glittering in the sun. Figg knew little Poe wouldn't last very long flat on his back, what with another blackie running up the aisle with all the speed God gave him.

In one motion, Figg's hands gripped the wooden box and swung it from the seat into the minstrel's face, driving him back, down, away from Poe. The box flew from Figg's grip. Damn it to bloody hell!

Now the man Figg had hit with the box blocked the aisle on his hands and knees, delaying the third man. Delaying, but not stopping him. He leaped over his fallen comrade and Figg backed away, swaying on the speeding train, seeing Poe crawl between the seats and disappear. Two down, one more to go.

Figg continued backing away, fingers tearing at the buttons of his frock-coat and vest. He felt his belt buckle.

The third minstrel slashed at the boxer, who leaned back out of reach as the train took a sharp curve. Both men tumbled into the seats. Figg hit the floor, down between seats, smelling tobacco juice

213

and urine, hearing the speeding wheels beneath him. The knife was in his hand and the roar of the rushing train filled his ears. He looked out into the aisle. Goddam Ethiopian was looking down at him, razor held high and ready to come down and draw blood.

Figg kicked out hard, driving the heel of his boot into the minstrel's ankle. For you, blackie. Enjoy it.

The minstrel hopped back, teeth clenched against the pain, his black woolly wig now lopsided on his head. In the sun his real hair was bright red and there was white skin visible at the top of his blackened forehead.

Now he and Figg faced each other in the aisle, both men crouched, swaying with the motion of the train. Figg's frock-coat dangled from his left forearm like a bullfighter's cape, hiding his right hand which held the small belt knife. *Closer, me darling, and we will 'ave our little dance, you and I.*

Figg shuffled forward in small steps. Wouldn't do to trip up now. The minstrel stayed in place. He was young, aggressive, and the old man in front of him had got lucky with that kick. Just lucky. The ministrel attacked, slashing shoulder level with the razor, then back-handing the weapon at Figg's face in almost the same motion. The train jerked, slowed, jerked, and the minstrel, leaning forward with his attack, was thrown off balance. He fell face down into the aisle.

Figg, falling backwards, grabbed for the edge of a seat with his coat-wrapped left hand. Got it! He gripped the seat edge, keeping his balance.

The minstrel was on his hands and knees when Figg kicked him in the head, sending him flying backwards, and then Figg was on the ministrel, coat pressed down on his face, knee down on his razor arm and digging into the bicep. The knife stroke that cut the minstrel's throat was smooth, deep; his feet jerked, his left hand came up to push Figg off, then it flopped back to the floor.

Crawling over the dead body, Figg grabbed the edge of a seat to pull himself to this feet.

*Jesus wept!*

Poe was almost done for. In front of Figg, the minstrel he'd hit with his pistol box was edging towards Poe who backed away along the aisle, arms outstretched. Where the bloody hell *was* Figg's pistol box?

The speeding train rocked from side to side and Figg fought for his balance. No gun. Damn it all to hell. And the tiny knife lacked the balance for throwing. Too small, too light in the blade and handle. It was for close work and, besides, who could throw anything on a train that moved like the engineer was in a hurry to get us all to hell in time for the devil's supper.

Nothing to do but have a go. Figg charged down the aisle, wrapping his arms around the minstrel, pinning the man's arms to his side, lifting him from the aisle. Then Figg slipped a hand between the man's legs and the minstrel was overhead, squirming in panic.

Figg heaved him through a train window. The sound of shattering glass swallowed the minstrel's screaming. Figg had only seconds to see the man disappear into a snow bank while the train sped on.

The boxer collapsed into a seat, chest heaving, eyes on the groaning minstrel he'd butted with his head. This one lay back on a seat, arm and leg dangling over the side, mouth opened because he couldn't breathe through his crushed, bleeding nose.

Figg glanced at Poe who stood trembling in the aisle, clinging to a seat.

Figg snorted. 'Thought these 'ere blackfaced blokes was only supposed to sing and dance.'

Poe closed his eyes and waited for his nerves to calm down.

'Mr Poe? Mr Poe?'

He opened his eyes.

'Yer about to tear off a hunk of that nice seat cover. Yer knuckles is white.'

Quickly Poe released his grip on the seat. Violence. It drew him as a bird was drawn to a hypnotising snake. But his love of it was disgusting. Why did he love it so? And there was the exhilaration of it, surpassing that of drugs and Poe had tried mind expanding substances on more than one occasion, suffering depressions at the conclusion of such an indulgence.

He'd wanted to embrace death, to end this life, but that was in the past. Now there was Rachel. His reason to live.

Figg was on his feet staring at him. Poe looked as though he was about to cough up all his insides. Got to get him talking, get him moving about.

'Jonathan ain't the kind to give up, it seems.'

Poe shoved his trembling fists into the pockets of his overcoat, 'Speak to the man lying there. That one in the aisle, he is—'

'No sense talkin' to 'em. 'E ain't got much to say.'

Figg looked down at the groaning minstrel now trying to sit up from the seat. Blood mingled with the burnt cork on the man's face and the sight was not a pleasant one even to Figg, who had seen more than his share of gore. 'Who sent you, mate?'

Behind Figg, Poe said, 'The attack lacks Jonathan's sorcery. These were paid hooligans, hired takers of life.'

Figg kicked the minstrel in the leg. The man flinched with pain and tried to back away in the seat. 'I says to you, mate, who's yer keeper? Who called the tune for this little dance?'

Figg slipped into the seat opposite the frightened man. 'Yer two friends is no longer with us. I can arrange for you to join them, if you wish.'

'M-Miles Standish. Hugh-Hugh Larney and Volney Gunning.'

Figg looked up at Poe, who nodded.

Poe said, 'Rachel could have told them where we were. We must find the conductor, the bearded gentleman with the nervous twitch. He is somehow involved, for he is the one who prevented others from entering this car.'

'After that,' said Figg, 'it's me for Miles Standish and his fop friend, Mr Larney. If they have any connection with Jonathan, I am all for beatin' Jonathan's whereabouts out of 'em.'

Poe nodded, chewing a corner of his mouth. 'I fear for the safety of Mrs Coltman. Events are moving swiftly and it is possible she is caught in this most treacherous current. When we reach New York, you seek out Miles Standish at his office and I shall go to the home of Mrs Coltman. If she is well, I shall join you at the home of Miles Standish as quickly as possible.'

Figg grunted, getting up from his seat and walking back down the aisle to the body of the man whose throat he'd cut. After looking down at it for several seconds, Figg stepped between the seats and opened a window. Returning to the body, he folded his frockcoat into a crude pillow, placed it beneath the dead man's head, then suddenly drew it away, letting the man's head fall sharply to the floor.

Gently touching the dead man's forehead, Figg stared at him for a few more seconds, then stood up. When he saw that Poe had been watching him, he blushed as though embarrassed. Wiping the tiny knife on the dead man's chest, Figg then stuck it back into his belt. 'Let us be gettin' on to look for that conductor, Mr Poe.'

He pushed past Poe, found his flat wooden box, then reached up into an overhead luggage rack for his carpetbag. Without a further word, the boxer limped up the aisle, his broad back to Poe who silently watched Figg walk away from him.

Figg is an extension of the ancient tribes, thought Poe. The rituals still live within him and customs lie deep within the recesses of his mind, and he knows nothing of how they came to be there.

Pierce James Figg. He opens the window in order that the soul of the dead man can easily depart. He makes simple the soul's departure by *Drawing the Pillow*, using his own coat and he *Touches the Dead* in a most respectful manner, to show that there is naught but harmony between the two of them.

His face reddens with shame at having me see him do these things, for he does not like to be reminded of what he and Jonathan share, what all mankind shares, for we here on earth are unified in more things than we choose to believe.

Poe followed Figg down the aisle and into the next car.

# CHAPTER TWENTY-NINE

Jonathan's fingers trembled with excitement, making it difficult for him to strap the scalpel to his left wrist. *The Throne of Solomon.* Within days it could be his. *Days.*

'Sproul has Mrs Coltman in the Old Brewery. Yes it is a fortress against the outside world, but Sproul is not secure from me. I shall enter the Old Brewery and kill him.'

He held out his right wrist so that Laertes could strap a second scalpel there. Laertes said, 'And you believe the body of Justin Coltman is there?'

Jonathan's eyes were bright. 'Yes. Sproul is where he feels totally safe. He is grief-stricken and his thinking has become more accessible to me, more predictable, though I did not forsee him revenging himself upon Poe, particularly in this manner. And note Poe's penchant for survival. In tandem he and Figg removed the cross-eyed Johnnie Bill Baker from this vale of tears. Our Sproul is making a final stand of sorts, therefore all that he considers dear or valuable must be near him. The body of Justin Coltman is not far from Hamlet Sproul. I shall have Sproul and he shall tell me the location of Mr Coltman's current resting place.'

Laertes said, 'It is a shame about Mrs Coltman. Even the police cannot help her.'

Jonathan sat down, extending a leg so that Laertes could pull a boot on it. The hunt was almost over and all that he had ever dreamed of was almost within his grasp. First Sproul, then the corpse of Justin Coltman. And the Throne of Solomon. He closed his eyes, dizzy with the thought of it all.

'Servants have described the Irish looters to the police, and it is a dolt who does not know where Irish thugs run to ground. The constabulary has detected her whereabouts as being in Five Points, but it has not pinpointed her as being in the Old Brewery. The police, as usual, will refuse to enter that building under any circumstances, preferring to live as cowards rather than die as underpaid heroes.'

Boots on, Jonathan stood up. He felt strong, invincible. Asmodeus would be pacified. One way or another, Jonathan would hold the demon at bay until he could complete the ritual. Just get the body from Sproul. That's all. And he now knew where Sproul was.

'Be grateful for the vices of men, Laertes. In Five Points the looters of Rachel Coltman's richly furnished Fifth Avenue mansion are selling their ill-gotten gains to buy the swill that passes for alcohol.'

Jonathan reached for his cloak. 'And drunken men talk, Laertes. They talk of a beautiful woman with long red hair, who is held prisoner in the Old Brewery. And those *I* pay talk to *me*. Yes, Laertes, one must drink a toast to vice.'

He paused. 'Sarah is overdue. Should she return while I am gone, tell her to remain here. She is to forget about Lorenzo Ballou until I come back, for if I have the body of Justin Coltman, then the ritual must begin at once. I will need help.'

Laertes nodded.

Jonathan sneered. 'I look forward to hearing of Sarah's visit to Poe cottage, where our indigent poet shares quarters with his aged mother-in-law Did you know, Laertes, that scandalmongers are busy with the tale of a romantic liaison between our Poe and his dear Muddy?'

Laertes snorted.

Jonathan said, 'Mr Poe avoids pleasures of the flesh, showing a discipline in this area that is missing in other parts of his life. I suspect, Laertes, that our poet is, forgive me, untouched. I suspect he is as virginal as new fallen snow, for his history indicates a lack of interest in carnal matters.' Jonathan chuckled. 'He *is* ill, after all, and where would he find the strength.'

He threw back his head and laughed. The laughter was the sound of Jonathan's triumph, for he *would* conquer, he *would* survive, he *would* get the Throne of Solomon.

First Sproul. Then Justin Coltman. Leave one dead body behind in exchange for another.

And suddenly Laertes was alone in the room, not having heard or seen Jonathan leave.

# CHAPTER THIRTY

The argument between Poe and Figg was bitter; they were contemptuous of each other once more.

The two stood near a water-pump on a crowded Broadway corner, keeping their voices low. Each was hot with his own anger.

Poe's eyes were those of a madman. 'You fool! I *know* the danger she is in. I have just come from her home and I demand you do as I say!'

'Demand?' Figg snorted. The little bugger had gone mental again.

'Yes, *demand*. Hamlet Sproul led looters in her home and now he has Rachel with him in Five Points. The servants told me—'

'Told *you* instead of bloody tellin' God almighty.' Figg jabbed a thick finger in Poe's chest. 'I been out 'ere in the bleedin' cold and I ain't departin' until Miles Standish shows 'is bloody face, *if* that is all right with you, Mr Poe.'

Figg looked over Poe's shoulder at the building housing Miles Standish's office. The building was towards the end of the block and just a short walk from where Figg stood.

Poe. The little man had come running up to Figg with the tale of Rachel Coltman's house being robbed and the lady herself taken along as part of the booty by Hamlet Sproul and some of his Irish brethren. Poe wanted Figg to leave with him now, to go to Five Points and look for Rachel.

Figg didn't see matters quite that way. Twice Standish had tried to kill him and now Pierce James Figg was going to put a stop to any future attempts. Standish was not in his office. Attending a medical demonstration, according to the clerk in his office. Watching a cut up, Mr Poe would say, and when that was over, Standish would return. The law clerk was alone, his desk and stool drawn up close as possible to the fire.

Time for hard questions to be put to Mr Standish. Time for him to tell Figg exactly where Jonathan was. If a man wanted Figg's life, the boxer was not going to turn tail and run, especially when he knew where to lay hands on the man. Meanwhile Poe was acting like a man crazed. Carrying on about Miss Rachel. Well, it was hard cheese to the lady until Figg concluded his business.

The two men moved aside to allow an old man to pump a pail full of brown water, water to be used in drinking and cooking. Even though the Croton Reservoir at 42nd Street and Fifth Avenue had brought water to Manhattan, pumps were still being used in some neighbourhoods, with a risk to pump users of diseases that were often fatal.

Poe clutched Figg's sleeve. 'I insist you come. *Now*!'

'Insist, 'e does.' Figg jerked his sleeve free. 'Me feet's in place right 'ere, mate, and 'ere they stay.' A carriage splashed mud on his leg. Mud and cold. Figg was up to here in both and he didn't like it one bit.

'She will die!' hissed an angry Poe.

'She will keep. Leastwise for a little time longer.'

Over Poe's shoulder and through the crowd he saw a cab stop in front of Miles Standish's office. Three well-dressed, attractive young women stepped from it, stood on the sidewalk and looked up at the lawyer's offices which overlooked the street on the second floor. One of the women carried a suitcase.

Figg shifted his eyes to Poe. 'You 'ave been a right nasty sort over this Miss Rachel business. I 'ave given me word to aid you, so why in 'ell can't you wait a minute or two?'

Poe raised his voice. 'If she dies, I shall kill you. My word on that, sir.'

'Kill me? You're daft. Fail to get your way and what 'appens? Turns into a snake, you does. Best watch yer temper, little man. Ain't had no food in me belly for a time and I got no love for this flippin' cold, so you just best watch your step.'

Poe was a nutter. The man had gone mental, that's all there was to it. Next he'd be foaming at the mouth. Look at him now, stabbing Figg with his eyes and breathing like a man who's just had a nightmare, which he does too often.

'I saved your life,' said Poe, drawing himself up as tall as he could. 'And this is how you repay me.'

Figg's patience was at an end. 'You were bleedin' drunk, mate. You didn't know *who* the bloody 'ell you was savin'.'

Poe stiffened. And Figg immediately regretted what he'd just said.

The boxer softened, laying a hand on Poe's shoulder. 'Lookee, I give you me word and I will stand by it. Just a wee bit longer, that's all I'm askin'. Let me talk to Standish—'

'One more, sir. Will you accompany me?' Now people passing by were slowing down to listen and watch.

Over Poe's shoulder, Figg saw him. Standish. Stepping from his carriage, tying the reins, then walking into the building. *Standish who could lead Figg to Jonathan.*

The boxer tried to step around Poe, who blocked his way.

'Outta me way, Mr Poe. Standish just wen—'

Poe swung at him.

Figg caught the small fist with his hand, squeezed it and said nothing. His eyes were slits. He spoke from between clenched teeth. 'With any other man, I'd 'ave—'

He didn't finish the sentence. Instead, he shoved Poe aside into the people watching the argument. Quickly, Figg limped towards Miles Standish's office. Damn that little bastard Poe. Why did he have to go and do that? Could have got himself knuckled good. Got the boot put to him. Why did he have to go and do that? Miss Rachel was turning Poe into a lunatic.

Jonathan could be at Figg's fingertips; he could be *that* close, Mr Standish would sing a pretty song. Figg would see to that.

At the bottom of the narrow staircase, Figg waited while three young men hurried down, passing him then rushing out into the street, disappearing into the crowd. One of the men carried a suitcase.

Damn Poe and his rotten temper.

At the top of the stairs, Figg waited until his eyes were used to the dim gaslight in the hall. Then he found Miles Standish's office and opened the door.

The clerk lay face down under his high desk. Blood seeped from under his head and chest and his crushed spectacles, lying between his legs, glittered in the golden sunlight shining through the window.

Miles Standish also lay face down. His head was in the fireplace, submerged in orange flames and the smell of burning hair and flesh was sickening to Figg. In the fireplace, and near the dead lawyer's head, a woman's yellow bonnet crumpled and blackened in the fire. Standish's arms were spread wide, as though he was being crucified. Both of his little fingers had been removed and his hands dripped dark pools on to the wooden floor. Somewhere behind Figg, a grandfather's clock chimed two o'clock in the afternoon. The boxer blinked, then covered his nose against the smell coming from the fireplace.

Outside on Broadway a nervous Figg breathed in cold air deeply, eyes darting left and right as he looked for Poe.

The poet had disappeared.

# CHAPTER THIRTY-ONE

Rachel Coltman, numbed with fear and naked under the blanket casually tossed to her by one of the Irishmen, cringed in a corner of a filthy room in the Old Brewery.

She kept her eyes closed and listened.

'No laddie, she is not sleepin',' said a male voice. 'She has her nose turned to the wall so she'll not be smellin' the likes of you, Sean.'

The three men laughed.

'Bleak moll she is, wouldn't you say?' Murmurs of agreement. *Bleak Moll*, a handsome woman.

'Love to give that one a flimp.'

'Sproul would drive steel through the back of yer neck and out yer mouth.'

'That's a truth, me friend. Dear Hamlet is not a fellow to cross.'

' 'E's not a fella what holds his liquor. Flat on his face, Sproul is, huggin' the earth down the hall. Grievin' does that to a man, it does.'

More murmurs of agreement.

And then a harsh voice. 'Hands off me diddle or I'll snitchell yer gig.' *Hands off my liquor or I'll break your nose.*

' 'Ere now, we all took her clothes off so we all owns the liquor. Jesus God, what miserable stuff I'm drinkin', but you know somethin', boys? I love it, God in heaven above I love it.'

They all laughed.

Rachel shivered. Her clothing, the little jewellery she'd been wearing, all of it torn from her by the three Irish thieves as soon as they'd brought her to this small, dark cellar room. She burned with shame at the memory of their hands on her body, their leers, the vile things they'd said to her. Her clothing and jewellery had been sold for 'Blue Ruin', bad gin, which the men now drank as they sat around a table and played cards.

Dear God, dear God, she would die here. Die in the midst of the most terrifying nightmare she'd ever known.

She as a prisoner somewhere in the Old Brewery, where men and women were stabbed for a handkerchief, where a child's throat was cut for a penny. Her bare flesh rested on damp, black earth and she now guessed she was in the basement of the building, somewhere close to the hidden underground passages connecting the Old Brewery to the tenements scattered throughout the slums. The people living in this hellhole had long ago burned as firewood the floor that had once covered the ground beneath her.

He had said that Rachel would die here. Sproul who wore that monstrous knife on a leather thong around his neck; who claimed that Eddy Poe and this mysterious Jonathan had slaughtered his woman and two sons.

A liquor-slurred brogue came from dangerously close to her. 'Warms ourselves with this goddam "Blue Ruin", we does and you know why?' 'Cause we ain't got no gold-plated fireplace or fur-trimmed cloak or no nigger servant to put the warmin' pan in our fuckin' beds like her in the corner has.'

'That's 'cause we ain't got fuckin' beds.' More laughter.

'Seamus, come away from her. Come on leave her alone.'

He was standing over her. Rachel smelled him. Liquor, the tobacco juice that had dripped down his shirt front. She clenched her teeth, arms wrapped tightly around her knees. Dear God, don't let him—

A hand clumsily stroked her hair.

'Seamus, I'll be tellin' you no more to come away from her.'

'Lovely little morsel, she is. I'm thinkin' I would like a bite of her.'

'Hamlet would kill you, Seamus. Interfere with his revenge and you'll end up on the sharp end of his knife. Know this for a fact.'

The hand quickly left her head. She heard him move away and she bit her lip to keep from crying out. From outside in the hall, she heard a baby cry and she heard the crash of a whisky bottle shattering against a nearby wall. So far, they had not raped her. So far . . .

'Hamlet Sproul is a drunken madman.' It was the voice who had stroked her hair. 'Killin' a handsome woman like this one.'

'Has his reasons, he does. Same reasons that made him take her from her home and bring her 'ere. Same reasons that now have him drunk and passed out in 'is room down the hall. Meets Ida's sister and the sight of her makes him weep.'

'Makes him drink until he cannot stand. Ida's sister is on the game, isn't she?'

'Aye, she is. Been a mab since she was ten and now she's fourteen and livin' in this grand palace with 'er ponce, she is. Lordy, this buildin' is a sin against the eyes and nose.'

'For sure. But you can't beat the rent. No spittin' into the bottle, if you will be so kind. Cards please. Like to ask you lads a question, after I take a look at me cards. Damn!'

Rachel heard the cards being slammed to the table in disgust.

'Me question is, what does Mr Sproul have in that sack he covered with earth and insists in sleepin' near?'

'You mean you don't know?'

A whisper.

Then silence.

Rachel waited, her eyes still closed.

'Oh I see,' said the brogue who had inquired about the sack. 'I sees indeed. But if he's gonna kill her, how does he expect her to pay for her husband's body—'

'Ah, Seamus, bite your tongue and look at your cards. Will do our guest no good to hear of such things. May I tell you, lad, that you are a poor poker-player and, for that reason, may you find the time to visit us in the grand hotel more often.'

'Blue Ruin has addled me brain.'

'And made you a *Billy Boodle,* thinkin' all the women love you.'

More coarse laughter. More drinking from the bottle.

A man broke wind and all three laughed and whooped. One said to Rachel, 'Beggin' yer pardon, yer ladyship. Please don't send me to bed without me supper.'

Rachel, sick to her stomach, felt tears roll down her face and into the corners of her mouth, leaving a salt taste there. Justin. His body was here in the Old Brewery with Hamlet Sproul, and soon her body would lie beside his. Oh, oh God, why are these terrible things happening to me? Why am I suffering so?

Her body shook with her silent sobs.

'See there, lads. Told you her ladyship wasn't sleepin'. Let's have a peek under that blanket.'

'Seamus, I'm warnin' you! We're to guard her, nothin' more.'

'A peek won't hurt. Lookin' never damaged the Queen of England and I've gazed upon her many a time.'

'Seamus—'

Rachel felt the blanket ripped from her hands and she brought her knees up close under her chin.

She screamed.

All three men laughed and moved closer.


'You may call me Mr Greatrakes and I shall call you Mr Poe. I know why you are here in the Old Brewery.'

Poe attempted to step around the man, who slid into his path.

'Mr Poe, if you refuse to stand and converse with me, I shall have to denounce you, and if you do not know what that means, I shall enlighten you, oh yes I shall. Mr Greatrakes, that's me, sir, will denounce you as being a nose, oh yes I shall. An informer for the police, a wretched spy. Look around you, Mr Poe. Any one of these lost souls in this room would kill you on the spot, oh yes they would.'

Poe licked his lips. He was twice frightened, for himself, for Rachel. Greatrakes. Bearded, humpback, with a left hand carried twisted over his heart as in some grotesque pledge. And he was preventing Poe from finding Hamlet Sproul and pleading with the grave-robber for Rachel's life. Poe had no other plan.

'Shall I denounce you, Mr Poe?'

'Speak, damn you, and quickly.'

'You wish to rescue Rachel Coltman. I shall help you.'

Poe looked left, right. He was in 'The Den of Thieves', the name given to the largest room in the Old Brewery. Montaigne had been his guide and together they had reached this hideous place through a hidden passage that began in the basement of a rotting tenement three blocks away.

The room was huge enough to contain more than one hundred Irish and coloureds, who clung precariously to life without the aid of any running water, sanitation facilities or even the simplest of furniture. Poe placed a hand over his mouth in a vain attempt to avoid breathing any more of the stench around him than absolutely necessary. Yes, he thought, the children here can indeed contaminate the wild pigs roaming in the muddy alleys outside.

No gaslight within these walls and only a window or two, minus all glass. The darkness was broken here and there by a bit of candle, a cheap lamp, a small fire. Men, women and children were thrown together in the severest of poverty, preying on the world around them, preying on each other. Crime was the only industry they knew or would ever know. Poe's nostrils flared in disgust at a nearby couple sexually entwined just feet away from him on the dirty floor. Only a few people of the many in the room even bothered to watch this prostitute entertain her customer.

Mr Greatrakes was correct. To denounce anyone as a police informer in these surroundings was to sentence him to death, and Poe, as a stranger, was especially vulnerable to such a charge.

'I said, Mr Poe, that I shall assist you in the rescue of Rachel Coltman.'

Poe eyed Greatrakes's matted beard, which reached to the man's chest.

'Ah,' said Greatrakes, wiping his nose with the back of a gloved hand, 'you are asking yourself, how can one such as Valentine Greatrakes assist the likes of Edgar Allan Poe. Well sir, I can lead you to Hamlet Sproul, oh yes I can, and you will admit that this is no small service in an inferno of vice as that in which we now stand.'

Poe nodded. It *would* be a service if he could trust Valentine Greatrakes, who appeared to be almost omniscient, despite having the look of a man far down on his luck. The Old Brewery was a different world, a world in which one moved with utmost caution merely in hopes of living one more day. More than one thousand Irish and coloured lived here, and some of the coloured, Poe knew, had white wives, a fact he found totally loathsome.

For the time being, Poe was safe, though his intelligence told him that anyone in the Old Brewery would murder him for the ragged clothes he wore, should he be so unfortunate as to meet someone so desperate. Greatrakes could guide him and Poe was desperate enough to take any assistance he could. Merely locating Rachel in time would be a problem, let alone talking Hamlet Sproul into releasing her.

There were twenty rooms in the cellar alone, plus almost one hundred other rooms scattered throughout the Old Brewery. There was no sunlight or fresh air in any of them, and even less humanity and decency. Dozens of people were crammed into some of the rooms, all living in unbelievable filth. The building was jammed with murderers, thieves, prostitutes, beggars and people whose imagination knew no limit in the committing of all vices known to man.

Poe *could* use the help of Valentine Greatrakes. But there were questions to put to the hunchback.

'How do you come to know of this matter of Rachel Coltman?'

Greatrakes sniffed, shifting his weight from foot to foot. 'Such a lady as her, sir, well her beauty is so out of place in the Old Brewery, wouldn't you say? She is under guard now, but still alive, still alive.'

'You have seen her?' Poe's heart pounded.

'Briefly, only briefly. Seen you, Mr Poe. The other night in the Louvre, you and the pugilist Mr Figg. Heard Johnnie Bill Baker and his coloured wench—'

'That is of no importance at the present moment. Mrs Coltman—'

'Alive. Now here is what I would like you to do.' He took Poe's elbow and steered him away from Montaigne, who now squatted near a small fire. On the other side of the fire was a large Negro man and his common-law wife, a teenage Irish girl, her stomach high and full with the child she expected. By the light of the fire, several men gambled with dice.

'You would have to do something for me, Mr Poe. Mrs Coltman has a great deal of money, which she won't be able to spend if she is dead. If she lives, I trust she will be, ah, grateful? You could see to that, yes you could. It is a known fact that you and the lady are, well, you are here to effect her rescue, are you not?'

'Lead me to her. I shall see that she rewards you but if you deceive me—'

'Oh Mr Poe.' Greatrakes leered. His teeth were yellow and black and Poe could have broken them with his stick. The man reeked of liquor. He winked at Poe. 'Did you know that Johnnie Bill Baker has friends even among those here in such a place as this? If they were to learn you are among them . . .' He shook his head, leering even more.

Poe pulled his elbow away from Greatrakes and would have fled the man, had he not looked over his shoulder and seen three thin-faced, dirty and ragged teenage boys staring at him. They were obviously trying to decide if Poe had anything of value, anything worth cutting his throat for. He had to find Sproul fast, talk to him, convince him Rachel had nothing to do with the death of Sproul's woman and sons.

Greatrakes again used the back of a gloved hand to wipe his nose. Poe noticed that the gloves were torn and stained. 'Ah, Mr Poe, I sense hostility in you. Ah, yes I do. Come, let us continue our stroll for I dare say those lads you are staring at may well be measuring your throat for a blade. Would it make any difference to you if I say Rachel Coltman is acquainted with me?'

Poe snorted. 'Acquainted with *you*, sir?'

'Oh, she is, she is. I was once a better man than you see before you. Educated, respected, a professional of some small accomplishment. I assisted Justin Coltman in a business arrangement or two. That is until demon rum trapped me in her embrace.'

'And you crawled into the bottle never again to crawl out.'

'Well now, who would know of such falls from grace better than you, Mr Poe.' Greatrakes grinned slyly, stroking his matted beard with the back of his gnarled hand. The man made Poe's skin crawl.

'Lead me to Mrs Coltman.'

228

'Well now, I do not know for certain where Mr Sproul is but the whereabouts of Mrs Coltman, ah, that is a fact of which many of us here are aware.'

'The two are not together?'

'From what I can gather, they are not. Mrs Coltman is being guarded by three of Sproul's men, while Sproul himself is somewhere in private drenching his grief in rum.'

Poe fingered his moustache. Sproul was drinking. Most likely, he would drink to excess, pass out and be unable to communicate with anyone. That meant Poe had a chance to talk with Rachel's jailers, to convince them to release her. But what if the pailers refused even to consider Rachel's release unless Sproul was present?

Valentine Greatrakes. The name was grand, a sweeping verbal gesture. Ridiculous that it be attached to this despicable-looking dunghill of a human being. Valentine Greatrakes. Poe had heard the name before, but where?

The hunchback sniffled. He leaks, thought Poe, like sap from trees in the forest. Valentine Greatrakes. I *know* the name. I *do*.

Poe said, 'Lead. I shall follow.'

'And you will inform Mrs Coltman—'

'Damn you, yes!'

'White of you, Mr Poe. Exceedingly white of you, sir. Oh, I would not leave your old friend behind. Already she has attracted attention, and her being so decrepit and all.'

Dear God! Poe hurried quickly to Montaigne's side, pushing through three ragged and dirty women who now squatted beside Montaigne in front of the fire. The women fingered the soiled rags she wore, her muddy boots.

Poe dragged Montaigne away from them, speaking softly to her in French, telling her to stay close to him.

Valentine Greatrakes leered at them, his twisted hand in place over his heart. 'Nice to see a man looking out after others the way you do, Mr Poe. Yes, I tell you it is a nicely thing to see. Well, sir, let us trek deeper into this jungle, and be of keen eye, the both of you. Won't do to go off on your own in the Old Brewery.'

He shuffled on ahead of them, reminding Poe of an insect in search of prey. Just let this leaking hunchback lead me to Rachel in time. It occurred to Poe that the story 'Hop Frog', on which he was working when he found time and energy, had a hunchback court jester as the main character. As for this Valentine Greatrakes, Poe's keen ear detected that his American accent was practised, an applied trait, something learned and acquired. It covered another accent, something from western Europe.

Greatrakes's original birthplace was not America; Poe was certain of it. And that name. *Greatrakes.* It scraped at Poe's brain as he and Montaigne followed the hunchback into a passageway blacker than the blackest midnight.

Greatrakes had produced a stub of a candle from under his cloak, lighting it from a lantern that rested on the floor between two drunken Irishmen with bloated, sore-encrusted faces. Poe, Montaigne and Greatrakes left 'The Den of Thieves' behind, the cries, curses and stench of the huge hall growing fainter. Now they were in a sour-smelling darkness leading to only the hunchback knew where.

A rat squeaked. From rooms along the passageway, some with doors closed, others with doors open, came more curses, screams, drunken laughter, the wail of babies and the toneless singing of those minds no longer concentrated. To Poe the darkness magnified the hellish odours and noises around them.

And his life and that of Montaigne were in the hands of a hunchback named Valentine Greatrakes, who shuffled noisily in front of them, candle stub held high and casting long shadows on the wall, as he led them deeper into darkness.


Greatrakes went inside of the room alone and talked to the men guarding Rachel Coltman. When the door had opened, a hard-faced Irishman with a scraggly beard pointed a flintlock pistol at Greatrakes's throat and drunkenly demanded what he wanted. Poe had not heard the hunchback's whisper, but the door had opened wider and he'd gone inside, the door slamming shut behind him. Poe and Montaigne had been left outside in almost total darkness: Greatrakes had taken the candle stub with him.

Now Greatrakes stood in the doorway, beckoning Poe and Montaigne inside. 'In with you now, you two. Your lady friend awaits and, Mr Poe, these here gentlemen will find it a pleasure to discuss with you. Come on, do not hang back there in the darkness. Come on.'

With Montaigne clinging to his sleeve, her tiny wrinkled face relaxed in a world of her own, Poe entered, blinking his eyes, trying to focus in the darkness.

Greatrakes was behind him. 'She is there, Mr Poe, resting in the corner.'

Poe turned towards Greatrakes's voice and a fist hit him in the jaw, spinning him around and sending him dancing into a barrel used as a chair.

They were on him in a flash, two men tying his hands behind his back and gagging him with a filthy bandana. In seconds it was all over.

Poe lay on the floor, his jaw aching. It had happened too quickly for him to be frightened, but the fear would come. He was sure of it.

It began *now*.

Greatrakes looked down at him. 'Oh dear, I told you, Mr Poe, an informer is not a welcomed man in these parts, no indeed, sir. I have told these gentlemen of your plan to betray them and Hamlet Sproul to the police. Hamlet will want a chat with you about his Ida and their boys.'

Poe struggled. He tried to sit up, to cry out. A booted foot was placed on his chest and he went down painfully.

'Bastard,' said an Irishman.

Greatrakes leered, gnarled hand stroking his beard. 'They do not appreciate the part you played in the death of me cousin, Johnnie Bill Baker.'

Suddenly Poe knew!

Greatrakes's voice had slid into an Irish brogue. 'No sir, me bucko, you cannot send me darlin' Johnny to the flames without me doin' somethin' about it, no sir. Hamlet Sproul is a true son of Erin. He said he'd help me 'ave me revenge, he did. "Corcoran," 'e said, "you'll taste 'is blood, you will. Swear it, I do. Me, 'amlet Sproul." '

Greatrakes's performance was skilful, convincing. It was perfectly tailored for his audience. A trapped Poe could only watch.

Greatrakes leaned down, his face just inches from Poe's. In the darkness and shielded by his own body, Greatrakes's hand could not be seen by the three Irishmen. He removed a glove. The little finger on his right hand was missing.

The veins bulged on Poe's forehead and neck with the effort of trying to cry out.

When Greatrakes stood up, the glove was back on his hand. His leer was deadly.

Poe cried out against the gag that was painfully tight across his mouth. He was dizzy with fear.

Greatrakes spoke to the Irishmen. 'Oh, before I'm forgettin' lads, Hamlet wants a word with one of you about a change in plans. He is not goin' to kill the woman. 'E's decided there's more money in her bein' alive. 'E's sellin' er to a white slaver for a tidy sum, in which you will all share.'

The men whooped.

Greatrakes leered. 'Ah, she's in the corner, is she? Quiet as a dead leaf.'

'Ain't dead,' said one of the men. 'Woulda been if Seamus had been allowed to 'ave 'is way with 'er. Pulled 'im back just in time.'

Greatrakes clapped a hand in Seamus's shoulder. 'Seamus, lad, you look the type me cousin Johnnie Bill would have loved. Hamlet wants to talk to ye about what 'e intends to do with the lady over there. I'm thinkin' that when you return, the three of you will be allowed a bit of fun with 'er, eh?'

He leered. The men whooped again. One sipped from a bottle and offered it to Greatrakes, who accepted.

After a huge swallow of gin, Greatrakes stepped over to Poe and poured gin on him. 'Last drink, Mr Poe. On the 'ouse, it is.'

The men laughed.

The gin burned Poe's eyes and wet his hair. *Jonathan wants to kill Hamlet Sproul. He has tricked these three into leading him to Sproul. And Rachel. These men will—*

A frightened Poe squirmed on the ground, lashing out with his feet, kicking at Jonathan, at the Irishmen.

'Liquor makes 'im dance, it does. Oils his tongue so's 'e can talk to the police.' Greatrakes's brogue was getting stronger. *Clever and dangerous*, thought Poe. *Arrogant. Manipulative. He challenged me face to face and he's won. The fiend has beaten me, and Rachel and I will die. First she will be degraded by these men, then two of us will die. She will take longer in dying and therefore suffer the more.*

Greatrakes and Seamus were by the door, Greatrakes's arm around the Irishman's shoulders. 'Seamus and I will be returnin'. You boyos keep Mr Poe amused and make yer plans for the lady. Come, Seamus, let us look in on Hamlet and tell 'im Mr Poe is arrived and has been welcomed.'

'The old lady,' said one Irish. 'What's to be done with 'er?'

Greatrakes's voice came from the dark hallway. 'Marry the wench or bury her. It's up to you, I'd say.' He and Seamus laughed.

The two Irishmen drank from the bottle, eyes on Montaigne.

'Ain't for marryin', Tom.'

'Nor I, Flynn.'

One lifted his bottle in a mock toast to Montaigne, who sat on the dirt floor, stroking Rachel's hair.

Had Rachel fainted or was she asleep? Or, dear God, was she dead? Poe couldn't tell and he was unable to ask Montaigne. *He was unable to warn her to flee for her life.*

The Irishman holding the bottle said to Montaigne, ' 'Ere's to you, old one. You'll get to heaven long before me. You'll get there today.'

'Before Seamus returns.'

'Before Seamus returns.'

The two nodded at each other, then stood up and walked towards Montaigne.

Poe's eyes bulged and he cried out as loud as he could. The gag strangled his words and the sound which emerged was that of a man powerless in the face of death.

# CHAPTER THIRTY-TWO

The pain was blinding. It exploded in the centre of his face, then squeezed his brain. Sproul jerked himself into a sitting position from drunken sleep, both hands going to his nose. *Pain.* Someone had slit his left nostril.

Crazed with pain, Sproul fumbled for the leather thong around his neck. His fingers were wet with his own blood.

'Sproul?' The soft voice came from the darkness.

*The knife wasn't there.* Sproul patted his chest in a quick, panicked search. *No knife.* A hand went back to his bleeding nose.

'Who-who is there? Speak, damn you!'

'Jonathan.'

Sproul went rigid, his stomach turning to ice. He tried to sit up. Something lay across his lap weighing him down, keeping him in place. Jesus and Mary! It was Seamus. *He was dead!* Lying across Sproul's lap, eyes wide and staring, a few inches of candle jammed down into his open mouth. The candle was the only light in the small, filthy room. Sproul shrieked, pushing Seamus away from him and sending the candle flying. It rolled on the floor, smothering its flame. A thin, pale blue wisp of smoke slowly floated up into the air.

'The body of Justin Coltman, I want it. It is in this room. You will tell me where.'

On his hands and knees, blood pouring down his face and into his tobacco-stained, blond beard, Sproul crawled left, right, seeking safety in motion. He whimpered in fear and crawled.

'You will give me the body, Hamlet Sproul.'

'Dear God, no! Do not carve me heart—'

Jonathan, scalpel in his hand, leaped on Sproul, sending him forward and to the floor. A hand covered Sproul's mouth, trapping the scream deep within the grave-robber's throat. Jonathan, strong in his triumph, began to chant softly.


Figg placed an ear to the door, listened, then nodded to the bowlegged dwarf who held the lantern. The dwarf, his black eyes expressionless in his large head, emptied the oil from the lantern, touched flame to it, then stepped aside. Figg, pistols drawn, waited and hoped he was not too late.

Smoke rose slowly from the floor. *Come on in there,* thought Figg. *Can't be hangin' about out 'ere breathin' this bloody stuff.*

The door opened and Figg stepped in front of it, kicking it, sending it back hard against the man who had opened it. The man ran backwards, fell on to a table, then to the floor. Figg blinked, eyes searching the dark room. Two men, no more. And Poe on the floor, wrapped like a Christmas goose and looking none too happy about it.

Against the far wall, the man huddled over a cringing Rachel now turned his attention to Figg. The man yanked at a flintlock pistol in his belt and Figg fired, sending a ball crashing into the man's jaw. The man screamed, spinning to face the wall, hands to his face, too late to save what had been destroyed. His tongue was mutilated and the sounds now coming from him could have been coming from an animal in agony.

The man Figg had knocked to the floor was on his knees, hands in the air. He trembled and wept, pleading with Figg for his life.

Grabbing his shirt front, Figg threw him in Poe's direction. 'Untie 'im and be quick about it! If he be hurtin', you'll answer to me!'

With the gag out of his mouth, Poe coughed, his face turning red.

'They-they have murdered Montaigne.'

'Who?'

'Montaigne. The old woman from the Louvre, she who warned us about Johnnie Bill Baker. These beasts made a game of it. They broke her neck and laughed about it.'

Poe was on his feet, rubbing his wrists. 'Rachel.' He turned and hurried to her, covering her with the blanket. She was silent, in shock, her face calm. Poe smoothed hair away from her eyes, then turned to Figg.

'Your coat, Mr Figg.'

The boxer tossed it to him, turning when he felt the dwarf pull at his trouser leg.

'We best leave,' said the dwarf, looking quickly at the smoke coming from the burning door. 'There will be others here soon, perhaps friends of these men.'

Figg nodded. 'Let us leave, Mr Poe.'

Poe walked towards them, an arm around Rachel, who looked small and lost in Figg's large coat. 'Jonathan. He is here, Mr Figg.'

'Where?' Figg clenched his fists.

'Ask him.' Poe pointed to the trembling Irishman who was still on his knees, hands in the air.

'Don't, don't know no Jonathan, sir. Don't know—'

Poe shouted, 'You know where Sproul is and Jonathan is with him! Now tell us, damn you, where is Sproul?'

Figg moved quickly to the Irishman, clapping the palms of his hands over the man's ears, making him shriek and fall backwards to the dark, damp earth. 'One time, Johnny boy. One time. Tell me where is Mr Sproul?'


Hamlet Sproul's heart and liver still burned on the dirt floor beside his corpse. The organs now a small grisly pile of flesh blackening in tiny blue flames. The smell of it was bitter. Not as bitter as Figg's heart. *Jonathan wasn't here.* They'd missed him by seconds. Figg's anger was almost out of control.

'Catchin' 'im is like tryin' to nail water to the wall. Christ Jesus, I want me 'ands on 'im! God above I want to kill that man!'

Poe pointed to an empty hole in the earth. It was shallow and not too long or wide. The dirt on the sides was freshly turned. 'He has taken Justin Coltman with him.'

Figg looked at Rachel Coltman who stood beside Poe. The woman's eyes were glazed, her hair all over her face, and she looked as though she was miles away. Shock, Poe called it. Figg had seen that look in the faces of boxers who had taken a bad beating, especially around the head.

Damn it all to bloody hell! Figg kicked dirt back into the hole.

'I suppose you are goin' to tell me that Jonathan is out in the bleedin' woods somewhere tryin' to get Mr Coltman to talk to him.'

'He shall try, Mr Figg. As soon as possible. And I fear the consequences.' Poe looked at the pockmarked dwarf who stood behind the boxer.

Figg, eyes on the hole in the ground, mumbled without turning around to look at Poe or the dwarf. 'Little fella what's with me is called Merlin. Works for Mr Barnum who gave me the loan of 'im. Mr Barnum claims Merlin has 'is own way of gettin' things done. Has 'is own kind of magic.'

Poe found the dwarf hideous. Big head, tiny eyes. Skin pitted by smallpox. And he kept staring at Rachel like some lascivious, deformed elf.

Figg turned to look at Poe. 'Merlin, he brought us through a passage he played in when 'e was a lad. 'E's from around 'ere, born and bred. Nobody would give 'im a job, save Mr Barnum.'

Save Barnum, who collects the bizarre, thought Poe.

Merlin waddled out of the room on bow-legs and into the hall. Then he stuck his head back into the room. 'Smoke is growing out here. Best we leave. Sproul might have a friend or two we have not met.' His voice was a high rasp, a sound that made Poe want to cringe.

'Nine days,' mumbled Figg, again staring at the empty hole. 'The bugger has got hisself nine days to do his little business.'

Poe moved near him, also to stare at the hole. 'If we are to stop him, Mr Figg, we have less.'

And then they were in the passageway, following the waddling Merlin. Figg was silent, brooding on how close he had come to Jonathan. When the bleedin' hell was he going to get his hands on him? Riddle me ree. Some bloody riddle, mate.

Poe, an arm around Rachel to guide her, said, 'Mr Figg?'

'Yeah.'

'Can't we walk slower? Rachel has no shoes; her feet are bleeding.'

'Don't hear 'er complainin'.'

'Her mind is temporarily damaged. She is in shock.'

'Merlin says we keep on. Got a ways to go, yet. Few blocks, then we come up in a tavern what ain't fit for a dog to piss in. No stoppin' now, Mr Poe. Got our lives to think about.'

*Got Jonathan to think about, mate.*

They continued walking in silence until Figg, his back to Poe and Rachel, said, 'Mr Poe?'

'Yes, Mr Figg.'

'Sorry 'bout me manners back there in the matter of Mr Standish. This is a pressin' business with me and I wants to end it quickly.'

'I understand, Mr Figg. I am again in your debt, as is Mrs Coltman.'

They continued walking in a darkness lit only by Merlin's lamp.

'Wants to ask you somethin', Mr Poe. You think Jonathan will get the thing 'e's after, you know what I'm speakin' of?'

'Mr Figg, I tell you this: I feel the worst will happen. My mind rejects the belief in these matters, but Jonathan is a creature out of the realm of possibility. He is improbable and therefore capable of anything. I fear for us all.'

'Why?'

237

'Jonathan is not through with us. I feel it to be so and that feeling grows stronger with each step. We are now in more danger than before.'

Figg limped, ignoring the ache in his bad leg. Chasing Jonathan was the same as toddling along in this blasted, stinking tunnel. A man could not go back; all you could do was go forward into something that might kill you—if you were lucky. And do a whole lot worse to you if you weren't.

Figg kept going forward. He was more frightened than he'd been at any time in his life.

# CHAPTER THIRTY-THREE

Hugh Larney felt light-headed with fear and exhilaration as he stood in his cold, dark stable listening to Jonathan speak with a strange new authority. The magician exuded power; the Throne of Solomon was within his reach.

Sarah Clannon was also within reach, but forgotten for the moment. She lay on the ground between them, eyes closed, her small, pretty face unnaturally white. Her breathing was shallow. Under her right side, the straw on the stable floor was red with her blood.

Jonathan said, '*Nonne Solomon dominatus daemonum est?* Had not Solomon dominion over demons? And so shall I. Solomon's wealth, wisdom, his rule over all spirits—this shall be mine.'

Hugh Larney, nervous and perspiring, nodded yes.

The magician's voice was a frozen hiss. 'I, not Solomon, shall ride the wind. Solomon's ring will be mine and like him I will call all demons unto me and impress my seal upon their necks to mark them as my slaves. I have the body of Justin Coltman; I shall bring him back from the dead to tell me how the Throne of Solomon is to become mine.'

Jonathan stood in shadows, visible to Larney only from the waist down. The magician's dark purple cloak was mud-splattered to the knees. In a stall behind him, a horse whinnied and shied as though disturbed by something evil and unseen.

Hugh Larney pointed down to Sarah Clannon. His finger shook. 'How long is she to stay here?'

'Until she recovers. I charge you with her care, Hugh Larney. Do not abandon her.' The words were a command and a threat. Larney understood this.

He quickly changed the subject. 'Poe. And the boxer. What about them?'

'Nothing to me. I have what I want. Poe is now more your problem than mine.'

'I—I do not understand.'

'Mr Poe and the persistent Mr Figg were seen at the office of Miles Standish earlier today, just before Mr Standish died. Having arrived there directly from the train, where they survived an attempt on their lives, it is logical to say they connected Standish to this failed assassination. From Standish to you and Volney Gunning is not far. You would be wise to assume they are on to you both.'

'What-what shall I do?'

'Survive.'

'Yes, but how?'

'More efficiently than you have up until now. Poe is weak in body but his mind is agile. Figg is primitive, a danger physically, and an underestimated danger in terms of thought. The forces of darkness lie within him, too. He does not acknowledge them, he does not need them, for he survives extremely well in this world with those abilities he chooses to recognise. But beware Figg. I tell you to beware this man.'

Larney chewed his bottom lip with tiny teeth. 'Shall I kill them?'

'If you must. If you can. I leave you now. Is the farm abandoned as I requested?'

'Yes-yes. It is yours for as long as you need it.'

'Nine days. And I am to be undisturbed. No duels in coaches, while your friends sip champagne and eat pâtés.'

'All in my employ are under strict orders to avoid the farm until further notice.'

Jonathan's voice was ice. 'Anyone approaching the ceremony will die. Those forces I seek to raise cannot always be controlled.'

'I understand. Yes, I—I understand.' As frightened as he was, Larney would have given all he owned to witness the ceremony, to actually see the Throne of Solomon appear. To see it!

But to disobey Jonathan—

No.

Larney found it easy to bow and scrape to those he feared. Since he feared Jonathan the most, he bowed to him deeper than to others.

'Soon the world will know and acknowledge your genius. You will—'

'You fool!'

Hugh Larney flinched.

Jonathan stepped forward into the light of a lantern hanging from a post. A gloved hand held his hood closed, hiding his face.

'I want neither the praise nor adoration of the world. I wish dominion over it; I shall rule as Solomon never did. It is written that in Solomon's palace the poor sat at tables of wood, the demons and spirits sat at tables of iron, while military chieftains sat at tables of silver. Learned men were at golden tables, where Solomon himself served them. *I serve no one.* All shall serve me and all shall sit at tables of iron. In nine days, Larney. Nine days . . .'

Hugh Larney tried to swallow and failed. Jonathan was a knife at the world's throat. Soon that knife would—

'I shall care for Miss Clannon. And if Poe should seek me out, I shall deal with him.'

'Or he with you.' Jonathan's voice was fading. He'd stepped deeper into the stable's darkness. He was leaving to begin the dark ritual of necromancy, to bring back Justin Coltman from the dead.

Hugh Larney shouted, 'If I find it necessary to kill Poe—'

He heard Jonathan's carriage pull away and head towards the country.

In nine days Jonathan would be the most awesome force upon this earth, controlling demons and challenging God. Hugh Larney would reap the advantage of that. Hugh Larney would have power through Jonathan, and then the people of New York who laughed behind Hugh Larney's back would laugh no more. *They would not.*


Poe sighed, crossing his legs and folding his hands in his lap. 'Valentine Greatrakes was an Irish mesmerist of the seventeenth century, who it is said possessed the gift of healing by the laying on of hands. Jonathan had his joke at my expense and I nearly lost my life because of it. At that moment I was too confused to think clearly.'

Rachel sat in bed sipping hot soup. 'It was as though he was daring you to discover him, to find him out. The man performed before you as would a travelling player.'

'Remember he is a man of the theatre, as well as one possessed of a powerful pride. He must be in control; he can accept no less. You frown, Mr Figg.'

The boxer, who sat at the foot of Rachel's four-poster bed, nodded. 'Jonathan is about 'is business. 'E's got what he come for.'

Poe said, 'We have less than nine days to find him, Mr Figg. I am convinced we must, for all our sakes. We are too involved to be let alone. Death has come to almost all of those who touched on this matter. The grave-robbers, Johnnie Bill Baker, Miles Standish. Destruction, no matter how unsought, appears inevitable. We cannot allow Jonathan to complete the ritual. Nor can we allow

241

him the advantage of seeking us out. We possess surprise and little else. We must use it and search for him and stop him.'

Figg cleared his throat.

Poe eyed him carefully. 'Afraid, Mr Figg?'

Figg rubbed the stubble on his shaven head, keeping his eyes on the rug. 'Must say as how I am. Indeed, I fear this man.'

Poe smiled. 'A sensible reply, sir. I fear him, as well.' He looked at Rachel, who had stopped eating. 'I fear him, but I cannot let him destroy as he chooses. Yesterday in the Old Brewery, Jonathan almost became the cause of my losing all that I hold dear in this world.'

Rachel blushed, looking down at the bowl of soup. 'I thank you, Eddy.' Looking up, she quickly added, 'And you too, Mr Figg.'

Figg nodded once, 'Yes, ma'am.' It was getting more and more noticeable: Poe and the lady were warming to each other. She was all the reason the writer needed to stick his hand into the fire. And in truth, a woman was Figg's reason for seeking Jonathan. His wife would have been twenty-three years old in another two months.

Figg said, 'Today is the first of the nine days. One thing is for certain: we won't be gettin' Miles Standish to lead us to Jonathan. The magician made sure of that.'

Poe used his fingers to comb dark brown hair back from his large forehead. 'Jonathan himself did not kill Miles Standish. He undoubtedly ordered it done, for reasons which elude me, though I have my suspicions. Someone else killed Standish.'

Figg flicked an imaginary speck of dust from the shiny black pistol box which he kept in his lap. 'Next thing you'll tell us is you been talkin' to that little fella you put down on paper. What's 'is name again? That Frenchie you made up for yer detective stories which I would like to read one day, if I may.'

'You shall have a copy of that book signed by me, Mr Figg. Not that it is a national treasure of any sort, but it will be my pleasure to present it to you. C. Auguste Dupin of Paris, at your service.'

Poe bowed. 'He appears in three tales—"The Murders In The Rue Morgue", "The Mystery Of Marie Roget", of which you have heard me speak in detail, and "The Purloined Letter". Ah, Dupin. Critics say he is I as I imagine myself to be, and I confess to you two in your private ear that there is some small truth to that. He is cool, analytical, aristrocratic, and a man of means. Cerebral, articulate, with extraordinary powers of reason.'

Poe leaned forward in his chair. 'Let us now examine the available intelligence. Had Jonathan murdered Standish and the clerk, taking time to mutilate the body of Standish, it is unlikely that he could have raced ahead of me to Five Points and been waiting for me in the Old Brewery arrayed in intricate makeup and costume. I have been an actor myself, as were my natural parents, and I know the detail involved in the application of makeup.

'No, my friends, Jonathan could not have committed the murders and the mutilation, then traversed the distance between Broadway and Five Points. Mr Figg—'

'Yeah?'

'For the moment I am Dupin, the French detective. Let us dissect what you have previously told me you saw. Begin with our meeting on the sidewalk near the office of Miles Standish. No, begin with your observation of Miles Standish alighting from his carriage. Was he followed into the building?'

Figg rubbed his bulldog jaw. 'Nobody follows 'im inside. He gets out from 'is carriage, which he drives 'imself, ties it, then he follows these three young ladies inside. One of the ladies is carryin' a suitcase—'

Poe frowned. 'Young ladies. There was little time between their entering and Standish following them. Mr Figg, you have already mentioned something to me. You said the bonnet of a woman was burning in the fireplace beside the head of Miles Standish. Forgive me, Rachel.'

She was pale, a hand to her throat. 'I am at ease, Eddy. Please continue. I know this is necessary. Please pay me no mind.'

'Yes, well, Mr Figg, the bonnet.'

'It was to the right of 'is 'ead. Yellow I think it was. Lookin' back on it, seems there was somethin' else in that fireplace as well. Some more rags burnin', seems like. I dunno . . .'

'Ah, Mr Figg, but you *do* know! Another sense within you sees and records. It was that bonnet which made me connect two things: the three women entering the building and the three young men hurrying down the narrow staircase.'

'I had to wait fer them to come down. Weren't enough room fer me to go up past them.'

Poe's eyes were bright with excitement. The problems of analysis thrilled him beyond measure. He responded to any challenge to his intellect *because he was Poe; he was the brightest, the very brightest of intellects*.

Poe's low, Southern voice was firm. 'The bonnet, Mr Figg. It has stuck out in my mind, and so has the suitcase, and now those rags you saw in the fireplace. Standish and his clerk were killed by those three young men. They entered the office disguised as women, committed the murders, the mutilation, then fled, passing you on the way down. The women and men had the following in common: their youth, their nearness to the crime, and a suitcase. I would wager the suitcase was used to carry some items of male apparel. As you noted, some of the female apparel used as disguise was burning in the fireplace.'

'Cor blimey!' Figg's mouth dropped open. Little Mr Poe had done it again, he had. Smart as a pen full of foxes.

'Something else, Mr Figg. Volney Gunning is a part of this business, and it is shameful for me to say this in front of Rachel but I must. Volney Gunning is a lover of young men. He is a homosexual, a man who pleasures himself in the flesh of his own sex.'

Figg snorted. ' 'E's a bloody poof, yer sayin'. Light as a feather.'

'Yes. And he is known to prefer the company of the Metropolitan Cleopatras to be found at the house of Venus called Scotch Ann's. No ordinary streetwalkers to be found here, Mr Figg. Here you find some of the loveliest-looking of women and all are available, sir. Except that these women are *not* women. They are young men in women's gowns and wigs and each young man has a most lovely feminine name. They sell themselves as street women do. Men such as Volney Gunning buy.'

Figg said, 'Mr Gunning and Mr Larney are friends. Them two and Miles Standish sends the minstrels after us. Now Mr Gunning sends some she-he's to pay a call on Mr Standish. Seems to fit. Yes sir, it seems to fit neatly.'

Poe sat on the edge of Rachel's bed. Figg saw her reach for his hand. Poe coughed into his fist, his body jerking. He quickly rose and continued coughing. You ain't healthy, mate, thought Figg. You had hard times but now you got a lady what cares for you and I am thinkin' perhaps that might be enough. For your sake, squire, I hope so.

Poe turned to face them again. 'Forgive me, dear friends. Despite being junior to you in years, Mr Figg, I am afraid I am nowhere near as fit.'

'Squire, I ain't fit. Jes' lucky, I am.'

'Your pluck creates your luck, Mr Figg.'

'Will take more than luck or pluck to get us to Jonathan, says I.'

'Let us begin with a carriage ride tonight. Let us visit Scotch Ann's establishment and see if we can find Volney Gunning. He, I believe, is the weakest link in their chain. After him, Hugh Larney.

244

Assume that Jonathan is no longer in the city. Assume, but above all, hope, that he has told one of these two men where he hopes to commit this awesome ritual.'

Figg's bulldog face was firm. 'In this place of Scotch Ann, beggin' yer pardon miss for havin' to mention it once more, you say all the pretty ladies is really pretty men?'

'Yes, Mr Figg.'

'This is a peculiar business, Mr Poe. I ain't never been in a place like this before.'

'Yes, Mr Figg. I note your rigid jaw when you speak of Scotch Ann's. You will not have to dance or embrace anyone there, you have my word.'

'I hold you to it, Mr Poe.'

Figg lifted his jaw in the air and sat firm, the picture of an Englishman who knew where the line had to be drawn.

# CHAPTER THIRTY-FOUR

**The night of the First Day**

As called for in the ritual, Jonathan slept during the day. He was scheduled to do this for the full nine days, waking only at night to perform the rites. Laertes, who would assist, lay beside him on the dirt floor of the abandoned barn; to make certain they slept, each man had sipped drugged, unfermented wine. Cold sunlight shone through cracks in the barn walls, throwing long, golden stripes across the bodies of the two sleeping men, both of whom wore stained, dirt-encrusted grave clothes torn from recently dug-up corpses.

Jonathan and Laertes slept within a magic circle nine feet in diameter, a circle dug in the ground by Jonathan, who had used an *Athame*, the ritual knife of the witch. Three feet away was another circle, this one around the plain, wooden coffin containing Justin Coltman's body, the severed head resting on the chest. Both circles were protection against those evil spirits who might be drawn to the ritual.

Preparation, summoning, dismissal. The three parts of the black art of necromancy.

Preparation. All items to be used lay within and just outside the circle. Torches. Flint for making fire. A bowl containing a mixture of opium, hemlock, saffron, wood chips mandrake and henbane. Six candles, salt, water, a mallet and sharpened wooden stake.

For food there was the flesh of dogs. And bread. Black, unleavened and unsalted bread, and more unfermented wine. The dog served Hecate, goddess of death. The bread and wine, lacking yeast, salt and fermentation, were without life and served as needed barren symbols. Jonathan and Laertes were to eat sparsely and only at midnight.

Midnight.

The summoning of Justin Coltman's spirit began.

Jonathan and Laertes had eaten, and both now sat within the first consecrated circle. Each had sprinkled human ashes into his hair. Laertes held a flaming torch in each hand, his eyes closed, his mind directed to Jonathan's chanting.

'*Powers of the Kingdom, be ye under my left foot and in my right hand! Glory and Eternity, take me by the two shoulders and direct me in the paths of victory! Intelligence and wisdom crown me! Spirits of Malchuth, lead me betwixt the two pillars upon which rests the whole edifice of the temple! Angels of Netsah and Hod, strengthen me upon the cubic stone of Jesod! O Gedulael! O Geburael! O Tiphereth! Binael, be thou my love! Ruach Hochmael, be thou my light! Be that which thou art and thou shalt be, O Ketheriel!*'

'*Tschim, assist me in the name of Saddai! Cherubin, by my strength in the name of Adonai! Beni-Elohim, be my brethren in the name of the Son, and by the power of Zebaoth! Eloim, do battle for me in the name of Tetragammation!*'

'*Malachim, protect me in the name of*. . .'

Jonathan's hypnotic voice lulled Laertes into a half sleep; he had to force himself to keep his eyes open. He listened.

His eyes went to the mallet and sharpened wooden stake which lay to his left. *Dismissal.* When the spirit had been raised and when it had done the magician's bidding, the wooden stake would be driven through its heart so that never again could it be used for such rites.

Laertes snapped his head up. Jonathan had just raised his voice.

'*Hajoth a Kadosh, cry, speak, roar, bellow! Our name is legion, for we are many.*'

*Our name is legion, for we are many.* So say demons and devils and their believers.

Behind Laertes, a sudden wind slapped loudly against the barn and the torchlight flickered, the flames snapping like whips. Laertes' hands shook. But he remained sitting, eyes on Jonathan's back as the sorcerer continued to summon the spirit of Justin Coltman who lay rotting in his coffin only three feet away.

The gaslamps had been lit, casting huge, pale yellow circles on the night-blackened streets of Manhattan. Poe's slight body gently swayed side to side with the carriage motion. Sparks flew when the iron-shod hoofs of the horses struck cobblestones.

Figg said, 'You are quiet, Mr Poe.'

'Next week, Mr Figg, is Valentine's Day. It will be the second such melancholy occasion since the death of my dear wife. I was thinking of the valentine she wrote me on February 14, 1846, the last Valentine's Day we spent together. She was dying even then. Had been dying for four years.

'Was it a nice one?'

Poe smiled, remembering. 'Quite nice. Simple and charming, as was she. The first letters of each line spelled out my name.'

'Say now, that's right clever.'

> *'Ever with thee I wish to roam—*
> *Dearest my life is thine.*
> *Give me a cottage for my home*
> *And a rich old cypress vine,*
> *Removed from the world with its sin and care*
> *And the tattling of many tongues.*
> *Love alone shall guide us when we are there—*
> *Love shall heal my weakened lungs;*
> *And Oh, the tranquil hours we'll spend,*
> *Never wishing that others may see!*
> *Perfect ease we'll enjoy, without thinking to lend*
> *Ourselves to the world and its glee—*
> *Ever peaceful and blissful we'll be.'*

Figg sighed, reaching over to pat Poe on the knee. 'Right sweet, it is. Yes, I did enjoy that.'

Poe touched his heart. 'It is written here and shall remain here forever. The document is too precious to me, so I do not carry it for fear of losing it.'

Figg said, 'You're smart to do that, squire. Where we are goin', a man can lose more than a scrap of paper.'

Poe chuckled. 'Scotch Ann's seems to have put you on the defensive, Mr Figg. You have my word that you do not have to partake of anything—'

Figg snapped. 'Ain't right fer a man to feel that way about another man. That sort of thing does not meet with acceptance in England, I'll have you know.'

'It is disgraceful here as well, Mr Figg. There can be nothing more loathsome than a man who engages in such unnatural practices.'

'The Queen herself has said that such things are an abomination. She says women don't do it, not ever.'

'I am afraid, Mr Figg, that the inhabitants of Scotch Ann's are not of a mind to be told they are in error in their proclivities. Pray that we encounter Volney Gunning there. One day has passed.'

Figg looked out at the dark Manhattan streets. The stench of a slaughterhouse reached his nose and as the carriage neared it, Figg heard the scream of an animal being killed. Jonathan. Did people scream when he killed them? Jonathan. One day gone.

'One day,' muttered Figg, eyes on the slaughterhouse. He continued to look back at it as the cab headed towards Scotch Ann's. The animal had stopped screaming. Its days were over.

Poe was an aristocrat in manners and morals, a romantic, a man fanatically chivalrous to women. His tolerance for people whose personal conduct fell below his standards of virtue was as low as his tolerance for lesser literary talents. Which is why he stared with utter disgust at the homosexual orgy he and Figg had interrupted on the third floor of Scotch Ann's brothel. A coin or two in the right hand had got them the location of this very private party. They'd entered the room to find six men—three nude, three in women's clothing—preparing to enjoy a lavish feast of erotic food and drink.

Volney Gunning quickly sat up, watery eyes rapidly blinking at Poe. Gunning had been reclining on huge lavender satin cushions, his long, balding head in the lap of a thin man who wore a shoulder-length blonde wig and a blue gown revealing bare shoulders.

'Poe, how dare you! This, this is a private affair. I shall have you and your friend thrown out immediately!'

Poe heard the cock of a gun-hammer behind him. That would be Mr Figg removing his flintlock from his pocket and undoubtedly depositing his rotund body in front of the only door in the room. Even with this assistance, Poe had no intention of remaining long in such decadence. From Gunning, he wanted only Jonathan's whereabouts. After that, it was retreat in haste from this temple of unnatural lust.

'Mr Gunning, you would be advised to tell us what we want to know. Where is Jonathan?'

Voleney Gunning's jaw dropped. He flopped backwards as though wanting the beautifully-gowned prostitute to embrace and protect him from a harsh world.

'J-Jonathan? I know of no such person. Who are you to come here and question me—'

Figg's soft rasp moved closer as the boxer stepped from the door. 'O "Oo are we," 'e says. We are the gents whats goin' to put a ball

249

through yer stinkin' brain if you do not tell us what we come to 'ear. *That* is 'oo we are, mate.'

A corner of Poe's small mouth went up in a bitter smile. 'Steady on, Mr Figg. I am certain that Mr Gunning believes us to be in earnest. Well sir?'

Gunning's deep voice trembled with fear. 'I know of no such per-person. I know of no such—'

'You lie, sir.' There was steel in Poe's gentle, Southern voice.

'You offend me, sir!' Gunning pointed a long, bony forefinger at Poe.

Figg stepped foward, arm extended, the flintlock aimed at Gunning's head. 'You offend *me*, you bloody poof! You sends nigger minstrels to carve me and I owe you fer that, mate.'

Poe's small hand was on Figg's pistol, gently pressing it down towards the floor. 'As you can see, Mr Gunning, my friend is upset at your twice having tried to murder him. I refer to the train yesterday noon, and also to the matter of gas leakage a few days ago at the Hotel Astor. My friend is vindictive and you could well be the worse for it.'

'I cannot speak of *him*. You-you must know that.' Volney Gunning, tall and extremely thin, cringed closer to his partner.

Poe looked around the room, grey eyes swiftly absorbing details. The room reeked of plush decay. Hanging from the walls were obscene tapestries explicit in their portrayal of the pleasures of Greek love between man and man, man and boy. *Explicit foulness.* There was the sweet smell of opium and amidst the esoteric eatables and beverages on the long, low wooden table, Poe saw the opium pipes. Faint wisps of smoke trailed from two of them.

There were red velvet drapes in front of the windows, gaslights on the walls, along with more obscene paintings. Spotted around the room were cheap copies of statues of slim, beautiful young men. On the floor were huge satin pillows of varying colours on which the naked men and their prostitutes reclined. All three of the prostitutes carried fans. Two wore thin, black lace gloves and one, Poe noticed, wore mittens. A few years ago, wearing mittens while dining had been something of a fad among upper-class New York women.

Poe said, 'Mr Figg, I cannot tell you the names of the so-called ladies among us—'

'Sarah,' said the one with his arms around Volney Gunning. Flicking his fan closed, *Sarah* pointed it at the other two prostitutes. 'Amelia and Messalina.'

Sarah, batting long lashes, smiled up at Poe. The male whore was stunningly beautiful and his lascivious gaze made the writer ill at ease. Poe continued speaking as though he had not been interrupted. The uneasiness he felt because of Sarah's glance, Poe would push aside by increasing his scorn. The tongue of Tomahawk had a sharp sting.

'Well now, Mr Figg, the ladies have introduced themselves, a fact which can either cause you to bow from the waist or retch until your stomach aches.'

The smile fled Sarah's face. He snapped his fan open with a delicate hand, hiding all of his face behind it, except for his pale green eyes and long lashes. The eyes gleamed with hatred.

Poe sneered. 'Let us now introduce the men, Mr Figg. Volney Gunning. You have made his acquaintance and are none the better for it, I warrant. Then there is Prosper Benjamin, the portly, bearded gentleman who has been holding hands with Amelia of the ivory-handled fan. Mr Benjamin, married and a pillar of respectability, owns ships of shoddy quality, ships used to bring cheap immigrant labour to the shores of this republic. How many of your ships are on the bottom of the ocean, Mr Benjamin? Obviously you cannot build quality vessels if you are to spend money in such a temple of Venus as this.'

'And there is Abe Pietch. Mr Pietch is a landlord, an approved bloodsucker. Notice, Mr Figg, how he blushes and inches away from Messalina. Could it be shame that causes such a breech? Who can say? Mr Pietch constructs slum housing and allows immigrants to live there in squalor unknown in the northern hemisphere. Surrounded by awesome filth and deadly living conditions, the immigrants are subject to such vagaries of fate as cholera, yellow fever, smallpox, turberculosis and a monstrous death rate that kills them in consistently large numbers. This state of affairs allows Mr Pietch to amass money which he lends or invests at usurious rates. Do not borrow money from Mr Pietch, Mr Figg. In return he would expect at least your first-born and three vital organs.'

Figg spat on the table of food. 'Lovely lot, they are. Maggots crawlin' over garbage 'ave a sweeter smell.'

Poe looked down at the table. 'Ah, honey mixed with peppercorns. Considered an aphrodisiac in the Orient. And this meat here, what is—'

'Partridge.' Sarah snapped the word at Poe.

Poe smiled at Figg. 'Throughout the ages, Mr Figg, impotent men have believed that the flesh of the partridge will return their sexual powers. Among fowls there is none more lecherous than the partridge. It is said to be so sexually adept that it has the ability to make pregnant its mate merely by using its voice.'

Figg snorted, pistol still pointing at Volney Gunning's head. 'Only the bloomin' voice? Saves a patch of 'ard work, don't it?'

Sarah, sardonically playing the hostess, fixed a cold smile on his lovely face, flicking his fan at the table. 'Goat's milk with the leaf of the Satryricon plant. Sip it, Mr Poe and you will be able to achieve sexual congress no less than seventy times in rapid succession. Assuming you have that objective. These are love apples, commonly called tomatoes and this, this dish is bull's testicles. Resembles an ordinary meat pie—'

Poe aimed his cold grey eyes at Sarah. 'Yesterday when you killed Miles Standish, did he beg for his life?'

Sarah snapped his fan closed, eyes still on the table. Amelia and Messalina quickly exchanged glances, looked at Poe then looked away.

Sarah stood up, forced a smile and slowly walked towards Poe. He moved with the grace of a woman flirting. Hips swayed, the fan fluttered, Poe smelled perfume, saw the flash of gaslight on jewellery. Sarah was close enough to touch him. Poe leaned back, uncertain as to how he should deal with this he-she, this lovely and evil *thing*.

Sarah closed his fan, placing the hand that held it on Poe's shoulder. Figg watched Poe stand rigid as a bird hypnotised by a slow crawling snake.

·'Dear, dear, dear Mr Poe.' Sarah's voice was soft, low, seductive. 'Can we not comfort you as well?'

Lord help us, thought Figg. This one really thinks she's a woman and if I didn't know the bloody difference, I'd think so too. And Poe, he can only stand there like his feet are nailed to the carpet. Nothing he ever learned about women has prepared the little man for this day, I'll wager.

Poe's jaw trembled. He gripped his stick with two hands. This was no woman, this was—

Figg heard the tiny click, saw the blade.

The knife was just behind Poe's shoulder.

Sarah's fan. Sarah had pressed a button, sending six inches of slim, bright steel out of the fan's handle.

Figg was in motion.

He did it all at once. Shift the pistol to his left hand, shove Poe

252

forward and out of the way and with his right hand, grab Sarah's fan hand.

Figg swung the arm behind Sarah's back, jerking it up hard, fast and high, jerking it up between Sarah's shoulder blades and driving the prostitute up on his toes. And with a sickening pop, breaking the arm at the right shoulder blade.

Sarah collapsed on the floor, blonde wig falling off. His face was white, his mouth open in terrible shock. He inhaled loudly through his opened mouth.

Figg levelled the pistol at the other two male prostitutes who were on their feet, fists tight around their fans. The blades in each fan glittered brightly.

Figg pulled his other flintlock from his pocket. 'I don't miss too often from this close up.'

Poe slowly got off the table. He'd fallen on it, smearing the front of his coat with erotic food and drink. His nostrils flared at the smell and he winced. 'My gratitude, Mr Figg.'

'Accepted, Mr Poe.'

Poe looked at Volney Gunning. 'Where is Jonathan, sir? And be quick about it.'

Gunning, vunerable in his pathetic nudity, began to weep. 'I cannot say.'

'You cannot or will not?'

'Cannot. I—I do not know.'

Returning a pistol to his pocket, Figg then bent over, picking up Sarah's fan knife. 'I could use this 'ere thing on yer tender parts, Mr Gunning. Bet you would converse with us then.'

Gunning shook his head, continuing to weep. 'I do not know, I swear *I do not know.*'

Figg sneered. Bloody poof. No spine, no spunk. Figg moved towards him.

Gunning was on his feet. He ran towards the drapes, disappearing behind them. Everyone in the room was caught by surprise. As the two other naked men were getting to their feet and the male prostitutes were looking in the direction Gunning had gone, they all heard the sound of window glass breaking and they heard Volney Gunning's fading scream.

Sarah moaned, but in the race to the window, Sarah was forgotten.

Through the broken window, they looked down at the bleeding body of Voleney Gunning barely visible in the snow and darkness behind the building. Gunning's head was at an ugly angle, an angle possible only in death.

Poe said, 'Jonathan terrified him, Mr Figg. More than you or I ever could, Jonathan terrified him.'

A shivering Prosper Benjamin moved quickly away from the window, rubbing his arms, muttering to himself. 'This is tragic. This is tragic. What shall we do?'

In the centre of the room, he turned to point a finger at Poe and Figg. 'You two! Your fault. You killed him and I shall see you hang for it. Yes hang!'

Poe said, 'And reveal to the world the degenerate you are? Unlikely, Mr Benjamin. Our modern times have not accepted homosexuality, and that, sir, is an understatement. There is nothing lower than a homosexual, and I, for one, would make sure that the press and public learned of your proclivities even if I had to write the article myself. No sir, you will not do anything to indicate that Mr Figg and I are criminally involved with the death of Mr Gunning. For your sake and that of Mr Pietch, I suggest you evolve a tale explaining Mr Gunning's sudden demise. I hear footsteps on the stairs. Think fast, Mr Benjamin. Your time is at hand, sir.'

Poe opened the door and Figg gladly followed him through it.

# CHAPTER THIRTY-FIVE

## The Second Day

The sun was a hard brillance; it shone down on the snow to create an eye-piercing glare. Dark shapes slunk in and out of the glare, heading towards the barn on Hugh Larney's abandoned horse farm. The shapes were starving wolves and they had heard the whinny of the two horses used by Jonathan and Laertes. The wolves, experienced and intelligent, had killed horses before. Made desperate by hunger and a bitter February cold, the wolves closed in on the barn.

There were seven of them and they moved in killing formation, spread out and alert, lean grey bodies loping easily and gracefully across the snow, heads turning left and right to sense danger. Their eyes glittered, their jaws hung down to reveal deadly teeth.

Suddenly the wolves stopped, freezing in their tracks. Their ears flattened against their skulls and a couple of them began inching backwards, mouths closed, heads darting left and right, eagerly seeking the source of the overwhelming danger they now felt.

There was no sound except the howl of the wind. Then came the howl of the wolf leader and the others took it up. The leader's sense of danger was stronger and he had warned the others. They felt it too and answered him.

The wolves turned and fled, leaving their tracks in the snow, and soon they had gone. Behind them all was quiet. No sound came from the barn where Jonathan and Laertes slept.

But the wolves had felt the danger and evil now accumulating around the barn, and even for these most vicious of killers in nature's scheme of destruction, what was now occuring there was more than they wanted to confront.


A worried Poe sat on the edge of Rachel's bed, holding her hand. Behind him the doctor said, 'She rests now but that is because of the medicine. According to the servants, her screams were heart-rending and occurred too frequently during the night.'

'Jonathan,' whispered Poe.

'I beg your pardon?'

'It is of no matter, sir.'

'There is a great disturbance within her, Mr Poe. She is deeply troubled and I would assume that her recent ordeal—'

'Yes doctor. She suffers from having confronted an evil most of us can barely imagine.'

*Jonathan. The corpse of Justin. The savagery of Hamlet Sproul. Near death and degradation at the hands of Sproul's cohorts. Yes, doctor, there is indeed a great disturbance with her and I pray to God it does not last, for she will grow to dread the night as I do and she will quake at the thought of what terror sleep can hold for her.*

'I leave you now, Mr Poe. Her maidservant has instructions as to the proper medication and she is to contact me immediately should the crisis reassert itself.'

Poe didn't turn around. 'Yes, doctor. You have my deepest gratitude.'

'Yes, well . . .'

Poe still did not turn around. He kept his eyes on Rachel, now deep in a drugged sleep. Was she again having nightmares about Jonathan?

Her fingers clutched Poe's hand and her lovely face suddenly contorted and Poe's heart fluttered.

He turned to look at the door, on the verge of calling the doctor back. Then Rachel relaxed her grip and Poe looked down at her once more. *My dearest, my dearest.* Leaning over her, he gently kissed her perspiring brow. *My dearest Rachel.*

A tear fell from Poe's eye, disappearing into the thick, soft redness that was Rachel Coltman's lovely hair.


Sarah Clannon screamed Jonathan's name over and over. She was delirious, thrashing about on the bed, and Hugh Larney could barely hold her down. The wound in her side was infected, turning yellow and an ugly green. *If she died if she died . . .*

Larney screamed over his shoulder, 'Get the bloody doctor, you fool! Get him!'

The servant turned and ran.

# CHAPTER THIRTY-SIX

'Yer here to bite the ken.' Wade Bruenhausen started his rocking-chair in motion again, slowly rubbing greasy hands on his shirt front. The Dutch procurer was fat, with a nose as long and as pointed as a carrot, and he smelled of shit. Figg, who found it easy to dislike him, turned his face away from the man's body odour.

'Ain't what we's 'ere for,' said Figg looking around the dirty cellar where Bruenhausen lived with his child whores. There was nothing in this house they wanted to rob.

'I says you are.' Bruenhausen rocked faster, moving in and out of the orange glow from the fireplace diagonally behind him.

'You can bloody well say what you like. We told you what we want. We want Dearborn Lapham.'

Bruenhausen stopped rocking. 'Do you now? The gentlemen want little Dearborn. Lots of gentlemen want little Dearborn. What makes you two so special, besides the fact that I do not much like either one of you by the sound of your voices?'

'We wants 'er. We will pay you for 'er time.' Figg looked at Poe standing several feet behind him. It was Poe's idea. Don't waste time searching for Hugh Larney. The hours were too few and too precious for that. Make him come to us. Dearborn Lapham. When Larney learned that Poe and Figg had her . . .

It will be too much for his vanity, Poe had said. Pray that it is, replied Figg. Poe was worried about Rachel, about her nightmares and her need for a doctor. He feared that as long as Jonathan existed, Rachel would live in terror. The spiritualist's continued existence would damage hers. So find Jonathan before the nine days were up, and destroy him.

Figg no longer had a woman to worry about, nor did he have nine days to find Jonathan. The second day was ending and that left one more week. Figg himself had barely been in New York a week. Seven days more and Jonathan would be beyond this revenge. Beyond *anyone's* revenge.

Make Hugh Larney come to them. Then force him to reveal Jonathan's whereabouts. So it was down to the Bowery and Wade Bruenhausen, who 'read' his Bible to his child whores and thieves by quoting long passages he'd memorised. The gross and smelly

Bruenhausen, with most of his black hair gone because of an earlier attack of yellow fever, was surly, suspicious. He wore a frilly shirt, knee-britches, silk stockings and high heels, the dated clothing of another century. All of the clothing was filthy, as if Bruenhausen had rolled around in coal dust.

He reminded Figg of a huge, vile toad.

Bruenhausen coughed up phlegm from his throat, spitting it on the floor just inches from Figg's boots. His voice was an ugly whisper, the result of a severed vocal cord presented to him some years ago by a broken bottle in the hands of a drunken acquaintance.

'Mr Poe ain't sayin' much. Then again he has been known to say too much. I still remember you telling that church committee that I should be hanged for what I was doing with little children.'

'Hanged, drawn and quartered, I believe I said.'

'Oh you did, that you did. *I* remember. Some folks took your words to heart, Mr Poe and I was forced to absent myself from New York for a brief turn. Might I inquire as to why you want the services of Dearborn Lapham, considerin' how you condemned my, er, business practices some time back?'

Poe stepped forward. 'She is the key to a mystery we seek to unravel.'

'Is she now?'

Bruenhausen leered and resumed rocking, lifting his dirty, white high-heel shoes off the floor each time he rocked backwards. Poe was a hypocritical bastard. Criticising Bruenhausen and now showing up with heat in his loins for the tender flesh of a child. Hypocritical bastard.

The Dutchman said, 'You cannot have her. She is reserved for a special customer and he pays well, more than you two can afford.'

Figg said, 'I have cash money. We know you sends 'er to Hugh Larney, but all the same we would like to 'ave 'er for a time. No 'arm will come to the child. We will pay you a good price.'

The man disgusted Figg, who would have preferred to hold the Dutchman's bare backside to the flames.

The rocking stopped once more. 'It is heartwarming, Mr Poe, to have you come to me after all these years. You are here to take—'

'To *pay*.' Figg was losing patience.

'No!' A smug Bruenhausen resumed rocking.

Figg looked around the dark cellar. 'Is she about?' Straw in corners for the children to sleep on. Cardboard boxes, empty barrels, empty whisky bottles. A junk factory smelling like a privy and Figg didn't want to spend any more time here than he had to. Near the front door, three dirty kids with long curly hair, their thin bodies covered by rags, stood watching the three men. Figg couldn't tell if they were boys or girls under the grime, but he knew one thing for sure—they would not not live long working for Wade Bruenhausen.

'Is she about, says the Englishman.' Bruenhausen stopped rocking. 'I would say that you are not a young man, that you are large and you are a plain man, lower station and you have little patience with matters which do not go your way.' The rocking resumed.

'The girl,' growled Figg.

Bruenhausen responded to the threat in the boxer's voice. He whistled sharply between his teeth—three shrill *tweets*. Instantly, the children ran from the cellar, leaving the three men alone.

As Poe and Figg turned to look at the empty doorway, Bruenhausen leaned to his left as though listening to the flames in the fireplace.

'Saint Luke, chapter four, verse ten. "For it is written, He shall give his angels charge over thee, to keep thee: And in their hands they shall bear thee up, lest at any time thou dash thy foot against a stone." '

Figg and Poe were staring at him, when they heard the noise behind them. Turning, they saw the dark cellar quickly fill with children. In seconds, fifteen of them crammed into the room, and most—boys and girls—held weapons. Knives, clubs, broken bottles. One who didn't was Dearborn Lapham, who stood uncomfortably in the first line of children.

Bruenhausen's rocking was slow and deliberate. *Menacing.* 'My rod and my staff, Englishman.' Bruenhausen reached for his own scarred neck with a hairy hand.

'Look at them,' he said. 'Abandoned urchins who know no loyalty save that which I have placed in their hearts and minds. No one dares challenge me so long as the little ones are around. Some are as young as five, none over fifteen, and I own them, Englishman, own them body and soul. And it is for fear and love of me that they will deal with you. You will not be the first to feel their wrath. When I clap my hands together—'

He stopped rocking, hands poised in front of his chest and only inches apart. 'Twice. That is the signal. And afterwards, we shall see if you are carrying anything of value. Dearborn?'

'Yes, Mr Bruenhausen?'

'You shall watch your friends be chastised.'

'Yes, Mr Bruenhausen.' Dearborn always did as she was told.

The Dutchman adjusted the tiny black spectacles which hid his sightless eyes. 'I owe you, Mr Edgar Allan meddlin' Poe, and a debt should always be paid. An eye for an eye, a tooth for a tooth, and so it is written. As for your English friend, I do not enjoy his manners.'

The Dutchman's smile was cruel as he lifted his hands from his lap and his hands were again in front of his chest and inches apart when Figg pulled the trigger on the flintlock, firing through his coat pocket, briefly setting fire to the cloth and sending a ball through *both* of the Dutchman's hands! Bruenhausen screamed, jerking backwards in the rocking-chair, sending it over and down to the floor. Now he was in the straw and dirt, arms crossed in front of his chest, blood pouring down the back and front of both hands.

'JesusJesusJesusJesusJesusJesus, oh dear JesusJesusJesus!' His tiny black spectacles dangled from one ear as he twitched with pain.

The advantage was Figg's and he used it.

Spinning quickly around to face the children, Figg removed the other flintlock from his pocket. His coat still smoked from the first shot. 'Only one ball. Well, 'oo wants it? Come on, you murderin' little buggers, 'oo wants to die!'

The boxer's bulldog face was terrifying. Poe had never seen him look this frightening, and it was easy to imagine the forces that had gone to create a Pierce James Figg over the years. There was a fierceness in the man that belonged to a trapped animal determined to kill or be killed. The boxer appeared to have accepted death and therefore no longer feared it.

His bold action had snatched away any initiative the children might have had. And Wade Bruenhausen lay in agony on the floor, unable to command or threaten.

Figg said, 'You, Dearborn. Step over 'ere and mind you do it carefully. Killin's a man's job and if anyone of you wants to try me, I will prove to you that this is so. I will kill one of you immediately and after that I will use a knife and me fists on the rest. More than one of you will die before I will, and that is a fact.'

The children hesitated. Dearborn stepped over to Poe who put an arm around her, his eyes darting from Figg to the children and back again. Violence hung around the boxer like mist around a high mountain peak. Poe held his breath. The children were capable of anything; children like these had killed before.

*But they had never seen Pierce James Figg before.*

He said, 'Get the bleedin' 'ell outta here, all of you. Go on, hop it!'

He took a step forward and they turned and ran.

Bruenhausen lay in front of the fireplace, trembling with incredible pain and continually repeating the name of Jesus.

Figg walked over to him. 'Do not come for the child, Dutchman. If you do, I will 'ave your life. You got me word on that. It is Pierce James Figg who tells you he will do for you if you seek the lass.'

Bruenhausen spoke through, clenched teeth. '*Jesus* will strike you down. *Jesus* will come for you.'

'Best you not be with 'im when he shows.'

Figg lifted his foot to stomp Bruenhausen and that's when Poe shouted, 'Mr Figg!'

Figg gently put his foot down to the floor, eyes on a frightened Bruenhausen.

The boxer dropped a gold sovereign on the procurer's bloody shirt front. 'Use it fer a gravestone, for if I see you again, that is what you'll be needin'.'

# CHAPTER THIRTY-SEVEN

Hugh Larney ordered Thor to follow the doctor who had treated Sarah Clannon's wound back to New York and kill him—*kill him in New York, not here.*

Larney, with Thor standing behind him like some huge, dark shadow, forced himself to smile, through the front window of the small country house, at the doctor, who placed his black bag on the seat of his carriage before climbing up himself. Once seated, the doctor leaned out of the carriage, waving to Larney who waved back.

Thor's brown eyes, spaced far apart, watched the two carriage horses lean forward in knee-high snow, lifting their hoofs to their chests, large nostrils snorting steam in the winter cold.

'Why do you not kill the doctor here? I think it save time.'

Larney let the green lace curtain fall back into place. He was angry at Edgar Allan Poe, for it was Poe who had made it necessary to have the doctor murdered. Damn Poe's eyes!

'You heard the doctor's words. He is treating Rachel Coltman who is in delicate health as a result of her misadventure with Hamlet Sproul. She does not sleep well; she dreams of unending horror, we are told. And who sits mooning at her bedside like a lamb bleating for its mother? *Poe.*'

Larney began pacing back and forth. 'Did not the healing physician confess that he has talked with Poe this very day, and how worried our literary friend is about his lady fair. Dear doctor expects to be asked once again to look in upon widow Coltman, and when that happens he will surely find Poe clutching her hand. A casual conversation *may* ensue and dear doctor *may* mention that he has paid a visit to my small country home to treat a woman for a pistol wound. This talk *may* transpire and it *may* not, but I cannot afford to sit idly by and have it occur. I am faced with cleaning up after Jonathan, for it was he who sent Sarah Clannon to Poe cottage where she received a ball in her side.

'And so, dear Thor of the hammer fists, you will prevent dear doctor from having words with that little scum E. A. Poe. You will prevent said scum from tracing Sarah Clannon here to me. I wish to confront Poe and his lumpish friend on *my* terms and when *I* choose. The two of them have probably called at my Fifth Avenue home; it is unlikely that they will seek me at the abandoned farm.'

'Which leaves this country retreat, a welcomed part of my secret land holdings. Let the doctor be disposed of in Manhattan, where one more crime statistic will go unnoticed in a city rampant with such numbers.'

Thor nodded, rubbing his right fist. He understood. 'They find the doctor not come back to New York, they come here. He die in New York, *nobody* come here.' He grinned, thick purple lips spreading across his wide, black face.

'You are not obliged to think,' said Larney, 'but it is gratifying that on those rare occasions when you do so, it is constructive. Yes, dear Thor, that is why dear doctor dies on familiar ground. Let the matter be pursued there rather than here. He will be mourned. I shall be among the mourners.'

Thor looked at the window. 'I go now. He be far enough in front of me and soon it will be dark.'

Larney stopped pacing. He looked down at his trembling hands. Sarah Clannon. Barely alive. Jonathan had charged him with seeing she did not die.

Poe. An omnipresent fungus. Well, Poe had held his last casual conversation with dear doctor. Sarah Clannon. Poe. Jonathan. So much to worry about. So much to fear.

Larney said, 'Thor, bring Dearborn back with you when you return. I have need for her exquisite solace and comfort.'

Thor grinned. 'It be done.'

He caught the gold coin flipped to him by Larney, payment for the beautiful child. Master Larney would be enjoying himself tonight, while the white woman slowly died in the room next to his and called out for the man Jonathan, who was on the abandoned horse farm doing things that Thor did not want to know about. Thor feared Jonathan as he feared no man born of woman.

*Voices called to her and shapes materialised out of the darkness and reached for her. Rachel turned to flee and instead froze with fear. Her husband Justin stood in front of her, bleeding from the mouth, reaching out for her with both hands. He called her name and she backed away from him, screaming. A hand holding a shiny scalpel moved closer to her face and she wanted to run, but couldn't! She waited for the shapes and the hand holding the scalpel to reach her, and when they did—*

Rachel was sitting up in bed, weeping, her arms around Poe who stroked her long, red hair and spoke softly. 'I am here, dearest. I am here.'

'Do not leave me, Eddy.' He felt the warmth of her tears against his cheek.

His love for her filled every part of him, lifting him to a height he had forgotten existed. He loved her deeply, terribly. 'I am here, dearest. I shall never leave you. Never.'

He felt her grip him tighter and the feel of her arms around him was a joy that made him weep, his tears blending with hers.

## The Second Night

He sat cross-legged in the protective circle, chewing the cold dog meat, his mind fastened to his quest: the Throne of Solomon. He was one day closer. Behind him he heard Laertes pouring unfermented wine into a small wooden cup.

Suddenly the wind rattled the rotting wooden doors, snapping the orange flames on the torches which were stuck in the ground. Jonathan sensed Laertes' uneasiness, and a second later Laertes said, 'Listen! Can you hear it?'

Jonathan listened. The wind. It seemed to call his name.

*Jonathannnnn. Jonathannnnnnn.*

There was danger hidden in the wind. Jonathan *had* heard his name and it had come from Asmodeus. The king of demons was here to fight the final battle, to stop Jonathan from securing infinite and eternal claim over him. Asmodeus would do all in his power to stop Jonathan from claiming the Throne of Solomon.

*Jonathannnnnnn.*

Laertes squirmed. Jonathan felt the man's fear and said, 'Silence. Stay as you are.'

*Jonathannnnnnn.*

The magician was himself afraid but at the same time he felt *free*, free to challenge Asmodeus in the last encounter the two would ever have. The exhilaration grew within him and he flung the dog meat aside and began to chant.

'*Raphael, Miraton, Tarmiel, Rael and Rex.*' The names of protective spirits.

'*Raphael, Miraton, Tarmiel, Rael and Rex.*'

The wind shrieked, rattling the rotting barn walls, threatening to uproot them. A torch fell forward and to the ground, its flame disappearing.

'*Raphael, Miraton, Tarmiel, Rael and Rex.*'

Jonathan spread his arms wide and chanted louder.

The wind blew faster, sending a bone-chilling cold down on the two men, then suddenly it died. *The wind was gone!*

Jonathan's chant became a mumble.

Laertes could not stop shaking.

Figg cautiously opened the door, to see Poe turn in his chair and smile at him.

Poe was exuberant. 'Enter my good fellow! You are not blessed with the grace of a gazelle, so abandon any attempt to enter this room like a gentle breeze.'

Figg stepped into the room. 'My, my. We are a chipper lot to-night. Come to tell you I am takin' leave of you fer me dinner with Titus Bootham.'

Poe put down his pen. He'd been writing at the desk in Rachel Coltman's study, working on the tale 'Hop Frog', and he was happy! For the first time in too long a time, he was happy. Rachel had brought him this joy. It was his and hers to share.

'Mr Figg, I wish you a merry dinner. My regards to Mr Bootham and to the rest of the English contingent he has gathered to make your acquaintance. I am sure they will find you to be a marvel, as have I.'

'Nice of you to say. Ain't much of a gatherin'. Mr Bootham and some of the English lads he knows are standin' me a meal at a good tavern, and I suppose they will ask me a thing or two about the prize-ring.'

'Regale them with tales of blood and triumph, Mr Figg. The audience enjoys a nice fright every now and then. I am hard at work, as you can see. I *feel* like working, Mr Figg, I do indeed.'

He feels too deeply, thought Figg. He's too high or he's too low. Takes the world seriously. Wonder what the widow Coltman and he talked about upstairs?

'I shall be lodgin' with Mr Bootham tonight. You take care of yerself.'

'Thank you, Mr Figg. Dearborn is asleep with one of the maids, and Rachel has told me the child can stay here for as long as we desire. It is here that Hugh Larney will come and it is here that I shall wait for him.'

'Well, you just let me ask Mr Larney the hard questions. I will be comin' back 'ere earliest. 'Ave cooky keep some food hot fer me. Nice to see you with a pen in yer 'ands again. It is a nice feelin' to do yer trade.'

'I cannot tell you how nice. Rachel and I, we have talked. There is a bond between us, Mr Figg, and it has come about as a result of this horrible business. I shall spend the night here in a spare room. By the way, you are not going to mention—?'

Figg shook his head. 'Mr Bootham knows a bit or two, but I ain't sayin' nothin' to the rest. Mr Dickens once taught me somethin' Mr Samuel Johnson said and that is "Three can keep a secret if two are dead".'

Poe threw back his head and laughed. The laugh was full, long. Feelin' too deeply, thought Figg. A man should have more control over himself than does little Eddy. That woman has got him runnin' a swift race at the moment. Hope she don't cut him off at the knees. It happens, Lord knows.

'Very good, Mr Figg. Very, very good. It is a thought that would nicely fill a space at the bottom of a column. When I have my magazine—'

Figg sighed. So that was it. Him and the lady and his bloomin' magazine. Did she promise to give him the money for it? No one else seemed ready to do so. What kind of reliable promise could be expected from a lady as sick as Rachel Coltman was at the present time. It was certain that the lady was out of mind a wee bit. Somewhat soft in the head due to the hard times that had fallen upon her in the old Brewery. Or so said the doctor.

Leave him be, it seemed best to Figg. Leave him with his dreams. He can ask his own hard questions when the sun arises. Or when the lady no longer graces her sick bed.

'In the mornin', then,' said Figg.

'In the morning, Mr Figg.' Poe's smile was wondrous.

He smiles, thought Figg, and I 'ave a hole in me one and only frock-coat.

Touching his hand to his top hat, he bowed slightly and left the room, his polished pistol box under his arm, his carpetbag in his hand. Little Mr Poe should know that a horse that runs too fast never makes it over the full course. He *should* know, but he doesn't.

# CHAPTER THIRTY-EIGHT

## The Third Day

The bitter winter cold that had been knifing through Laertes' body began to fade. He was being hypnotised by Jonathan.

As ordered, he gazed into the magician's eyes, fascinated by the colours that spun around and around—the reds, blues, greens. They drew him deeper into a pleasant warmth and he relaxed, smiling gently with no idea of who or where he was. *He felt warm.* The numbness left his hands and feet and never in his life had he heard a sound as pleasant as the voice that now filled his life; it was the only thing in the world worth living for.

As Laertes slept on the hard, cold earth, Jonathan sipped the drugged wine and thought of last night's triumph over Asmodeus. The demon king would return. He *had* to. He had to stop Jonathan from getting the throne, for possession of the throne meant dominion over all. It meant dominion over Asmodeus.

So long as Jonathan remained within the magic circle, he was safe. But he wanted more than mere safety. He wanted power. And when Asmodeus returned, Jonathan would fight him again.

And win.

Nothing could stop the magician now. Nothing in heaven or hell or on earth could stop him or keep him from the Throne of Solomon.

Hear me, Asmodeus. Hear me. Bow to me, as you must. Bow to me, bow to me, bow to me.

Jonathan fell back into a drugged sleep.

*Bow to me!*

# CHAPTER THIRTY-NINE

An angry Hugh Larney, backed by Thor and two more men, stood in the snow on the sidewalk in front of Rachel Coltman's mansion. He drew his ermine-trimmed cloak tighter around his small, elegantly-dressed body and aimed his pointed chin at Poe, who stood alone at the top of the grey stone stairs leading into the mansion.

'I *will* have the girl, Poe. Hear me well on this. For the last time, I order you to stand aside.'

'I will not stand aside, Hugh Larney. You have been refused entrance into this house and that refusal will not be withdrawn.'

'As usual, you go far beyond yourself. I cannot have you oppose me. I cannot and I will not.'

'Since I do not utter your name in my prayers, know that I oppose you in all things.' Poe shivered. Fear. And the cold. And, as always, from the excitement he felt when near to violence.

Where was Figg? He was supposed to have returned early this morning, but it was almost noon and he had not shown. Was he alive? Dead? Lying wounded in some vile grog shop, the victim of Jonathan's minions?

'The child is mine whenever I choose, *Mister* Poe, and I so choose now.'

Hugh Larney looked at the men with him. Thor and two others. More than enough to wipe something as insignificant as Edgar Allan Poe from the face of the earth, and at the moment that was exactly what Hugh Larney was strongly inclined to do. Last night. Thor had returned with the news that Poe, assisted by his friend with the face of a ravaged bulldog, had removed Dearborn Lapham from Wade Bruenhausen, leaving the Dutchman with hands containing holes where God had made none.

Thor had murdered the doctor but that news did not affect Larney as much as hearing that Poe, *Poe* had Dearborn. Hugh Larney took no such blow from any man, particularly from a man such as Poe, who spent more time lying face down in gutters than he did standing on his feet. Larney's stables were cleaned with better rags than the clothes Poe wore. Poe was a thing to be stepped on, not knelt to.

'For the last time, Mr Poe, will you stand aside and allow us to enter?'

'No.'

'Then the consequences be on your head, and, let me say, I relish this fact, sir. I most certainly relish it.'

'As you did the death of your friend, Miles Standish?'

Larney moved his tiny mouth in circles. Poe's query was leading to something. Larney was uneasy.

Poe clenched his fists to keep them from shaking. He wore neither greatcoat nor suit jacket. When told by a servant that Hugh Larney was at the front door, he had rushed from the study, his mind clouded by the desire to protect Rachel. The last time men had pushed their way into her home, it had resulted in a terrifying ordeal for her, one from which she had not recovered. Poe was not going to let that happen again. Not so long as there was breath in his body.

*Where was Figg?*

Poe stepped down, slowly walking towards Larney. A foolhardy act, perhaps, but Poe was a man of pride, of strong loyalties, particularly towards women, and at the moment he saw himself as Rachel's only protection.

'Tell me, Hugh Larney, where has Jonathan taken the body of Justin Coltman?' Poe continued his slow walk down the stairs, his fear a slithering icy mass within his stomach.

The smile passed swiftly across Larney's face. 'I see the game now. I do see the game. You hold the child and lure me to you in hopes that I give you the information about—'

He paused, then smiled once more. 'Thor will answer all of your questions, Mr Poe.'

Poe was now on the sidewalk directly in front of Larney and, without warning, he slapped Larney in the face.

The act caught everyone by surprise. Including Poe, who was almost unable to breathe because of the excitement.

*Figg where are you?*

The strains of a piano came from a nearby home. A horse-drawn ice-wagon pulled away from the house next-door and, overhead, birds huddled together for warmth on the wires of telegraph poles.

Larney, his face red where Poe had struck him, spoke in a barely audible voice. 'Do you realise what you have done?'

'I-I have challenged you to a duel.' Poe kept his eyes closed.

He heard Larney say, 'And the choice of weapons is mine. I do also take it upon myself to declare time and place. I prefer the combat to take place here and now and I choose as a weapon—Thor!'

Poe opened his eyes. Wide.

'Thor, Mr Poe. And so you lose, as always, sir.'

Poe looked up at the towering Negro, whose smile covered almost the entire bottom half of his round, black face.

Thor's grin was malevolent. 'Lit-tul mon, you and me is goin' to—'

'*A moment if you please!*'

Figg strolled towards them, as always favouring his lame right leg. Behind him, Titus Bootham, in tiny round spectacles and grizzly fur coat, climbed from a carriage. Another man waited in the carriage for Bootham to step clear.

'Ain't goin' to be no duellin' with Mr Poe,' growled Figg. He stopped, his right hand taking the black pistol box from under his left armpit.

Hugh Larney's voice became more arch, more British. He began using his hands to talk, his wrists going limp. His gloves were grey, handmade, expensive.

'Mr Poe has often claimed to be a man of honour, a Virginian aristocrat, though one finds it difficult to see how such lineage falls in line with being born of travelling players. It is a fact that duelling is frowned upon, but it is also a fact that it is an almost daily occurrence among men of honour. I repeat, among men of *honour*. No man of honour backs down from a challenge. It reflects poorly upon himself, upon his lady, who must of course suffer his lack of courage, I would trust. As Mr Poe's friend, you, ah Mr, Mr—'

'You know the name, mate.'

'Yes. Figg, was it not?'

'Was and is. And you would be Mr Hugh Larney, the man 'oo pleasures hisself with little girls.'

Larney bowed. Thor's back was to Poe, his widely-spaced eyes on Figg. The two fighters locked eyes.

Poe seemed crushed. His eyes were on the ground, as though seeing his sad life pass before his eyes. Challenging Hugh Larney had been an impulsive act, one born of pride, ignorance, an unholy attraction for violence. He was no warrior and pride was not enough to save his life this time. Not this time. And he did so want to live now. There was Rachel and there was the future, and Poe wanted to live.

He looked up, eyes on the grey clouds high above him. 'I am a man of honour, sir. I will not subject myself or Mrs Coltman to ridicule, particularly by such a relentlessly mediocre organism as yourself, sir.'

Larney flinched, his nostrils flaring.

Figg said, 'The blackamoor 'ere will thrash you into a red ruin. Look at 'im. Tall as a tree, 'e is, and 'e enjoys 'urtin' people, don't you, Mr Thor?'

The Negro's smile was sly. 'Ah only does what Master Larney says fo' me to do.'

'I jes' bet you do mate. Well now, why don't we all say *ello to this 'ere gent what's a policeman.* 'E's 'ere to ask Mrs Coltman about her doctor, what got 'isself murdered last night.'

Poe looked quickly at Figg, who continued. 'Murdered, 'e was. Face all beat in, neck broke. 'Orrible mess, it was.'

'*Quelle tragédie.*' Hugh Larney's eyes went to Thor, then looked away.

'Sergeant Tully is me name and I am here to talk with the lady.' Tully was Irish, a gruff, round man in a brown cloth coat that reached down to the snow. He had a walrus moustache on a red face and kept one hand on his tall top hat as if afraid it would be stolen, or driven away by the wind. 'I do me talkin' inside.'

He went on ahead, climbing the stairs, one hand on the railing, the other on his top hat.

Figg said, 'Since 'e's a copper, I think it best there be no trouble inside the home of Mrs Coltman. Is that not a wise way of lookin' at matters, Mr Larney?'

Larney said nothing. He continued to move his mouth in tiny circles. He was still in control of the situation. Or was he?'

Figg said to Poe, 'Spent the mornin' with Mr Bootham 'ere. 'E gets told about the murder of the doctor, Mr Bootham bein' a newspaper writer and all. When I hears it was Mrs Coltman's doctor what got hisself kilt, I says to meself you best see what is what, so's you can tell Mr Poe and 'e can do some thinkin' on it. You look to catch yer death of cold out 'ere. Inside with you, Mr Poe.'

Larney said, 'Mr Poe and I have business, or is Mr Poe's honour a thing of the past. All that concerns him seems to be a thing of the past.'

A shivering Poe said, 'The duel shall pro-proceed, sir. I request t-time, for it is not in the duelling code that you alone set time and p-place. Time, sir. I-I shall face your weapon.' He looked at Thor.

Poe drew himself up as tall as he could stand. Dear God, if only he could stop this trembling.

The coughing. It started again.

'Dear me,' said Larney, smirking at Poe. 'Such bravado. Mrs Coltman is blessed beyond belief. If only she knew how much. Or cared.'

Poe, coughing into his fist, snapped his head up at Larney, who said, 'Very well. Time. One day, two, three? How many?'

'Tomorrow, the next day, the following—' Poe's coughing became severe.

Larney gently laid a hand on Poe's arm. 'Do take the time to find a handkerchief. Say six days from now. I have guests arriving from Europe then and they do so enjoy native amusements. Perhaps on that day you will decide to crawl and beg—'

Poe spat in his face.

Larney almost lost his balance leaning backward. Thor caught him, then glared at Poe.

Figg had the pistol box open, his hand inside. His eyes took in Larney and all of Larney's men. 'Now nobody do nothin' sudden 'cause there is an American policeman inside with Mrs Coltman and if somethin' 'appens out 'ere, we are all in a spot of trouble.'

Poe was close to fainting. The cold. The coughing. His poor health. The excitement. But he stood on his feet, grey eyes boring into Hugh Larney.

'I shall die, sir, before retracting anything I have said to you today or any other day.'

'And so you shall,' Larney wiped spittle from the side of his face. 'And so you shall die, you snivelling little excuse for a man. Thor will grant your death wish, which you have laboured under for oh too long, sir. Your wish will be granted. And I shall have the child. Together she and I will look down upon your grave and—'

Figg said, 'Mr Larney.'

'Keep out of this, Englishman!'

'But I'm in it, mate.'

'As a second, perhaps, not—'

'As a fighter, Mr Larney. As a fighter.'

Larney's jaw dropped.

'Mr Poe, 'e ain't no fighter and you bloody well know it. You picked yer weapon, now 'e picks 'is. 'E picks me.'

'Mr Figg, Mr Figg—' Poe gripped Figg's arm and then the world around Poe began to spin and blood ran from his mouth and he slid down towards the snow.

Figg caught him, held him in both arms and stared down at him for long seconds. Without looking at Larney, the boxer said, ' 'E ain't fightin'. Mr Bootham?'

'Yes, Mr Figg?'

'I would be pleased if you would be my second. You have jes' 'eard us speak of the duel. It will be boxin' between me and Mr Larney's man 'ere. Kindly speak to Mr Larney about the details of time, place, conditions.'

Figg looked at Larney. 'Yer man beats me, you gets the child. You try and take 'er before the duel and somebody will die and the police will know more than we wants 'em to know.'

Larney nodded. 'I look forward to it, sir. It shall be a pleasant interlude for me.'

'If I win, mate, it won't be. I am comin' fer you then and when I 'ave you, there will be nothin' on earth to stop me from makin' you tell me what I wants to know and we need say no more about that, do we?'

Larney, cold fear trickling into his brain, nodded once more.

Inside the mansion, Poe said, 'It occurs to me, Mr Figg that in six days, Jonathan concludes his evil quest. You fight on the day that could be Jonathan's biggest triumph.'

'It is the night time we 'ave to fear, squire. If I remembers correctly, 'e will not 'ave 'is way before midnight. We 'ave until then.'

The two men were alone in the marble foyer. A tall grandfather clock ticked away the minutes.

Poe said, 'I am grateful, Mr Figg, for your offer.' He coughed, spitting blood into his fist.

'Squire, you best clean up a bit before seein' the lady.'

Poe looked up towards the first floor. 'Yes. I assume Sergeant Tully is with her now. I must go to her.' He looked at Figg. 'I shall deem it an honour, sir, if you allow me to be with you on that day.'

Figg sat down in a chair near the entrance to a small bedroom. 'Thankin' you muchly, Mr Poe. Been a while since I been in a prize-ring. Ain't set foot in one for seven years, not since me leg. I am forty-eight now and I have been a teacher of the science, a bodyguard to those who could afford it, but the ring, well, squire, that is another world. Another world, indeed.'

'Bootham will be of a great assistance and I should suppose he will rally the English contingent around you.'

'I believe so, squire. Well get you gone and wipe the red away before comin' upon yer lady.'

Halfway up the winding, white marble staircase, Poe stopped

and turned to stare down at Figg who sat alone with only the tick of the clock for company, the black pistol box on his lap, his tall top hat resting on the box.

For seconds the two stared silently at one another, and Poe bowed his head in a gesture of respect, something he had not done in the presence of another man for more years than he could remember.

Figg, who sat with an almost regal presence, nodded back. Poe turned and, clinging to the railing, walked slowly upstairs.

# CHAPTER FORTY

**The Fifth Night**

Asmodeus raged outside of the magic circle, filling the barn with his screams, his stench. Jonathan's powers were tested to their fullest extent and twice, he held on to Laertes to prevent him from fleeing, from leaving the circle and being torn apart.

Asmodeus wanted a blood sacrifice. He would name the victim. Before he could do so, contact between him and Jonathan was broken by the magician's strong will to survive, and the demon king disappeared. But Jonathan knew he would return to demand that the blood rite be given him. It was a test, one final obstacle between Jonathan and the Throne of Solomon. If the magician refused the test, Asmodeus would return again and again and Jonathan's will would be damaged, for he now knew that he could not concentrate on the ritual while simultaneously opposing the final, furious onslaught of the demon king.

In a spurt of incredible confidence, Jonathan conjured up Asmodeus and agreed to the test. From within the barn and without leaving the protective circle, he agreed to perform the blood rite on the person Asmodeus named.

In a swirl of howling, frozen winds and shrieking devils, Asmodeus named his victim.

Jonathan touched his ash-covered head to the hard, cold ground in acceptance of this final test.

# CHAPTER FORTY-ONE

Four days before the duel.

Poe said, 'By deduction, it appears that Hugh Larney had a hand in the brutal death of Rachel's doctor.'

'We are listenin'.' Figg sat on the bed massaging his right knee-cap, while Titus Bootham sat in one of the two chairs in the small room. The three were in Bootham's home.

'I have made inquiries,' said Poe. 'The doctor was summoned by a servant of Larney's, one Jacob Cribb, and Mr Cribb declared that a woman was in need of immediate treatment for a pistol wound. There are people in the area where the doctor resided who remember Mr Cribb, who it seems beat his horse to excess, thereby drawing attention to himself. Cribb is in the employ of Larney. Cribb was heard to mention the words "pistol shot" and "woman".'

Poe eyed each man. 'Given the association of Larney and our missing mystical friend, is it not an extension of the logic I have just presented to assume that the woman in difficulty is that same woman who appeared at my cottage, Mr Figg, and to whom you gave evidence of your excellent marksmanship?'

Figg nodded, impressed. 'Yer deductin' jes' fine, Mr Poe. Larney is keepin' the hurt woman while our mystical friend keeps hisself involved in other ways. I take it Mr Cribb is also avoidin' people?'

Poe sighed. 'He is. Mr Bootham?'

'Yes, Mr Poe?'

'You are dealing with Prosper Benjamin in matters of the duel?'

The little Englishman leaped from his seat. 'Oh yes, Mr Poe. Indeed I am. Mr Benjamin says he speaks for Mr Larney and his coloured. Mr Benjamin has made it plain that he has no love for you, Mr Figg, or for you either, Mr Poe.'

Poe smirked. 'I assume Mr Benjamin did not make himself explicit as to why he refuses to utter our names in his prayers?' He thought of Benjamin naked in Scotch Ann's brothel.

Bootham shook his small head. 'No, Mr Poe, he has not divulged the matter of what I sense is a private quarrel. He and I have quarrelled concerning conditions of the forthcoming combat, but fortunately we English are familiar with the rules of the prize-ring, a sport which owes much to us, sir.'

He nodded once for emphasis. Hardly pausing to take a breath, he continued. 'Mr Benjamin has more or less agreed to abide by the London Prize Ring Rules of 1838.'

Figg muttered, 'Do not wager yer last penny on that, mate. What's 'e agreed on?'

Bootham counted on his fingers. 'A single line—'

'Comin' up to scratch,' said Figg. He looked at Poe. 'You draw a line in the dirt and both fighters meet there. If a man cannot come up to that line what has been scratched in the dirt, then he loses. What else, Mr Bootham?'

'A round ends when a man is knocked down. He has thirty seconds to get up, eight to come up to scratch. We, my friends and I, argued with Benjamin concerning whether or not you come to scratch alone or with your seconds. In England a man must come up alone. Too often has an injured man been carried to scratch by his seconds, sir, and the result has been that an exhausted man has been made to fight when he should have been allowed to walk away. You must come up to scratch alone, Mr Figg. We insisted on it, for your own safety.'

The boxer nodded. 'A round is a man knocked down.'

Bootham nodded. 'We are quarrelling over the choice of an umpire, but I think that can be settled. There will be two time-keepers, one English, one American. Two seconds per fighter, seconds to be allowed in the ring.'

Poe said, 'I count it an honour to be the other second if I may, Mr Figg.'

'I would be pleased to have you in my corner, Mr Poe. Well, that is a matter done with. I hear, Mr Bootham, that there is a fair amount of bettin' goin' on?'

'Indeed, Mr Figg. The English to a man are supporting you. Most of the Americans are with Larney's coloured, who has not yet been defeated. He has also killed two men in the ring.'

' 'Is killin' don't stop there, I'll wager. When can I talk with them what's been in the ring with the coloured?'

'Tonight.' Bootham adjusted his steel-rimmed spectacles. 'We are seeking those you requested. Three men who have faced Thor in the prize-ring. One is nearly blind and the other two have bitter memories. The Negro is a brutal man. Strong and, it would seem, a formidable foe. But our prayers are with you, sir.'

'Thankin' you muchly. Please inform the men what talks with me that there is a shillin' or two in it for 'em. It is a help to me to know what Mr Thor does in a prize-ring.'

'He kills and brutalises. And Larney gloats. Larney is said to have wagered ten thousand in gold that Thor will kill you.'

'Blimey! Ten thousand? Ain't that much money in the bloomin' world.'

Bootham coughed to clear this throat. Bending over, he picked up a small cardboard box and opened it.

'Handkerchiefs, Mr Figg. I took the liberty of ordering them. Mr Poe informs me that you are partial to the colour lavender.'

'Me wife was, yes.'

'May we distribute them?'

Figg nodded yes. It was the custom among British prizefighters to hand out handkerchiefs to their supporters. If the fighter won, each person who accepted the handkerchief was to pay the fighter five pounds.

Bootham's eyes gleamed as he slowly, gently pulled a handkerchief from the box and held it up as though it was spun gold. 'Thank you, Mr Figg.'

Bootham held the box out to Poe, who swallowed and looked down at the floor. 'I am aware of the custom, Mr Figg, but I am in the worst of financial straits and upon your victory, which I hope for with all my heart, I fear I could not pay as called for.'

Figg took a handkerchief and handed it to Poe. 'Yer me second, guvenor. It would not look well to 'ave you in the ring and not sportin' me colours. I would feel proud to 'ave Mrs Coltman carry one, though she is not to attend the fight.'

Poe accepted a second handkerchief. 'Mr Figg, the honour will be hers, I am sure.'

The writer looked at Bootham. 'I suggest that we ourselves bottle the water Mr Figg will drink in the ring on that day. And seal it. No one but you and I, Mr Bootham, is to go near that liquid. It is not above Larney to somehow manage to poison the water on that day. Also, those who attend the fight in support of Mr Figg are to sit on his side of the ring, to prevent assassins and blackguards from doing him harm during the contest.'

Bootham nodded vigorously. 'Yes, Mr Poe. That seems to be a wise course.'

Poe took his hat, stick and greatcoat from the bed. 'I go to Rachel now. She is somewhat better, though still in the grip of nightmares and horrendous deliriums. I shall also continue my attempts to locate Hugh Larney. I am convinced that the death of Rachel's physician means that Larney can tell us where our mystical friend is. Larney knows, Mr Figg, and that is why he is avoiding us until the day of the fight. He enjoys his games, does Hugh Larney. He enjoys mortal combat from a distance and I am sure he is intoxicated at the idea of watching it once more, while harming you and me.'

Figg nodded. 'Guard yerself well, squire. Larney is a black-guard.'

'I am of no consequence to him until the conclusion of the duel, Mr Figg. By absenting himself, he not only aids Jonathan, he also avoids having to confront our pressing inquiries. I assume my life is safe until the termination of the duel. I do not wish to think of Larney and his Negro triumphing over you, but should that happen, I believe my life to be forfeit. And the child Dearborn becomes his. Good day Mr Figg, Mr Bootham.'


Larney watched Thor punch the sandbag suspended from a beam in the barn. The Negro was barechested, sweating, hitting the bag with powerful blows.

Larney, several feet away, turned to the man who had ridden out from New York to report to him.

'Poe is askin' all over town,' said the man. 'He's inquisitive about the dead doctor, your whereabouts, everything.'

Larney frowned. 'I would say kill him but there exists a peculiar truce between our camps and this fight is attracting much interest. A dead Poe would cancel the occasion and what would I tell my guests, who expect some diversion after a long and tedious sea voyage.'

He tapped his chin with his forefinger. 'Let him live. And on the day of the fight, on that very day, I think, I think I shall re-enter Mr Poe's dreadful life, to his undying displeasure. Undying, dear friend.'

Larney threw back his head and roared.


Martin said, 'Hammer-blows he uses. Brings his right hand high and down on your head, relyin' on his strength. Will crowd you if he can. Likes to grapple, hug you close, squeeze your back 'til it hurts.'

Figg nodded.

'Watch yer eyes,' said Tabby, pointing to his eye-patch. 'Took out mine, he did. Thumbs. Presses down. Nigger's a tall one. He jes' presses down.'

Figg said, ' 'Ow's 'is moves left and right?'

Martin shook his head. 'Ain't got none. Straight ahead, right Tabby?'

The one-eyed man nodded. 'Black bastard is like a damn train. Straight ahead and nothin' else. Both of his hands are like the wrath of God. Long arms and he can keep you at a distance, if he wants. Punches down. He's almost seven feet.'

'Nahhhh,' said Martin scowling. 'Over six to be sure, but under seven by five inches or more.'

They argued over Thor's height until Figg gently stopped them. There was agreement over the Negro's boxing skills; the two men drinking Figg's whisky in Bootham's parlour estimated that Thor had defeated more than thirty men in the ring.

There was no way to estimate what the Negro had done outside the ring. Only Larney and Thor himself knew those deadly figures.

Thirty fights, resulting in cripplings, blindings and at least two deaths. Figg was facing the challenge of his life.

When he'd given the men a few shillings and the remainder of the whisky and sent them on their way, he returned to Bootham's cellar where he trained alone and in secret, despite the pleas from Bootham's English friends to watch him prepare. Figg was taking no chances that Jonathan or Larney had planted a spy anywhere near him.

Tomorrow Figg would talk to another survivor of Thor's boxing ability, this one a man who Bootham said was half blind and addled, but who could talk. Several men who had fought Thor refused to talk to Bootham. Larney would not like it, they said.

And, as Figg reminded himself two boxers wouldn't talk because they were dead, as dead as Rachel Coltman's doctor.

In the cellar, in candlelight and musty heat, Figg trained.

And worried.

# CHAPTER FORTY-TWO

**Jonathan. The Sixth Night**

Asmodeus had given him the name of the victim selected for the final blood rite.

Rachel Coltman.

The rite was to be performed in the barn, without leaving the circle; Jonathan was to lure the woman here, then carve out her heart and liver, burning them. If the husband is to be removed from the world of death, let the wife take his place; she was the price Jonathan must pay before reaching the end of the rite.

*Kill Rachel Coltman here on the final day, on the ninth day.*

Poe closed his eyes, rubbing the corners with his fingers.

Figures, names, dates all swam in front of him and he saw nothing. But he *had* to see, he had to!

He wanted liquor, he wanted its warmth and protection, but he would have to deny himself that salvation. Does a man gain salvation by denying himself salvation?

Poe opened his eyes wide, drawing the lamp closer. He had much reading to do. He was checking land records to learn what Hugh Larney owned and where. The musty smell of the Property building's cellar was abominable and Poe was too sick to stand it for much longer, but he owed Figg.

He owed him a great deal.

Poe continued to turn the pages of the large book that recorded those dealings by which a handful of men were profiting on land that was becoming more and more valuable with each passing day.

Later the clerk found Poe asleep, head down on one of the books.

# CHAPTER FORTY-THREE

**The Seventh Night**

Jonathan, the evoker; Justin Coltman, the evoked. Magician and a dead man's spirit drawn closer by a thought transmission unknown to human reason, a transmission that had been growing stronger for seven days, seven nights.

Jonathan's obsession with the Throne of Solomon gave him the physical and mental strength needed to proceed with this dangerous ritual, one which few magicians ever attempted. He was now in a world inhabited by the rarest of sorcerers, a world he'd conjured up with all of the magic at his command. He sensed the increasing presence of Justin Coltman and, with it, that knowledge which could yield the Throne of Solomon.

The dead man knew the secret of the grimoires, those books of black magic stolen by child thieves in London. That Justin Coltman lacked the knowledge to use them was a sign to Jonathan that *he*, and not anyone else, was meant to triumph.

In performing the ritual for the past seven days, Jonathan was no longer functioning on mere reason; his mind had now achieved a level of comprehension known only to those with faith in powers denied mortal men. *Be it as your faith.* So said Jesus Christ and so say all beliefs. Be it as your faith, and Jonathan's faith in his power as a sorcerer was never stronger than now.

Behind him in the protective circle, Laertes sat chewing the raw, rancid dog meat. He chewed slowly, eyes glazed, face dusty with human ashes, a man with only the remnants of a mind and will of his own. The ordeal of the ritual had drained him and all he could do was mechanically obey Jonathan; his existence was in the magician's hands. The restoration of his sanity was a matter that could wait until Jonathan had obtained the throne.

Jonathan's chanting was almost finished. 'Hasmalim, enlighten me with the splendours of Eloi and Shechinah! Aralim, act! Ophanim, revolve and shine! Hajoth a Kadosh, cry, speak, roar, bellow! Hallelu-jah, Hallelu-jah, Hallelu-jah.'

Two more days. And then he would have the greatest prize man had ever dreamed of.

Suddenly the barn was filled with bright orange flames and the strong, foul smell of demons. Animals shrieked, threatened, and the cries of dead men were everywhere.

Asmodeus!

Again he had returned to demand his sacrifice.

*Magician*, he cried, *the woman offends me.*

*Torment me not*, thought Jonathan. *I renounce her.*

*Give her to me, magician. Bring her here and give her to me in sacrifice.*

*I will. Before the ninth day ends.*

The fire disappeared. Asmodeus, the fire, animals, the dead men's cries all vanished.

Jonathan sat rigid. When his fears had eased and his hands had stopped trembling, he looked over his shoulder at Laertes who sat unseeing, showing no reaction to what had just occurred. I will save him on the final day, thought Jonathan, for then all power will be mine.

Since demanding Rachel Coltman's death in exchange for the soul of her dead husband, Asmodeus had not ceased to torment Jonathan. The demon king, in all his hideous fury, had appeared daily; the sight and smell of him would have defeated all men except Jonathan. But Jonathan, tiring and fighting hard against collapse would need all of his concentration for the final day. Let Asmodeus have Rachel and leave Jonathan alone.

The magician was working at full strength, exhausting himself and his powers, but the prize was worth it. The prize was within reach and Rachel Coltman's life was a small price to pay for it.


'Mr Figg? It is I, Poe.'

'I said no one was to come down 'ere. No one!'

'It is Poe.'

'I know 'oo yo are. I said no one, you hear me?'

Poe stood in the middle of the cellar stairs, squinting down into the darkness. 'Mr Bootham and the others are worried about you. You seemed to have cut yourself off from them and I am told you eat very little. Why are you down here alone in this oppressive, foul-smelling darkness? Would you please light another candle? I cannot see—'

'No candle!' Figg's voice was a primeval, guttural sound coming from the blackness. He was hostile, unfriendly and Poe was shocked.

'Is there anything wrong, Mr Figg?'

'Jes leave me be, mate. Climb back up them stairs and leave me be. Tell the others I says to keep away and leave me be.'

Poe stared down at the two candles flickering on top of barrels; the candles cast a pale red glow on the brown dirt cellar floor. Something was wrong. Figg was spending all of his time alone in Titus Bootham's cellar, eating vegetables, drinking plain water. No meat, no milk or foods made from milk. If anyone saw him it was Bootham, and then only briefly. With the duel less than two days away, an anxious Bootham had begged Poe to go down into the cellar and talk with the boxer. Because of Figg's odd behaviour the Bootham household, servants and family, was afraid to approach him.

A thought nagged at Poe. Figg's choice of diet. His living and training down here in the cellar. And those two candles. Could it be—

Poe said, 'There is a crowd of Englishmen gathered in the street at the front of Bootham's home, Mr Figg. All are enthused over the forthcoming combat. Word of the duel has spread and you are the man of the hour—'

'They want blood. I know what they want.'

'It is true, Mr Figg, that this duel has assumed the proportions of a holiday and a circus in the eyes of many, and for that I am deeply sorry. Mr Barnum has twice been to this house and twice Mr Bootham has turned him away—'

'On my orders.' Figg was still invisible in the darkness.

'I understand and my sympathies are with you, dear friend. Mr Barnum has offered any assistance you may need and he wishes you to know that he is among your most fervent backers. I understand that Mr Barnum has offered the use of one of his warehouses for the duel.'

'Talk to Bootham about that. Will you leave me in peace?'

Poe took one more step down into the cellar. 'Mr Figg, I know what you are doing. And I understand, sir.'

'Understand what?'

'The ritual. Your preparation.'

There was a noise in the darkness directly in front of Poe; he cocked an ear.

'What is it that you know, Mr Poe?'

'Jonathan fears you. Let me say with good reason, for he sees in you those forces which are deeper and darker within himself, those forces you continually deny. All of us see in others only those things which are in ourselves, and Jonathan knows and can recognise the occult. You are fasting, dear friend. Not an ordinary fast but the black fast.'

Poe could *feel* the silence in the dark cellar. Meaning he was right in what he'd just said.

'The black fast, Mr Figg. To aid the concentration, to strengthen the powers of thought. Abstain from meat, avoid all milk and milk foods. If I recall correctly, an Englishwoman was executed in the sixteenth century after having been accused of using this particular fast in a witchcraft plot to kill King Henry the Eighth.'

Figg's voice was softer. Nearer. 'I 'ear tell that witchcraft is called "the old religion", the one the English useta 'ave long before Christianity come to our island.'

'That is true. It is also known as "the cult of the wise" and history shows how important it was to the ancient tribes of Britain, the Angles, Saxons, the Celts. Your ancestors, Mr Figg.'

'I do not fast in order to kill anyone, Mr Poe. It's stayin' alive I am after. The fast you speak of is also used to bring misfortune to an enemy, not that I am admittin' to what yer sayin'.'

'I understand, Mr Figg.' Poe sat down on the stairs. 'Forgive me, but I am tired and not too well. Much time has been spent in tracing the land transactions of Hugh Larney, no easy matter in these days of speculation and questionable business dealings. Everyone is anxious to become a millionaire, a new word coined by the envious to describe the avaricious.'

'What is so interestin' concernin' Mr Larney's dealin's in land?'

'Note, Mr Figg, that Miles Standish and Volney Gunning are both dead. Which eliminates either man being of much use to Jonathan. Note that the recently assassinated physician who attended Rachel, was contacted by a servant of Hugh Larney, one Jacob Cribb who, as I have mentioned, beats his horse too severely in public and shouts aloud the urgency for needing a physician. Now if as I surmise, and I believe myself to be correct, the physician died because he had come directly from Rachel and myself to treat the wounded woman used by Jonathan to deceive me, this means that Hugh Larney has the woman. But where?

'We know, Mr Figg, that Hugh Larney is in hiding, most likely on property he owns. He needs space enough to properly prepare his man for the duel. Larney is wealthy, far wealthier than most people know. By long and arduous effort in reading tax ledgers and records of land sales, I have learned that Hugh Larney owns three well-appointed homes here in Manhattan. He also is in possession of numerous tracts of undeveloped land, which he expects to be worth a fortune to him as Manhattan expands northward. To be exact, he owns nine parcels of land, parcels of various sizes. And he has not made his holdings public. Most are abandoned, which is to say they show no record of development and only carry the minimum of tax liabilities. Larney, his man Thor and the wounded woman are on one of these tracts of land. It has taken me until today to learn this. To investigate all of this land, which lies in most rugged areas, would take days if not weeks.'

Figg said, 'We don't 'ave days and weeks.'

'I am aware of this, dear friend. I suggest that on the day of the duel, we somehow force Larney to tell us—not where he has hidden the woman—I suggest we force him to tell us where on his land Jonathan is performing the dark ritual.'

Figg's voice was nearer, but still he remained hidden in darkness.

'You tellin' me for certain that Hugh Larney is hidin' Jonathan?'

'It cannot be otherwise. The dead physician, the wounded woman, both indicate a contact made between Larney and Jonathan. At this most important time, who else could Jonathan turn to for a place that would allow him privacy? Volney Gunning owned real estate but most of it is here in Manhattan, acres and acres of abominable housing given over to immigrants. He had some land outside New York but it is settled on; it is only a modest amount of productive farm land. Miles Standish had stock investments, no real estate at all. That leaves Larney.'

Figg said, 'Perhaps Jonathan had land of his own.'

'I doubt it. He was in Europe until recently, was he not? He roamed the world, and he was always in need of funds, funds which he secured from such as Larney and Gunning, from others he humbugged as Doctor Paracelsus. I have been to Jonathan's home.'

' 'Ave you now.'

'A Mrs Sontag, pointed out as a patroness of Doctor Paracelus, escorted me. She fancies herself a poet and was flattered at my asking if she would consent to show me some of her poetry. In exchange she took me to the site of her spiritualist experiences, costly ones I might add. The house no longer stands. It was burned to the ground a week ago.'

'When 'e left to begin his dark deed.'

'Exactly. He is elsewhere, Mr Figg, and that elsewhere is known to Larney. I stake my life on it.'

'All of us, we are stakin' our lives on this business.'

Poe pointed his stick. 'Red candles. Red is the colour of life. The

Celtic ancient tribes believed that to dance around flame was a method of raising power. That is also why certain rituals are performed naked, to allow the power to flow unobstructed.'

Figg cleared his throat. 'I does what makes me comfortable. I ain't been in a prize-ring in seven years and I will be facin' a younger man, a stronger man, a killer. I does what is comfortable, Mr Poe.'

Poe smiled. 'I have been told that when one speaks of black magic, one speaks of what others are involved in.'

Figg snapped, 'Ain't no black magic bein' done 'ere.'

'Forgive me, dear friend. I—'

'Jes' doin' what's comfortable, is all.'

Poe looked around in the darkness. Blankets over the windows, a stale, musty odour inside. Darkness lit only by two red candles. Figg was returning to the strength of his ancestors. No matter how much he denied it, 'the cult of the wise' was within him.

The boxer must be a desperate, frightened man. Suddenly Poe started coughing and couldn't stop. His head spun and he blacked out, a pitching forward and down the stairs.

When he opened his eyes, a worried, sweating and naked Figg was hovering over him.

'You been workin' too hard, squire.' The hostility was gone from Figg's voice.

'I *am* a man of honour, Mr Figg, and I have a debt. I owe you for agreeing to fight in my stead, and so I am doing all I can to locate Larney and Jonathan. I feel certain,' he coughed, 'certain that Larney knows Jonathan's hiding place and that hiding place is on property owned by Larney.'

He coughed again. Figg bent down, lifting him into a sitting position.

'Bet you ain't been eatin' much.'

'I take my cue from you, sir.'

'I does what must be done.'

'I know.'

Figg sighed. 'I feel the need of this, Mr Poe. Them crowds outside, they look at me like I am an animal, something penned up in 'ere for their amusement. It's a game to them, somethin' to cheer on. For me it could be me last fight. The blackamoor is strong, and I do not mind tellin' you in the quiet of this room that I am a man with more than small fears within 'im. I have been in this country almost two weeks and it could well be that I die 'ere. I feel tired, Mr Poe, tired and alone. Huntin' Jonathan has taken much out of me. I'm not a young man any more and me skills are not what they used to be. I feel the need to prepare in this fashion, and I would be thankin' you muchly if you were not to tell anyone what you have seen down 'ere or what you have deducted with yer thinkin'!'

Poe nodded. 'You have my word, Mr Figg. Nothing that has transpired in this room will pass my lips. And I shall insist that Bootham stop your exuberant fellow Englishmen from rapping at your window.'

'Blankets can keep their bleedin' faces from me sight, but not their knuckles from tappin' on the glass. They are enjoyin' themselves makin' wagers and cursin' the Americans. I figger to be their bleedin' saviour, it appears.'

He and Poe smiled. Poe said, 'A residue of the two wars between our countries, dear friend. It is harmless, this patriotic excess. Barnum is growing impatient to see you. He is your champion.'

' 'E sees me on the day of the fight. Make it known that anyone what comes down them stairs is riskin'.'

'Done. I shall calm Mr Bootham myself. Allow me to return here on the day appointed to escort you to the site. The police have wind of the duel and will do their best to prevent it. Prizefighting and all forms of personal combat are prohibited, which does not in any way stop them from occurring. They merely occur in secret.' *And men bear their pain in quiet forests and on secluded farmland.*

There was a light tapping at a tiny cellar window. An English voice shouted, 'Hello in there! You are our man, Pierce James Figg! Our money is on you! A cheer for Figg. Hip hip hooray! Hip, hip hooray! Hip, hip hooray!'

An unimpressed Figg looked towards the sound. 'Like to kick them all in the bleedin' arse with a pair of hobnail boots, I would. But Mr Bootham's neighbours got their own thoughts on all this 'ere noise what's goin' on.'

Poe took a bloodstained handkerchief from his greatcoat pocket and coughed into it. It was the lavender handkerchief given him by Figg.

'I shall give your regards to Rachel and to the child, Dearborn. She is a delightful creature, little Dearborn. So much like my Sissy.'

'Make sure you eats some decent grub. You looks like a horse sat on you.'

Poe smiled. 'I dare say I do not resemble a dashing beau. My gratitude for the use of your room at the boarding house. With my perennially impaired financial position—'

'It's yers, mate. Rent has been paid fer two weeks. If I get meself kilt by the blackamoor, you got a place to mourn. If, if somethin' like that does 'appen, there are some private things in me carpetbag: a ring that belonged to me wife, a tiny paintin' of her and Will. There is a family Bible and —'

Poe swallowed hard, forcing the words out. 'I shall see that they are buried with you, Mr Figg.'

'Thankin' you muchly. Now please leave me be. There are some things in me mind and it's bein' alone that will 'elp me deal with 'em.'

Poe looked at the sweating, naked man. Scars on the outside of him, scars on the inside. And, as for all warriors, the day he had long dreaded had come to Figg, the day when he doubted if his fighting skills were enough to keep him alive.

Poe was halfway up the stairs when he stopped and turned. 'Thus thou shalt possess the glory of the whole world; and all darkness will flee from you.'

Figg had stepped back into darkness. 'Sounds like the Bible.'

'No. It is from an ancient occult inscription which some claim was discovered by Sara, wife of Abraham, and others say was found in a cave by Alexander the Great. Medieval students were quite found of quoting it, though the entire inscription runs much longer.'

'Sounds pleasant. I appreciates you sayin' it to me.'

'With all my heart, dear friend. I say it to you with all my heart.'

'You ain't startin' to believe any of this, this "old religion", are you, Mr Poe?'

'Be it as your faith, Mr Figg. So Christ said to one who came to him for a miracle. May your faith in whatever you believe be strong enough to bring you victory.'

Silence.

Poe turned and continued up the stairs.

# CHAPTER FORTY-FOUR

**Sundown of the Ninth Day**

An exhausted, drugged Laertes, more dead than alive, slept. Jonathan sat inside of the protective circle and conjured. Fatigue and strain were forgotten. The sour taste in his mouth from the uncooked dog meat no longer disturbed him; the excitement of being mere hours from obtaining the Throne of Solomon gave him added strength. The goal was within reach.

Jonathan's power was almighty. There was no one on earth to equal him. *No one.*

Across space and time, his mind sought out Rachel Coltman. His eyes were closed, his arms extended to the side, his thoughts all directed to him.

*Come to me, come to me, come to me. Come . . .*

She would! He knew it. She could not withstand his power; she would have to obey him. And when she was sacrificed to Asmodeus, her dead husband would be next to obey the command to appear and all power that could be imagined would belong to Jonathan. The Throne of Solomon would be his as it was destined to be.

He directed his mind to Rachel Coltman miles away in her Manhattan home.


Less than two hours later, Dearborn Lapham looked down from a first floor window and watched Rachel Coltman climb into a coach a servant had brought around to the front of the mansion. Mrs Coltman had not looked well and Dearborn had thought that Mr Poe, for one, would not care to see her going out on such a cold evening as this. Better to stay in a warm bed, with servants bringing you sweets and hot tea.

Mrs Coltman had said little. Just a quick order to a servant, then down the stairs in one of her many beautiful capes and she was out the door. She had walked by Dearborn without saying a word. Someone else had also not spoken or waved to Dearborn either. Mr Poe.

Dearborn was almost sure that it was he who had leaned from the carriage just before Mrs Coltman had climbed in. Mr Poe, the friendly man from Virginia, the soft-spoken man who so loved to talk about travelling players and life upon the stage. Dearborn had waved to him from the window, trying to catch his attention, calling his name, but he had ignored her. Why hadn't Mr Poe waved back?

When Mrs Coltman climbed into the carriage, the man beside her, *whoever* he was, flicked the reins and the carriage moved out of the yellow circle cast by the gaslight and rolled into darkness.

Perhaps it wasn't Mr Poe after all. It *was* dark outside and . . .

She let the curtain fall back into place and turned around to see Hugh Larney and two of his men staring at her. Paralysed with fear, the child stood silent and rigid.

Larney smiled. 'So much beauty in so small a treasure. I am not in the habit of entering a home through the back way, but for one so lovely, I gladly make an exception. It is just as well that the lady of the house was leaving as we were quietly making our way to you, for there is no time to tarry and pay our respects to her.'

His eyes caressed her small body. 'We are leaving, my dear, for we are to watch another duel together this very night. Such events please me more when I am with you.'

Larney tapped Jacob Cribb on the shoulder with a silver-headed cane. 'Take her.'

In the carriage, a frightened Dearborn sat between Hugh Larney and Jacob Cribb. Three men sat across from her. Two were Larney's men. The third was bound, gagged and unconscious in the seat directly across from her.

It was Mr Poe.

*But if he'd just left with Mrs Coltman, how could he be here?*


*The duel*

Thor jabbed three times with his left, then swung a roundhouse right hand that would have knocked Figg down—again—had it landed. Figg circled backwards, leaning out of reach. He'd been hit tonight by the Negro and the blows had hurt; strong right hands, stinging jabs with the left. Thor could punch and, though occasionally awkward, he had good speed.

Figg's left cheekbone ached where the bare knuckles of Thor's left jab had made contact several times. The Negro's arms were inches longer than Figg's. He was only twenty-four, half Figg's age, but, at six foot seven inches, almost a full foot taller. Figg weighed 190 pounds, Thor weighed 250, with all of the arrogance to be expected in someone who had never lost a fight.

Thor was also certain of tonight's outcome; three times he'd put the Englishman on the ground. Three knockdowns, three rounds to Thor, who'd been promised $100 in gold by Hugh Larney if he would kill the white man. There would be no police involved, since a death in the prize-ring was merely an unavoidable hazard of that trade. And the $100 in gold was more money than Thor had ever imagined he'd see in his lifetime. With that in his pocket he was king among all the coloureds, so he had quickly promised Hugh Larney that the Englishman would not leave the ring alive.

Thor lunged, swinging his left arm wildly and with all his strength. Figg leaned to the right, the blow missing his face by inches and Thor stumbled forward, off-balance. As the Negro stumbled past him, Figg hooked a left into his right ribcage, then stepped behind him driving two quick hooks, left, right, into Thor's kidneys. Another man would have cried out, perhaps dropped to his knees in pain. Not Thor.

The Negro *was* hurt, but not nearly enough to stop fighting. Arching his back and reaching behind him, he stumbled forward faster until he crashed into a ring post, knocking it out of position. The crowd of shouting men in the cellar of Phineas Taylor Barnum's warehouse was on its feet, whisky and rum bottles now forgotten. Thor was tangled in ropes and the spectators seated within inches of the ring. The ring post lay across his thighs.

He fought to get to his feet. 'No knockdown! The man he no knock me down!'

Titus Bootham and Phineas Taylor Barnum—Figg's seconds— ran to the centre of the ring shouting and waving their arms, trying to convince two umpires and two timekeepers that *yes*, it was a knockdown.

'Knockdown!' yelled Barnum in his squeaky voice, his round face red with anger. 'You blind ass, can't you see he knocked the nigger down?'

'I *insist* it was a knockdown!' yelled Bootham, the shortest man in the ring.

More arguing, shoving, threats.

Figg kept the crowd between him and Thor. God above, let them continue arguin', for I can use the rest. Need time to catch me breath, 'cause ring fightin' is a hard road to travel. Go for a man in an alley and you could surprise him and end it quickly. But

292

there were no surprises in the ring. Your man knew you were coming and he was ready. When the timekeeper called *time* and the umpire signalled *fight*, you got up from your second's knee and you went to the centre of the ring. You came up to scratch and fought for your life.

Tonight's crowd, still on its feet, roared opinions, prejudices, preferences. Tonight's a man could be for white vs. black, Americans vs. English, Larney's enemies vs. Larney. It was a crowd made noisy and dangerous by liquor, by lingering hatreds from two wars between America and England, by money bet on either man, by a love of bloodsport.

Figg, bare-chested, in knee-britches, stockings and a borrowed pair of shoes, breathed deeply and rubbed the swollen knuckle on his right fist. He eyed the screaming, bearded faces around him. They want to see somebody killed tonight, they do, and they don't much mind who it is. They don't know what the quarrel is about and they don't care. They want to see me or the coloured lyin' here in the dirt with the breath of life gone from either one of us. They can all go to bloody hell, they can.

Once Figg had loved the prize-ring, the excitement of it, the camaraderie, the women who spoke against its violence but who whispered their names and addresses to a boxer when the fight was over. It was in the bones of the Figg family for its men to love it, for its women to curse it. But Figg had become disgusted by the corruption in boxing—fixed fights, doped fighters, by the unending call for blood. Tonight in New York, far from his home and everything he held dear, he knew he was a happier man outside the ring. The life for him was teaching boxing and swordplay in his London academy, seeing young boys learn the science of self-defence, seeing the pride on the faces of fathers as a son took his first steps towards manhood by learning to protect himself.

That was the life for Pierce James Figg; God would decide whether or not he lived to return to it. Too many boxers had gone back into the ring for that last fight and died there. To be in the game too long was to stand on a scaffold; you could only go down. You could only entertain the people by dying for them.

*Where was Poe?*

He hadn't appeared at Bootham's home to escort Figg to the fight and a runner had reported Poe was neither in Figg's room in the boarding house, nor at the *Evening Mirror* newspaper. Figg had been forced to ask Barnum to be his second. Not only had the master showman enthusiastically agreed, but he had offered one of his several warehouses as a site for the duel. Both sides had accepted the offer of the warehouse cellar, and a delighted Barnum had set about bribing the police so that the duel could proceeed uninterrupted. Several policemen had been paid to follow a false scent, to head out into the country on a 'tip' that the duel—illegal under New York State law—was to be held there.

In addition to the money given them, each policeman received a pass to Barnum's American Museum, entitling him to a year's free admission. Barnum bribed well.

*Where was Poe?*

In trouble, Figg was sure of it. Not in his cups, as someone had laughingly suggested. Not face down in a Five Points gutter. Not tonight. Figg was certain that nothing, except a serious illness or interference by someone, could have kept Poe from acting as his second. Poe was a man of his word, a man of strong loyalty. He'd proved that by the manner in which he had stuck by Rachel Coltman.

Figg looked across the ring at Hugh Larney, who sat with his arm around a pale Dearborn Lapham. The bloody bastard. Surrounded by his friends and pretending to be as British as the Prime Minister. He'd never have dared o take the child unless certain that Poe would not interfere. Larney knew what had happened to Poe. Figg sensed it.

Thor was back in his corner, sitting on the knee of a second, and the ring was more or less cleared. Umpires and timekeepers remained, continuing to discuss the last knockdown among themselves. 'Round Mr Figg!' announced one, and the crowd booed, hissed, cheered.

By tradition seconds placed one knee on the ground, with the other knee upraised for the fighter to rest on between rounds or while recovering from a knockdown. On Larney's orders, Thor was taking his rest. Larney moved to stand behind Thor, a hand on his broad, sweaty shoulders, his lips close to the Negro's ear. Both men smiled across the ring at Figg, who thought: *Damn them.* If they think I am to worry about what they say to one another, they got another think comin'. I could die here tonight but I'm dyin' like a man. Like an Englishman. With pride.

'*Time!*'

Figg rose from Barnum's knee, shuffled forward, both arms extended stiffly towards Thor. When both men reached the line drawn in the dirt cellar floor, the umpire yelled, 'Commence fighting!'

294

Thor jabbed quickly with his left, his long reach making Figg lean backwards and, with Figg off balance, Thor put his head down and charged, butting Figg in the stomach, knocking the wind from him, and then the Negro had Figg's arms pinned to his side, squeezing, threatening to break them.

He lifted Figg in the air and hurled him to the ground, throwing his own body after him, trying to crush Figg's chest with his 250 pounds. Using instinct learned long ago, Figg rolled clear; Thor missed him by inches.

But Figg was hurt.

His arms ached, his chest felt on fire. The crowd roared and Figg struggled to get to his feet. He was on his hands and knees, trying to clear his head. Two umpires and a timekeeper struggled to keep Thor from kicking him while he was down.

Behind a dazed, pained Figg, Bootham yelled, 'Up, Mr Figg! Please get up, sir!'

Figg tried to push himself up and collapsed. He lay open-mouthed on the ground and tasted dirt.


With only four hours to midnight, Jonathan prepared to summon the spirit of Justin Coltman. He sprinkled salt and water, symbols of life, around Coltman's coffin. Laertes, shuffling like a man almost dead, lit the two white candles, one at the head, the other at the foot of the coffin.

The incense—a combination of opium, hemlock, henbane, wood, saffron and mandrake—was burning in two wooden bowls. Soon Jonathan would wave eleven puffs of it to Qliphoth, the evil spirit of damnation. And there would be the use of the Athame, the ritual knife, to be held in both hands, point up, and offered to the four powers in turn, east, south, west, and at the north he would stop.

To the candle burning at the north point of the magic circle, he would offer eleven more puffs of the incense, then touch the northern point of the circle eleven times with the ritual knife. North, the compass point sacred to devil-worshippers.

The forces would gather at Jonathan's command and he would charge and command the spirit of Justin Coltman through the power of Astoreth, Demon of Death and Lord of the Flies, of Loki, Qliphoth and Satan, all of whom would be ordered to return the body of Justin Coltman to this earth from whence it came.

It was then that Justin Coltman would speak to Jonathan,

telling him where the grimoires could be found, the grimoires that would lead the magician to the Throne of Solomon.

*Speak and tell me what I want to know.*

Yes, there was the matter of the sacrifice, but that was easily taken care of. Asmodeus' challenge had been a pitiful one, one simple to deal with. Jonathan had projected his mind to Rachel Coltman, giving her a strong reason for leaving her home immediately and coming to Jonathan.

Rachel Coltman was more drawn to Poe than she would admit and Jonathan, ruthlessly using that weakness, sent Poe's image to her. He let her hear Poe's voice. To Rachel's mind, disturbed by her kidnapping by Hamlet Sproul and by the shock of learning that Paracelsus was indeed the murderous Jonathan, the projected image of Poe was quickly and easily accepted as the writer himself.

She heard and saw Poe in her bedroom. It was Poe who ordered her to get a carriage and team of horses and come with him to an abandoned barn where she would see Justin Coltman *alive*.

It was Poe she believed, but it was Jonathan she obeyed.


The wine had been drugged; he sensed it more than knew it for certain, for Poe was now in a world that he had dreaded all his life, a world that he did not want to focus on. Was he buried alive? Had it happened to him again?

He was in darkness, musty-smelling darkness and his mind fought to cling to sanity. What did he remember? The note from Muddy saying come quickly, she needed his help, and Poe had gone with the man who'd brought the note to the boarding house, a man claiming to be a farmer in Fordham, employed at the nearby college of Jesuit priests.

Poe, edgy about tonight's duel in which Figg was risking his life in Poe's stead, had naturally followed the man from the boarding house. Yes, he remembered that much. Then he'd climbed into the carriage, wondering if he could get to Fordham then back into Manhattan in time for the duel. Someone, no it was two men. Yes two men had forced him to drink wine, held the bottle to his lips, holding his nose so that he had to open his mouth and the bitter taste of the wine had told him it was drugged.

He'd heard Hugh Larney's voice, then turned to see the man's little face. After that there had been blackness. For a brief moment or two Poe had been conscious and he'd seen Dearborn Lapham sitting across from him in a carriage, a smirking Hugh Larney beside her. Then it was into darkness and distance again. Had Poe died?

And now his mind tormented him. The darkness would not leave and he cried out against it. He saw Jonathan's face, the face of Valentine Greatrakes, and he saw Rachel lying dead while beasts tore at her flesh. The drugged wine claimed him and he passed out.

Passed out in a coffin buried two feet under the earth in a cemetery directly across from City Hall.


Merlin held the bottle of water to Figg's swollen lips. Barnum, whose knee was being used as the boxer's chair, wiped blood from a cut around an almost closed left eye.

'Twenty-three rounds, Mr Figg.' The showman frowned with worry. 'That left eye of yours is all but closed, I fear. The coloured has gone after it with a vengeance, the bastard.'

Figg's chest heaved. 'Doin' what I'd be doin', if I was in his black skin.'

Titus Bootham was close to tears. 'Let me throw in the sponge, Mr Figg. You have taken enough punishment for Poe, who is not decent enough to come here tonight and support you. He has no right to carry your colours, sir.'

'I ain't quittin'. Never quit in me life and ain't of a mind to now. All I got left is what I am as a man. You throw in the sponge and you are no friend of mine.'

The tears rolled from Bootham's eyes as he gently wiped Figg's face. 'Yes sir. I-I had no idea it could be like this. The blood, I mean.'

Figg's smile through swollen, bleeding lips, was hideous. 'Always been that way, mate.'

'Time!'

Figg pushed himself off Barnum's knee, forced his one good eye open as far as he could and limped forward to meet Thor. The coloured had given him the worst beating of his life. Worse, Figg had never hit a man so many times and not have him go down. Thor had taken Figg's best blows, most of them to the body and still he was on his feet, still strong, aggressive. Like now.

Thor threw a right uppercut that barely missed Figg's jaw, then brought his huge left fist straight down as though it were a hammer, missing Figg's head but hitting his shoulder and sending him staggering sideways. *Panic.* The blow numbed Figg's shoulder for a few seconds; he could lift the arm but there was no power in

297

it. All he could do was back away, keep out of range of those long, powerful arms.

Thor jabbed with his left. Figg leaned away, then ducked under it, hooking a right into the Negro's side. The punch had nothing behind it; the shoulder was still numb. Figg rushed him, grabbing Thor around the waist, trying to lift him from the ground and throw him down. *Panic.* Thor was smiling down at him. Figg hadn't moved him.

Thor brought his knee up into Figg's groin and a series of harsh and blinding white lights exploded in the Englishman's head. The pain was searing, speeding from his groin to his head and back again and Figg fell forward to the ground.

Dimly, he heard Barnum and Bootham yelling 'Foul', heard the Britons in the huge cellar take up the cry. 'Foul! Foul! Foul!' Someone threw an empty whisky bottle and a half-eaten sandwich into the ring.

Figg, still on the ground, fought to breathe. His knees were drawn up to his stomach. Pain squeezed his brain, his stomach, his groin.

And suddenly—from far away, he heard the voices of a chorus of old men. *'You have called. We have come. Celts of old have come.'*

Figg rolled over on his stomach, forcing himself to his knees. The roar of the men in the cellar filled his brain and he could not hear the voices of the old men. His one good eye went to a window high and to the right. He saw the moon. Large, round, full and yellow. It seemed to grow right in front of him.

He remembered. *Power grows when the moon grows. When the moon grows strong, all beneath it grow strong.*

*Show your new money to the moon so that it may grow as the moon grows. Sow crops just before a new moon. Wish on a new moon, bow to it and turn around nine times.*

In his travels throughout all of England, Figg had heard these things many times. Old wives' tales, he'd thought. Superstitions remaining from the days of the ancient tribes, left over from the Druids, a priesthood so powerful that not even Julius Caesar could stamp it out.

*'Celts of old have come.'* The sound of the old men once more.

*'Mars Cocidius,'* said the old men. *'He is with you. You have called upon him, upon us and we have come. We are we and we are you.'*

Mars Cocidius. The Druids and Celts had adopted those Roman gods which coincided with theirs. Mars, the Roman god of war, became Mars Cocidius, god of war for Britain's ancient tribes. Had

Figg called on him for help? He couldn't remember. Perhaps he had during those lonely, frightened days spent alone in Titus Bootham's cellar.

*Figg could not remember.*

Merlin the dwarf poured water into Figg's mouth. Barnum was shouting something in his ear and Mr Bootham, little Mr Bootham was weeping because he could no longer stand to see Figg take a beating. The Englishmen in the crowd had pushed to the edge of the ring, screaming, threatening to kill the umpires, timekeepers. Thor, Hugh Larney and his friends. The situation was ugly.

Again Figg, and Figg alone, heard the voices.

*'Widdershins, widdershins, widdershins . . .'*

Widdershins. The counterclockwise motion used by witches in casting spells. Christianity had outlawed 'the old religion', and in retaliation 'the old religion' had declared itself the opposite of all Christianity stood for.

In medieval times, armies marched counterclockwise around a castle before attacking it, the better to work up strength and increase their chances for victory.

Figg pushed himself to his feet, swayed, blinked and tried to focus his one good eye. There was Larney, bloated with arrogance now, accepting the congratulations of his friends on his *victory,* and there was Thor turning to him and grinning. On their side of the ring, men cheered, whooped, drank and jeered at Figg. The bettting in the cellar had got out of hand; Larney had increased his wager to $100,000 in gold, and the English, in the heat of patriotic fever and a hatred for the Americans, had matched the bet among themselves.

*Widdershins.*

*'Be it as your faith,'* said the old men.

'Me faith,' muttered Figg.

He looked at the moon. As he did so, the pain in his body seemed to ease. Suddenly there was some sight in his left eye and the right eye was fine. Perfect. He blinked. He could lift his right arm.

*'Time!'*

Figg looked into the moon once more, then limped forward to meet a supremely confident Thor.

*Widdershins.*

Figg limped to his left. Counterclockwise.

Thor stalked him.

Rachel felt secure, safe. She sat in the carriage beside Eddy, dear Eddy, and soon she would see Justin once more. Eddy had done this for her, he had made it possible for her to see Justin again. Both men were so dear to her; how fortunate she was to have them in her life. She felt peaceful now, rested. There was nothing to worry about.

The carriage rolled slowly, steadily through the moonlit night, along snow-covered roads, through woods, over low hills and across flatlands.

Towards Hugh Larney's abandoned farm.

Towards Jonathan.

And a mesmerised Rachel, not knowing she was in a trance, sat contented beside an apparition.

Poe awoke. He was still in darkness. And there was the dampness around him, the stale air. The coffin lid. He kicked it, punched it, cursed it.

He screamed and screamed and the sound of his voice remained as trapped in the small, hellish prison, as did Poe himself.

Thor was confused. He frowned, licked the blood from his lips and charged once more. Waiting until the last second, Figg sidestepped to his left, hooking his left fist into the Negro's rib-cage, then driving his right arm fully extended, into the same spot. Thor's eyes became all whites. He staggered backwards.

For the past few minutes the Englishman had been hitting him in the same spot, the right rib-cage and the pain was growing. All of the white man's blows had been concentrated there, nowhere else, and Thor was feeling it. What Thor hated most of all was that the white man had knocked him down three times, and the last time Thor had found himself getting up slowly.

The Negro, more cautious now, flickered his bloodied left fist at Figg's face. The Englishman stayed out of reach, continuing to circle to his left. Two more swings by Thor, and again they missed, and when the Negro was leaning forward, slightly off balance, Figg flicked a small jab at his face. The blow stung.

*Widdershins.*

Every man in the cellar was on his feet, shouting, cursing, encouraging. Some who had been against Figg were now for the squat, bulldog-faced Englishman. His courage had impressed

300

them, his ability to absorb punishment and not quit had won their fickle allegiance. A worried Hugh Larney chewed his tiny lower lip as Figg faked right with just his head, drawing a reaction from an anxious Thor, then stepped left, punching on the move, hooking his left fist under the Negro's heart.

Thor staggered backwards, surprised, but he didn't go down. He'd never seen a man punch and move at the same time. Most boxers planted both feet, then swung from a firm stance. Suddenly the old man in front of him was running all over the ring, hitting while he ran and the blows were hurting Thor.

Thor was angry. He wasn't going to lose a fight to this old white man, this man who could not walk without dragging a foot behind him, this man with scars on his face and body. Thor was going to kill him, and not just for the $100 in gold. He was going to kill him because he now hated him more than he'd hated anyone in his life.

Figg felt strong, confident. He gave no thought as to how that had come about. That it had come about was all that mattered. If he was a part of a tradition that had lived long before Christ and was still alive in the hills and dark woods of England, then so be it. All he was certain of was that it was now a different fight between him and the blackamoor. A very different fight.

He noticed something. The Negro kept his right side farther back than before. It must be painin' him. Didn't want any more taps on it. But keeping his right side far back had thrown Thor's stride off. His stance was too narrow; both feet were one behind the other instead of being wide apart for a firmer grip on the earth. A weak stance meant a weaker punch, even from a man as big as he.

Thor jabbed with his left, shuffling forward cautiously, keeping his right side away from Figg, who moved quickly to his right, forcing Thor to lean after him.

Then Figg changed directions. Counterclockwise. As Martin and Tully, two of Thor's opponents, had said: he cannot move sideways too well. Figg took a chance. He lunged, leaping forward and swinging his left in a wild roundhouse at Thor's right side. He connected. The blow was one of Figg's strongest of the fight and drove the big man across the ring. The crowd roared.

Thor was against the ropes and Figg was on him. The Englishman's hands reached for the Negro's throat, squeezing, digging in, weakening him. Backing off, Figg hooked to the body with both hands. Again, again, digging his fists into the Negro's flesh. Thor leaned off the ropes, hands reaching for Figg, who backed off and stepped left, hooking a left into Thor's temple. Then a right cross and the crowd shrieked, stomped its boots on the damp, black earth. Thor fell forward on his face and Figg staggered backwards.

Thor's seconds dragged him back to his corner. Barnum's squeaky voice cut above the shouting crowd. 'Start counting, time-keeper! Count, I say!' Barnum had $10,000 in gold bet on Figg.

Figg sat on Barnum's knee, his head flopped back against the ring post, eyes on the moon. *Widdershins.* They were all congratulating him. Barnum, Bootham. Merlin. The Englishmen sitting at the ringside. The cheers, the screams, the yells. It was something from an old tribal rite, it was. Nothing's changed, thought Figg. Nothing at all. We are them and them is we. The old ones, the new ones. We are all the same.

He looked across the ring. Thor was leaning backward, trying hard to breathe. One of his seconds gently touched the Negro's right side and he cried out, shaking his head from side to side.

'Time!'

Figg was on his feet, limping forward, reaching the line before Thor.

Thor came up to it slowly, doubled over, left side facing Figg, left hand pawing the air. In adopting the cautious, defensive posture, the Negro had reduced his height. His chin was where Figg wanted it to be. Jes' keep it there for a while longer, mate. Jes' a while longer.

They circled each other, Thor with his right side back to protect it. Figg was moving to his left, looking for that opening, that opportunity to end the fight. He knew he could end it, he knew he could win. *Be it as your faith. The old and the new are as one, for nothing has ever changed in this world save the eyes of those who view it.*

Figg charged, stopped. Thor backed up, then stood confused. Someone booed and shouted. 'Hey Larney, yer nigger wants to go home!' Laughter.

Again Figg charged, stopped. Again Thor backed up. More boos, all aimed at the Negro. He looked around, his bloodied face confused, with only the remnants of pride left in it.

All right, white man. You come again and Thor will not run. Not this time. This time Thor will run to meet *you.*

Figg faked a charge, two steps, then stopped. Thor lowered his head and charged him and Figg swung a right uppercut that began almost at the ground. The blow caught the Negro on the move, half in the throat, half under the jaw, and lifted him in the air and into the ropes.

As Thor bounced off the ropes, Figg stepped to his own left and hooked his left fist into the Negro's temple. Thor fell forward into the dirt and didn't move.

The cellar erupted with cheering, roaring, yelling men. There were no boos, no jeers. They had seen what they had come to see.

They'd seen a fight.

Back in his corner, Figg, surrounded by cheering Englishmen, Barnum, Bootham and Merlin, breathed deeply through his open mouth. His face was bloodied, swollen, as were both fists. His back was to Thor, now being dragged back to his corner by his seconds. Figg knew there would be no more fight tonight.

There wasn't.

'*Time!*' The timekeeper could barely be heard above the cheering, yelling crowd.

'*Time!*'

Thor's seconds frantically worked on reviving him. But the Negro was unconscious, blood pouring from his nose and mouth.

And now the ring was filled with men, almost all of them English, desperate to be a part of Figg's victory, to touch him, speak to him, listen to him. There would be no raising of Figg's hand in victory by an umpire. The umpire couldn't get through the crowd.

As men fought to be near him, Figg pushed his way to Barnum, and when he was close to the showman, Figg whispered in his ear. A jubilant Barnum nodded vigorously. 'It will be done, Mr Figg, exactly as you asked. You have my word on it.'

Barnum looked down. 'Merlin? You have work to do.' A delighted Barnum picked up the dwarf in his arms and kissed him on the cheek.

The Englishmen picked up Figg and carried him triumphantly from the ring.

# CHAPTER FORTY-FIVE

In the abandoned barn a proud and arrogant Jonathan spoke to the freezing winds raging around him. 'Soon the woman will be here.'

'Sacrifice her,' replied Asmodeus, 'and you are forever free from me.'

Jonathan, eyes closed, spoke to the demon king with his thoughts. 'But you will *never* be free from me. *Never*. You will serve *me* as I wish. You will serve *me* forever, for soon I shall hold dominion over you.'

The howling winds suddenly disappeared. He fears me, thought Jonathan. *He fears me.*

Jonathan remained seated, eyes closed. He waited. It was less than three hours to midnight on the ninth and final day.

Holding Dearborn's hand tightly, a nervous and bitter Hugh Larney hurried from the doctor's small clapboard house and rushed down the stairs towards his carriage. Thor was still bleeding from the nose and mouth and he couldn't talk. That last punch in the throat had crushed something and Larney didn't know or care what it was. Let the doctor worry about it. Larney was concerned with Figg. The Englishman was alive and the smartest thing Larney could do was flee to his small farmhouse and hide there.

Figg. Damn him, damn him, damn him! He'd cost Larney $100,000 *and* the best prizefighter in New York; Thor would never be the same man again, no matter what the doctor did for him. And what bothered Larney more than anything else was the loss of prestige, to have this defeat occur in front of his friends.

Jonathan had been correct. Beware Poe and Figg. Well, little Poe was no longer a bother to anyone, not where he was at the moment. Lying in a coffin, in an unmarked grave, perhaps still drugged by wine, perhaps screaming and begging to be let out. Perhaps dead from fright by now. He deserved it, the snivelling little bastard. Larney was not going to be humiliated by the likes of a shabby, dirt poor writer who lacked even the money to bet on the man who was taking his place in the prize-ring. Larney had money, position. Poe had none of these things, so why should he be proud? He had nothing to be proud of. Let him now be proud in his coffin let him parade and boast in front of the worms who would soon be drilling holes in his sallow flesh!

Larney had left two men with Thor, to bring the Negro back to the farm when the doctor said he could travel. Jacob Cribb was waiting in Larney's carriage to drive him out of Manhattan, away from Figg. It would be wise to get as far away from Figg as possible.

At the carriage, Larney lifted Dearborn up, then climbed inside himself.

His jaw dropped.

Figg, in the seat across from him, rasped, 'I'm here to get yer congratulations, Mr Larney. You left without sayin' "Well done, Mr Figg." '

Larney looked at the horrible dwarf who stood on the seat beside Figg, a flintlock aimed up at the back of Jacob Cribb, who sat outside on the driver's seat.

'How—how did you—?'

'Find you, Mr Larney? Little Merlin 'ere, 'im and another one of Mr Barnum's friends followed you and one of 'em comes back and tells me. Little fella like 'im must be hard to see at night.'

Figg leaned forward. 'And now you are goin' to tell me, mate. Where is Mr Poe and where is Jonathan?'

'I do not—'

Figg leaned over and backhanded a slap in his face. Larney fell to the side and lay there, whimpering.

Dearborn said softly, 'They took Mr Poe to the cemetery and left him there.'

Figg grabbed Larney's hair, jerking him upright again. 'If Poe is dead, you will lie beside him, me promise on that. Merlin!'

The dwarf jammed Figg's flintlock into Jacob Cribb's back. The carriage jerked forward, pulling away into the night.


'Sweet Jesus,' muttered Figg.

He, Dearborn and Merlin stood beside the open grave as a dishevelled, dirt-covered Hugh Larney and Jacob Cribb pulled the cover from the coffin with bloodied hands.

Poe lay curled on his side. He didn't move.

'Take 'im out, you two, and pray to God 'e ain't dead, 'cause if 'e is, then you two will be as well.'

Larney and Cribb supported Poe between them. Was he breathing? Figg watched him carefully. Poe's head snapped up and his eyes widened in his pale face. There was dirt on his wide forehead and on his moustache.

Figg grinned. 'Even', squire.'

'Mr—Mr Figg. You, you do not look well, sir.'

'You ain't no 'angin' tapestry yerself. Glad to see you, I am.'

'And I you, sir. And I you.'

'Little Miss Dearborn 'ere, she tells me she saw you twice tonight. Sees you drive off with Miss Rachel, and quick after that she sees you tied up in Mr Larney's carriage. She is the one what told me you were 'ere in this awful place.'

'The-the duel, Mr Figg. Did you—'

'We were victorious, Mr Poe.'

Poe's smile was weak. 'I am delighted, sir. I am extremely delighted and pleased beyond measure.'

Pushing himself clear of Larney and Cribb, Poe staggered forward, found his balance and straightened up. 'Wine, that bane of my existence, in essence saved me, for through its drugged mercies I slept much more than I screamed and clawed at the coffin lid. Even now, I am not entirely in control of my mental faculties, but soon I shall be. Soon. I never imagined myself as ever being grateful to alcohol, but it was that which gave me welcomed sleep. Welcomed sleep.'

Poe stepped towards Figg. 'You say I drove away with Mrs Coltman?'

'That's right.'

'I most certainly did not. I have not seen her in two days, having spent my time securing intelligence regarding the property owned by Mr Larney. It is for that reason that I feel I know where Jonathan is.'

Figg held his breath. 'We gots barely two hours before—'

'I know, Mr Figg. I know.'

'One thing, squire. If it was not you what drove off with Miss Rachel tonight, then 'oo was it?'

Fear descended on Poe with sickening speed. 'I am terrified, Mr Figg. Not for myself but for Mrs Coltman. Only one man has the power to create such forceful illusions, for it was not I who took her tonight. It was Jonathan. Even though he cannot leave the site of this evil ritual, somehow he managed to convince her that it was I who was beside her and so she succumbed to his illusion. Mr Figg, let us leave this place. We shall need fast horses, for we ride to the country, to the north of the city, to a certain abandoned horse farm—'

'No!' Larney took a step forward, then stopped. 'I mean—'

Poe coughed. 'You mean, Mr Larney, that you pay the least taxes on that particular piece of land, that it has been under the least scrutiny by municipal authorities, that it has been without human habitation for over two years. You mean that Jonathan is there, as opposed to being on land of yours that contains tenants, cattle, hay, buildings. It is all there in the records, sir. All except where Jonathan is, and you have just admitted that I am correct in my assumption.'

Poe looked at him with contempt. 'That is why you and this swine, Jacob Cribb, deceived me with a false note from my dear Muddy. You deceived me, then did this to me. There is no hell on earth that could properly torment the both of you.'

Figg looked at Larney and Cribb. 'We needs a guide, Mr Poe, and that would be Mr Larney, willin' or unwillin'. I am certain I can convince 'im to make the journey with us. Merlin, you and Mr Poe take the child with you back to the carriage. You go with them, Mr Larney. Merlin, should Mr Larney prove difficult in any fashion, put a ball in 'im. Aim for his stomach.'

The dwarf leered and nodded.

As the men left, Jacob Cribb started to follow them. 'Not you, Mr Cribb.' Figg's hand was inside his frock-coat. In the moonlit darkness of the graveyard, Figg looked terrifying. Jacob Cribb trembled.

Figg walked towards him, the hand still inside the coat and on the belt buckle. 'Somebody's got to stay behind, Mr Cribb, and I reckon it should be you.'

Seconds later, Figg joined Poe, Merlin, Larney and Dearborn at the carriage. No one asked why Jacob Cribb was not with him.

# CHAPTER FORTY-SIX

As Poe tied the horses to the trees, Figg pulled Larney down from the saddle.

'You goin' in first, mate. And remember: you get the idea to shake a loose leg and I will put a ball in you before you have run very far.'

Larney closed his eyes. His hands were tied in front of him and he'd ridden through the night on the same horse as Figg. There had been the hell of Figg literally breathing down his neck for the three-mile ride, and the worse hell of knowing they were speeding to meet Jonathan. Jonathan who would soon be completing the nine-day ritual. Jonathan, who tonight would unleash dark forces that no man on earth could contend with. Larney had wanted to see Jonathan conjure the Throne of Solomon, but he had not wanted to come upon the magician in this fashion. Not as a prisoner, not with Poe and Figg at his back.

The three men stood in the small grove of trees, eyes on the barn that lay across an open expanse of moonlit snow. Poe shivered. His fears for Rachel were stronger than his fears for himself. Thanks to the drugged wine, the experience of being buried alive had emerged as almost unreal.

Figg looked at his pocket watch, squinting to see the hands in the moonlight.

'Gone half eleven, it has. We be gettin'—'

From the barn, a woman screamed.

Poe clutched Figg's arm. 'It is her! It is Rachel!' He ran, loping through the snow, lifting his knees high, his dark brown hair wild around his head and face, his mouth open, a man obsessed with saving the woman he loved.

He screamed her name.

A frozen wind suddenly blew swirling snow around him and he was temporarily blinded. Then he saw the barn again, saw the candle glow within it.

'Rachel!' He fell forward in the snow, rose, his front covered by the soft, cold white powder, and he ran towards her, towards Jonathan.

Figg jammed his flintlock in Larney's back. 'You too, mate. Let's go.'

'I-I—'

'You will die 'ere or you will run towards that barn. Which is it gonna be?'

Larney, weeping and moaning stumbled forward, following the gouges in the snow left by Poe.

A frightened Figg followed him. But first he looked up at the moon.


Inside the barn, Rachel scratched Laertes' face, frantically struggling with him as he tried to keep her down on the ground. Jonathan stood holding the ritual knife point up towards the ceiling. Both men were gaunt, haggard, dusty with human ashes and foul-smelling from the grave clothes they had worn for nine days and nights. The men and Rachel were within the protective circle.

The wind howled around the barn.

Asmodeus. He has come, thought Jonathan. Let him receive the sacrifice, thus freeing me from him forever. Let him receive—

'Stop!'

Poe stood in the doorway of the barn. The wind grew stronger. Two candles around the protective circle toppled over.

The wind tossed Poe's hair around his face. 'I command you to stop!'

Jonathan turned quickly to face him. 'Fool! She has to die! Only she stands between me and the Throne of Solomon. Asmodeus has claimed her and—'

The wind was stronger, rattling the rotting wood of the barn. Poe clung to the inside of the barn door. 'You cannot kill her! You cannot!'

Figg, pushing Hugh Larney ahead of him, reached Poe. Figg and Jonathan stared at each other. For a few seconds, neither man moved.

And then Jonathan *knew*. 'No! Nooooo!'

The wind blew louder, filling the inside of the barn with dust and dirt, whipping the dirt into the eyes of Poe and Figg, stinging their faces.

Within the wind, Asmodeus spoke only to Jonathan, who alone heard him. The demon king's laughter was cruel. 'You fool! I have tried you and now I shall have you! I have won, and you have lost.

Your pride has been your downfall, for you have attempted to be as God, and no man, not even Solomon himself, can long hold dominion over us.'

Jonathan turned frantically, listening, listening.

Asmodeus spoke within the wind. 'Your pride made you accept the challenge, magician, and in drawing the woman to you, you drew the one mortal man you fear, the one mortal who can and will destroy you. He followed the woman as I knew he would, and now you will be sacrificed to me.'

'Noooooo!' Jonathan screamed at the top of his voice. The incredibly strong wind pushed Poe, Figg and Larney into the barn. Laertes straddled Rachel Coltman's body, a knife in his hand, the blade raised high.

'Kill her!' shouted Jonathan. 'Let her die! The sacrifice will save us.'

Figg had been looking behind him. There was a blizzard in the open field, a vicious swirl of blinding, stinging snow and there was nowhere to run but inside the barn. It was as though he, Poe and Larney were being pushed inside the barn, *forced* to enter it. Figg was convinced of it.

Jonathan shouted again. 'Laertes! Kill her!'

Figg turned and fired quickly. The ball went into Laertes' side. He jerked, remaining on top of Rachel Coltman. Figg squinted, trying to focus in the dust storm. He fired his second pistol and Laertes' face turned bloody and he fell backwards.

Figg pushed Poe ahead of him. 'Into the circle! Quick, run!'

Poe ran. The strength of the wind increased and both men leaned into it, feeling the frozen air gnaw at their faces, pull at their eyes, lips, jam their throats with dirt.

Jonathan was pained and angered at having been tricked; he knew the *power* was also within Figg. He recognised a kinship, but one opposed to all that Jonathan believed in. The spirits rested within Figg though he had little awareness of it. Figg sought no power, sought no gain, and the spirits in touch with him were benign, restrained and would never appear unless summoned for no less than survival. But they were spirits and Jonathan feared them, for he could not dominate them.

And now Figg was here, Figg with the unknown forces that had helped him all his life. Jonathan, half crazed with fear, faced the boxer.

Somewhere in the dust storm filling the barn, Hugh Larney cried out. 'Jonathan help me! Help meeee!'

Figg and Poe reached the protective circle. Figg crouched, his swollen face hideous in the dust storm. 'Me and you, magician! It has come down to that, it has! Me and you!'

Poe crawled to Rachel, taking her in his arms, holding her tight, burying her face in his shoulder. The eerie storm around them was filled with howling winds, shrieking sounds as though men and animals in pain were calling out for help.

The ritual! Jonathan had raised forces that were out of his control! Or was this just a sudden, vicious storm. *Was it just a storm?* On the ground, Poe clung tightly to Rachel. Through the dust, Figg and Jonathan were only vague shadows.

He heard Figg's voice over the shrieking winds. 'Do not leave the circle, Mr Poe! Whatever you do! Do not leave! Your life depends on it!'

'Jonathannnnnnnn!' Again Hugh Larney. 'Jonathan, they have me! They have me! Oh, God, no! Dear God, I beg you do not . . . Aieeeeee!' And his voice was swallowed up in the howling winds.

Jonathan, his grave clothes flapping in the wind, gripped the Athame, the ritual knife, in both hands. He crouched, squinting in the swirling, stinging dust, trying to see Figg, trying to . . .

Figg was on him, a hand pressing the knife down, the other hand punching him in the face, punching, punching, knocking him to the ground.

Then the Athame was in Figg's hands and the boxer gazed down at the man he had come so far to kill. Suddenly Figg stopped and listened to the wind.

He listened, and Jonathan screamed, 'Nooo! Noooo!' The magician had heard what Figg heard. They had both heard the order for Jonathan's death.

Figg heard the voices of the old men. *'We are you, we are one. All is one, all is one . . .'*

Figg, his top hat long blown away, straddled Jonathan, quickly slashing his throat. The magician's feet jerked; his blood spurted up on Figg's hands and coat.

As the wind continued to howl in a ear-piercing, murderous fury, Figg tore at Jonathan's filthy, grave clothes.

Instantly, a shocked Poe knew that Figg intended. 'Good Lord, man! Are you mad? What are you going to do?'

*Poe knew.*

Figg snapped his head towards Poe. 'Lie down flat and cover the woman's face! She must not see me do this, this thing! The wind, it will destroy us all if I do not act! There is no choice, Mr Poe, and I think you know what I am sayin'.'

'But we cannot act as *he* would have done!'

'Damn it man, I tell you we will not leave this place alive unless we do, unless I do what has to be done! I have jes' been told that it must be this way! My, my spirits tell me! I do this on their orders, not because of Jonathan's devil god! Jonathan has begun a thing and a promise must be kept! He, the thing, he cannot have the woman but he must 'ave somebody, do you understand what I am sayin'?'

The wind tore at them and Poe knew they could not stay much longer in this brutal, unearthly storm, this sudden storm that screamed around them and pulled at their flesh like the claws and teeth of a thousand rats. The storm that Poe also knew could kill them, unless—

It *must* be done and Poe was sick to his stomach. Almost completely blinded by the stinging dust that filled the barn, he fell to the ground and held Rachel to him, a hand behind her head, keeping her face in his chest. Figg the primitive was sensitive to forces that Poe could only imagine.

*And that's why Jonathan had feared the boxer.*

Poe screamed over the wind, 'Do as you must! Do as you must!'

Still straddling the dead magician, Figg rubbed dirt from his own eyes.

And with a trembling hand, began to cut out Jonathan's heart.

*My Dear Mr Figg,*

*In this letter, I am forced to acknowledge some things which should not be acknowledged at all. I am certain that you do not wish my gratitude in the matter of the two gold sovereigns you left behind in my cottage. One could say you forgot them, mislaid them, but Mr Figg, I am not of a mind to underestimate your intelligence, which regrettably, once was the attitude I carried with me in viewing your existence. I do not accept charity, sir, but my dear Muddy, Mrs Maria Clemm, assures me that your intentions were honourable and that in no way did you seek to demean me. Therefore, let me say that the receipt of the money is appreciated and Muddy and I will make the wisest use of it possible, though money does not long remain in my company.*

*The recent events which involved the both of us in this city are still strong within my mind. There can be no logical explanation for much of what occurred and I find that I am unable, unwilling as well, to discuss this matter with others. I cannot explain the sudden, brutal winds that surrounded us that night on Hugh Larney's property, any more than I can explain their quick cessation upon your completion of a business best left unsaid. I am forced to repeat what I said to you that night, that you saved our lives even though it was done in a fashion which I personally find abominable. Do not take this as criticism upon yourself, since neither Rachel nor I would be alive had it not been for your swift action. I acknowledge that there are forces beyond my ken, and as yet, I am not sure if it is good or bad for me to admit this.*

*To sum up recent happenings, the death of Volney Gunning was proclaimed to have occurred in a traffic accident, thereby explaining the broken bones he incurred. The demise of Miles Standish is still a matter for police inquiry, though I have learned that Prosper Benjamin is active in keeping that inquiry at a standstill. I surmise that Mr Benjamin is reluctant to have the homosexual killers of Scotch Ann's temple of lust traced to him, so I must tell you that it appears as if the matter of Miles Standish will remain a mystery for some time to come.*

*Hugh Larney was ruled to have been killed by wolves made ravenous and daring by the winter, a conclusion drawn from the condition of his corpse which appeared to have been shredded by*

313

*wild beasts. I leave a closer examination of this matter to you, dear friend, who I am sure can give a more detailed explanation should you be so inclined.*

*When the burned ruins of Hugh Larney's barn were examined, no human remains were found. The fire which immediately ravaged the building after we fled it must have contained flames capable of destroying human bone and tissue in a fashion not yet encountered on this planet, but, as I have stated, there are things I prefer not to acknowledge.*

*Barnum and others with wagers to collect from Hugh Larney are not ecstatic with his having gone on ahead, as the religiosos are apt to proclaim of the dead, but it was agreed by one and all that the fight between you and Larney's coloured was worth any price. The coloured is a broken man and at loose ends since Larney's transportation to other planes, and I fear he will end up in Five Points, a soul lost to vice and numerous human weaknesses. Dearborn Lapham, sad to inform you, has run away with a group of travelling players. I wish her* bon chance.

*Of Rachel I can say little since her recovery is slow, if not nonexistent. Doctors have told me it is her mind and not her body that is the source of her ailing. The shocking experiences she encountered have proven too much for her, and I fear for her sanity, dear friend. Again I say there is much I would prefer not to acknowledge but life, as always, is harsh, relentlessly so, and I am forced to consider the intelligence that she may not ever again regain her correct faculties.*

*I do so love her and cannot avoid dreaming of a time when she will be well and I have my magazine and she and I will be as one. All of my life I have yearned for love, for the comfort of a warm and tender heart, and I would rather die than renounce this ideal. I spend as much time as possible by her bedside and on those days that she recognises me, I can truthfully say that I feel no greater joy, no greater euphoria.*

*She has made no inquiries about her husband, whose body also perished in that peculiar barn fire. I have not spoken of him, for I fear the mention of his name would only increase the darkness which now seems to have gripped her mind. At this stage he can only remind her of the horrible events of recent days.*

*Like all writers, I place my life in my work and the aforementioned, recent events are no exception in terms of being grist for my literary mill. I cannot use the events as they transpired, again for fear of offending Rachel or of reminding her of things I am certain* she would rather not be minded of. However, in the tale of 'Hop Frog', which is still much on my mind, I shall deal with revenge and the destruction of those men who have offended a lovely woman.

I do hope you read some of my tales. The book I presented you before you sailed for London is one of many copies clogging a portion of the attic in Poe cottage. Some publishers do not pay in cash. The literary life is rewarded by them in terms of free copies of whatever books they deign to publish. The literary life, while exciting and spiritually fulfilling for me, is far from lucrative, as you have heard me say before. Publishers lack morals and vision and until the copyright laws are changed throughout the world, as our mutual friend Dickens has urged, the literary life will lack protection for its much needed essence, namely the author.

I am still in an emotional and mental turmoil over the events that you and I shared, but I am sure that they will have their influence on me, opening my imagination more to things unheard, unseen but still in existence on planes of their own choosing. I struggle with the matter of intemperence and I fear that should something happen to Rachel, and she and I fail to achieve a union, I may well fall into a serious breach of this issue. It would be better for me to be done with drink forever, but it is not so easy to renounce as it once was.

Let me hear from you. Please send your reply to my home in Fordham. With the most sincere friendship and ardent gratitude.

Believe me your true friend,

Edgar A. Poe

London, April 23, 1848

*My Dear Mr Poe, Esquire,*

*Please excuse my way with words since I am not at ease around them as are you, but I am proud to say I learnt my letters from my dad when I was young and I can letter after a fashion. You wrote to me of gold sovereigns and I write to you that a man pays his way if he is a man, and I am a man. I ate your bread and I slept under your roof, so if I choose to pay, that is my concern not yours.*

*Like you, there are some things I much prefer not to say. I acted as I thought correct, haven to save three lives and all, so I did to Jonathan what I was told to do. I will not say more except to write you that a man has things in him he does not always know of and they come out of him when they want to come out. I have told no one of what I did, not even Mr Dickens, except to tell him that I met up with Jonathan and the matter was settled.*

*I am getting on well, thank you, and the hurt from the duel is going away better than any hurt I ever had in any fight I ever had. Still I do not want to step again into the ring and if I never have to come up to scratch again in my life, I would like that just fine, thanken you muchly. I teach young lads and their fathers are proud to watch them become good men, which is what learnen to box can do for you. I am sorry about Mr Barnum not collecten his gold from Mr Larney, but we could not help Mr Barnum in this matter.*

*May God carry the little Dearborn in his hand. I do not think the life of travellen players is correct for a child but she must learn this on her own stead. Before I close I say hello to Miss Rachel and wish her well and tell her Mr Figg tips his hat to her, a fine and pretty lady. Pray that the doctors can aid her in recovering her true mind and that she put behind her these sad events. It is a hard thing to do for I know and I must put them behind me as well. Yes I am readen your book of deduction and I tell you that no one has a quick and clever mind as do you. Mr Dickens thinks the same and he says you will one day be a grand gentleman of letters and Mr Dickens is a smart fellow himself.*

*I take my leave of you.*

*Your obedient servant,*
*Pierce James Figg*

# INTERVIEW WITH THE VAMPIRE

## *Anne Rice*

'The most seductive evocation of evil I have ever read. It is enthralling.' *Detroit Free Press*

In a darkened room a young man sits telling the macabre and eerie story of his life . . . the story of a vampire, gifted with eternal life, cursed with an exquisite craving for human blood.

'A supernatural thriller raised to the level of literature.' *Philadelphia Inquirer*

'A spine-chilling nightmare . . . highly accomplished . . . an impressive feat of imagination.' *Sunday Times*

'A voluptuous dream.' *Boston Globe*

'Compulsively readable . . . From the beginning we are hypnotized . . . The reader feels he has glimpsed experiences no mortal ever had.' *Chicago Tribune*

'Thrilling . . . a strikingly original work of the imagination . . . Sometimes horrible, sometimes beautiful, always unforgettable.' *Washington Post*

FUTURA PUBLICATIONS
FICTION
0 7088 3170 2

# THE VAMPIRE LESTAT

## *Anne Rice*

'Ah, the taste and feel of blood when all passion and greed is sharpened in that one desire!'

Lestat: a vampire – but very much not the conventional undead, for Lestat is the truly alive. Lestat is vivid, ecstatic, stagestruck, and in his extravagant story he plunges from the lascivious stews of eighteenth-century Paris to the Rome of Augustus and the Britain of the Druids, from the demonic Egypt of prehistory, to fin-de-siecle New Orleans, to the frenetic twentieth-century world of rock superstardom – as, pursued by the living and the dead, he searches across the world and time for the secret of his own dark immortality.

### THE VAMPIRE LESTAT

The brilliantly decadent, sensual sequel to the bestselling INTERVIEW WITH THE VAMPIRE.

'Dizzying narrative flights . . . as brilliant as the first; it is funnier, wilder and more disturbing.'
*New York Times Book Review*

'A vampire bonanza in appropriate dark, humid, spider-web narrative.' *Kirkus Reviews*

'A rich and unforgettable tale of dazzling scenes and vivid personalities.' *Library Journal*

FUTURA PUBLICATIONS
FICTION
0 7088 3153 2

All Futura Books are available at your bookshop or newsagent, or can be ordered from the following address: Futura Books, Cash Sales Department, P.O. Box 11, Falmouth, Cornwall TR10 9EN.

Please send cheque or postal order (no currency), and allow 60p for postage and packing for the first book plus 25p for the second book and 15p for each additional book ordered up to a maximum charge of £1.90 in U.K.

B.F.P.O. customers please allow 60p for the first book, 25p for the second book plus 15p per copy for the next 7 books, thereafter 9p per book.

Overseas customers including Eire please allow £1.25 for postage and packing for the first book, 75p for the second book and 28p for each subsequent title ordered.